THE
WELL

THE WELL

A NOVEL

CATHERINE
CHANTER

ATRIA BOOKS

New York London Toronto Sydney New Delhi

ATRIA BOOKS
An Imprint of Simon & Schuster, Inc.
1230 Avenue of the Americas
New York, NY 10020

Copyright © 2015 by Catherine Lloyd
Originally published in Great Britain by Canongate Books

First Atria Books hardcover edition May 2015

ATRIA B O O K S and colophon are trademarks of Simon & Schuster, Inc.

For information about special discounts for bulk purchases, please contact Simon & Schuster Special Sales at 1-866-506-1949 or business@simonandschuster.com.

The Simon & Schuster Speakers Bureau can bring authors to your live event. For more information or to book an event, contact the Simon & Schuster Speakers Bureau at 1-866-248-3049 or visit our website at www.simonspeakers.com.

Interior design by Paul Dippolito

Manufactured in the United States of America

10 9 8 7 6 5 4 3 2 1

Library of Congress Cataloging-in-Publication Data
Chanter, Catherine.
    The well : a novel / by Catherine Chanter. — First Atria Books hardcover edition.
        pages cm
    1. Water-supply—Fiction. 2. Great Britain—Fiction. I. Title.
    PR6103.H3655W45 2015
    823'.92—dc23
    2015010422

ISBN 978-1-4767-7276-9
ISBN 978-1-4767-7278-3 (ebook)

For Simon, Christopher, Jeremy, and Jessica

Oh fair enough are sky and plain,
But I know fairer far:
Those are as beautiful again
That in the water are;

The pools and rivers wash so clean
The trees and clouds and air,
The like on earth was never seen,
And oh that I were there.

—A. E. Housman, A *Shropshire Lad*

CHAPTER ONE

The Well has won me back. Tonight will be my first night under house arrest. First of how many? I scarcely dared hope they would allow me to return, yet when it came to the last night in the unit, I clung to the comfort blanket of my sleeping pills and section order, desperate to stay. Security. National security. Secure accommodation. An insecure conviction. It may keep me in, but all the security in the world will not keep the ghosts out; if I am home, they will be also.

In between the nightmares I have been daydreaming my way through three months of enforced idleness: picturing myself escorted from a prison van into the house; running my fingers through the dust on the half-moon table we were given for a wedding present; picking up the photo of the three of us, taken the first day we ever saw the place, me crumbling the damp earth between my fingers and laughing. I thought I might throw open the bedroom windows, listen to the insistent buzzard, stare out over the cracked hills and wonder how it came to this. I thought I would turn on the taps and watch the water stream down the drain, like liquid silver, lost. Things I knew I would not do: pray, write, work the land.

I do not follow that script. In the end, something rather bustling and pragmatic takes over. Maybe it is nerves. I am conscious from the moment that we pull out of the gates that my mouth is dry and I am picking at my cuticles as I used to when I was a child. I can't see, of course; the windows are blacked out. I wonder if there is a sack under my bench seat, ready to pull over my graying hair and gaunt eyes, just as you see with rapists and pedophiles, when the absence of a face makes them more, not less, terrifying, only the hands that strangled the child or the legs that ran down the alley visible to the waiting press.

Are these the palms of a saint or a sinner? I scratch my hands over and over again, hoping they will wake up and tell me.

Even the ruling that I am to be sent back is to be kept sub judice, as they say. I like that phrase. Underneath the justice. If you can only limbo long enough, then the law is upheld and everyone is happy.

"If we're prepared to act within the Rapid Processing Regulations, they'll reach a settlement. All we have to do is withdraw our intent to sue the government for illegal occupation, and then they'll let you serve out your sentence under house arrest. Deal done." That's what my lawyer told me. I asked him what was in it for the state, and he talked about overflowing prisons and adverse publicity, drought and scientific research. I interrupted him, asked what was in it for me. It sounded so simple, his answer.

"You get to go home to The Well," he said.

The first part of the journey from the women's wing seems "stop, start, and slow," and takes place against a sound track of sirens. Petrol rationing has solved the capital's traffic problems, but no one seems to have told the traffic lights. Then the feel of the journey changes to the relentless flat, forward impetus of the motorway heading north. I know that route so well, and once we exchange the straight line for the swerves and lurches which take you over the hills and down into the valley, my breathing slows and I feel the saliva run again against my sandpaper tongue. Fifteen minutes for the long, slow climb past the Little Lennisford church; twenty-five minutes before meeting the stretch of flat, straight road beside the poles of the hop fields (the last chance to overtake, as we used to say); forty minutes and the sharp right-hand turn past Martin's farm, grinding up through the hairpin bends, through the gears, through the clouds as often as not, to the brow of the hill, to the top of the world. Then, at last, the swing to the left down the quarter mile of unfenced, rough track which leads through my fields to The Well.

"Nearly there now."

The guard's words are unnecessary.

The van is going too fast for the potholes. Surprising they haven't done anything about them, but then again, we never got round to it either. It takes the wearing down of water to grind holes in stone, and The Well wore her puddles like a badge of honor. We are stopping. The grille is pulled back.

"We'll just be a couple of minutes while we check everything. You OK back there?"

It is kind of them to ask but not clear to me how I am meant to answer. That I am totally at ease with being brought back to my own notorious paradise in a prison van?

"I'm fine. Thank you."

I sit very still. Part of me doesn't trust the ruling even now. Bizarre ideas from old war films tug at the rubber mat under my manacled feet, and I see myself taken from the van, led to my dear oak tree and shot there, falling in a crumpled heap among last year's desiccated acorns and the sheep shit. The soldiers are getting out now, slamming the doors behind them.

"It's unbelievable, isn't it?" That is the woman with the Birmingham accent. "It's just like they said, just like on the web page."

"What is?" The driver. I could tell from his choice of music on the journey that he had no insight.

"This is. It's like going back three years. Green fields. When did you last see grass like that?"

So, my fields are still green.

New voices. Greetings. Slightly formal. Then a younger man talking.

"You should talk to the locals. They say it's true what it said in the papers. When she was here, it rained; when they arrested her, it stopped."

"Where did it happen, then?" asks the driver.

"Down in the woods."

"I'm with those who think the old bag's a witch, not a savior."

"Quite a sexy old witch, all the same."

They must be moving towards the house because I can't catch the rest of their conversation. The knowledge of the space outside is somehow suffocating me inside and I feel nauseous. Not now, I think. No more of these visions, no more drownings. Sweat breaks out on my forehead; I try to raise my hand to wipe it away, forgetting the weight of the handcuffs. I too am being pulled under the surface. I am not mad. I put my head down between my knees to stop myself fainting, and the darkness of the van slowly steadies itself, the thick water recedes, and I become myself again, just as the footsteps grow louder on the gravel and the back doors of the van are opened.

"Home at last!" she says. "Out you get!"

There is no blinding flash of sunlight; rather, the washed-out blue of an early April afternoon merges with the bleak interior of the van in the way that paints on a palette mix in water and reach a gray compromise. I try with some difficulty to get out, stooping under the low roof of the van, holding my handcuffed wrists in front of me like some bizarre posture of prayer.

"Tell you what," says Birmingham woman, "sit on the edge here and I'll take those off you. Home sweet home! Hope someone's done the washing up. That's all I ever want when I get back in the evening." She punches various codes into the keypads attached to my limbs.

The driver has joined us now. "Bet you don't get your lily-white hands all damp and dirty in the sink."

"Tell you something, have to, now. The dishwasher used to cost a fortune on the water meter. Still, every cloud has a silver lining, as they say, washing up's about the nearest I get to a bath nowadays." She fiddles with my unattractive ankle bracelet. "This one stays on, it's what we call the home tag."

I am sitting on the edge of the back of the van, childlike, my legs not quite touching the ground, and when I am free, I feel each of my wrists in turn and then stand uncertainly and take a few steps away from the guards. In front of me, the stone front of the house stands even and steady; it is my spirit level. I turn, and then I am facing my fields which rise up and fall away before me, their hedges like ley lines, feeling the contours, the forests like velvet folded into the valleys. A hand takes my elbow. I shake it off but follow the guard to the front door all the same. We don't use this door, I am about to say, we use the back door. Kicked off our mud-clodded boots on the tiled floor there, once; hung the fishing rods on the hooks above the raincoats there, once. We. Me and Mark. Me and my ex. Front door. Back door. River. Ex. Words.

"This is as far as it goes for us," says the driver. "Job done. I expect your new friends will introduce themselves once we've signed everything." He waves towards three armed young men in uniform who have appeared at the fence between the house and the orchard and are standing with their backs to us, pointing towards Wales. That was one of the reasons they agreed to house arrest, apparently, the fact that there were government soldiers here already, keeping watch over their crops by night.

"It must be good to be home," comments the guard, and I nod because I am trying hard to be human, just as she is. She waits until her companion strolls over to the soldiers before continuing in a quieter voice, "I've never seen anything so beautiful. You are a special woman for it to have happened like this."

I mutter something like maybe or I don't know. I have long ago ceased to trust people who seem to worship me.

She says, "I'm sorry about the van and the handcuffs and all that. About the whole thing. None of it should ever have happened. I hope you'll be happy now you're back and . . ."

"And?"

"And I hope it rains again, here, I really do and . . ."

"And?"

"And, if you still pray, pray for me."

She tries to grasp my hand. I see she is crying. The tears and the prayers at The Well have been out of balance; there will rightly be more crying than praying from now on. I pull away, and for a brief moment she is left staring at her own empty palms, then she turns abruptly and strides back to the van. She gets in, slams the door, leans over and blasts the horn. At the fence, the driver punches something into his phone and halfheartedly salutes the soldiers. Just as he is about to get back into the van, he bends down as if he has dropped something and scoops up a handful of earth to examine like a gardener. He looks up, sees the soldiers watching him and chucks it into the hedge, laughing out loud, then dusts his hands down on his khaki trousers, climbs in, and starts the engine. The prison van beeps as he reverses towards the oak tree, and he yells out the window, "Don't worry, lads! We'll pray for you on your frontline duties!"

The guard sits in the passenger seat, staring straight ahead at the track which will take her away. The driver turns up the music and they are gone and then there is nothing except silence, three soldiers and me. They kick the fence with their heavy boots, one lights a ciga-rette, and suddenly I think of a picture of Russia I saw once, taken during the Second World War: young men silhouetted against a barren landscape, staring at the horizon, waiting for relief. We face a different onslaught. I stand, halfway in and halfway out of the house, my legs shaking with exhaustion.

"Shall I go in?" I call, and immediately regret my weakness. "I mean, are there any other formalities to be completed?"

All three turn, as if mildly surprised that I can speak. A sudden officiousness seems to come over the short one, as it does for all people newly appointed to small amounts of power. He marches over; the other two hang back slightly.

"There are a number of regulations and procedures we need to go through with you. I therefore suggest that we meet . . . er . . ." He has a tight voice.

"Around the kitchen table?" I suggest.

"That would be satisfactory, yes—there, in one hour."

"You may have to knock and remind me."

"We don't need to knock," he replies.

The thinner of the other two tries to make some joke about drinks at six. I don't quite catch it, but try to smile all the same. *Pour encourager les autres.*

What do I do now? I try to summon old habits. Like a frightened bride, I force myself over the threshold and then kick off my shoes and go into the kitchen. It is a sparse version of its former self, being robbed of its clutter and wiped down. I run the cold tap just to make sure and then fill the kettle. While it is boiling, I take down my favorite mug and trace the delicate painting of the grayling, trout, and perch which swim the porcelain river and wind themselves around the handle, wipe the dust from the rim with the tip of my finger. Instinctively, I go to the fridge, which is working normally. There has been no shortage of wind in the last few years. For us, if our turbine is working, the pump is working, and if the pump is working, we will have water from The Well. Water, but no milk. I loathe the powder substitute, it tastes of the city, but the drought has forced a lot of substitution one way or another: no rain, no grass; no grass, no cows; no cows, no milk. We were going to have a cow in Year Three of the dream, but we never got that far.

Most of what Mother Hubbard had in her cupboard is gone, but there is a half-empty box of tea bags on the counter, so I use one of those. Sitting at the empty kitchen table, I trace the grain of the wood. Such silence. I shiver, the Rayburn is not lit. That would help, I think, I could warm the place up a bit, but the matches have deserted their home in the top left-hand drawer of the dresser and I don't know where they have gone. Easily defeated, I wander into the sitting room where the curtains are drawn, my hand hesitates at the window, but even tweaking them opens the way for a javelin of daylight and I leave them closed, for the time being. Moving to the stairs, I put one foot on the bottom step but make the mistake of looking up. That is too high a mountain to climb now.

The sofa feels damp. Yesterday's newspaper lies on the table, with the ring of a coffee mug over the face of a topless model. "Dress for drought!" A pale, hollow-cheeked woman in the photo on the opposite page reminds me of Angie, although my daughter would not thank me for the comparison. Flicking through the pages, it is as though I am in a waiting room, regretting not having brought a friend with me to soften the blow.

My name is called, but I am slow to respond. For a few moments, I can't remember who they are, these men I can see sprawling against the sink and spilling all over the kitchen as I sit obediently, rigid, feeling the wood of the kitchen chair hard against my fatless thighs. Have these men come because of the investigation? No, that was a long time ago and that was the police, not these oversized boy soldiers.

A ringless hand, cuffed in khaki, places a brown file with my name on it in front of me, then opens a laptop and hammers in a password. A voice says the purpose of the meeting is to remind me of my legal status, the reasons for that status, the nature of that status and my rights while subject to that status.

Ruth Ardingly is subject to house arrest under the terms of the Drought Emergency Regulations Act, section 3, restriction and detention of persons known to, or suspected of, or deemed likely to act in a way liable to: (i) Disrupt, interfere with, or in any way seek to manipulate the supply of essential goods or services, in particular any service relating to the provision of water for drinking, irrigation, manufacturing processes, or commerce not covered by exemption clauses outlined in the Drought Emergency Regulations Act, section 4.

I find this funny, being the only subject in Her Majesty's kingdom who appears to have unlimited access to water and who has no need to siphon it off for my own purposes. The judge and jury in front of me don't seem to have a sense of humor. What is less amusing is that the period of detention is described as "indefinite but subject to judicial review at periodic intervals," and my questions about what that means in practice are unanswered.

Ruth Ardingly has also been subject to the following Finding of Fact judgments, as used under the Emergency Drought Protection Order Regulations for the Rapid Processing of Justice:

   (i) that Ruth Ardingly started a series of fires with intent to cause grievous bodily harm or death;

   (ii) that Ruth Ardingly was derelict in her duty towards a minor, resulting in death.

I put my hands over my ears. I will not listen to that. I will not have that said.

The small man drones on.

Under the civil jurisdiction of the Emergency Drought Protection Orders, it is confirmed that the property known as The Well shall remain the principal domiciliary residence for Ruth Ardingly, but that under the terms of the Occupation Order 70/651, Ruth Ard-

*ingly agrees for the said property to be temporarily used for the pur-
poses of research and development, including, but not limited to:
soil sampling; the planting, management, and harvesting of crops;
the drilling and sampling, but not extraction, of bedrock water as
defined under the Extraction for Use Act (amended); the collection,
sampling and testing (but no distribution of) rainwater runoff.*

Despite the small print of my Faustian pact, they don't own The
Well—I won that much. It is still mine; underneath the wire and the
helicopters and the men in brown, The Well is still mine. Half mine.
It is not clear to me what has happened to Mark's share.

"That's the legal status. Have you got any questions?" he asks.

Sinking a little, I shrug. He hands over the file to the fat, anonymous man who is apparently going to deal with the "nitty-gritty" of
house imprisonment. He reads haltingly, finding it hard to make
sense of the interminable regulations. It is as if I am listening to a foreign language, but the broad message is clear. They are my guards.
This is my home. Words slide across the paperwork and set off randomly around the room, sliding down the sink, fluttering up the cold
chimney, trying to crawl their way out like wasps from a jam jar. The
photo we took of Heligan Gardens in the spring and hung to the side
of the kitchen window is tilted, and this makes it look as if the lake
is flowing over the banks and about to trickle down the cream walls
and onto the vegetable rack, empty except for the brittle brown flakes
of the outer layer of an onion.

Curfew
Bread
Electronic
Rights
Request
Exercise

A sort of Kim's Game, by which a large number of disparate things are being laid out before me and named in expectation that when they take the tray away, I will remember them.

"No need to worry about all of this tonight." That is the first time the thin one with glasses has spoken since we sat down. He is also the only one who has looked me in the eye.

"I won't," I reply.

"Good night, then," he says, for apparently it is bedtime.

"Good night," I reply.

I stare after them. "I'm sorry, where did you say you were sleeping?" I ask.

The small one stops at the door. "We didn't," he says, and he and Mr. Anonymous leave.

The thinner, short-sighted one lingers for a couple of seconds. "We're in the barn," he says. "Not far away." He is just a boy. I shall call him Boy.

Little did I know when we plowed our time and money into renovating the barn that we were building a barracks for my own guards. They're not the first to move in there and try to control me; they are following in Mark's footsteps, and his footsteps went out the gate and straight on till morning and I haven't seen him since. I doubt the guards will forget me so easily.

These guards of mine, what will they do all day? What do they eat? What do I eat? Now their commands have receded, questions appear in their place: thousands of questions about blankets and the Internet and food and telephones and children and tomato plants and sheep and baths and books and cutting the grass and, oh my God, everything. I am a toddler again. I want to run after them and hold on to their legs and ask them why, when, how, who. I am in my own house, but I have no idea how I am going to live.

Bedtime. It seems I am going to have to force myself to go upstairs. My fingers remember where the light switches are, but I prefer the dark. I find my way to my bed and, still fully dressed, slide stiffly between the sheets and the duvet, which do not smell of prison but do not smell of home either. Even though it is cold, I leave the shutters open just so I can see the moon over Montford Forest. I will lie here and ask The Well what it thinks of the day just gone and we will reach our conclusions. I will count the sheep I have lost as a way of avoiding sleep, because sleep avoids me. I will compose letters to the ones who are no longer here, because they are no longer here. They no longer hear. I like that pun. I will allow myself the pleasure of the occasional pun. Mark, for instance. I say his name very loudly to confirm his absence. Mark my words. Marking time. And despite the silence, despite the fact that only a wall separates me from the fathomless emptiness of a dead child's bedroom, I am suddenly knocked sideways with happiness because I am back.

I wonder if it will rain.

CHAPTER TWO

S tiff in my stale clothes, I wake. I could lie here all day, all week, all year, and the hairs on my skin would grow through the wool of my sweater, like the tendrils of ivy through a green knitted sweater dropped in a wood. The sun would make its rounds, from the fairground picture above the bed, to the chest of drawers, to the blue, painted mirror, and back again, and I would still be here, thinking and getting thinner, until one day I would have found the answer, but by then there would be nothing left of me, just an imprint, the shell of a tall woman as brittle, straight, and empty as the hollow stalks of the Queen Anne's lace that line the drive in summer . . .

––––––––––

Your search has found 83 matches.

Click. "A little piece of paradise on the banks of the Severn . . ."

Click. "Want to get away from it all? Look no further than this 3 bed, 2 recep . . ."

Click. "Looking for a project? Turn this barn into your castle and be lord of all . . ."

That's how it started. Mark and me in London, hunchbacked slaves to the laptop, squabbling over control of the mouse, believing that the bricks and mortar and land just a virtual second away would eradicate the bickering and divisions which had increasingly become our coat of arms after twenty-two years of marriage.

"It can't be that hard to find somewhere," said my colleagues at school.

"With the price you'll get for this . . ." said our neighbors.

Moving out of London, living off the land, that was the dream. It always had been Mark's dream, but he had mortgaged it for me and, although he never put it this way, he was calling in the debt. He had paid out for so long and now he was bankrupt, whereas I had been investing and accumulating in people and work and ways of living that to sell out now seemed, at the very least, daunting.

Standing like a child on tiptoe at the edge of the diving board, I wanted to jump and yet was terrified of jumping; I wanted to grasp the handrail and walk back down and yet the cold concrete world at the bottom was also slippery with fear. To plunge into a new, freshwater pool, live with a different energy in a world unpolluted by hatred, to come up for air at last, like Mark I was in love with the idea of getting away from it all and starting again in the country. But if we slipped, it would be a long, long way to fall and we would be far away from anyone familiar who might throw us a lifeline. As far as Mark saw it, it was the right thing to do at the right time. I was an inarticulate advocate and found it strangely hard to voice my worries in the face of his enthusiasm, not to mention his desperation. His central thesis was convincing; he might have had a fair hearing at the tribunal, been found innocent, but he had no hope of an unprejudiced future if we stayed. He had things to get away from; I had things to stay for. And whose fault was that, I thought, when I was at my lowest, even though that was neither true nor reasonable.

Mark had further supporting arguments in his brief: there may have been a lack of rain for a while, but these cycles had a habit of correcting themselves, didn't they? Money wasn't an issue; the sale of our semi in the suburbs covered the price of a cottage in the west with land and some to spare, and his payoff for his unfair dismissal from the local authority plus what I had inherited from my father was going to give us enough to live on for a bit; we had savings. Angie had turned out to be the cheapest of teenagers: hers was the one problem you cannot throw money at, and the NHS, Social Services, or HM Young Offenders had spent more time looking after her than we did. We spoiled our grandson Lucien, of course, but as I think of that word, I regret its double-edged meaning. Anyway, the theory was we would be fine for a couple of years, if we were careful, until we knew whether we could make a go of it. It, ostensibly, being the smallholding. It, in reality, being our relationship.

We almost didn't bother to get the details of The Well. There was no video link and anything that wasn't instantly accessible online seemed like too much hassle. We wanted to be able to view heaven now, without an appointment.

"It's got to be worth a real look," Mark said.

"Only if there are two or three to see on the same day," I replied.

There were, but one was sold two days before and the other was taken off the market, so that left The Well. We argued about it but went anyway. Lucien was with us. He had been staying for two or three weeks while Angie tried yet again to sort herself out. He must have been four at the time. "He's a lucky little boy to have grandparents like you." That's what our friends said, whenever we took him on again. I don't expect it's what they're saying now.

It was an unnaturally hot autumn day, a sort of savage last stand by the sun after what had been yet another dull, dry summer following yet another dull, dry winter—dry, that is, according to the statistics the weathermen had then. The various restrictions in the southeast had already been extended to the rest of the country, even by April, and the serious papers carried editorials on the introduction of compulsory water meters, while the tabloids alternated between the threat of Armageddon and close-ups of celebs wearing very little in the sweltering heat. No one knew then where the downward trajectory of the rainfall graphs would eventually take us.

The map was magnetic. The Well was on one of those pages where the red and yellow lines of the roads skirt around the edge, and everything else is white space with lanes penciled in: lanes which skirt the boundaries of private estates of long-dead lords of the manor; lanes which make long detours seeking out old stone bridges, following the packhorse routes, from market to market. Mark preferred the satnav, but as we got close to our destination it let him down.

"Where the hell are we? You've got the map."

"Don't shout at me. This was your idea, traipsing around the middle of nowhere looking for a bolthole!"

Silence.

Me. "Sorry. I didn't mean that." I turned the map upside down and squinted. "I think it's back the way we came."

Mark attempted a three-point turn in a gateway with a ditch on either side. He wasn't an angry person when I met him—purposeful was how other people used to describe him—but the allegations which had led to his dismissal had really got to him and his fuse was shorter, even by then. We crawled slowly back up the hill until we saw the footpath sign with just the symbol of a man with a pack on his back and a stick in his hand and no named destination.

We turned in and Mark stopped the car, took his hands off the steering wheel, and held them in the air, like a priest. There was no sight of the cottage itself; it was not that, rather it was the circle of the world running in a blue rim around us which left us breathless. Far in the distance, hills upon hills shadowed each other to the north and the west until somewhere, far out of sight, they sank into the Atlantic. The closer ridges on the other side of the valley were forested and, in that heavy autumn light, the conifers were charcoal etchings, smudged against the dust gold of the recently harvested fields below them. To the east, the amber land was mainly scorched pasture, hedged and squared by centuries of farming and, behind us, the bleak scree of the Crag.

"Have we arrived yet, Granny R?"

"Yes, Lucien, we have arrived."

The track ahead of us was a dotted line awaiting our signature. There it is, we said to each other, as we spotted first the barn, then the mottled redbrick chimneys rising up from the Victorian stone cottage, and suddenly we were children together, going on holiday and the squabbling in the backseat suddenly stops as the cry goes up from the first one to see the sea. There it is! Look at it! We're here! We signed up the moment we stepped out of the car, but we didn't know what for.

The estate agent was waiting for us, propped up against a bright red 4x4 and smoking.

"Shouldn't do that really," he said, squashing the cigarette under his deck shoes, "not with the fire risk nowadays."

We shook hands. He seemed to me to stare a little too long at Mark, then withdraw his hand a little too quickly. I felt the familiar increase in my heartbeat; there had been times during Mark's hearing in London when I had been very afraid of what people might do. There had been other cases like his in the press, in other towns when the public had forgotten the concept of due process and taken things into their own hands. I looked over my shoulder, back up the drive. Maybe there is nowhere to run to, I thought.

But the estate agent had turned his attention to his car and the moment was gone. "You'll need one of these," he joked overloudly, stroking the hood, apologizing for the state of it, what with the car washes closed and the hosepipe ban.

Breathing deeply to control my voice, I humored him. "Think

we're more likely to get a donkey. What percent did they say petrol had gone up this year?" I asked.

"One hundred and twenty!" He called the words as if it was a darts score.

Mark engaged in manly talk about clearance room and low ratio gears; I could see he was impatient to look around, but he was good like that, putting himself out to make other people feel at ease, and his charm was dismissing whatever doubts the estate agent might have had. That was what he did with me when we first met, the morning after a party, in the last term of the last year, exams over and the future waiting somewhere beyond the overdraft and cleaning the fridge to get the deposit back. I was sleeping in an armchair, some-one else's overcoat covering my bare shoulders, and when I woke up there was a tall, dark, slightly foreign-looking gentleman offering to get me a coffee. He came back and never left me again. We spent that night together, we spent the rest of term together, and we altered our plans and spent the summer together. Four months later, I was five months pregnant and we were at the registry office. We went from young to old very quickly.

The slam of a door brought me back. The estate agent was getting the details out of his car, disturbing a lone white butterfly which had settled on a late-flowering buddleia by the gate. Everything is out of season this year, I thought, and where has the time gone, I won-dered, all caught up in the past, and look at us now, moving to the country as middle-aged people do. In some odd, instinctive gesture, I put my hand on my stomach. "I love children," I remember Mark saying when I told him I was pregnant.

Lucien climbed out of the back of the car, smelling of crumbling chocolate and hot skin. Still sleepy, he held my hand and pointed to a gray squirrel skulking up the trunk of the great oak tree. Our eyes followed it up through the branches until we lost it among the gilt-edged leaves, light falling like dappled water on dry ground at our feet. A police car or ambulance was making its way up a main road somewhere over towards Middleton.

"You can't always hear the road," said the estate agent, keen to market the dream. "It depends on the wind."

"But that must be westerly," I concluded, taking my evidence from both the sun and the Welsh hills.

"Westerly? Probably," he conceded. "That's certainly where the prevailing wind comes from. But I bet you can hear a pin drop at night."

Screech owls, I thought, and barking foxes.

I asked where the nearest neighbor was. Oh, he was saying, miles away and can't see another house, but in truth, I was already feeling the distance between this place and the rest of the world and wondering if I could manage that. Maybe I looked to him like someone who wanted to escape. Much later, Sister Amelia would certainly reach the same conclusion the moment she met me.

A heavy velvet curtain hung inside the front door, which the agent held to one side for us, like a stagehand. It didn't take long to look around. There was the back passage, the kitchen and Rayburn unchanged since the 1960s, Mark's study—well, the room that he made into his study—and the little sitting room with a wood-burning stove, the one we had to replace after the chimney fire. From there, we went upstairs and crowded into the small bedroom and the tiny bathroom and then in here, the main bedroom with the view, this alchemy of a view. Well trained, the estate agent left us to it and Mark felt for my hand and pulled me closer, kissed me once, slowly, on the cheek, and I felt him breathe in deeply, as if he could taste oxygen for the first time in a very long while.

"Just about enough room for Angie and Lucien," I said to Mark as we stepped apart. We both knew my daughter well enough to know that our home would always need to be big enough for both of them, and not just physically.

"I love it," said Mark. I hadn't heard him as enthusiastic about anything since before the tribunal. "A place to start again," he said.

Lucien loved it too, running up and down the creaking staircase, opening cupboards in the kitchen, peering into the fireplace. The sunlight coming through the bay window was showing up the cracks in the banisters, the stains on the carpet, the damp patches on the ceiling, but the place itself felt solid as though it could contain whatever we poured into it.

"Ready to take a look outside?"

We followed the agent up to the "stone outbuilding with electricity and water, currently used as a garage/barn. Scope for development." If the old lady had owned a car, it was clear she had never put it away in there, jumbled as it was with stepladders and spades, broken sun loungers, and coal buckets without handles. No problem to upgrade it for a holiday let, we agreed; no problem to convert it into temporary accommodation for a displaced family.

Along one side of the barn were neatly stacked and recently split logs.

"How long had the old lady lived here?" Mark asked.

The agent didn't have the answer to that, but he did know that since her husband died, a lot of the land was let out to a neighboring farmer, who had also been lending a hand, with the wood, that sort of thing. "They're a tight-knit bunch round here, but the Taylors, they'd always help you out if you were in a fix, I'm sure."

The synonyms for tight-knit must be interesting, I thought. Introspective, xenophobic? At what point does tight-knit become hostile? The agent was explaining that the letting agreement ran out on March 31 the following year.

"Thirty acres of field and woodland. Just the right size," Mark commented, as if there was such a thing as a right size for a piece of paradise. It sounds small, thirty acres, for the havoc it has caused. We visited the orchard, picking up apples and pears which were feeding the worms, wondering at the old fruit cages hung like discarded hairnets over strands of growth, sticks leaning at odd angles like old-fashioned hairpins. The vegetable garden showed signs of more recent work.

"Look at this, Mark." Lucien had his small hands clasped around a fat marrow which had obviously continued swelling all summer, oblivious of the death of its planter. With a huge tug, it broke off the plant and he fell backwards. "Can we take it home? Can we eat it?"

"It's not ours, Lucien," I said.

"It's a good size, considering how little rain there's been," said Mark.

"Who's going to mind? Give it a good tug and Mummy can carry it for you," said the agent.

It was a familiar error, which Lucien corrected. "This is my granny. My mummy's away at the moment."

"Well, your granny certainly doesn't look old enough to be a granny," smarmed the agent.

Lucien stared at him, crossly. "Well, she is," he insisted. "Everyone's always doing that," he said to me, as hand in hand we went over to join Mark who, like an art lover in a gallery, was drinking in the burnished woods, mentally clearing brambles, thinning poplars, planting Spanish chestnuts where the pines had fallen in a strong wind, like spilled pencils in a dark classroom.

We told the estate agent that if it was OK with him, we would eat our sandwiches there, under the oak tree. We promised to call, and he talked the talk about quick sales and all the usual nonsense in a housing market dried out by a lack of faith in the future.

Mark called after him; there was just one thing he had forgotten to ask. "What about the water?"

"It's got its own supply. It's not connected to the mains and doesn't need to be. A well has kept this place going for a couple of hundred years. I can't see it failing now."

I pointed out that now might be just the time it would fail, since there had been so little rain for so long.

"Obviously," he conceded, "you need to get a professional opinion. But it's not called The Well for nothing." He went on to tell us about the water table. That was what made the land so good. Look at it. In fact, as far as he was concerned, we were probably better off here with our own supply than being linked up to the mains and suffering all the shortages and standpipes and allocations everyone had had to put up with for the last couple of summers.

"Anyway"—he gesticulated away to the west where the wind was bullying the clouds—"most forecasters think the drought's coming to an end. This winter will be one of the wettest on record, they reckon."

We believed him because we wanted to.

The dust hung in the air long after he had disappeared. I got a bag out of the back with some sandwiches and crisps we had bought at the service station. We sat on a rug, Lucien cross-legged and upright and Mark struggling as always to organize his long legs which had been forced to live under a desk for almost twenty years. We passed a bottle of water from one to another, sipping judiciously, listening to the repetitive sheep and the blackbird warning us off, and then suddenly, spontaneously, we both burst out laughing.

"I can't believe this." Mark rubbed his eyes and looked up again, as if it was all going to disappear in a puff of smoke. "Well?" he asked.

"You first," I replied.

"No, you."

"Granny R, you go first."

"I don't know," I said. "It's incredible. Look at it. It's got everything we're looking for."

"Everything," repeated Mark. "Talk about the land of milk and honey."

"Yes, it's beautiful," I continued. "And the land is just what we want. And the view is out of this world. It's just that . . ."

"And nobody would know us up here. Know me. No looks in the supermarket, no sniggers from kids on the bus. A clean sheet, Ruth."

"That's probably right . . ." I admitted.

"You think it's too good to be true?" suggested Mark.

"Yes. No. I don't know." The place was breathtaking, I too was dizzy with its beauty, but I needed space to think. I got to my feet, stepped away from the rug, and looked over the wooden gate leading into the field. If someone was looking to escape to the country, then they would be unlikely to find anywhere better than this. "If," I started.

"If what?" said Mark.

His hope was warm on my back; I did not even need to turn around to see it on his face. I counted the cost of what I might lose if we moved here and that only added up to things that could be maintained or replaced—job, connections, and surely my friendships were strong enough to survive the distance. So then I counted the cost of what I might lose if we stayed in London. Mark. And The Well—I'd lose this one-off miracle of a place, this Well.

"It feels like such a responsibility." I looked at my grandson, sitting on the edge of the rug and poking ants with a stick in the gravel. "What do you think, Lucien?"

"I think it's the best place in the world," he said.

We put in an offer on Monday morning, some way below the asking price, as if there was a part of us that couldn't cope with the dream coming true. "Offer accepted," said the agent and I sat on our front doorstep—mobile in my hand, smelling the exhaust from the cars trapped by the city heat, hearing the plane overhead circling for Heathrow, watching the old man opposite scooping up his dachshund's crap from the pavement with a blue plastic bag— overwhelmed with a ridiculous sense of loss. What's done cannot be undone. By the time Mark came home, I had pulled myself together for his sake and we toasted the future like newlyweds. We played old favorites, Mark did his dad-dance around the kitchen, and we got ridiculously drunk. The cottage was taken off the market and the self-timer photo we had taken that day was uploaded and greeted by a chorus of envy from our fellow suburban sufferers.

"Hope you're having a going-away party, because you're sure as hell never going to come back," was one comment.

We pinned the picture up next to the toaster in the kitchen in London, as a reminder. It moved with us, graduated to a frame, propped up on the half-moon table in the sitting room.

———————

I creep downstairs and approach it like a communicant, hold it up to the light. In the beginning was The Well.

CHAPTER THREE

One week. One summer. One night. One week is all that it has taken for all my good intentions to come to nothing. I was going to stand strong against their assault on my freedom, but in truth, I am a sloth, lying in bed for hours and hours, subdued. One summer was all it took before our dream started to curl at the edges and stain like picked primroses. One night is enough to swallow a lifetime of lives.

Outside is a space now devoid of human landmarks. Inside, this is a sentence with no punctuation. Nobody comes. Nobody goes. Nothing happens. I have christened the guards: Anon, Boy, and Three. They own the present tense: recording, monitoring, signing. That leaves me with just the past and the leaden weight of what might have been, the grammar of the human condition.

The reality of house arrest sinks in. I lie here, my sheet a shroud, wondering how long it will be until the end. I will not write. Music slaps like the tide on my mind. To start with, I was wandering a lot, understanding a little more about why caged animals pace, picking at the food my keepers left on the table, but now I stay in bed. I do not take my medication. Drifting through these days on a river of memories, rarely pulling into the bank, sometimes a light flickers in the distance, reminding me that I need supplies to stay alive, but it all seems a long way inland and I push off again and rejoin the current of the past.

Yesterday I saw in a local newspaper that one of the guards had chucked out. "Welcome Home for Well Worshipper!" read the headline, with a picture of women with roses lining the Lenford Road and a white prison van passing. I scrutinize their faces, none of the Sisters are there. We had one year here before The Well made the headlines for the first time. Our first year, my blue remembered hills and one remembered summer.

We sold our house so easily; it slid through our hands to a couple like us, pregnant with plans for the future—only half our age—and spent our last Christmas there with Angie, who was, as they say, "in a good place," if sticking to your script can be described that way. We gave Lucien the blue bike, telling him we would take it with us to The Well so he could play with it there when he came to stay. It must be rusting in the barn, unless the police took it away as part of their investigations. The last Christmas, the last day of term, and the last day of work. And then the stupid lasts: the last book club; the last night in with a takeaway from the Balti House and the ten o'clock news on the television, in the sitting room which had been the stage set for so many acts; the last night out, roaring drunk and hysterical with laughter, with the girls at the George and Dragon (because the girls had stuck with me through it all, and what was I going to do without them?). The last of the obscenities spray-painted on the garage door and the last of the headlines in the local press and the last of the sideways glances in the queue at the checkout. Swings and roundabouts.

As we worked our way through the house preparing for the move, we sorted out the last twenty years. The books, for a start: Mark's unloved law manuals; novels I used to teach at school which had seemed cutting edge at the time and now looked dated and pale; travel guides to places where we had been on holiday with Angie—in a baby carrier in Morocco, in a pushchair in Granada, on the seat on the back of a bike in Normandy, nowhere to be seen in Rome.

There were books on how to adopt, which we never did, and how to manage difficult children, which we never mastered, and how to stay married, which somehow—goodness knows how—we did. I showed that cover to Mark, who had come down from the loft with a boogie board and a moth-eaten sleeping bag.

"Shall we keep it?" I laughed.

"We've made it this far and God knows against the odds," he said. "Bin it."

As a teenager, working as a waitress in a hotel as a holiday job, I used to be able to recognize the couples who had finally managed to leave work on time, get a babysitter, find the money, make a reservation, and get out for a night together. They would sit at one of the highly prized tables for two, looking out over the famous view of the gorge, having survived everything the day could throw at them separately, totally at a loss as to how to make it through the evening together, their hands touching across the white tablecloth, seeking the reassurance that they still loved each other. Well, I thought to myself as I sealed the boxes with tape and took the black bags to the dump, we have made our booking.

We moved on the first day of the cruelest month. Angie and Lucien were meant to turn up on our last morning in London to wave us goodbye.

I checked my phone.

"She's not coming. You can never rely on her. Come on, we need to get going." Mark, sitting in the driver's seat, drumming his fingers on the wheel, the packing cases in the vans, and me, standing like a plastic figure in an empty dollhouse.

"Two more minutes?" I pleaded.

As I was driven away—rather, as we were driven away—I craned my neck. There was still no sign of her and the street was empty as if someone had just wiped our story from the whiteboard.

That evening, after the removal men had gone and we had done all we could for the first day in our new home, he gave me two presents: the first was the glass heron—even then it seemed impossibly fragile, its beak as sharp as an icicle, its neck a script in italics; the second was a bottle of vintage champagne from the fridge, which we had been given some time ago in London and had agreed we would put away until our silver wedding anniversary.

"You don't think we're jumping the gun? We only hit twenty-two last month." I laughed.

"Who cares? We're never going to have a bigger reason to celebrate than this."

I wiped my hands on my sweater. "A bottle of fizzy piss breaks the bank now. That stuff must be worth a fortune. Besides, I'm not exactly dressed for the occasion."

"You've no idea how beautiful your bum looks in your dust-covered leggings with your particularly appealing unkempt hair," he replied, digging out a couple of beer glasses from a packing box.

"Not to mention your unintentional designer stubble." He looked gorgeous to me at that moment, in jeans and a baggy sweatshirt covered in grime, the tight-suited man well and truly consigned to the charity shop.

"Come on outside," he called.

She hadn't texted. I put the phone down before Mark could catch me checking it.

He balanced the glasses on the fence post under the oak and popped the cork, sending lambs scuttling out onto the cold hillside.

"To us!" said Mark.

"And to The Well!"

It was bitter outside, so we finished the rest of the bottle in bed, like we used to when we first fell in love, and suddenly it all felt right, I really believed we had left the worst of it behind, and the future, like my screensaver, was green and blue and beautiful. I embraced my reclaimed, revitalized man, my husband, my Mark.

You have no new messages, the phone said.

It was the best year, our foundation year. We had spent hours and hours in London timetabling the dream and agreed that we should take year one slowly, learn a little, live the idyll. The Taylors, the neighboring farmers mentioned by the agent, were a sort of umbilical cord to the unfamiliar world of our new rural community, lending us equipment and expertise with equal generosity. Our first lambs came from Tom Taylor, skidding down the ramp into the field and looking as bewildered by the beauty as we had on our arrival; I was so bewitched by their innocence I almost failed to close the gate in time, and Mark, more familiar with office paraphernalia than trailers, struggled to fix the bolts. We were city-weak and street-feeble in those days. Then there was Bru, our beautiful puppy, one of the litter from Tom's border collie bitch; he became our therapy dog from the moment he bounced into our lives and chewed my gloves until the moment he was gone, taking his healing powers with him.

This is something I can hardly admit to myself, but there were times in London when the sight of Angie at the door had made me want to close the curtains and pretend I was out, but when we moved to The Well, if I had had a Union Jack, I would have run it up the flagpole to show we were at home in our castle, I would have instructed the guard to throw open the gates for her. She finally came to stay, just for a few weeks before the festivals began, and it was Tom who showed Lucien how to feed the orphan lambs with a bottle, holding on tight with both hands as they tugged at the teats. Getting the hens in at night, that was another of Lucien's favorites, a lengthy and ridiculous pastime which involved us flapping more than the birds. We got battery hens, which needed rehoming, but their experience of prison seemed to have left them wholly incapable of dealing with the outside world; they were decidedly resistant to being shut up and ill inclined to ever lay eggs again. But it was fun.

Every morning, Mark used to stand in the doorway with his mug of coffee and point at the distant hills. "No one," he used to repeat like a mantra, "no one for miles and miles and miles." Company wasn't much of a problem for Angie, not only because she had Lucien and all over the world children are a passport to conversation, but also because it seemed that once you had a dealer, you had a whole network of acquaintances. I was the one who was struggling, taking my first faltering steps at building a social life: yoga in the village hall with two enormous women who ran the post office in Lenford and a Portuguese au pair from the large house by the river; cinema club at the Assembly Rooms; a wine tasting at a local vineyard, whose crop was one of the few that didn't seem to suffer from the lack of rain.

"Give it time," Mark used to say, when I despaired of ever making new friends, "small steps."

One such small step was our invitation to dinner at Cudecombe Hall with Lord and Lady Donaldson, apparently a sort of rite of passage for any incomers, so that they could be weighed up—and definitely found wanting in our case. After a lot of braying and barking around the long dining room table about the state of the gardens in the dry summer and what a hell of a job it was keeping the horses watered, the conversation turned to the forthcoming Lenford Foxhounds Hunt Ball.

His Lordship turned to Mark. "Now, tell me, who do you hunt with?"

"My wife and my dog," replied Mark, catching my eye over the table and winking while the other guests tittered in a sort of nervous recognition of what they hoped must be a joke.

"We've got to post that," I said as we laughed uncontrollably all the way home, "I'm sure Lord D. doesn't use social media."

We had set up a Facebook page in the name of TheArdinglyWell, mostly as an easy way of keeping in touch with everyone in London, because it turned out we didn't pop back as often as we thought we might. Our photo album might as well have been titled "An Exhibition on Paradise," except we were hardly Adam and Eve. Neither of us was strong enough to lift a bale of straw, although actually we were growing upwards and outwards, firming up individually as well as a couple. I noticed it one day when I was standing Lucien against the kitchen doorframe and marking with a pencil and a date how tall he was compared to the first night he ever slept there. As a joke, I stood Mark up against the woodwork and flattened down his now rather wild hair with my copy of the *Vegetable Gardener's Handbook*.

"Has Mark grown?" asked Lucien.

"Oh, yes."

"How do you know?"

"Because now I have to stand on tiptoe to kiss him. And he's changed color," I added. Lucien looked particularly puzzled. "He always used to look a bit yellow in London," I explained.

"But now he's gone brown," observed Lucien. "Like me."

Our technical competence did not develop as quickly as our tans or our muscles. Mark had no idea how to reverse a trailer, despite having been the parking king of southwest London, and I was caught on film being attacked by a piglet the size of a miniature poodle. Our total incompetence was epitomized by our attempts to build the greenhouse, which was like a flat-pack furniture episode on a grand scale. Mark lost it.

"Don't just stand there laughing. Look what you've made me do!" He sucked the blood from his finger, trying to stop it dripping onto his white T-shirt.

"For fuck's sake, I thought you said you'd secured the frame."

"No, we can't just get another one because we've bent this one. This is costing us money. You live in bloody never-never land, you do, when it comes to money."

It went up in the end; the windows never really opened properly and we had to rig up some complicated system by which the door stayed open but the rabbits were kept out; perhaps it knew it was too fragile to last. We posted pictures of us triumphant and reunited in victory with the first pots and seedlings; we didn't post pictures of the rows it provoked, of course, just witty comments like "fallen out big time about the greenhouse, expect Mark back in the office on Monday." It all got the thumbs-up on The Well page, but despite the good intentions, our friends came to visit less and less, apologetic about the spiraling cost of travel, and our contact with the old world relied more and more on anxious emails from them about the price of a pint in our old London pub and the smell of sewage in the streets and, in response, self-deprecating emails from us about the wrong sort of chain saw oil and inedible nettle soup. Increasingly, it seemed wrong to revel in our good fortune and we did what we could not to appear smug. You can do that online: spin, select, make things seem just a little different from how they really are.

Gradually we explored the countryside surrounding The Well, toddlers venturing out in ever-increasing circles from their mother, picking up fence posts from the timber yard the other side of Lenford, or saplings for the hedge we were planting from the tree nursery which was struggling to stay solvent. Once we saw a notice in the post office from a farmer selling up quite some way away, and we drove over on the main road to buy a saw bench and small rotavator from him. He was a nice old boy and talked in his broad accent about the struggle to make ends meet now everything was expensive and how he'd got rid of the dairy herd because the water meter was costing him a fortune. As we bumped back down his farm track, we were sorry for him, but we saw his demise and our ascendancy as the natural order of things and were buoyed up with enthusiasm, our new toys in the back of the Land Rover.

"Let's go back another way," suggested Mark. We took the old road which climbed steadily through the black conifers of Montford Forest and he pulled over into a rather derelict picnic area, the faded walkers' map on the notice board and the outdated calendar of events testament to the rapidly imploding tourist industry in the area. We quite liked the lack of visitors, but we were ignorant and selfish in those days.

"I reckon if we climb to the viewpoint at the top, we should be able to look back and see The Well," Mark said. The climb took us longer than we thought. Bru ran ahead hunting in and out of the larch and we walked hand in hand, only a little self-consciously at first; I remember thinking that it was the sort of thing people do in films. There was no need to talk. It was soft underfoot and silent and we breathed in the pine, noticed the scent where the fox had crossed the path in the night, felt the thud of wings when we disturbed the buzzard. Finally, we broke free from the tight, dry forest and stood in a clearing on the top of the hill, a panoramic view, the great scenery of the world stage spread out on the other side of the valley in front of us, painted in a thousand shades of brown and gold as if it was autumn already. We took our time getting our bearings, noticing small landmarks by which we now oriented ourselves: the sharp curve in the Lenn where it doubled back on itself at Tanners Pool; the famous white church at Nelworthy, catching the evening light; then from there following the line of the lanes through the jigsaw of fields and farms and hamlets until we could recognize the orchards in the valley next to the old cider farm in the valley beneath The Well.

"Which means we must be almost directly above there and over to the east," I said. Several minutes we spent, pointing, thinking we had it, there, that must be our barn, that must be First Field, then realizing no, we were looking too low, too close. In the end, of course, we recognized it not by the one chimney which showed above the rhythm of the contours, nor by the pinprick beauty of the solitary oak, but because it shone—our Well gleamed green like a tiny emerald pinned to the breast of a tired old lady towards the end of the dance.

"Who needs friends and neighbors," said Mark, "when we've got the whole world on our side."

Not us, apparently, because as we found more and more to love about our home and each other, and as we received fewer and fewer invitations from the locals, we went out less and less in company. Mark laughed at me one time, seeing me slipping on the muddy bank coming back from the henhouse—you look as though you've got all your eggs in one basket, that was what he said. I think he was right, although neither of us knew it. It wasn't just the hens on overtime; our vegetable garden was also a lot more productive than our social life. Lucien chose "The Magic Porridge Pot" story night after night, because we said we had a magic porridge pot of a garden all our own and no matter how much we took from it, it made more: perpetual spinach, beans, mangetout, courgettes which became marrows because we simply didn't have mouths enough or hours enough to eat them. Like children, we were amazed by the world we found ourselves in and threw open the window every morning, promising each other that we would never, ever take all this for granted.

We even won third prize for our basket of mixed produce at the Middleton Agricultural Show in late August.

"Not bad for a couple of townies," I joked with Martin, who farmed to the south of us.

"You've got your own secrets for your success, I suppose."

"Secrets?"

"Ay. Don't know what you're putting on your land, but it's nothing that the rest of us can buy in county stores, that's for sure."

The resentment shown to successful incomers was legendary, and real, as I was discovering, but in fact the whole show was tainted by the talk of drought. The dairy section was depleted, although there were still sheep, with the Exmoor mules and other breeds used to picking their way through scrub and moorland proving popular. Everyone said it wasn't like other years—the numbers were fewer, the jokes flatter, and there was not so much money swilling around in the beer tent.

When we got home that night, Mark said, "Come and take a look. There's something I want you to see."

We crossed First Field, went down towards the ancient trees at the edge of the wood, and reached the brook which marked the boundary between our land and the Taylors'. Like many small rivers, the low level meant it had forked around recently created islands, and on the far side there were no prints in the banks where animals had come down to drink, no wet pebbles glistening in the evening light, just a line of barely connected mud puddles. But all the way down, our side was different. The stream was singing. Above our heads, the ash showed no signs of the stress which was bringing a premature autumn hue to the landscape beyond The Well, and beneath our feet in the suppurating bog were worms and flies and larvae and all the microscopic teeming stuff of life.

"Does it run down all the way down to the Lenn?" I asked.

"I've tried tracing it," he said, "but it goes underground just before the boundary hedge."

"This is mad." I said. "No wonder Martin thinks we're cheats or witches or worse. It doesn't make sense."

It didn't then. It doesn't now.

Mark said it was all down to the spring which surfaced at the pond in Wellwood. We were lucky it was miles from the road and hidden away like that, or he wouldn't be surprised if people tried to siphon water from it. You should take a look, he said, it's pretty special. It was our turn for a bit of good luck, he added, that was all.

CHAPTER FOUR

I t was a Keatsian autumn for us. With their roots starved of mois-
ture, trees across the country were brought down in the battering
winds, but in our orchard the only things that fell were apples
and plums and damsons and pears, and we stumbled on the cooking
apples lying unharvested in the long, wet grass because we simply
didn't have enough space to store them. In high spirits, we got tickets
for the village harvest lunch. This was the sort of event which we
thought epitomized the rural community spirit we had signed up for.
Mark and I sat down at one of the long trestle tables, but as everyone
else arrived, they sat somewhere else. I was furious and told Mark
that it was ridiculous that we were treated like lepers, after all my attempts to get involved.

"Do you think it's because of . . . ?" I took a large swig of cider and
immediately regretted saying what I had been thinking.

Mark met my gaze full on. "Because they think I'm a pedophile?
No actually, Ruth, I don't. I think it's because we have water and
they don't. So leave it," he said, "it won't get you anywhere."

But I crossed the hall to the table where over a dozen of our clos-
est farming neighbors were squashed onto a table of eight. The men
looked up, stone-gray, embarrassment flickering over the red faces
of their wives. One or two of them at least managed a hello before
straightening the cutlery.

I said they looked pretty squashed and there was plenty of room on our table. "We're not infectious," I said.

"Some of us wish you were," said Maggie. Someone had told me that she had won Local Farming Entrepreneur of the Year only a few years ago for her parsley farm. Now she was bankrupt. I couldn't think of anything to say.

I watched Mark, taking his drink outside. Other tables fell silent, and then people resumed talking just that little bit too loudly to make it look as though they weren't listening. The locals stared at the menus, designed by the children at the village school where Jean's sister was the secretary, run off on the photocopier at the post office where Alice Pudsley ran the counter, laid out on the tables along with the corn wreaths made by the Altons who lived at the end of our drive and turn left, and the flower posies arranged by the Clardles, who used to run the pub and were now retired, Perry taken up with the largely redundant role of chairman of the River Lenn Fishing Association. I wanted to tell them that we'd done nothing to either deserve or receive or create this fertile land: we'd added nothing to the fertilizer, we were not diverting their streams, we had no way of dragging the clouds to our hill and emptying their leaden sacks of rain on our earth. Somewhere, underneath it all, they were logical people and they knew that must be the case. The vicar gave thanks, the ladies carried in the trays with bowls of steaming parsnip soup and homemade bread, the cider flowed, and Mark and I left. Our harvest was the most prolific, but it seemed we had the least to celebrate. We walked back along the river, where the exhausted salmon hurled themselves from the shallow pond against the dribbling weir, again and again, until the heron picked off their flapping bodies from the dry stones on which they landed.

We knew what it was like to be ostracized. Try having your husband accused of keeping child pornography on his local authority laptop for a pretty swift introduction to the paranoid world of the outcast. But given what has happened since, it's clear that we didn't even know the meaning of the word. We so wanted to believe that we had left the plague behind us in London, and that The Well was the cure, that we minimized the symptoms of its return. True, Tom still helped Mark with the autumn plowing and sowing of our first winter wheat; we bought the ten ewes in lamb from him as well. But it must have all stuck in his gullet, as one evening when we called him for some help with the driller, we left a message on the phone, but he never rang back. In retrospect I can plot the course of our fall from local grace through incidents like those, although they were just the skin-deep symptoms of far more serious disease.

Christmas, which now will always be the bleakest of festivals, was then still glitter and stars. The barn was just about habitable, the wood burner was put in just in time, and our first and last guests were friends from London who'd stuck with us through the allegations and we put on a good show, as if to thank them. There they were with their talk of short-time working and escalating crime, concreted gardens and milk shortages, of reduced services on the Underground and half-empty shelves in the supermarkets, while we delivered a lunch of our own chicken, our own potatoes, and our own broccoli, parsnips, and cranberry sauce, and everyone toasted The Well and agreed we'd got away just in time. Then, just as they left and I was staring at the blank pages of my new diary, Angie showed up again without warning, this time with Lucien and a guy called Des, who spent the short days helping Mark fence the woods ready for the piglets he planned to run in them in the spring and the long nights drinking too much cider.

"This is fucking paradise, this is, Angie. Why don't you stop here? You and Lucien. He'd be growing up in heaven," Des said.

"Then there'd be nothing for him to look forward to, would there?"

She always had an answer, Angie. Her teachers used to say she

was clever but lacked concentration. I called her a dreamer. Then
a rebel. Then an addict. Sometimes, a daughter. January became
February and they stayed on and I wasn't lonely any longer because
this was my Lucien winter: Lucien, running after the pheasants and
yelling with delight at the power he held over them, forcing them to
heave their heavy bodies over the hedges and flap laboriously into
the frosted woods; Lucien, sitting on Mark's secondhand tractor, all
gloves and woolly hat and scarf, driving to the ends of the world and
back; me sawing logs, Lucien carrying them one by one to the woodpile, staggering under the weight and falling asleep on my knee, in
front of the fire, long before bedtime. It was a physical existence for
all of us, and it felt so good to be tired, to ache, to feel the newfound
roughness of Mark's hands on my breasts, because we made love
again that year, night after night. My body felt good once more; even
the drunken Des hit on me in the kitchen one night: "you could be
my Mrs. Robinson," he slobbered. I told Mark and we laughed and
he ran his hands up under my sweater, humming the theme tune to
the film.

I can only assume that Angie overheard us, because all of a sudden
she had come over from the barn and was packing Lucien's things.

"Are you off?"

"Yeah."

"Both of you?"

"Of course." She was stuffing Lucien's clothes into a well-traveled
holdall, nothing folded, nothing counted.

"If you want to travel again, you could leave Lucien here, you
know."

"Why would I want to do that?"

I had bought him some slippers and I held these out to her. "You
would be more free and Lucien could go to school here, make
friends."

She snatched the slippers. "Like you've got such good relationships with the villagers that they'd all be asking him round to play, would they? Haven't you noticed, Mum, none of them want to be around you any longer?"

"I don't think that's totally true."

Angie left the room and I could hear her crashing around the bathroom. "Because you don't want to. But I hear stuff. You're up here with your green fields; they're all going out of business. They think something's not right," she shouted through the wall and then came back into the bedroom. "What the fuck's he done with his toothbrush?"

The room felt too small for both of us. I moved out of her way and looked out the window. "You're going away from the point, Angie. I was just offering Lucien a bit of stability. He loves it here. All this could be his one day."

"You can stuff your middle-class idyll. This is all about you. You always wanted another kid. You always wanted a boy. Actually, what you always wanted was Lucien . . ."

I turned back to face her. "Angie. You were barely seventeen. If we hadn't stepped forward, you wouldn't even have had Lucien, the state you were in. Adoption, that's what social care were talking about."

Angie is mouthing the words as I am speaking them. "Yeah, yeah, yeah, like I haven't heard all this before. And the social workers weren't so keen when Mark got accused, were they?" She zipped the holdall closed.

"Angie, don't stoop that low. You know as well as I do that he was completely exonerated. So don't you ever, and I mean ever, pull that one again."

"OK. For God's sake, don't get so stressed. Mark's in the clear. All's right with the world. Things have changed. I've changed."

"Have you?" I called after her.

Sitting on the end of the unmade bed, I tugged the duvet straight.

I had never doubted Mark's innocence, not once throughout the whole sordid affair. I just knew—I thought I just knew—that he could never do anything like that. It would have been impossible to have allowed myself to think any differently. The sound of Angie slamming the back door brought me back to the present. I noticed my broken nails and pressed hard against the blisters on my fingers from the wheelbarrow until they hurt and wept.

By sunset they were gone, but she had got Lucien to write a note on a page from his farmyard coloring book with huge, irregular letters, half facing the wrong way round. It was her way of saying sorry—that and taking only half the money from Mark's wallet.

Dere Grany R Thank you for having us. Look after the lams. Tell Bru I love him. XXXXX Lucien

I keep it as a memento mori in the dressing-table drawer I dare not open.

The second half of February was cold, gray, and difficult. It snowed once or twice at The Well, but only after Lucien had left.

"He would have loved this," I said to Mark.

"So would everyone else," he replied as we stared over our sparkling, sugar-coated plow towards the black fields and forests beyond.

We saw virtually no one from London or Lenford until the end of the month at the meeting with the spokesperson from the Department of the Environment. The parish hall was crowded out with farmers exhausted from lambing, smelling of sleeplessness, the windows steaming. Patience, like water, was in short supply.

The chairman of the local National Farmers Union introduced the speaker. "I hope he's going to be our Angel Gabriel and bring us good tidings."

But it was clear from the start that the man from the Emergency Committee on Drought Relief (ECDR) had letters after his name but no wings. His was an exercise in panic reduction and spin, and the heckling rose.

"What are you going to do about it?"

"What's going to happen to this country's food supply?"

"Someone needs to do something about it."

"What can he do about it?" muttered Mark to me. "He's not God."

"And what are you doing about places like The Well? They've got enough water to make a fucking reservoir."

The official encouraged any such landowners with possible answers to contact the Drought Help and Information Line on 0816 . . .

"Witchcraft," interrupted an old woman, standing at the back with a baby on her hip.

"Chemicals."

"Stealing other people's water."

Our neighbors were not short of suggestions.

Mark elbowed his way through the crowd and we stumbled across the car park in the dark, me shouting at him to wait. We walked home in single file in silence, went to bed in silence, turned out the light in silence. We'd made promises when we moved here that we would not let the sun go down on a quarrel; we tried so hard to stick to our resolutions, but like the smoker in the pub on January 2, the world was full of ways of failing.

The next morning, I got up first, opened the shutters, and looked out the window. "I can't stand it," I said to Mark.

"Can't stand what?"

"The loneliness. The scent of overnight rain."

"Then you're the only person in this wonderful United Kingdom of ours who feels that way," he replied, sitting on the side of the bed, pulling on his jeans, shivering. Despite the cold, we had scrupulously avoided touching each other all night, so that when my knee had brushed his back, we had both recoiled like strangers.

"Do you know what? I've had just about enough of being on the receiving end of the general public's accusations. We did that in London and it was no fun. Now I just want to be like everyone else. I'd actually prefer to be part of their fucking drought."

Mark came to me, put his arm around me. I wanted to pull away, but I thought no, if I do that now there will be no going back. He'd asked me one night after a long interview with the police about the laptop, "Do you find me repulsive?" We couldn't go back to that. But as for The Well—Mark had no answers, just platitudes. It's not called The Well for nothing. History. Geography. Geology. Logic. The lawyer and the farmer, his alter egos kept each other company, but his schizophrenic platitudes were not for me. I pushed him away, told him to use his eyes, look at our green grass, the snowdrops under our hedges, our tight-budding trees. Now look beyond our boundary, at the landscape iron-gray and stubborn in its sickness. That's not normal, I said. That's not logical, Mark. Nor is the rain.

"What about the rain?"

"The rain. Like last night, it must have rained. We hardly ever see it rain, we don't usually hear it rain, but it has clearly rained. And just here. Nowhere else in the whole glorious country has it rained properly for almost two years, but it rained here, last night, again. Here, we have unlimited access to our best friend the Rain God and we don't even beat drums for him."

Mark thundered downstairs without replying, ostensibly for break-fast, but from the little window on the landing I watched him, in that green sweater, standing between the rows of our fledgling winter wheat with Bru beside him, looking up at him with unconditional loyalty. He crouched down and picked up a feather, brushed it across his unshaven face. When he came back into the kitchen, I didn't know if it was rain or tears on his cheeks, but whichever it was, I wanted to kiss them away, but there was a gap between us and my love didn't seem wide enough to bridge it.

Instead, I wiped my own eyes and made a suggestion. Perhaps we should contact the man from the ECDR or go ahead and get a supply license and run a pipe down to the other farmers. Then at least the locals would see we were not just taking our luck for granted.

"Your 'locals' were so unbelievably rude last night that they can go hang themselves for all I care," said Mark, then he sat down heavily at the table, rubbed his head in his hands. "Look, one drainpipe's not going to solve their drought, Ruth." He picked up the spoon as if to start eating, but paused and held it up to his face, studying his distorted reflection for a moment before continuing. "It wasn't what we came here for, a load of prying bureaucrats traipsing all over our land with their measuring equipment and weather stations and forms for this permission and data for that. The next thing you know they'll slap a compulsory purchase order on the place. We came here to get away from all that crap and we've been doing so well, we've been doing so well," he said, stirring his cereal round and round. Congealed porridge. Hard-boiled eggs. Burned toast. I pointed out that the crap seemed to have caught up with us and he pushed his chair back and grabbed his scarf, saying he needed time to think about things. I said fine, take all the time you need, I'm sure it's not urgent; then fed the toast to the dog, put the eggs to one side for lunch, scraped the porridge into the bin, missed and made a filthy mess because of the rage and the tears and the hair in my face. Couldn't be bothered to clear it up. Kicked the bin. Threw the bowl in the sink, cracked it.

The first letter from the Drought Monitoring Watchdog arrived the following morning. Aerial photos showed a higher than normal level of water retention in the soil on our land and they wanted to drill a small exploratory testing hole. The second letter arrived only three days later. As we had failed to lodge an objection to the first letter, within the specified time limit, the drilling would commence shortly. Third, fourth, fifth, innumerable letters asserted the rights of the state to use, take, drill, occupy, requisition our land. Mark ripped the envelopes into shreds, filed the forms in his desk, the lawyer in him furious at the breaching of proper procedures and the man in him railing at the disregard for his rights. He was going to fight it, he said, fight, fight, fight, thumping the table in time to his rage. Resting my hands on his fists, I tried to still him, pointing out that we could be entering a world where having the letter of the law on our side was not enough.

Events proved me right, of course. We watched, at first incredulous and then fearful, as events unfolded at a smallholding in Devon called Duccombe, which, like ours, seemed to benefit from unlikely rain. The compulsory purchase order became an eviction order, the eviction order was enacted by bulldozers and bailiffs, and the groups of protestors who had camped out at the farm in defense of the old couple who lived there were shown on the news with bloodied heads and placards stamped into the mud, as the riot police moved in. An ambulance was driven up to the house and it was confirmed later that the farmer had apparently died of a heart attack. Two days later, the farmhouse burned to the ground and conspiracy theories swept the Internet as violently and rapidly as the flames which had consumed the thatch. The national uproar was deafening. Anyone with an interest in the environment, human rights, farming, legal aid signed a petition. Duccombe seemed to act as spark to the smoldering confusion about who was to manage this drought and how. Pent-up fury erupted: fury about profits being made by big businesses trading in water while elderly people's homes were rationed and nonemergency operations were delayed, if not canceled; fury about ministers filmed drinking wine on green lawns at Chequers while workers at car plants were put on a four-day week; fury about the exclusion of Westminster from proposed Level 5 drought restrictions, while children in some parts of the southeast attended school only in the morning to save electricity. A march in central London drew half a million people. The government faced a vote of no confidence in its handling of the water crisis. Three people died in clashes with police at a private reservoir on Lord Baddington's estate.

"What's going to happen to us?" I asked Mark, hugging my knees tight as I watched the news. The question was a familiar one; I had asked it before when we were under a different sort of attack in London, but Mark didn't seem to hear the echo.

"Not that," he said, aiming the remote at the television and silencing it. "They won't force us from The Well. They wouldn't dare now. They'll be looking for some sort of agreement. We're in a stronger position, because of Duccombe, even if we have to go all the way to court."

"I hope you're right," I said. "I'm off to bed!" I damped down the fire, gave Bru a biscuit, and kissed him good night.

Mark was partially correct. The official attack on us abated, but the locals were fighting a far more vicious war. Bru had been out hunting and failed to appear for his supper. We stayed out as dusk turned to dark, calling him, banging a spoon against his metal bowl, convinced that any moment now he would rustle up through the brambles, exhausted from hunting, slinking towards us with his tail wagging, expecting a scolding for being out late. We left the back door open for him. Mark said he'd be home, but I slept badly, creeping downstairs in the middle of the night, hoping I'd touch his soft body in the dim light, asleep by the Rayburn, or believing I could hear the click of his paws on the floorboards, coming upstairs to let us know he was safe. Mark felt the emptiness of the cottage as soon as he opened his eyes. He woke me and we dressed quickly in thick sweaters and boots and separated out over the fields to resume our search, our legs making slow work in the heavy mud, our shoulders hunched against the gusting easterly wind. Caught on barbed wire, stuck down a badger set, hit by a car—I went through all the possibilities. I wondered if he could have been shot as a sheep worrier, spotted in the distance, out among the pregnant ewes, but it seemed unlikely when the only people out on the land would have been the Taylors and they would recognize him. I beat the boundaries of The Well, praying that we would find him, calling his name over and over and over again. Someone told me later that if you're searching you should not call relentlessly, because although the frantic clamor might seem purposeful at the time, it's actually only ever in the silence that you can hear the cries for help.

It would not have made any difference for Bru. He was lying among the sodden leaves and dead wood, camouflaged by the undergrowth and the detritus of the winter wood, soft feathers of a white pheasant resting like snow on the mold and the mulch around him. One front leg was bent at the joint with the soft paw towards me, the other straight, just like they used to be when he was twitching and dreaming in front of the fire. His head was stretched out before him at an unnatural angle, his eyes were open, but there was no love left in them. He was unmarked, undamaged, as perfect as he had ever been. I might have wished he was just injured, prayed that he would lift his head, convinced myself that his ribs were moving with the rhythm that signifies breath, swore blind that there was a twitch in his tail when he saw me — although I might have and I did wish all of those things, there was no point, because he was dead.

Maybe people do fall on the bodies of those they love and weep into their stiff, cold hair, but I hardly dared to touch him. I shouted for Mark. I ran to the edge of the wood and screamed. He was too far away. I stumbled back, but there was no hurry. Bru was still there, nothing had changed, he was dead. How, it was not clear. Finally, I found the courage to feel the velvet of his ear between my fingers and stroke the long length of his young body, but there was no injury that I could feel. As I cried, I tried to lift him and as I tried to lift him, I cried. He was heavy. Fifteen bags of sugar; I was weighing my dead dog in bags of sugar. And awkward, rigid. He slipped from my circled arms and thudded to the ground and I had to start all over again, trying to be gentle, as though I were trying not to wake him. George's is a wild wood, long neglected; nobody has thinned the trees for generations, and the undergrowth, left to its own devices, has become tight and mean. The brambles pulled their knives and the roots raised their boots to trip me unawares. It was impossible to climb the fence carrying him, so I had to drop him over the wire. He landed as if he was worth nothing. Mark, I called again and again, I've found him, I've found him. When I was just within sight of the house, he saw me, came running, took Bru and laid him in front of the Rayburn, gently placing his beautiful black-and-white head on a cushion and we clung to each other, worldless.

The vet said it must have been deliberate, almost certainly a dead bird laced with a restricted strychnine-based pesticide, and he advised us to trawl the woods and dispose of any more bait.

Mark dug the grave in grim silence, forcing the spade into the earth as if he could root out the pain, but I wept, noisily and helplessly. He said we had to wrap his body in plastic so the badgers would not disturb him, although how he knew such a thing about burials I've no idea. There were some rolls of polythene in the shed left over from the work on the barn roof, but I could not bring myself to fetch one. Then I struggled to help Mark fold the awkward sheeting over Bru's stiff legs, couldn't find the end of the tape to seal it over his dry muzzle, couldn't control the scissors. I heaved from the bottom of my stomach; I did not know death smelled so rancid. We buried Bru at the top of the garden, the nonjudgmental member of our family, who loved us unconditionally and who healed us, just by being between us.

Bru's death felt catastrophic to me. Inside the house, in the daytime, on my own, his loss tripped me up at the bottom of the stairs where he used to wait for us in the morning and got under my feet in the kitchen when I was cooking; the loneliness got under my skin when I sat in the silence and listened for him barking to be let back in.

In the evenings, there were just the two of us again, our only company the unspoken memory of nights in West London with the front door double-locked and the security lights on in the driveway going on and off for no known reason.

Outside, at night, it was fear which rustled the hedges and slammed the stable door unexpectedly behind me.

"It's as if someone has poisoned everything," I said. "Just to know there are people out there who hate us that much."

However much they hated us, Mark hated them even more in return. I had never seen hatred in his eyes before that time.

Someone told me once how quickly it becomes difficult to picture the dead. That has not proved to be the case for me: the dead are with me always—but the living? Angie I can see clearly, her absence is so painful that her presence in my mind is almost tangible. With Mark, I struggle to recall his face. There remains an Impressionist's portrait of him, or maybe a Cubist version, with disconnected parts of him lying against each other in conflict on the canvas: the hint of his half-Greek missing mother in the sallow complexion, the thick, dark hair, the straight lips where I used to rest my fingers, those eyes, those deep-set, brown eyes. But these things do not make a face, maybe because he has not visited me once since the funeral, maybe because I fear what I may see reflected in those eyes. I cannot hear his voice either and I dare not imagine what he might say if he were to speak. And then there's Sister Amelia, whom I can see and not see. Her hologram is always flickering just out of reach; she conjures herself up whether I want to remember her or not.

I pull the blanket up over my head and hide.

CHAPTER FIVE

B oy stands at the kitchen door and says something about needing to check the monitor. He doesn't exactly knock, but at least he hesitates—unlike the others. "Boyish enthusiasm" springs to mind, a cliché, but true in his case, I imagine. His eyes smile a lot, even when he is supposed to be looking serious, and he has thin, dislocated limbs a bit like a yearling. He must be over six foot, but even so he can't quite reach, so he drags a chair across the room to the corner where one of the cameras is mounted, climbs up, and removes a wire.

"I thought you might want to know," he begins, "that the shrink has called. He was asking if your medication needed to be increased."

"The answer is no," I tell him, biting my black fingernails.

Still on the chair, he looks down at me, the battery in his hand, his head at a ludicrous angle against the beam, squashing his spiky blond hair. "It's just that if they think you're not taking it, then they'll move to a patch or injections. You're still sectioned, and apparently they can do that whether you want it or not." He pauses and turns his attention back to the monitor, as if a little embarrassed. "I thought it was your right to know, that's all."

He reaches up to reconnect the wire.

"I'd better get washed and dressed, then," I say.

He steps down, turns his back to the camera, and makes a thumbs-up sign. "Good idea," he mouths and leaves.

It occurs to me that I smell, but there's no one here to tell me. Anyway, for some reason, this boy soldier seems to have risked something for this unwashed woman and his warning energizes me to take control. I wrestle my mind into logic: I do not want to be medicated or hospitalized because I need to be here and I need to be able to think; I need to stay here because here is the only place I am ever likely to find out what happened; there are things which were never found here which mattered—like the sweater, the rose, the truth.

Only when I have found the truth will my sentence be over.

I must therefore take control.

Having won the debate with myself, I plan an assault, concentrating on Anon, because being devoid of personality he seems the weakest of the three. The guards have requisitioned Mark's study and he is in there on his own, feet on the table, dealing a hand of solitaire, and when I stand in the doorway, he swings his boots to the ground, knocking the cards onto the floor. I never did like heavy-set men.

"Is there a problem?"

Bending down, I pick up the run of spades and lay them out on the table. "Eight, nine, ten, jack, king, ace. You're missing the queen."

"I never get it to work out," he says, shuffling the cards back into one pack. "I usually end up cheating on myself."

He sounds faintly American, but I am sure it's just that he thinks the role he has been given is an American soldier sort of part.

"Sunday today, isn't it?" I ask.

"Sure is."

"I've been thinking I'd like to go to church."

Silence. All three of them have been well schooled in being noncommittal; maybe that's module one in the policy, practice, and psychology of internment.

"You know," I persist, "to take communion. I think that must be one of my human rights, the right to worship, don't you?"

Anon pulls out a cigarette, seems to remember my house rules, and puts it away again. "You can ask, I guess. I'll get a request sheet sent over."

"And I'd like to visit the woods. I assume that's not a problem?"

"Depends on which wood and what you plan on doing there." Anon takes his jacket off the back of the chair.

"Wellwood," I offer helpfully, "the wood at the bottom of First Field."

The blank look doesn't fool me. They have a map of The Well which Three spread out in front of me on my second day, wanting to ensure that I was clear about where I was and was not allowed to go. They know what has happened where in the history of this land.

Anon looks at his watch, looks at me, looks out the window.

"One minute," he says, and leaves the house via the back door. I can hear him, calling over to Three, saying he needs a word. Three has some authority over the other two, although as yet I don't quite understand the rankings. Anon calls him Sarge, but whether that's part of the script he's written for himself or a real reflection of Three's status, who knows. She wants to go to that pond, Anon is saying, and Three is replying, but they are walking away like a panto-mime duo, little and large, and it seems from the words I can catch that they do not agree: arse-licker, grave, fucking, shit hole, old, then rather oddly, boo to a goose. That makes me smile.

Later, Boy lollops over to the house with some papers in his hand—marching was never going to be his thing. "You're going to need to fill out these," he says. "The pond is beyond the current agreed limit."

"Do I put both requests on the one form? The fields and the priest?"

"You seriously want to see a priest? I was surprised. I wondered if it was some sort of joke on Adrian's part."

"No joke and yes, I do."

"That's what he said. So I brought two forms over. If it was up to me . . ."

Those six words are a windbreak where cowards hide during a storm. I let him stew for a few moments and with his complexion, he blushes easily. I am a vindictive old cow.

He breaks the silence. "It's quite straightforward." He is showing me which boxes to fill in. Not many people have stood this close to me recently and I can smell the soap he uses for shaving, breathe in the maleness which saturates his cotton shirt.

"The usual bureaucratic crap. Date, name, signature," he says. As he puts the papers down, his hand touches mine accidentally, and after he has left, I examine my hand as if this brief moment of contact might have left an imprint in the shape of normality on the flesh.

Having signed in all the required places and frustrated by the tedious processes which confine me more effectively than any ball and chain, I wander as far as the beginning of the drive, from where I can see the government workers planting strips of trial crops in geometric patterns across the top fields. Apparently they moved in with their Portakabins and GM crops virtually the day after I was moved out. The land still looks fertile enough, as if beneath the crust the seeping springs are still working their magic, but I have been gone for more than two months and apparently there has been very little rainfall even here in that time; and I have been back more than two weeks and it has still not rained. I don't know what to make of this. Perhaps the clouds don't like these khaki farmers and are waiting for me to pick up the plow, but I won't fall for the same trick twice. Back in the cottage, I pick up the pen instead. I will apply to walk my land, not work it. As I complete the form, I remember the worksheets I sometimes set at school on Friday afternoons, inspiration gone. They were called "cloze" exercises and consisted of blocks of text with words missing and all the pupils had to do was to put the right word in the right place. It was a mindless exercise designed to control behavior as much as anything else. Then, later, I would pack up the marking for the weekend and head home on the Underground. Minding the gap. Filling in gaps. Staring at the bottom of gaping holes. This is my business now.

Permission finally arrives in the form of an amendment to the terms and conditions of the house arrest, reluctantly shared with me by Three. I am to be allowed into my beloved vegetable garden, into my heaven of an orchard; I am to be allowed to sit and lean against my oak tree and look through the latticed world of branch and leaf to the untouched sky above, and I am to be allowed to visit the Wellspring.

As he walks away, Three turns casually and says, "Oh—and there's a letter for you. I'll send it over later."

"I didn't know I got post," I say suspiciously.

"This was for our attention, to be directed to you if I judged it appropriate. If you did receive post in your own name, it would be read by us. Whether or not it was passed on to you would be my decision. But"—Three smiles—"this is all hypothetical because no one has directly written to you, have they?"

The wait for the letter is unbearable. It could be from Angie. It would start, *"Dear Mum, I forgive you . . ."* It could be from Mark— confession or accusation, who knows. Or from one of the Sisters; I really thought Sister Amelia would write if no one else. Sister Amelia. What would we say to each other if we were to meet again? Since my return, I have fought against her shadow, which has tried again and again to stand between me and the light, but the idea of imminent, direct contact from her is too strong, and the thought of her dries my mouth with hope and fear and thoughts, wild and screeching as crows at dusk, scattering into the darkness.

Breathe, breathe, I tell myself, slowly, imagine you are blowing out a birthday candle in one long breath. There. She is gone, for now. The spring sun moves in millimeters across the sky and I am beside myself with dread and hopeful expectation.

Finally, Boy bangs on the window. "Post," he says as he comes in. I can imagine him as someone's son, or holding out a birthday card for a girlfriend. "Read it."

"I fear the Greeks," I say, and am surprised when he replies.

"I'm not bringing any gifts. Not on my wages."

These children must be part of the new breed of "community conscripts," much disputed in Parliament but introduced in the face of the drought on that most tenuous of premises that "needs must." He is probably doing his stint after university, and there is no reason why an army private shouldn't be quoting Virgil nowadays, but I have become predatory and recognize in him not only a possible source of conversation but also a potential source of information from the outside world. Right now, though, I am consumed with anticipation about the letter and am torn between ripping it open and a more reverential approach which would allow the moment to last.

The Reverend Hugh Casey has written from The Pumphouse, Middle Sidding, to say he has been contacted by the Prison Welfare Division in relation to my request to see a priest. He is pleased to let them know that it would be a pleasure to visit. Not Angie. Not Mark. Not Amelia. Disappointment punches me in the stomach.

"It's good news isn't it? This priest bloke will come on Sunday."

"This Sunday, then." I don't want any of them, even Boy, to know how much I have lost track of times and dates.

"Yep. Two days. Be a bit of an event for us all. Perhaps we should have a party." Boy clicks his fingers and reggaes his way around the kitchen. "Red red wine . . ." he croons. I think he's one of those people who can't tolerate other people's unhappiness and feel a personal responsibility to cheer them up. I manage to laugh just because I feel sorry for him: he has his work cut out for him here.

This must be a boring posting for three young men. No doubt their mothers are pleased that they are safe in the English countryside, with running water and the task of guarding some inoffensive crops and keeping a middle-aged nutcase in a field, rather than out on guard duty, firing off rubber bullets at protestors or policing the marches which I am sure must have continued—the motivated and the mad stamping their thirsty way up and down Whitehall, demanding rain. The news used to be on constantly in the dayroom at the unit, blaring from the TV hung too high on the wall: pictures of soldiers guarding the reservoirs, the lakes in Cumbria, the building sites where the first desalinization plants are under construction, or shots of the RAF droning overhead in their helicopters, sights trained ready for unscheduled activity on the ground—an old woman with a bucket, a black kid with a hose, a group of men rigging an illegal pump next to an unauthorized factory. These jobs carry a lot more risk than this one, I am sure. Here the risk is of insights into one's own dry soul, and that has never worried anyone's mother unduly.

Needing to do something to wash away the taste of abandonment, I hold up a mug and he says please.

Small talk. That will help. "It must be quite boring for you here," I begin.

"The job description's pretty dull," he admits, "but the location, now you can't call that boring. The science of it, if you like."

"What science?"

"We were recruited because we've all got science degrees of some sort. Typical army. They thought, oh, he's got a degree in particle physics, he'll be good at taking rain gauge readings, although of course it hasn't actually rained since we got here."

"And have you? Got a degree in particle physics?"

"I did a geography degree," he tells me. "This is my payback year. They were asking for science graduates, and then when they found a bunch of us, they pulled out the ones who would be no good on active service and came up with us three. The blind, the deaf, and the dumb."

"And you are?"

"The blind. Lenses—very strong. Adrian—Anon as you unkindly

insist on calling him—he's asthmatic. Mind you, it's hard to find anyone who isn't nowadays, with the dust and everything."

"His weight can hardly help," I add. "So that makes Three the dumb one."

Boy looks away. "Hardly," he says. "He was already in the Volunteers apparently, so one step ahead as always. He was telling us how he's already had experience policing the demonstrations as a reservist. So I told him I was probably one of those marching."

"What were you marching about? Not me, I hope."

"I'm afraid not. I'm not religious. Other stuff. Human rights mainly. I think there have to be ways to manage a drought without chipping away at all our civil liberties. And the land, of course, the way we're messing up the climate. Have messed up, past tense for all we know. I'm not a geographer for nothing." He glanced at the camera. "Anyway, I got the rest of my degree in footie and beer."

I would have liked a son. I turn away and pour the remains of my drink down the sink.

CHAPTER SIX

Sitting outside, my back to the stone wall at the rear of the house, inviting the spring sun to repair my prison-pale face, my heart is beating a little faster in the knowledge that today I will have a visitor. I wait, half in hope, half in fear, counting the minutes. Then, through the haze, I spot a black lumbering shape at the top of the drive. For a split second I think a Friesian has got loose, before remembering that there are no cows around here any longer. A few moments later the cow becomes a man wearing a dark suit, a black hat, and a billowing black raincoat and carrying a white plastic bag. He must be the only person in England who still possesses a raincoat. The man is limping slightly, inching along the track and, like most people, when he reaches the crest of the hill, he stops and looks around him, but he stays there much longer than most, sitting on the raised verge beneath the turbine for a few minutes before getting up heavily, brushing down his trousers and picking up his bag, and continuing on towards the house. Here is my priest. Enter the Reverend Hugh Casey.

God knows the last thing I need is another persuasive religious, let alone a male version. This distrust of men is the legacy of Amelia and her sisters, I tell myself: you should rid yourself of this prejudice. On the way into the house, I pick some daffodils from the wilderness of weeds straggling along the edge of the drive, stick them randomly in a redundant milk jug, and put them in the middle of the table; it isn't something I've done since I returned here, but today I am entertaining.

Boy announces the priest's arrival like a maître d'. "Ruth, meet the Reverend Hugh Casey. Come on in, sir."

"No, no, I'll wait for the good lady of the house to invite me in."

It is a polite, cultured voice with a hint of an Irish accent. The body which accompanies it is large and the face is flushed, although whether that is from the walk or embarrassment, I don't know. I play my part and greet him; he takes my one thin hand in his two warm palms and holds it slightly longer than I am prepared for. In the kitchen he introduces himself again, takes off his coat and hat, and hangs them over the edge of the chair.

"Not your local man, I'm afraid. They dug me out of retirement for this. I can only suppose it's because I live relatively close and many years ago used to be the chaplain at a military hospital. Hardly guaranteed secure, but that's the way their minds work, I suspect."

"Well, thank you for coming anyway." I offer him a cup of tea.

"Ah. Now, that's where I can make myself useful," he says and rummages in his plastic bag. He pulls out a Bible, which was to be expected, a small wooden box with a cross on it which he says contains the holy sacrament, and a little flask. "I gather you have the water," he says. "I can provide the milk."

This is proper milk, milk that we drank as children in great gulping mouthfuls, milk that we poured onto cocoa on bonfire night. The smell of it spills over my mind and I am drunk on the memory.

"I have my own cow," he pronounces. "A Jersey, Annalisa by name."

Giggling in church at Christmas was always my forte when I was small, and something about the priest in my kitchen is making me revert to childish ways. That or hysteria. I stick my head in the drawer, ostensibly rummaging for a spoon.

"I'm sure you'd love her. She is particularly beautiful. I have to say that she is the love of my life."

"They let you keep her?" Now I am really hunting for sugar, because although I am not familiar with the clergy, he looks like the sort of vicar who takes sugar—a lot of sugar.

"Let them try and stop me, that's what I said. Truth be told, I played the holy card. Said that the priest of the village had ancient rights to graze one cow on the common land and if they tried to remove her, I'd take it up to the House of Lords. God seems to be exempt, you see, from the effect of their emergency powers, and it would have been a frightful nuisance for them, so they went away like most bullies do in the end."

Interesting though this line of thinking is, I want nothing to stop me savoring the taste of tea with real milk, so we sit at the table together, sipping in silence like connoisseurs. As predicted, he adds a lot of sugar and gazes around the kitchen expectantly. I wonder if he is expecting cucumber sandwiches and bourbon biscuits arranged in a circle on a porcelain plate, because he is not only old but also old-fashioned, a sort of living anachronism. It has to be a possibility that he, too, is not what he seems. I pick up the thread of his conversation.

"I didn't know that. I'm surprised no one suggested the ecclesiastical legal route to me for The Well. After all, it had become a religious place of sorts by the time I was arrested."

"Not the same at all, my dear, not in their book. God forbid anyone might start accessing eternal life by any means other than the Church of England. Now, are you going to show me round?"

Having explained the limitations of my imprisonment, we set off, past the back gate ("This must be where you got the daffodils," he says, "such a wonder to see a vase of real flowers on a kitchen table nowadays'), on through the budding orchard, and then down through First Field. He apologizes for repeating himself, praising God like it was Easter Day all over again. "But you must see the wonder of it for me, can you not see the wonder of it, the green of the grass and that pink color you get when the trees are in bud?"

Once he calms down, we walk slowly and we talk freely. We talk about varieties of tomatoes, we talk about dust, we talk about the Holy Land and about water and a shared childhood experience of swimming off the coast of Exmoor, where the pebbles gang up with the waves to drag you under. He describes being a prisoner of war, and we share an understanding of freedom based on barbed wire and spotlights. We find ourselves, inevitably, I suppose, looking down at Wellwood, and he says, so is that where it all happened, and I say, yes, that is the place, but I don't go there, and he asks me if I mind if he prays. He closes his eyes and bows his head and his prayer is silent; mine is written in dried leaves floating on the surface of the water out of sight, under the trees. I appreciate the way he asks no questions, offers no answers. Making our way back up the hill to the house, I am conscious that I am emaciated and unfit, but that for him this is really hard work, he is definitely overweight and rather purple in the face. I am no doctor, but it's not hard to diagnose high blood pressure and to hazard a guess at a root cause: too many years putting too much Jersey cream on too many scones when it would have been rude to say no.

"I was surprised you requested a priest"—he puffs and pauses and puffs again—"after all that has happened here with the Sisters of the Rose of Jericho. Who was the one? Sister Amelia, was it? Haven't you had enough of religion?"

His question reminds me that I had not intended to like him. "I wanted a visitor," I say.

"Any old visitor?"

"I am not spoiled for choice. You were one they couldn't refuse."

"No other reason for a priest, then?"

I hesitate, deciding to be economical with the truth. "I am haunted," I say. "I thought you'd bring some answers with you."

"Who haunts you?"

"There are any number of ghosts here. It depends on where I am, what I am doing. There are the Sisters, there are . . ." I stop myself, I will not name the others. "There are others, I'm sure you've heard all about it." We pause at the top of the hill and look out over the fields and onto the yellow ocher hills beyond, and I continue, "But here, at this spot, I am haunted by the ghost of a farmer. He was our neighbor, Tom. He was an absolute lifeline for us when we moved in. I don't know how we would have survived without him, ordinary things, everyday stuff. It's difficult to explain, but it almost came as a shock to us, his kindness, after everything we'd been through. We could hardly believe it was real."

The roof of his old milking parlor is visible from here; the corrugated iron which patched up the roof is catching the afternoon light. Fool's gold.

"Sometimes, if I am sitting out here, I see him walking the hedges, checking the lambs. He had a habit of tying baler twine around the gateposts in a clove hitch. They hung around for ages, the bits of orange string, like those gaudy flowers people tie to lampposts after an accident. Then it seems as though he is coming over to chat to me, but he looks straight through me, walks straight through me. My only visitors are ghosts."

"Times have been hard for farmers," acknowledges the priest, but I am not listening to him. I am both the storyteller and audience.

"We did try to help. They used to farm The Well land, you know, before we arrived. Eventually, we offered to run pipes from the Wellspring down through his farm and Martin's, but they were very suspicious of us by then, wanted to know what was in it for us, pointed out we hadn't got a license to supply, and then Mark wouldn't apply for one because he'd never wanted to do it in the first place and the whole idea fell flat."

"I'm sure you did what you could at the time."

"It wasn't enough, was it? One night, after supper, with his wife in the kitchen doing the washing up and the brown envelopes piling up on the sideboard, he swapped his slippers for boots, his cardigan for his tweed jacket, and pulled on his cap that he kept for market days. Then, it seems, he slipped out of the house, across the yard, and wedged the barn door closed behind him with two fifty-pound plastic sacks of chicken feed. I expect he wanted to make sure that only a man could find him, do you think that's why?"

The Reverend Casey half raises his arms, empty-handed; he doesn't offer an opinion, he doesn't have answers. "I think I know where this story is leading, Ruth. You don't have to do this." He reaches out as if to touch me, but I flinch him away. He is wrong. I do have to do this.

"It was new rope, you know, brand-new, slung over the oak beam and secured around the handlebars of the quad bike. They owed a lot of money on that. Imagine him, taking time to steady himself as he climbs onto the old chair, clutching at the fractured ladderback until slowly, like a tightrope walker, he straightens up and catches the end of the rope and ties the knot. He was very good at knots, did I mention that? He still had his cap on when they found him; that would have mattered to him."

"The suicide rate among farmers has been something dreadful, may God rest his soul."

The priest crosses himself and we sit on the grass in silence. I respect people who are good at silence. I've been to two funerals at Little Lennisford; Tom's was the first. It wasn't as hard as the second, but it wasn't easy. Both of them—guilt and grief—hand in glove.

Finally there is a question from the audience. "Can you say why you are telling me all this? Were you thinking that I might be an exorcist?"

"It's far too late for that. Maybe if you—if any of you—had come along earlier. But you weren't there when it mattered, and I fell for it, the whole religious scenario, and now it's too late." I get to my feet. He takes longer to struggle up and I am torn between offering to help him and watching him flounder.

"Is it our fault, then?" he asks when he is finally standing.

"Whose?"

"Those of us who weren't there when it mattered."

I kick at a molehill without replying.

He continues. "God was there, somewhere. For you. For Tom. It is never too late to face the ghosts, you know." Now he is wheezing in his attempt to keep up with me, breathless by the time we get to the gate. "Come on, you wouldn't expect to invite a vicar for tea and to get away without a sermon, would you?"

"I became rather used to doing the preaching myself," I tell him. "I was probably as good as the next charlatan. Because that's what it is in the end, isn't it? All lights and mirrors. Besides, I'm not interested in the meaning of life any longer. There is only one question to be answered, as far as I am concerned, only one truth to be found. Nothing else matters."

"To not know who killed your own grandson is a terrible thing. I can only imagine the pain of not knowing," he says.

Three is waiting for us, ostentatiously checking his watch. "Your pass expires at five p.m.," he says.

The reverend smiles beatifically. "The Lord alone knows when our time is up."

Church: one; army: nil. I hate to say it, but I like his spirit.

"I don't want to outstay my welcome, or indeed jeopardize my chances of coming again, so I'll be off. If my parishioner and I might just have a moment?" The reverend holds the silence and under pressure Three retreats. "Now, about the Eucharist . . ."

I put my hands in my pockets. "You've probably gathered by now that it wasn't . . ."

"Exactly as I thought." Reverend Casey goes inside, and through the kitchen window I can see him busying himself with the plastic bag, the Bible, the little box, the flask, while Three and I wait at a distance from each other without talking. The priest comes out and smiles benevolently towards the waiting soldier. "Ruth and I have shared a very special time here today." He raises an eyebrow quizzically as he looks at me.

It seems I have a choice, an unfamiliar feeling, but it doesn't take me long to make up my mind. Apart from anything else, I think this old priest could be easily manipulated and will have his uses. "Thank you, Reverend," I say loudly. "I look forward to seeing you next week."

"If I'm to come again, then you must call me Hugh. I will be here, same time next week. God bless you both."

The priest—Hugh, as I must learn to call him—begins his slow walk back up to the road, pausing again at the brow of the hill where I think I see his right hand rise and fall in the sign of the cross, although he may just have been adjusting his hat.

"A very holy man," I comment to Three.

"I wouldn't know," Three replies.

Nor would I.

The whole house feels different, even the air hangs awkwardly; neither of us is used to visitors. I walk through my garden in the dying light and reclaim it, surprised by how disoriented I am at this contact with another human being. He was right about one thing: there are ghosts to be confronted here. I turn back and go inside, but it takes a long time before I get as far as the landing. I stare at the closed door which separates me from Lucien's room and strain to hear beyond the silence. My thumb is on the latch, my fingers around the black metal handle. I press and release the catch and open the door, just an inch or two, just enough to check the night-time breathing. Without going in, I reach around the doorframe and fumble for the switch, stepping into the room for the first time since

I have been back. It is virtually empty, except for a black bin liner of Lucien's things returned to us by the police, tied in a knot which I will never be able to undo. The mattress on the bed lies sullen and ugly—no sheet, no duvet, no pillow to grace it. No head on the pillow. No hair on the head. No carved wooden rose hung with a leather thread around his neck. To not know who murdered your grandson is a terrible thing. If only I were to find the wooden rose, I would be one step closer to knowing.

I move the bedside light as if the rose necklace might have just dropped down behind, in the way that in more ordinary times pound coins find the gaps between cushions or earrings rest between floorboards, but there is, of course, nothing. On my stomach I force my chewed fingernails between the cracks in the floorboards, lie facedown with my mouth licking the dust, squinting into the darkness; on my knees I crawl to the bed and drag it from the wall so that the spiders scuttle from the skirting boards. Not this room, then, not here, but surely somewhere there is a small rose carved in wood and threaded with leather, and if that was found, then the truth would be next.

In the bathroom, the medicine cabinet has been emptied by the guards, all cleaning fluids locked away, but I can still rip up the carpet and tear down the false hardboard wall which conceals the pipes, cutting my arm on the screws sticking out of the plaster. Downstairs, I can claw the curtains from the rails, and I do; I can empty the coal dust from the bucket and shower the sitting room black so that it too can be in mourning, and I do; I can pull the emptied drawers from the sideboard and dislocate the sides from the front, the bottom from the sides, the brass handles from the front, and I do. I must, because somewhere is the small wooden rose which my grandson wore and which has never been found and if I can find it, if I can only find it . . . Nothing will stop me searching, nothing, nothing, nothing.

———

"Can you speak to me, Ruth?"

There are men on my brittle arms, over my wasted legs, the weight of men on top of me. Sister Amelia warned me about the weight of men, holding you under until you cannot breathe any longer. I am offered a drink in a small, cardboard beaker, and I know it is poison from the moment it sleeps my tongue.

CHAPTER SEVEN

Sleep is a malevolent force. It lurks around the edges of my bed like a sick dog, its bad breath hanging on the night air. There are many explanations for what I may have done. It is not unusual for people to be unable to remember the heinous deeds committed by their own hands, conceived in their own minds even in broad daylight, while wide awake. Then there are those who do terrible things when they are asleep. Then there have been those throughout history who have done things of great importance, both good and evil, when it was not clear if they were awake or asleep or in some half world, as yet unclassified by scientists. This is another grammatical construct I have not thought of until now. I have been thinking about what I may have been, what might have been, but now my mind turns to what must have been.

My thigh is branded with the sign of the Rose. One night, during those last days, I must have stood over the Rayburn and heated the metal emblem until it was white, must have held it with an oven glove as I pressed it against my own flesh, must have smelled the burning, must have felt the million pins pierce me. Sister Amelia blessed and tended the burn the next morning with honey, I do remember that. The mark is here now, I feel its uneven writing with my fingers and it reminds me of the pain I could suffer and the pain I could inflict in an ecstasy of unknowing.

Although the psychiatric assessments dismissed as unlikely the possibility that I was one of those people capable of terrible acts of destruction while in a state of sleep, there are those who still consider it a possible solution to Lucien's unsolved death, myself among them. The press, of course, loved it.

"The saint: did she sleepwalk her way to murder?"

"Was this a visionary death?"

I will never be able to dismiss that possibility until someone else is found guilty—and until that happens, I cannot sleep. When I do finally fall asleep, which is usually when it grows light (as if the diminishing darkness takes with it the possibility of destructive acts), then I dream of footprints leading into the reeds, of a heron cast in iron on the far bank of the Wellspring, staring. If I am not to become a prisoner not only of the state but also of my own self, I must go to the Wellspring again.

The grass in First Field is becoming sparse; the thistles scratch my ankles and I can feel the flints through the soles of my shoes. We always thought the water table here was close to the surface, but as the rest of the country has proved, that cannot last forever. There is a strange quiet in this empty field. The guards told me that the government disposed of the remaining livestock, by which they meant my lambless ewes, my harebrained hens, Mark's feral piglets. Disposed of. Shot. Hundreds of years these fields have hosted sheep, cows heavy with milk, and the wind whispering the barley, and now they are barren, unless you count the sterile strips of engineered produce patrolled by the guards, and I don't. Reaching the crest of the hill, I stop. The history of the River Lenn is embodied in the landscape around me: the position of the church close to the bridge, its Norman tower clearly visible now that so many of the trees, weakened by drought, have come down in the gales; the ribbon of cottages along its length, road following rail following river as our industrial past snakes its way towards Wales. Then to the north, the

Crag, a bitter and rugged hill keeping its bald head bullish above the simpering lowlands. I bring my eyes away from the horizon to the nearby landscape and the footpath descending the hill in front of me, down to the stile into the wood, between brambles and low-hanging boughs of budding ash, until it reaches the Wellspring.

Despite the afternoon sun slanting through the canopy, the water looks black and the reflections of the surrounding trees blur as three or four mallards dip their heads for food in the thickening sludge. Sister Amelia would not have liked the brash dominance of the male birds, their harassment of the muted females on her reservoir of femininity. There is a flash of blue over yellow as the kingfisher takes flight over and is gone, then it is still and quiet apart from the intermittent warnings screeched by the vulgar crows in the treetops. The water level is low and parts of the old moss-covered stones are exposed, but they hold in their memory the marks showing where the surface usually lies. Matter holds memory, they say, in which case these are sad stones. I approach the pond, kneel down and dip my fingers in, feel the coolness, cup my hands and wash my face and let the drips run down the front of my shirt, trace their way down the veins on the inside of my arms. Staring into the dark mirror, it is as if I can see his face, as if he is about to say something.

With my eyes closed, I can banish the specter of the Sisters encircling the water and pray. No. It is not a prayer. It is rather a saying out loud of things which need to be said, but I do not anticipate being heard or answered. *Tell me how he died.*

There is a time to cast stones and a time to gather. I pick three flints from the dust-dry floor of the forest. I toss the first into the water and watch the ripples in perfect circles pulse towards the reeds which are just breaking the surface with their lurid spring-green confidence. Screeching, the ducks take flight, heaving into the air with a gross flapping and a pandemonium.

It could have been the Sisters.

I throw the next flint, a little harder; it falls off center, creating cavorting waves which cross the paths of the ripples and revel in the anarchy.

It could have been Mark.

The third flint fits my hand. I draw the sharp edge across the thin transparent skin of my wrist until a red weal rises up, with just the smallest beads of blood, congealing, not spilling.

It could have been me.

I stand and hurl the last stone into the pond. Water does not forget either. The blackness makes my head swim and, feeling faint, I grope towards the log where I used to meditate, staying there long enough to regain some sort of equilibrium and for the ducks to alight on the water again as if nothing has happened there. As I retrace my steps back to the house, the breeze swings to the southwest and the horizon, far beyond Edward's Castle and Cadogan Top. Clouds gather, great shafts of light ruling lines of fool's gold across the forests on the other side of the valley.

Last night I slept. This morning I wake and it has rained. I went to the Wellspring. It rained. It just depends which conjunction you choose to link the sentences. For me, it is a sign that The Well will give up its answers to me one day, but for others it is a justification of the paraphernalia which has been plowed into this place. A convoy shudders down the drive. Government officials get out and crawl all over the fields with their probes and electronic gauges and high-tech equipment, while members of the press are invited to take photographs of the crops. Three is in his element, marshaling the parking like the science teacher at sports day. Boy and Anon are children, jumping in puddles.

"Is this what it was like before?"

"Yes," I say. "Just some rain, falling here and not anywhere else. Everything else went from there."

"Did you know it was going to rain?"

"Will it rain again?"

I have a question of my own: can there be rain without visions and voices? That would be something worth having.

There is one last emotion, though, which I have not anticipated. I am feeling smug. There, you thought you were just guarding a middle-aged crank who had delusions of grandeur, but now you'll have to think twice, smart-arse.

Rain, rain, go away. Come again another day. I dance like a witch doctor around the sitting room.

Boy sticks his head around the door, looks a little taken aback, and I fall onto the chair, laughing. "I forgot to tell you," he says. "We go off duty tomorrow. One month on, one week off."

Rain comes. Duccombe burns. Boy goes. I stay. World turns. I skulk off to my bed, out of control once more.

Three relief guards have arrived, ill at ease. One of them is a woman, and I am not sure what to make of that. I spy on her through the upstairs window, notice how her hair is scraped back off her face and pinned under her cap, how her feet look as big as the men's in the regulation boots. She is sour faced and brusque when she comes into the house to complete the battery beep test on my tags, and I am relieved by her monosyllabic responses to my attempts at conversation. I thought I was ready for a bit of female company, but I was wrong. All three of them keep to the barn when they are not on duty, and when they are on duty they adhere to rigid routines, patrolling the boundaries, testing the alarms, inspecting the house. It is not enough to be known by three soldiers, male or female. I used to have friends, a family; I had neighbors, I had followers, for God's sake—no irony intended. I was a person in the middle of a web. But all that was cut with one stroke of the knife, and here I am alone, my very own living Gordian knot. The worst is that I don't know if anyone has tried to contact me or not. I grow more and more suspicious of this regime; someone out there must be thinking of me.

Sometimes I hear people, a lorry reversing somewhere on the lane and someone shouting directions. Once I heard shots and then saw two men walking alongside the hedge which runs between the Great Nunton Lane and the old parsley farm. They had guns and every now and again they stopped and took aim and the valley cracked as they fired. Without beaters, the birds have no reason to fly, so I don't know what they hoped to kill. Today, I can hear wedding bells ringing in the village. We didn't have bells. We got married in a registry office, with our favorite duet from *Porgy and Bess* playing on a CD in the corner of the soulless room, vows and the weight of his mother's lifelong absence sitting on Mark's suited shoulders. I overheard Mark's uncle saying how they had always thought Mark would take over their farm because he'd loved it so much as a child, spent all his holidays there with them, and then my dad agreeing with him that there was no money in farming, and being a lawyer, that was the way forward for a man with a kiddie on the way, the two of them standing outside the hotel, stamping their feet and flicking the red ash into the slush.

It snowed at our wedding, a desultory sort of snow that fell from the aimless sky that day as if it was just a way of getting rid of the leftovers, and I realized that everything Mark had ever planned was being suffocated in white.

The peal continues to ring across the valley, but even that song is not strong enough to bring me to prayer. Births, marriages, deaths. Angie was born three months after the wedding, and three years after that we sat in another soulless room hearing it confirmed that Mark would never be able to have children of his own. Neither a farmer nor a father be. They made a lot of that during the investigation, as if not being able to have your own son would make you more likely to abuse other people's, or murder other people's, I suppose. It seemed a ridiculous theory then, but what happens to a man who loses his dreams, not just once or twice but over and over again?

The bells have stopped. The silence cannot hold. It is replaced by the relief guards conducting the weekly alarm test, the siren sending the crows circling and screeching over the treetops. Even the birds fight over our fields—the robins attacking the dunnocks, the rooks nipping the wings of the buzzards in flight—but none of them can take on the helicopters. The beating of their metal blades whip up my day-sleep memories.

———

The eggs were warm and perfect spheres in my cold hands. We had spoken about marking our first anniversary at The Well, but the time for celebration seemed to have passed. Even so, in my head I was planning a soufflé as a special dinner, for a surprise or a salvage operation, I'm not sure which. The sound of blades slicing the morning sky made me look up and there was a helicopter hovering, a man with a camera leaning out at an angle. It made me jump, I think, and as I grabbed the post from the washing line to steady myself, I smashed the eggs, I do remember that. Then, moments later, in the kitchen, washing my hands and sponging down my trousers, Mark came in and flung the paper on the table.

"Wonder Well. For Christ's sake, look at this headline, Ruth, look at it!"

———

I still have that cutting. It looks small, as things of import often do when you revisit them.

———

Wonder Well? It was an aerial color photo. It needed to be, because its sole purpose was to highlight the difference between our land and that of the surrounding countryside. The land of milk and honey vs. the land of Sodom and Gomorrah. Our house was in the center of

the photo, tilting slightly, and you could see the drive carving between the two top fields, although the gradient isn't clear from above.
The Land Rover was parked up by the chickens for some reason; it
never was usually. I don't know what was going on to make that necessary, maybe we'd been lugging some new posts up for the fencing
because we'd lost a lot of hens to foxes around that time.

"What on earth . . . ?" I stared at the photo. "What's it about?"

"I don't know. I haven't read it yet. No need to go running to your
precious government adviser now, is there? The whole world will be
fascinated by our back garden."

"How did the press . . . ?"

"The same way it always does. By sticking its snout in the gutter."
Mark left, the door slammed, and moments later I could hear the
whir of the chain saw and the scream as it bit into the logs. Mark
had taken about as much as he could with the media coverage of the
tribunal and this would be more than he could cope with. Although
I felt keenly for him, I was also wondering how many more of his
last straws I could carry before this camel's back broke. I spread the
paper on the kitchen table and began to read. The caption said that
only two weeks after the disturbances at Duccombe, their investiga-
tive reporter revealed another place mysteriously unaffected by the
drought: The Well. It referred readers to the full article on page 4
and 5.

Then the phone rang.

It was the first of a relentless barrage of calls: the *Mail*, the *Express*, the *Edinburgh Herald*, *Figaro*, the *New York Times*, the *Phnom
Penh Post*. The email in-box filled as I watched it, the bold black type
of the unread messages pouring down the page like an oil spill. The
answer machine lived its own existence in the corner of the kitchen,
dutifully recording old friends, the press, weirdos, PR agencies, until
the messaging service was full. Eventually, I stormed around the
house ripping plugs from their sockets, watching the blinking green

lights of communication with the outside world flicker and go dead. We turned the mobiles onto silent and then when their crazed vibrating dances drove us mad, we turned them off completely. Outside, the helicopters continued to drone overhead. Mark shouted at them to fuck off and they nodded and bobbed in acknowledgment before leaving in their own time.

Not so much a Well as a sieve. We could not keep them out. The first car jolted down the track. It brought a couple from Birmingham on their way to visit their son; set out ever so early this morning, they said, heard it on the radio, had a bit of time to spare, thought they'd come and see what the place looked like and who would have thought it? As they turned round, they met two more cars arriving: one was a local journalist, the other a water diviner who had driven all the way from Essex, and behind them, more cars. Impotent, speechless, I hid behind the kitchen window watching Mark leaning into the drivers' windows to talk to them, pointing at the main road and shaking his head. Strangers, all of them. If only one of them had been Angie, or a friend from London, or anyone I knew, who I could talk to, if only I wasn't so scared of anyone and anything that came from beyond our Well.

By four o'clock we had locked the gate at the top of the drive. The wood was slightly rotten and the bottom bar broke when we yanked it free from the long grass and weeds entangled around it. We padlocked it to the metal post, aware that it was a feeble defense against this new army of the curious. It was the first barricade.

CHAPTER EIGHT

The next couple of days were bitter, and we lived tense from both cold and the threat of invasion. The stove in the sitting room was working overtime, we were getting through over a basket of wood a day, and our last lamb to be born, a weakling, was in a cardboard box in front of the Rayburn, her head heavy compared to her unsteady legs. The ewes were still in the barn; Mark was fretting, wanting to get them and their lambs out onto the spring grass, but he was worried they might not be safe. I liked them there, protected and smelling of vigils with flasks of coffee and torches, nights spent rubbing the lambs into life, seeing our flock give birth to our future. On the third evening after the article, we had been going to relax for the first time, there had been fewer calls, fewer trespassers, and we decided to make a conscious effort to toast the success of our first year as shepherds before getting a good night's sleep.

"Don't even think about logging on," said Mark.

"Don't answer it."

We did turn on the news—The Well featured briefly, pushed to the end by a fire at one of the British Museum's warehouses which could not be contained because of the low water pressure. Watching forced us to talk about our new state of siege. I tried to be the positive one, saying that they'd all go away, that today's news was tomorrow's fish and chips, as we had discovered before. Mark said that might be the case if the rest of the world wasn't dying of thirst and had just discovered their nearest oasis. I told him not be so melodramatic, he told me not to stick my head quite so far in the desert sand. It sounds like an Aesop's fable, the tale of the badger and the ostrich.

I took my plate to the kitchen to wash it up and stared out through the window into the darkness, my own reflection distorted in the panes and beyond that a full moon making the bare branches of the oak smooth like a skeleton. Turning on the tap, I stood watching the water run in a single stream from the tap to the white sink and down the plug. Perhaps if I left it long enough, there would be a spluttering and a coughing, then the flow would stutter before dwindling to a trickle, a drop, a nothing. Then the phone would stop ringing, we could unlock the gates and be as dry and as desperate as everyone else. But the water ran on.

When Mark had gone to bed, I gave up pretending to cope. I took the bottle out of the fridge and my head out of the sand. I logged on. I had learned a lot about online porn addicts when Mark was accused, did research about what sort of men looked at images like that and why, just so I could be doubly sure that it couldn't be true of him, I suppose. The social science articles told me how impossible such men find it to log off and here I was in the same predicament: the laptop became a puking monster, an excretor of filth, but I could not get enough of the poison.

Condemnationuk. A place, it boasted, where the citizens of the UK could openly condemn those who were ruining society. It was one of the most popular sites at that time, with rants and diatribes about illegal immigrants drinking all our water, videos from homemade CCTV cameras showing the children next door playing with a bucket. I would never have gone there, had it not been for the alert on my screen:

You're popular today on the following sites: condemnationuk, watchthis, spotthespongers, newsday, weakeningplanet, smalholderweekly, waterwater; natmeteo . . .

The list was endless. I went to the first.

F***ing spongers like this should be locked up and allowed to die of dehydration.

Selfish drought breakers.

How stupid are these farmers? Did they really think no one would notice? Duh. People that thick don't deserve to have lives, let alone water.

Wait for it. It's going to be the Good Lord who has blessed them. I bet they are perverts and pedophiles.

No need to bet. The owner was done for kiddie porn. That's why he left London.

I felt sick. If the locals didn't know before, they would now and it wouldn't matter how loudly we shouted from the hilltops that he was innocent; all anyone ever hears is the accusation, not the acquittal. And God knows, they hated us enough already without more fuel for their fire. I continued clicking.

This is our water, not theirs. The government should take it over NOW. If not, we will do it for them.

F*** off the land and DON'T COME BACK.

Then I reached the comment where I overdosed.

I know these people. Their daughter's a druggie and a whore and their grandson's a moron.

Who wrote that? Surely no one who knew us could write that? But if they didn't know us, then how did they know about Angie and Lucien? All at once these people were not invisible, they materialized. I could hear them scratching at the keyboard, I could see their faces leering at me through the screen, they were crawling out of the Internet and I smelled their threats as they breathed down my neck. So many of them and me on my own: I could not think of one person I could call on for help. Transfixed, I scrolled through my contacts: Angie, autorepair, Becky and Richard, on through Mark (office), Sophie (mob), Youth Addictions Support, Zahira . . . I hammered the keyboard with my fists, smashing the letters and symbols for what they no longer offered; over and over again I beat them, beat back the baying crowds.

Mark must have been woken by my hysteria. When he found me, I had thrown the laptop across the room, where it had smashed a mug but lay still alive on the floor. Between sobs, I tried to tell him that they could not be contained, that these people would get together, they would be here, smashing our windows and slaughtering our lambs—tonight—they were probably out there now and there was no one in the world who could help us. I was hard to hold, but Mark was so strong by then. His pajama top smelled of shower gel and sleep, and as he rested his chin on my head, I could feel the steady beat of the heart of a man who was now physically fit.

"What do you mean, there's no one? I'll look after you," he murmured. "I love you. You don't know how much I love you."

There was a time when I thought the risk lay in the fact that he loved me too much; now, after such a long silence, I know he loves himself more.

Mark turned the laptop back on. "This stuff isn't helpful, Ruth," he said. He brought up TheArdinglyWell Facebook page and went straight to Settings. "There," he said. "One click, gone. Deleted. We can do without crap like that just making things worse."

Later, he asked me a question. "What came over you to trawl through that sewage? Why didn't you just log off when you saw what it was like?"

Because there was a quality of connectedness for me when I was online that was both affirmative and addictive, regardless of the voltage. That is the truth. The psychiatrists talked about the third person in our marriage. Sometimes I think that person was the web.

————

When Hugh comes this week, for my so-called communion, he finds me less jolly company.

"It smells beautiful here," he says, closing his eyes and breathing deeply. He puts his weekly offering of fresh milk on the table and then pulls from his bag a bunch of early yellow roses, losing their petals and smelling of the piano room at home when I was a child. My mother was a piano teacher. *Mrs. Alysha Rose. Individual Piano Tuition, Beginners to Grade 8.* The card in the newsagent's was confident, but my main task as her daughter was to tell the little girls clutching brand-new bright pink music cases and their huffing mothers leaning out of 4x4s to go away because she wasn't well. Again? they would say. Again. She devoted her life and her health to "giving me a little brother or sister" by whatever means science could offer. At least that's how she framed her quest. My father devoted his life to her and that meant working every hour God sent to finance her dream. It never happened. She died at fifty from an excess of procedures, breast cancer, and a lack of meaning in her life beyond menopause. I like to imagine her reunited with all her unborn fetuses, happy at last. The smell of rose petals and furniture polish . . . that is all it takes to bring back her unmourned absence.

"Don't roses make people happy?" he comments. "If you look in the mirror you might catch yourself smiling."

"I smashed the mirror the other night," I told him, wiping the cobwebs from a pottery vase and filling it with water for the roses. "I kept looking at this gaunt old witch who lives in there. I can't take my eyes off myself."

"If you'll forgive an old man for his forwardness, you're a good-looking woman."

"You don't understand. I was becoming like a budgerigar that spends all day on his perch, pecking at his own reflection in the hope of connecting with his own gene pool. I've been thinking a lot about connections," I add, leading him out into the orchard to the old bench. "Do you use the Internet?"

"The Internet? Of course."

He sits; I stay standing.

"Sorry."

"I may be old, Ruth, but I'm not totally decrepit. Why?"

"I miss it. I miss it and I don't miss it."

"It brought a lot of trouble to your family, I understand."

"How do you mean?"

"I had my briefing papers coming here, about you and your husband. Maybe they thought the priest needed protecting against the molester for a change, rather than the other way around."

I laugh, in recognition of his effort. "It was ridiculous. At least I used to think it was ridiculous." I pull a bough down towards me and pick some apple blossoms. "What do you know?"

"That your husband was accused of having viewed child pornography on his work laptop. That he was suspended, fought the allegations, and was found to be innocent."

"I stood by him. I thought the whole thing was ludicrous at the time. Mark, for God's sake." I pulled the pink petals off, one by one. "But when everything is stripped away, do we really know anyone, Hugh, or is that just your God's privilege? Omniscience?"

"There's no hiding from him in the garden, that's for sure, unless you happen to have a supply of fig leaves." Hugh is doing his best. "So why were you asking me about the Internet?"

Taking my place beside Hugh on the seat, I lower my voice. "I'd like you to find out some things for me. Will you?"

"Searching is certainly part of the job description. But I'm not convinced the World Wide Web is a wholly benevolent force, so it depends slightly on what it is you want me to find out."

"I just want to know about my family. That's not too much to ask, is it? I need to know if Angie is all right. And Mark."

Hugh shifts uncomfortably, fiddling in his pocket for a handkerchief. "If you don't mind me asking, does Angie have contact with her biological father? Might she be with him?"

"No." What else was there to say?

Angie's father. There was nothing wrong with him, as far as I could remember from the eight hours we had spent together when I was all of twenty-one, but not much right either. By the time Angie came to want to know about him, he was dead and she was angry. We had never pretended, but even so, was that when she changed the vocabulary from Daddy to Mark? Was that the only reason why? She blamed me, of course, although omnipotent as I was for a while I can hardly have been held responsible. Car crash in Kenya, aged twenty-eight. Turns out my one-night-stand nerd was a rally driver, a bit of an adrenaline junkie. Junkie. Maybe that was where she got it from.

Hugh persists. "You have no idea then where either of them might be living?"

"No. But I'm worried about Angie. She could be anywhere, you've no idea how low she can get." There are nettles now, growing tall alongside the bench. I reach out and grasp one to stop myself crying. "Maybe she and Mark are together. I haven't heard from either of them since . . ."

He waits to see if I can finish the sentence, then replies, "I'll see what I can do, but I can't see how the Internet would be of much help."

"You'll need it because I also want to know what has happened to the Sisters. To Sister Amelia, in particular. Where she is, what she's doing, anything relevant about her. Would you search that for me? I have to know more about her, Hugh, if only to discount the possibility that it was one of them that did it. You could print things out and slip them in the Bible—or just in your bag. I don't think they'll search that again."

"So we didn't come out here for the sunshine." He hands me a dock leaf to press against my nettle stings.

"No."

"Because you are asking me to do something which contravenes the rules of your imprisonment and therefore my visits."

"Yes."

"And if they find out, my visits will be stopped."

I hadn't thought it through as far as that. I look down at the bench and peel off the splinters, finding myself surprised at how thrown I am by the idea that Hugh would not come again. Perhaps he won't come again anyway now I have asked this of him. There is no choice for me. My hair has grown, and as I look up, I pull it back off my face and fix it with a band so he can see me clearly.

"Probably, but it's a risk I'm willing to take. More than that, I'll risk everything to know the truth."

"I will pray about it, Ruth. I can't promise you more than that."

Pray for as long as you like, I thought. But Google for longer.

CHAPTER NINE

The relief guard is gone, my boys are back: Three conducting the 7:30 a.m. alarm check which wailed across the valley, a cross between an air raid siren and a call to prayer; Anon slumping in front of the bank of screens playing computer games while "Sarge is out"; I find myself hoping to catch sight of Boy. Finally, he knocks on the door and I am so very, very pleased to see him.

"Morning."

"You're back. I didn't even know the other lot were gone."

"Thieves in the night," he said. "You must be sleeping better. Actually, I've brought you something. That's not strictly true. In fact my mum sent you something."

"Your mum?"

"Yes. I was telling her and my dad about you and Mum made up a sort of Red Cross parcel for you."

Boy hands me a shoe box–sized parcel, taped up. In one corner, in neat handwriting, I read, "All the best, Andrew and Helen."

"Shall I open it now?"

"Why not?"

I sit on the doorstep and take off the lid.

There was a jar of marmalade, a CD of *Ten Greatest Classical Hits*, some bath essence, and several packets of seeds.

"The bath essence isn't new, but she said she didn't know anyone else who could use it now, so you might as well have it," said Boy. He sits down beside me. "It was meant to cheer you up."

I nod, just about able to speak, and ask him to thank them for me.

This is a terrifying awakening which embraces me like a wave that curls itself around the child at the edge of the beach and sweeps him off his feet. How much easier it is to believe that nobody cares and that I care about nobody, how much harder the truth that Boy matters to me now, and that maybe I matter to him and mothers matter to their children and children matter to them.

"You'd like Angie," I said to Boy. "If she ever came back and met you, I think you'd like her." If.

"She was a traveler?" he asked.

Oh, yes, she was a traveler. I nodded.

"And she sort of came and went?"

Extraordinary, the comings and goings at The Well.

Some sort of sixth sense woke me to the fact that we had visitors. Regardless of the age of their children, mothers have a particular way of sleeping, always on alert for the slightest of cries from the cot, the night terror, the key in the front door, and the click of heels on the staircase far later than the time we'd agreed she'd be home by. Tense, I strained my ears to hear what had woken me; I looked into the shapeless corners of the bedroom, nothing; nothing except my heartbeat and the steady breathing from Mark, curled away from me and sleeping soundly. It was constant and familiar, the thick darkness around me, and I was on the point of accepting it for what it was when the room changed. A beam of light shone through the gap in the shutters, slowly sweeping the room like a searchlight, and was gone. There was really only one explanation: a car at the top of the drive. Then it happened again, a son et lumière illuminating first the picture, then the mirror, then the crack where the wall and the ceiling meet, before leaving me in the audience with nothing but shadows, ill at ease and unsure if the show is over. I gave it half a minute, no more, before I shook Mark.

"Mark! Mark! Wake up!"

He woke instantly, startled. "What the hell are you doing?"

"There's someone out there!"

Feeling my way around the end of the bed, I found my way to the window, opened the shutters just an inch or two, and stared out into the night. There was no moon that I could see and it seemed as if the cloud must be low because even the trees were strangers.

Mark came up behind me. "There's nothing there, what are you talking about?"

"Just wait a moment, will you? It was headlights, shining into the room, but I couldn't hear anything so they can't have driven down here."

"Are you sure?"

"I'm not making it up, am I?"

"I don't know, you're a nervous wreck sometimes."

"I felt safer when we had Bru," I said. We stood together in the blackness, close but not touching, waiting. "There! What's that?"

There wasn't anything or anyone on the drive, but there was an orange glow on the other side of the rise in the field between us and the road; it grew, then went out as instantly, as if someone had flicked a switch, then came on again.

Mark opened the window, and a gust of cold, damp air blew into the room. A few drops of water fell onto the windowsill. It had been raining again.

"Listen!"

It was as if we had been suddenly blinded and expected to make sense of the world only through sound, random noises, devoid of context or clues. We named them as they found their way through the mist to us: a car engine, revving as if reversing or getting stuck in mud; a dog barking; a snatch of music, turned off abruptly; and finally voices, muffled and indecipherable human voices.

"Who is it?"

"How the fuck do I know?" Mark reached for the light switch.

"Don't turn that on!"

"Why not?"

"Because they'll know we're here!" I slammed the window closed, pulled the shutters together. Mark didn't even bother to answer, but he left the light off. He sat on the edge of the bed, pulling on his sweater and jeans over his pajamas.

"What are you doing?" I didn't know why we were whispering.

"I'm going out there!"

"Don't be ridiculous! You don't know anything about who it is. They might be dangerous. There's obviously quite a few of them and there's only two of us!" I sat beside him. "Please, Mark. Unless we call the police—why don't we call the police?"

The breath sagged out of him, he put his head between his hands. "I don't know. I can't think in the dark," he said. "What's the time?"

I fumbled for my mobile. The illuminated screen said 12:43; my hand looked luminous under the glare. "What difference does that make?"

Mark's idea was to wait until first light and then he would go up there and see what was going on. "They don't seem to want to rape and pillage straightaway," he said.

Part of me was relieved that we weren't joining battle with this un-known enemy in the middle of the night; the other half of me knew that it was going to be a very, very long time until dawn.

2:11 a.m. 2:56 a.m. 3:42 a.m. 4:29 a.m.

"Ruth, where's the phone? For Christ's sake, where's the bloody phone?"

Under the duvet, that's where it was, my hand wrapped around it, warm and safe like a new baby checked on the hour, every hour. I must have finally fallen asleep, but here was Mark, in the bedroom in his coat, yelling at me, clumps of mud falling on the floorboards, it didn't make sense. And then I remembered the night visitors.

I sat up in bed. "Oh, God, have you been up there? Who are they?"

"I need to phone the police!" He chucked the pile of books from the bedside table onto the floor, turned over the heap of clothes on the chair. "Bloody travelers, it's travelers parked up beyond the drive, against the hedge up there. It must have been them in the night, breaking in!"

"Travelers? What sort of travelers? How many?"

My heart beat a little faster—fear of these travelers, fear of Mark, fear for Mark. His voice was rising, "Where's the phone?" He turned back to me. "Travelers, about a dozen, I don't know what sort, I didn't stop for coffee and a chat."

"How did they get in?" I began.

Mark interrupted. "God knows! I didn't think it was possible. I haven't checked."

"Didn't you ask them?"

"They weren't up, were they? Because they don't have jobs to go to, do they? But there they are, with their flower-power tents and ecowarrior Dormobiles, not to mention the dogs, just waiting to attack my lambs. Just find the phone, Ruth, we need the police to help us get rid of them now."

New Age travelers, then, from his description, probably totally peaceful people. Probably quite good company. It was the fear of the unknown I couldn't cope with any longer, but Angie had hung around with people like that before, so my breathing slowed and, feeling a great wave of relief, I got out of bed and the phone slid to the floor.

Mark lunged for it, but I got there first and snatched it back.

"Wait! Calm down! It doesn't sound half as bad as we thought it was last night," I said. "Why don't we just talk to them? Ask them to move on? It doesn't need to be some massive confrontation." Holding tight to the phone, I stepped out of my pajamas and reached for a towel. Mark followed me into the bathroom. He wanted the phone and he wanted it now. I held the towel tight in front of me; he held his hand out with a sarcastic sneer on his face. Our eyes met.

Then he turned away to the door. "Have your shower, get dressed, bring the phone downstairs. This whole thing is ridiculous."

There was a time when me getting up in the morning, sleepy and standing by the shower with nothing but a towel between us, would have brought him closer, not driven him away. Alone in front of the mirror, I dropped the towel on the floor and, naked, studied myself. Thinner than before, that much must be good, surely. And browner, at least around the edges. But sort of dry, brittle. I cupped my empty breasts, noting to myself that I didn't even check them any longer. I couldn't remember when I last wore makeup. Scrunching my hair up into a bun, I held it above my head, exposing my white neck. I couldn't remember when I had last gone to a hairdresser, either. We never saw anyone else, it never seemed worth the effort, but maybe I owed it to Mark to do something about myself for him. Take myself in hand, that was my mother's expression, although pot, kettle, and black spring to mind. And, for that matter, it wasn't as if Mark was doing a hell of a lot for me. I washed quickly, and in the same unwashed jeans as yesterday, the same shapeless fleece as every day before that, I picked up the phone and went downstairs. At least I wouldn't have to dress up for our visitors—the travelers wouldn't mind what I looked like.

In the kitchen, Mark had made tea. I broke the silence. "What's wrong with just walking up there, explaining our situation, giving them a time scale for when we'd want them gone?"

"A time scale? We want them gone now."

"Why?"

We might as well have been speaking different languages: Mark speaking loudly and slowly, gesticulating at me, the foreigner in my own country. "Because they are trespassing. Because we have spent the last weeks trying to keep people out, not inviting people in. Because they have no right to be here. Because once we've let them in, then the rest of the world will follow. Because, because, because, . . ."

"*The Wizard of Oz?*" I tried to joke.

"Yes, and let's get our traveler friends to do a bit of paving for a yellow brick road while we're about it, shall we? That's what they're good at, isn't it?"

"You never used to be such a bigot."

"No, you're right, I didn't. If you remember, I was too busy fighting the bigots off to have time to be one myself."

Change tack, that used to be a behavior management strategy advocated at school for angry adolescents. "Have you had any breakfast?" He shook his head, so I put some bacon in the frying pan, cut some bread, got the butter out of the fridge, found the honey, talked with my back to him, watching the toaster. "I'm sure you're right, but we don't lose anything by meeting them. And you never know, it might even be nice to have them around for a bit."

"Nice?"

To talk to. To share things with. To change the landscape around here just a little. Two pieces of toast, two plates, two knives—I put them all on the table and thought I could think of a thousand ways it might be "nice" to have some company at The Well, but I suggested just the one. "Not nice, I didn't really mean that. I was thinking they might help out, odd jobs, that sort of thing, there's so much to do."

"We don't need help, Ruth. We've proved that. We can do it on our own if we work together."

Sitting opposite him at the table, passing the spoon over the net, receiving the butter on the baseline, I wondered how long this game of singles could go on. I tried one last time. "The other thing, though," I said, "is that we can do without the police coming here again. The last thing we want is to draw any more attention to The Well. We've got all those legal letters outstanding and they'll start asking questions about more than the travelers."

Game, set, and match. Mark agreed I was right. If we could avoid the law, that would be better. I volunteered to go up there, check them out, and report back; he said it was probably better if he kept out of the way, given how he was feeling. He'd clear up breakfast and hoover up in the bedroom.

The rest of the bacon was going begging and we had a load of rolls which needed eating, so I heated them up, squirted some ketchup in them and made a thermos of coffee. Just as I was setting off, it occurred to me that they were probably veggies, so I went back and grabbed a handful of apples from the store before heading up the drive. With no news from Angie, I had a sort of karma theory that if I looked after these people, then someone might be looking after her and Lucien. What goes around comes around. The sheep scattered, nagging their lambs as I crossed the field towards the tents and vans which splattered lurid oranges and yellows against the spring grass, reminding myself that if it wasn't for the wet grass, these people, whoever they were, probably wouldn't be here at all. The tents were arranged haphazardly at the bottom of the field, close to the hedge, as Mark had said. A lurcher appeared from behind a rusty van and ran towards me, howling, followed by a young man also apparently from the 1960s, limping after it.

"So this is the barking dog," I said.

The man grabbed its collar and pulled it back. "Sorry, did she wake you up last night? I tried to get her to shut up."

"I heard you," I said. "Is she OK with sheep?"

"Yeah, she'd never attack anything, just got no manners."

I made some comment about having lost our dog recently and

he said sorry about that, the two of us standing there with my bacon butties dripping and my flask and the dog looking hopeful from a distance.

"Are those for Angie?" he asked.

"Sorry?"

He smiled. "You must be Angie's mum. I'm Charley. I'll give her a shout."

Before I had time to understand what was happening, the man had gone over to a small green tunnel tent. It bulged, lurched a little, and the sagging guy ropes tightened and loosened and raindrops showered from the door flap and then there was Angie, struggling out, pulling on a sweater over her cotton pajamas. Her blond hair, always curly, was a total mess, her nails were black, she smelled of smoke, and her sweater had holes, yet I knew the moment I saw her that she was well. It was something about the fact her eyes could meet mine without flinching, the honesty of her hug, how it wore its heart on its sleeve and did not conceal requests for money or loans or "just this once" or "I'll pay you back"; something about the way she didn't mind looking dirty, because she was not having to pretend to be clean.

"Angie . . ." I found it hard to speak. "Dad didn't say you were here! I didn't know . . ."

"Hi, Mum!" She hugged me, she put her arms around me and hugged me.

"You look so good. So well. I am so . . ." I couldn't finish. I stepped away from her and wiped my face on my sleeve. "I'm sorry, it's just that we haven't heard from you."

"Looks like your mum's brought your breakfast," said Charley. "Now that's what I call maternal!"

"It'll get Lucien up, for sure," said Angie, and Charley obligingly left us to it and went over to stick his head in the tent and called to Lucien to wake up. Angie read my thoughts.

"Usually it's just Lucien and his friend Henni who sleep in the tent and I'm in the van with Charley, but everything got a bit messed up last night because we got lost and arrived really late and it was dark. We didn't want to turn the headlights on in case we woke you up and you were freaked out. We didn't, did we?"

"Not really, we thought we heard something, but . . ." There was no point in starting off with an argument, but I did have questions.

How had they got in? It turns out the police had got wind of their arrival without Mark ever having to phone and there was a police car at the gate when they pulled up at midnight. But it was the same "copper" who had been round to The Well to Identimark our farm machinery when we moved in, and Angie and Lucien were around. He recognized them and let them in.

Why hadn't she kept in touch? Apparently they didn't use phones much, these people she was traveling with; they tried to avoid television and the Internet, she said. She didn't even own a mobile any longer.

"It helps us focus," said Angie.

Focus on what?

"The important stuff. The land. The community."

What brought them here?

Word of mouth, apparently. When Duccombe went down, everyone was talking about this other place which had been in the paper where it still rained and how people should mobilize to protect it. She didn't even realize at first that it was The Well they were on about.

You could have written, I wanted to say. The recriminations were rising; I swallowed to keep them under control. Every reunion for the last five years was like that: relief, then shock, joy, resentment, anger, regret, played out over and over again at different intervals and with different emphases, but always the same excuses, the same pain. I was saved this time.

"Granny R!"

Lucien. I see him now. I see him often. Curly hair, reddish-gold like the sun, brown, barefoot. I give him a bun and he eats it, splats of ketchup landing on his bedtime T-shirt with a picture of a bee on it. A bee and a buttercup. Bees and buttercups have an unbearable beauty for me now.

CHAPTER TEN

Mark was furious. Day after day, following the article, we had faced relentless petty incursions onto our land and all the adrenaline aroused in him when he first saw the travelers' vans turned into bitter accusations for letting Angie turn my happiness on and off like a switch when she chose to appear or not to appear in our lives.

"She can't just come and visit her parents like any normal daughter, can she? She couldn't possibly have called ahead. No. She has to arrive in the middle of the night and bring half of la-la land with her, as if we didn't have enough problems with trespassers."

His anger was familiar, in part fueled by relief that she and Lucien were OK and in part by fury that she always turned up with other people in tow, without ever asking. We never dared say no; if we pushed her away, then we risked never seeing her or Lucien again, and we owed it to both of them to keep trying.

Angie and Lucien came down to the cottage to say hello, and I think it was Lucien who persuaded Mark to come up and meet the travelers. Mark could never resist Lucien. He strode up to the camp, pressing down the ruts where the vans had driven over the field with his heel, picking up a leaflet about benefits which had blown across the drive from the camper and dropping it ostentatiously into the fire. Once there, though, I think even he was won over. It was company apart from anything else. We were both starved of company. Bru's death had deprived us of our one mutual friend, and we didn't feel ready to replace him. We never did. Mark got involved in a long conversation with a couple of the men about the shortage of temporary work and ended up saying he'd probably have some odd jobs around The Well over the next few weeks, as if he'd thought of the idea in the first place. There was a lot of fencing which needed doing if we were going to keep people out, he said. He couldn't even do his usual rant about parasites and junkies because everyone who traveled with them took a pledge not to use. One of Angie's friends was telling me how they helped each other keep clean, for the sake of the kids, for themselves, to be true to something, and I found myself seduced by their thoughtfulness. I blocked out the distant whine of a siren in the valley and instead relished the prospect of company and conversation which Angie and her travelers brought with them. The siren grew louder. It had turned off the main road and was coming up the lane.

Angie spoke to the group. "While we're all here, I just wanted to thank Mark and Mum for letting us stay, and I just want to say to everyone to respect the land, because this is like a working farm with sheep and stuff."

"Thank you," I mouthed at her across the group, but she was distracted because the siren had become deafening. From the other side of the distant hedge, I could see blue lights on our lane.

Mark jumped to his feet. "It's coming this way!" he shouted, running towards the gate.

I half stood up. Angie held Lucien tightly by the hand, presumably to stop him following Mark. Everyone stared at him running up the hill, with two kids behind him making *nee-naw* noises. The men closed ranks, asking each other what sort of shit was this? I moved away from them until I could see Mark talking through the window of a police car that had pulled up in front of our gate. He looked more at ease talking to the officer than with his daughter. I looked back at the travelers.

"Go and help him, Mum," called Angie.

Out of breath, I caught up with Mark. The two police cars had now been joined by an ambulance and a crowd of people were milling around, like extras in some cheap TV drama, waiting for the action to begin. Mark gesticulated at a line of cars and vans stretching down the narrow lane.

"Hundreds of them, apparently, on their way here from all over the bloody country, thinking we're the Promised Land. I told you. Enough company for you now?"

The policeman lived in Lenford. I recognized him as Morgan's brother-in-law.

"Sergeant Willis, isn't it?" I asked.

"Afternoon, Mrs. Ardingly."

He said they had reinforcements coming down from the north of the county and I said I didn't think that was necessary, that once people realized they couldn't camp here, then they'd satisfy their curiosity and be gone.

"Are you crazy, Ruth?" Mark was uncoiling barbed wire which he had brought up to the top hedge days ago when he had found a photographer snooping. He had no gloves and it was tearing his fingers, but he didn't notice. "They're believers, they won't get fobbed off that easily. Not now they've escaped from the asylum and seen the Promised Land."

His reference to my daughter was unmistakable; his love affair with the travelers short-lived. The sergeant moved away as he talked into his radio, and over by the gate a roar broke out from the gathered crowd as they started banging on the doors and roofs of a police van which had just pulled up.

"Help me move the wire, Ruth," Mark shouted.

"No, wait! Someone just needs to talk to them," I called back. Behind me, several of the travelers were lined up, watching, waiting, when a couple of disheveled young men started to break through the hedge from the road and aggression agitated the crowd. Mark picked up a fencing stake.

"Get off this land before I make you!"

Sergeant Willis moved between them, his raised hand lowering the wooden pole. "Leave that to us, sir," he said.

Mark dropped it. "It's because we've let this lot in," he ranted, pointing at the group of watching travelers. "That's what the police think. She did this. Word spreads."

She didn't even warrant a name, right then. I wanted to argue but it wasn't worth it. Already explanations and listening were valuable commodities in short supply. Mark set off at a run down the drive to pick up the most recent investment in our smallholding: padlocks, bolts, chains, electric fencing, the stage props of imprisonment. Gradually the police took control, the shouting diminished, the vans maneuvered onto the verges to do awkward three-point turns and head back to wherever it was they came from. Turning my back on all that, I walked slowly towards Angie and Lucien as Mark hurtled towards the house. I tasted separation in the back of my throat like sour milk and retched. My head swam, and when the world stopped turning, Mark had disappeared out of sight.

Later that evening, he asked me what was happening to him. "I would have hit them, you know, if Willis hadn't stopped me. I would have done it." His face was hidden in his hands on the table.

"We're so tired," I said. "We were up half the night and it's been a long day." I kissed the back of his head. "It's because this place matters to us, that's why. And I don't think you would have hit them, Mark, not when it came to it. You're just not that sort of person."

Like poachers-turned-gamekeepers, the following days were spent with Mark and Charley and one or two of the other men from the camp repairing fences and locking gates and towing boulders into gaps where ancient tracks met new roads. I ferried to and fro, between the house and the camp, bringing food out to the travelers, bringing questions home. Lucien was often with me at my side. The sightseers, soothsayers, and naysayers gradually drifted away, the police presence was scaled back, but they left a code which we were to give to the station if more people turned up or tried to break in. But it wasn't just travelers who had us under siege. The newspaper article had opened a floodgate of obsession. We were contacted continuously by everyone from estate agents to extraterrestrial enthusiasts. The guttural pulse of helicopters droned over the house like bees in winter. Several times one or other of us would come across a reporter, trespassing on our land, with his long lens and thirsty pen. Despite the assurances I'd given him, I was actually worried that Mark, who was once probably one of the most cerebral and least physically aggressive people you were ever likely to meet, would get into a fight. I watched with foreboding when he headed out at dusk to check the fences, his shotgun cocked under his arm.

The post lessened slightly over the weeks, but still piles of envelopes pleading and promising and prying lay unopened on the spare room floor. We changed our email address, answered only our new mobile phone, and gave up going out unless we had to. We did attend Tom's funeral, taking two of the extra chairs which had been laid out at the back of the packed church, but we were unwelcome mourners both for the publicity we attracted and for our perceived complicity in the drought which had caused his death. After that, we relied increasingly on the Internet to connect with the outside world, shopping online, putting a large crate at the top of the drive where curious supermarket delivery drivers could dump their orders over the fence. Unless we collected our deliveries quickly, they were stolen, now that the price of even basic foods like sugar and bread was becoming unaffordable for so many people. Either that or the locals were trying to win the siege by starving us out. At home I struggled to concentrate on doing what I had planned to do, making a poor job of preparing the vegetable garden. Mark immersed himself in the farm, preoccupied with the arrival of his piglets. He settled them in like a foster mother, fussing over them, gradually increasing the size of the pen until they were free to rummage in the wood at will, clearing the undergrowth for us. He found refuge there; I had Lucien. For a while, we muddled through, but not for long.

There was the evening I suggested tackling the backlog of post. Tired and unenthusiastic, having spent the day sawing up the wood left over from the improvements to the barn, I was slumped in front of the television watching a bleak documentary about the plight of the growing number of homeless people, victims of the now snowballing financial crisis. I imagined them scratching their legs as they scrabbled over hedges, stinging their fingers on the nettles covering the stiles as they struggled onto our land, with Mark and me trampled underfoot on our own doorstep. I didn't want to share my doomsday scenario with Mark; we were beyond sharing nightmares, or dreams, or beds even, since for two nights now he had slept in the little bedroom. We pretended it was because he was coughing a lot; we knew it wasn't. I had an idea: a wastepaper basket full of unopened post. We can't just throw it all away, I reasoned, we can't assume it's all from nutters. Let's do it now in front of the television, just clear the backlog. He didn't want to, but he agreed. It was at least something we were going to do together. We even managed to laugh at some of the letters.

Dear Sirs,

You will be interested to know that I have been bequeathed the seeds of an ancient pea from the Holy Land, handed from genera-tion to generation since the birth of our Lord. I am offering you the chance to buy these seeds for £100,000 to plant in your holy land . . .

That seemed hilarious at the time, but it is perhaps even more hilarious now to think that I did spend a year worshipping the floral equivalent of the sacred pea. The Rose of Jericho mocks me and minds me still.

We pressed on. Mark emptied one bottle of our homemade damson gin and opened another, and we sat next to each other on the sofa, sharing some of the more bizarre offerings. Behind us the ten o'clock news showed 271 in the corner of the screen next to Big Ben—the number of days since it had rained on the London weather center—but nevertheless we were laughing, letting our bodies touch each other in quite an ordinary way. I was even wondering if he might sleep in the same bed as me that night.

Mark had no inkling that I had an ulterior motive. I had loved him once for his straightforwardness, his truthfulness. I was convinced he was never a man who dissembled and I think he thought the same about me. I pulled out the formal letter to both of us, which I had in fact opened some days before and had been rereading on my own over and over again. It was typed on paper headed "Cranborne, Cranborne and Chase, Solicitors." They were acting on behalf of a private client who wished to remain anonymous, who was prepared to offer in excess of £5 million for the freehold of The Well and all its land.

"Yes, and pigs might fly," Mark said. "Next you'll be showing me an unmissable offer from Nigeria from someone who says we just need to give him our bank details and ours is the kingdom of heaven."

There were plenty of those if he wanted to read them, I said, but there were plenty of serious offers too. I showed him one from a philanthropist who wanted to buy the place and use it for research (I scanned the letter for the right wording), so as to "reduce the harmful effects of drought on the most vulnerable in our society." They were not all from selfish bastards or big corporations, I told him. He took a plain piece of paper, with a beautiful italic, handwritten script. It was from a religious order which had been given the money to buy the place as a center of spiritual peace and contemplation in difficult times.

"We don't need the brotherhood for that," I said. "Your own daughter's busy doing that off her own bat down the end of your garden, if you were only prepared to notice." I filled up my glass, half empty, half laughing.

But Mark wasn't laughing; he had suddenly realized I was seriously recommending selling up.

"Don't talk to me about not making a go of it," he said. "I've put more of myself into this place than you. All of myself, in fact."

"This was, *is* my dream just as much as yours."

"It's me who's done the planting and the plowing. I've invested a hell of a lot more in this place in practice than you have." He chucked the envelopes on the floor.

"So you should have done. It was you who needed to get away."

"So we're back to that, then? Never going to be allowed to forget that, am I?"

"You know that's not what I mean. For God's sake, turn the telly off."

Mark stood up and got the remote. "No. I don't know what you mean because you never really knew what you thought, did you?"

With the volume on mute and the news playing out like a dumb show behind us, the room was silent for a pause between our ranting. I tried to continue in a quieter voice. "It's nothing to do with that. Nothing to do with the money either. It's about us."

"Exactly. That's what I'm saying."

"No, it's not."

Mark stood with his back to me, staring at the silent screen, and said, "You're not listening."

"Yes, I am. I want to leave, but not without . . ."

He swung round. "Well, fuck off and leave, then."

He turned the sound back on, racking up the volume notch by notch. I had to shout to make myself heard. ". . . not without you, Mark. I'm saying we both go. Hand this land over to someone who can make better use of it than us."

"I'm staying."

"Why?"

Mark did not reply immediately. He turned the television off completely and spoke slowly. "Because I love it here. Because it's what I've always wanted ever since I was a kid. Because it was what I was always going to be until . . ."

"Until what, Mark? Until I spoiled it for you? Because I got pregnant with some other bloke and produced a daughter who turned out to be a nightmare. That's what you've always wanted to say out loud, but haven't dared."

Mark sat back down. Having opened the door to the wood-burning stove, I started chucking in the envelopes one by one. The flames illuminated half of Mark, biting his fingernails, leaving the rest of his face in the dark. I reached for some more of the begging letters. He put his foot on the handwritten one from the religious brotherhood, then reached down and took my hand. Exhausted, I laid my head on his knees.

"We're in over our heads here. If we leave, it would free us up," I said, trying again.

I wanted so much to try again and again and again. I was a believer.

Before we went to bed, he opened the back door and called to me to look at the night sky. The Plow was low and clear; I followed the line of the constellation all the way to the North Star.

"Wish upon a star?" he said, slipping his arm around my back. From behind we must have looked like the perfect couple.

———

I found it hard to stop shivering then, and I shiver again now, thinking about the black night, the North Star, everything it saw, the way it turned a blind eye when it mattered.

CHAPTER ELEVEN

Dear Mark,

I haven't heard from you. I don't know if that's because you haven't written or because they don't let your letters through.

I only want to know if you have heard from Angie. Nothing more.

Do you think about The Well? It thinks about you. The coppice unharvested in the woods, last year's spinach cropping up again, the damson blossom, you are part of all of it and more. Do you remember the night when I suggested we sell, when you said, "Wish upon a star"? I wonder what you wished for.

I am lonely. I cannot make sense of the fact that you have not contacted me once after over twenty years of being together. What am I meant to make of that? I am asking you to please visit me, visit The Well. I never was anything without you and now I am less than nothing.

I do not know who killed Lucien. If you know, and if you ever loved me, then you must come back and tell me, however awful that might be. If it was neither of us, we will be stronger in our search for the truth together than apart.

Ruth

Boy knocks on the door. Nothing important, he is just warning me that the electricity is going to be turned off for a couple of hours while they repair a break in the fence. That explains the alarms going off. I am encouraged that someone wants to break into my prison. Oh, there's no end of people wanting to do that, he laughs. I love the way he laughs, so won over by his innocence and idealism that I tell him, quite unexpectedly, that I have just written to my husband asking him to come and visit me, but what a waste of time it has been, since I don't expect to be allowed to post it. Boy looks at me, then at the floor, and I know immediately that I have put him under pressure to post if for me and that is unfair.

"But it doesn't matter. It was a load of self-pitying drivel anyway," I say. "Probably better not to send it even if I could. That's the good thing about letters, rather than email . . ."

Boy interrupts me. "I can post it for you."

He is an adolescent, all impetuosity and risk taking. With a terrible lurch, he crosses a line and everything changes. The room fills with awkwardness: the lid which doesn't match the teapot, the way the fridge rattles and dies as the electricity goes off, the squeak of the soles of my shoes on the lino. Although it is no later than six, it seems dark in the kitchen now with the lights off.

"No, you mustn't do that," I say quietly.

"I will," Boy insists, "but you need to understand that I would have to read it."

I turn to look at him.

"It's not that I'm into censoring stuff, or any bullshit like that, but at least if I was caught I could say that I'd followed the protocol. Because if I was caught, I'd be sent away, wouldn't I, and then I wouldn't be any use at all."

I keep my thumb and forefinger on the edge of the envelope but do not tear it, yet. "It's not worth it, it really isn't," I say. "What little life I have will continue to stutter along, but you'll have served your time soon and then you've got everything ahead of you. If you walk out of conscription without a reference, you're done for, if that's the right expression."

Boy pulls up a chair to the kitchen table and sits down and immediately looks embarrassed. It is the second thing he has done in the last five minutes which has usurped the ordained order of things.

"No, stay there," I reassure him, as he half rises to his feet. I sit down opposite him. "Where's Three?"

He smiles. "I can't get over the way you persist in calling him that. He has got a name, you know."

"So have you, but I still call you Boy. Just terms of endearment."

He answers the original question, spinning an apple around on the table. "He's with Adrian down at the bottom of the Brook field, mending the electric fence. They'll be ages."

Saliva moistens my mouth; I catch myself scratching the back of my neck, an old nervous habit I'd quite forgotten. Signs of life. Across from me Boy bites into the apple, teeth on skin in silence, and I think, that was my apple, and the chewing and the swallowing are audible, physical violations or invitations. He has said he will post the letter, so let him post the letter. I move around the table, dragging the chair behind me, sit down beside him with the letter in my hand. I take it out of its envelope, unfold it, and spread it out in front of us.

"If you don't want me to . . ." he begins, but I shush him by shaking my head.

It is difficult to decipher in the gloom. The rays of the lowering sun are at the one point of their daily cycle where they shine between the oak tree and the corner of the house and through the kitchen window. So we move up a bit, to take advantage of their temporary light. Our eyes follow the shapes of the words in front of us, up and down the uneven letters, but we are blind people reading. Touch is the only sense left in the room. I know that my leg is barely an inch from his.

Not only can I feel my own chest rising and falling, but his too, his shoulders lifting imperceptibly beneath the khaki shirt, his rib cage swelling and retreating, his breath invisible but felt. Like a teenager myself, I shift fractionally until our legs are touching. He does not move away. There has been time enough to read the first page and turn over, but we sit in this magnetic state unable to go forward or back. The thought that this boy is beautiful finds space in the closed ecstasy of my mind—the boy is beautiful and he is touching me.

His radio buzzes in his pocket. Our legs divide. He gives some confirmation to Anon in an unnecessarily loud voice and then tells me the others are on their way back and he stands up abruptly. I walk without reason to the sink, turn the tap on, and let the cold water run. Staring at the sink, I think, do not look at him, do not think about what has just happened. Then he is leaving, he is gone.

So is the letter.

————

The gap is flooded with Mark. Adultery comes dressed in many different garments, but when I am stripped naked, it is Mark who is there, Mark is everywhere tonight. He is sitting at his desk, sorting out the bills, he is leaning forward, cheering at the television, England vs. Wales: 24–23 in the last three minutes. When I go upstairs to bed, I meet him coming out of the bathroom, his pajamas low around his waist, his chest bare, rubbing his wet hair with an old fraying towel. He has a farmer's tan. But when I close my eyes, I hear him: not the Mark that was meant to be, but the Mark he became, the Ruth and Mark we became. The scuttling of the mice behind the skirting boards becomes the relentless scratching of our arguments, the screech of the owl outside my window, the cuts we inflicted on each other.

An example: Mark is pouring himself another glass; I am deciding to stay sober. He is brewing up for a showdown; I crack the eggs into a bowl for an omelet. Lucien has asked to stay the night with us, but he is upstairs crying.

"I expect he'll settle."

"He's very restless at the moment."

"I don't think he's very happy."

"He's not the only one around here."

"Who do you mean?"

"Who do you think I mean?"

"We can't go on like this."

"Like what? Just joking."

"It's not funny. It's not fucking funny."

Mark stays drinking. Lucien starts crying again.

Another breakfast, another argument: Mark throws a pile of letters and printed emails onto the kitchen table and embarks on a monologue.

"Forget the crackpots, the druids, the parish council, the society of rain dancers. These are serious. These all need a reply. Have you even bothered to read them? This one is from the Drought Environment Agency Force—something about compulsory access to the place. And this one is threatening to prosecute us because we haven't replied to the first one. And this one is some sort of newly dreamt-up legal notice of right of government, something which we have ten days to respond to and which never existed on the statute books when I read law. Fucking interfering bureaucrats!"

A response to the monologue by me: "Don't walk out, Mark. That's so childish. Like all this is just going to go away if we pretend it doesn't exist and we can carry on planting broad beans—wake up! This isn't our land anymore anyway. Not our land, not our lives. It's just our problem. Let's leave, before it drives us mad."

He has gone.

"Before it drives us apart," I say to myself. The post stays on the table.

A third example: at night, when we were still in the same bed. We'd separate, try again; it would start conciliatory, then end up at loggerheads. I'd go to bed first and often pretend to be asleep.

"I still love it here." Mark with his back to me, closing the shutters. "I know I'm going to get up tomorrow morning and look out this window and think, how could we ever leave?"

I open my eyes. "Do you think I don't feel that? But I don't know how long we should give it. There won't be anything left of us before long. Sometimes I think it may be better to cut and run."

He gets into bed. "Where to?"

"Take the millions and buy a farm somewhere else. Scotland, maybe? There's still a bit of rain in the far northwest."

"Don't be ridiculous. Any land there that was for sale has been snapped up ages ago. Can't you see? We're the only two people in this country who have what everyone else wants. That's why they hate us." With an exaggerated lurch, he turns away from me, grabs the duvet, and pulls it like a shield around his head. "We've got what everyone else can only dream of. And we dream of being like everyone else. There is no choice but to stay. We've nothing to go back to."

Wasn't he the one who set fire to the bridges?

Mark continues to talk to the wall. "We took on the responsibility of this place and we're not going to walk away."

"You talk as though it's your baby. Like we might hurt its feelings."

"Maybe it is. And don't start your pseudopsychotherapy on me!"

It is my turn to roll away. "You never used to be so sarcastic."

"You never used to be so selfish." Mark takes his pillow and moves into the small bedroom.

That is how it was.

———

Those days before the Sisters came, Mark was working hard at the land, exhausting himself struggling to make a success of something, whereas I became more feckless, drifting from one task to another, leaving the hen shed unmended, the seedlings unwatered, and in between these desultory attempts at putting something into the farm, I would find endless excuses to go to Angie and look after Lucien, until one day she actually said that if I wasn't able to give her a bit more space, she'd be moving on. I craved company, but I never went out because I couldn't face the town. I found excuses, always leaving it just too late so the shop was shut, or planning to go to the post office on a Wednesday, knowing it was early closing, or suddenly finding out I didn't need new socks after all—but it was the sweat on my palms and my desiccated tongue that told the truth. Mark went on the rare occasions when there were supplies we really needed and came back tight-lipped and tense. I had no friends, but nor did he. If it wasn't for Lucien, I would have gone mad. Mark grew physically stronger in direct correlation to my mental deterioration; two sides of the coin which landed his side down when we tossed.

"All I ever wanted to be was a farmer!" There, he'd said it; I don't know when, possibly one of those hideous nights, probably before the Sisters came.

"I know. And all I've ever done is stop you."

"Maybe that's the price I've had to pay to be with you," he replied, just a little too quickly.

Into all this stepped Sister Amelia.

CHAPTER TWELVE

Sunday. I expect Hugh to come with news of Mark and Angie and the Sisters, and I am feverish with expectation, cleaning the kitchen floor to rub away the waiting time. When I hear him arriving, I tap three times on the wooden draining board, just to make sure it's good news, then welcome him in. He arrives with an apology.

"I'm so sorry I'm late, with you probably watching the clock and the hands going so slowly."

He has come later than usual because his daughter has come to stay for a few days. Fussing, he calls it. Certainly his breathing seems shorter with each visit. The sun is not yet on the back wall—our usual spot—and it is a cloudy, oppressive day so we go inside and I pull up the stool for him to rest his swollen leg.

"My daughter drove me up as far as the gate and that was a pala-ver. There's been a lot of trouble in Lenford. She doesn't seem to trust me not to smash the windows in the bank or riot in the public car park."

"I'm glad you got here safely."

My lack of tolerance for small talk must have been obvious, be-cause having checked that Three has left, Hugh goes straight to the heart of the matter. "So that's Lenford and my daughter and I'm sorry to say I don't have any other family news at all to cheer you up."

"None at all?"

"I'm afraid not."

With the excuse of getting him a glass of water, I leave the sitting room, but in fact I can barely walk straight, the disappointment feels so catastrophic. There seems no point in returning to Hugh.

His voice comes through the open door. "That's not to say I might not be more entertaining on another visit. Now, come and sit with me because there's something I've been wanting to ask you."

There is no need for social conventions to apply here. There is nothing to stop me behaving badly, slamming the door and going up to my room to sulk. Inexplicably, however, politeness prevails.

"Have you changed your mind?" he asks.

"About what?" I place the glass of water for him on the little table beside the armchair.

"About working the land." He corrects himself, "about not working the land."

No. I haven't. I have remained steadfast to the three vows I took at the beginning of my sentence here, and as a result mere anarchy is loosed upon the little bit of the world left to me.

"Why do you ask?"

"I noticed the little field at the back of the orchard."

I haven't been there for a while, the nettles are too high, the ground is littered with broken glass, and there is no view from there anyway. Now I prefer sky and a sense of space.

Hugh persists. "Someone's been weeding the old vegetable plots up by the broken-down greenhouse, hoeing them, planting maybe, by the look of it."

My face gives everything away.

"You didn't know?"

I shake my head. This is small-scale stuff, not exactly an organized assault on the wilderness by the department, like the experimental strips on the top fields. I wonder out loud why someone would do that.

"A much more rational question would be why someone wouldn't," Hugh said. "Why this refusal to work this land you love? It's hard to believe you sacrificed everything for The Well—your life, your marriage, your freedom—all for this dereliction."

"I choose not to." Even as I say it, it sounds adolescent. Shan't. Won't. Can't. Don't want to. It's boring. Why should I? I say that out loud. "Why should I?"

Hugh closes his eyes for a moment, then takes his Bible out of the plastic bag and turns it over in his hands. He looks old, his head nodding and his shoulders sagging.

"Are you all right, Hugh?"

He opens his eyes. "I am all right, Ruth," he says, "but I am worried about you. It seems to me something has changed here, though I can't for the life of me put my finger on what it is exactly."

I reassure him. I am getting on well with the guards—God knows I am not about to start confessing about my moment with Boy, although I desperately want to talk to someone about what happened. I am sleeping at night from time to time, getting up in the mornings, I think I may have even put on a bit of weight as my jeans feel tighter. As I speak, I am unpicking the loose thread on the fringe of the cushion on the sofa and it is unraveling in my hands.

"Why are you worried?" I ask.

"I'm worried about the choices you are making,"

The last remaining thread snaps off, the stuffing is falling out of the cushion. "I am glad that you acknowledge I have choices. I thought your God was more in the business of choosing rather than allowing choice."

"Because you did feel chosen, didn't you, Ruth? You did believe you were one of the chosen ones, for a while."

Pick, pick, pick at the next loose thread. "Other people believed that. Amelia, the Sisters, they chose me to be chosen if you like, and I acquiesced. But they were wrong, we were all wrong."

"It rained, though, didn't it? And there's no denying it's still raining here." Hugh takes a sip of water, his hand shaking as he raises the
glass to his lips.

"Well, I wish it would stop fucking raining here."

"You should try to understand what it might mean for the rest of
the country that it still rains here. Do you really understand what it's
like out there, Ruth? People are struggling. Think of the price of a tin
of soup, and the women with the little ones to feed and the old folk
trying to find the pennies to keep the budgie that's their only friend.
And it doesn't just rain here, it drizzles, pours, comes down cats and
dogs. Just to say those words, Ruth, that's a blessing in itself. This is a
holy water one way or another, however you look at it." He looks at
the glass. "This is a blessed place."

"That's what the Sisters used to say."

"Then they got one thing right."

The cushion is a mess now; I'll have to mend it or bin it. I've had
enough of his preaching. He may not have had news about Mark
and Angie, but he hasn't said anything about what he might have got
from the Internet about the Sisters. He can't share it here, not with
the camera winking at us. We need to move outside, but he looks
settled in for the duration, sagging in the armchair as if he is in the
lounge of a five-star hotel after a good dinner.

"Let's go outside."

Hugh nods. "As you wish." And starts to ease himself forward in
the chair with difficulty.

There are many ways to become a monster; I do not know why I
feel the need to explore them all.

"You know, it's not that nice out there. We're fine here." I perch
on the arm of the sofa. I want him to go now. He has brought me
nothing and I don't have the patience for an afternoon with the elderly, but I persevere.

"Thank you. It is probably easier for me here, today. Now, you

wanted to know how I was getting on learning about the Internet,"
he continues. "I'd say I'm making steady progress." He looks up at
the camera and back to me. "I think there is a great art to searching
successfully. Like life, you have to know what you're looking for, otherwise you get led a merry dance. And to know what you're looking
for, you have to know what you know already."

All right. We'll come at the truth this way round.

————

Breach: a noun which became part of our vocabulary, but an act
which had in fact lessened in frequency over the weeks since the
article. Mark put this down to his habit of firing off a few rounds over
the heads of intruders to "get the message out there," and there was
no arguing with him about the legality of this. Breach birth, those are
words which come to mind now to describe the arrival of the Sisters.

There was no strange glow above the Hedditch field, where we
planted wheat, no heavenly host on high in the evenings announcing
their presence, no sense of peace spreading throughout our increasingly war-torn paradise. But there were four campers, four nuns, and
one mission. It sounds like the beginning of a shaggy dog story and,
in a way, I suppose it was.

The tire tracks left the gravel and crossed the grass. Mark had no
need to drive that way, and the travelers had learned not to incur his
wrath by carving up the fields with their vans. I stopped to listen to a
cuckoo, the first I'd heard that year. His duplicitous call was echoed
by singing. It was a damp heat that evening and the notes clung to
the low cloud like scent. It was a chant more than a tune, and the
lapses and surges suggested that someone, whom I could hardly
hear, was leading, with others responding. As the cuckoo took to the
skies to the east, the music seemed to grow from the valley to the left
of the track, its base notes reaching their stems down into the roots
of the forests, its treble climbing high over the stave to where the

lark flutters like a tremolo. It swelled with the rise of the breeze and dropped as invisibly, moving in unison like wind through wheat. It was an English music, I thought, our history in the breathing in, our future in its exhalation, and I was captured in the present moment of it being sung.

There was still no one to be seen even when I reached the hedge which marks the edge of the field. I sat on the stile with my back against the wood, my knees bent, my feet on the ground, but losing touch with the turning world so completely that I was unaware of Angie's arriving behind me. She touched my shoulder, I turned, she held her finger to her lips and together we listened. Finally, the singing ceased and there was silence like clear glass; through it you could see in a way you had not seen before. We crept forward until, at the solitary oak in the middle of the field, she motioned for me to stop. Below us there were the campers and women moving between them, a silent pageant so strange I wondered if it was real at all.

"I knew you wouldn't mind," Angie whispered.

Now I look back I can see it always was a game of power with Angie, and it seems to me she held most of the cards. Three-handed whist we played, Mark, Angie, and I, with her calling trumps and splitting our longest suits. I wonder now, did we manage to stay married for so long in spite of Angie, or because of her?

"You know them?" I ask her.

"Yes. No. Well, I know about them." Even in her newfound truthfulness, dissembling was still a habit for her. She told me what she knew of their story. These women had all met for the first time on a retreat at a priory in Wales. Their leader had some sort of revelation about a new way forward and they all joined up. To Angie that seemed quite straightforward; I had my doubts, to say the least. Are they Christians? Sort of, she thought. Angie had let them in. Apparently, someone in the village had seen the campers arriving and had phoned the police, who turned up "all guns blazing," as Angie put it. Then there was something of a standoff until she arrived and told the pigs—"sorry, Mum, I meant the police"—that the nuns were there with our permission. I made some feeble complaint, about it not being her decision and all those tired lines I'd used before when she had invited other sorts of people to sleep on our floors and puke in our bathrooms. But this was different, she insisted, these people have been led here.

"By whom?"

"By their god, the "Rose" they call her. You heard it in their music as much as I did. Mum, there's something special going on here, you can't deny that."

I could deny whatever I wanted to, I said. What I couldn't do was to deny what Angie had done and that it would need to be explained to Mark. I told Angie I was going to talk to these seminuns before I made up my mind, and besides, who was looking after Lucien while she was up here being spiritual? How ridiculous that I doubted her ability to look after her son, but I did and I must live with that. She didn't take offense, she hugged me, told me to go and meet them.

"You'll like them," she called back as she climbed back up the field. "They don't come empty-handed, they bring something for you. They know all about you."

By the time I made my way down the hillside, the women had disappeared and the little encampment was mute and a little less awe-inspiring. I hovered in the middle of the circle of campers, unsure of myself, the wind catching a couple of T-shirts hanging from an improvised washing line. Close enough to peer through the window, I saw inside, obscured by condensation, four pale statues in a tableau around a fold-out Formica table. One seemed to be reading out loud while the others ate. It was the reader who caught sight of me. She passed the book to her neighbor as the other eyes looked up at the window. I half raised my hand in greeting; they bowed their heads, folded their hands, and appeared to pray, food apparently no longer of interest to them.

With the click of shoes on metal steps, the reader came round the camper. I psyched myself up to be assertive, but was left disarmed when the tall woman dropped to her knees, her long auburn hair covering her face, kissed the hem of my shirt while whispering something under her breath, and then stood again with tears in her eyes and her hands open wide. She was imposing, statuesque and, apart from the strikingly erotic hair, curiously androgynous.

"Ruth!" she said. "Ruth Brigitta Rose!" And the wind picked up my maiden name and took it away along with the rest of myself and lost it in the gathering clouds.

Later she said, "We have traveled a long way to find you."

She also said, "Welcome. I am Sister Amelia."

She pulled the land from under my feet. There were some paltry attempts on my part to define ownership and boundaries and explain that Angie had no right to let them in, versus Sister Amelia's repeated assurances that all this was meant to be, that all shall be well and all manner of things shall be well. Finally I managed to turn away, saying something about getting back, lunch, needing to talk more tomorrow, but I knew already that I would not be asking them to leave. Angie's words played again in my head. They bring something for you. Pull yourself together, Ruth, and see them as they are: a bunch of weird and hopeless women resorting to mind games. But then, what was wrong with belief? I had to believe in something. Everything else was quietly sliding to nothing.

———

I have had long enough to think of explanations and have a lifetime left ahead of me to think of more. I have conversed with psychologists, psychiatrists, scientists, priests, psychics, and myself. I have consulted the stars and the tea leaves, looked for answers in the shapes of clouds and faces in the bark of trees, strangely wrought. Some people see Jesus in a packet of processed cheese: that would have been as close to the truth as any. Who can blame me for choosing the cheese.

––––––––––

That day, pausing beside the lonely oak on my way back to the house and looking down at what, after all, was nothing more than four tin boxes with four lost souls, choice slipped through my fingers. True, I could have gone up to the cottage, phoned the police with my special ID number, and sided with Mark—but when I got back, Mark was out. We never went anywhere, but an old school friend of his had been in touch, doing a valuation at yet another estate selling up about twenty miles from The Well and he had suggested meeting up for a drink. That day of all days, he was not there for me. The phone call from an old friend had been a bright moment in a difficult month for him and I thought it would do Mark good to get out. God knows when he had last seen any friends. This way he could have a few beers, regain a sense of perspective, maybe calm down. He was never much of a down-the-pub type, slightly on the edge of conversations about league tables and play-offs, but Will had been a good mate to him in the past, never wavering, and Mark had gone to meet him after I reassured him that nothing could go wrong while he was away. Later he rang from the bar, clearly a little pissed, to say he was too drunk to drive and would be staying over and would I be all right on my own at The Well. Yes, I said, I am fine on my own at The Well.

So, for that one evening only, out of all the evenings, I was on my own. The lights from the houses way over the other side of the valley were dimmed by low cloud, shadows of sheep moved out of the mist towards me and away again, and an owl swooped low over the Hedditch where it found a branch and perched, motionless. It smelled of rain. So often, I had woken in the morning to damp grass and puddles, the drip from the gutters into the water tank, the sudden shower when the squirrel shook the oak, but I rarely actually saw it fall or felt it. Upstairs, under my duvet, the wind lifted the latch on the half-open window and drifted me in and out of sleep. It was not unusual for me to sleep alone, but now that Mark was actually away, I craved him, the round of his back, the warmth of him, his absence was a reminder of how well we fitted together.

It was in this half haze of a sleep that I dreamed about the rain: I was trapped in a metal matchbox and the rain was splattering on the tin roof of my miniature home. Outside people were dancing to the drums of the raindrops, trying to rouse me; inside, the beating of my fists on the walls was mistaken by them for rhythm and rapture. Half awake, I struggled to divide the dream from the night but realized they were one and the same thing and, disoriented, I groped my way downstairs and out of the house. There were shapes in the darkness: the oak reaching heavenwards; the night-purple poplars pulling the veil of cloud over their faces and weeping into the brook which ran at their feet; the fields, like me, lying naked, the better to feel the rain on their skin; and the outcrops of rock on the Crag washed clean by new streams. The shower slowed and was gone, the diminishing clouds released the moon and allowed her to regain her place, illuminating the silver puddles on the gravel. I had tasted the rain and it was good.

When I woke, it was dawn and I was not sure what had happened in the hours of darkness. Only the trace of footprints, writing in bare feet and mud across the kitchen floor, told the story of where I had been. Even more disheveled than usual after my restless night, I didn't bother to wash or do my teeth, but pulled on Mark's dressing gown and retraced those footsteps in an attempt to recapture the night. I went out of the kitchen into the back passage, out through the back door, unlocked as always, then followed the barely visible path through the long grass, ending up at the huge oak at the gate, and there was the woman, the woman with the long auburn hair.

She was standing in a rainbow-colored nightshirt, with the sun just cresting the horizon behind her and the concerto of the dawn chorus around her.

"Good morning, Ruth," she said. "Welcome to the first day."

"Morning," I replied. "You're up very early." I sounded absurd, as if I had bumped into someone on the way to catch the 6:45 to Waterloo.

"I was very excited," she said. "I haven't slept, I wanted to know every drop of rain; like you, I wanted to feel it on my skin."

I didn't know if I had heard her correctly, or understood her. She was implying that she was with me last night, or at the very least knew where I was and what I was doing. She seemed to know everything about me. I pulled the dressing gown tight around me. I was naked last night. I was on my own then and now. What was this woman doing prowling around my cottage at dawn?

"Oh, yes, the rain, I suppose we've become a little blasé about it," I lied. "No, that's stupid. What I really mean is that we've become used to it and it has brought problems as well as solutions, you know."

"Blessings," she said.

"Sorry?"

"Blessings. Solutions are blessings."

I wished the dressing gown had not lost its cord. "And problems are problems whatever you do with the language," I told her. "You've obviously come here thinking this is some sort of paradise, but actually it's a bit hellish, stuck up here, no company, hated by everyone around, trying to make ends meet. You need to understand that."

Amelia came towards me, her arms outstretched, and hugged me, but at the point at which a stranger should have let go, she carried on holding me and at the point at which I should have politely wriggled free, I found my face hidden against her shoulder, her hair smelling of lavender; ridiculously I found myself close to crying. She said that she knew how hard it had been for me, but that she was there for me now, her and all the Sisters, that I wouldn't be alone any longer. I was going to say that I was not alone, that I had Mark, but I didn't say that, and when we broke apart, she turned and left, diminishing as she crossed the field towards their campers, but growing larger and larger in my mind.

CHAPTER THIRTEEN

Mark arrived back midmorning, hungover and fraught. People are getting desperate out there, he said. He had had a difficult time at the gate: some woman with a kid had run alongside the car holding onto the handle and when he'd got out to undo the padlock, she'd tried to push the little boy into the car, saying that now he'd have to let them in. He hardly paused to dump his bag before pulling on his boots as he continued to talk.

"She was crying about how she didn't have a job, how she'd work for us. It was horrible, Ruth. Horrible. I had to shove her aside and slam the gate. Then the kid started climbing and I thought he'd get an electric shock and I was shouting to her to make him get down." He reached for the shed keys.

"Come and sit down," I suggested. "It sounds awful."

He looked at the keys. "I suppose it can wait," he relented and came back and kissed me. "Will was reminding me that I married the sexiest girl at uni," he said.

At the table, he moved on to more ordinary-extraordinary news. The price of beer: apparently it takes forty-five pints of water to make one pint. And Will had then joked that Jesus would be turning wine into water if he was around now, though he'd do better as a dealer: cocaine is cheaper than cider, and it seems half the country is permanently stoned. They had been drinking at the hotel bar, because there were hardly any pubs left. We had realized of course that our local, the Bridge, had closed some time ago but had no idea the problem was so widespread.

"I've spent a fortune, I'm afraid. We'll have to take out a mortgage just to pay for the booze. Still, it was a small price to pay for a bit of escapism."

Other things he'd noticed: standpipes, boarded-up garden centers, the army in convoys escorting water tankers on half-empty motorways. It crept up on people, he said, that's what Will and he reckoned. Year after year of below average rainfall, the odd farmer in the southeast going bust, car washes out of order, and then before you know it, drought. He wasn't surprised The Well was such big news.

"We've lost touch with what it's really like out there," he said.

"You could have let her in," I said quietly, "the woman and the little boy."

Mark finished his coffee and chucked the mug in the sink. "Oh, yes," he said sarcastically. "Every single one of them who leaves begging notes for jobs pinned to the gatepost. We could let all of them in, couldn't we? But then there'd be no room for us. You just don't get it."

"Are you interested in my news?" I asked.

"Sorry." He wrapped his arms around me. "Let's not argue."

The break had done him good; he even tasted of the outside world—smoke and borrowed toothpaste. Perhaps my news could wait, because in some way I felt I had betrayed him and The Well that morning, with the hug and telling a complete stranger how bad things were, and I wanted to repair that infidelity. Then again, perhaps it couldn't wait. It was more than likely that he and the nun would meet and she would mention what had happened.

So I told him about the Sisters. I lied for the first time that morning and said that it was me who had let the nuns in and given them permission to stay, not Angie. He said he thought I was mad, that he could scarcely get his head around it. Just before he slammed the door, he asked if I'd checked the sheep and I replied of course, indignantly, and wondered how I could possibly have forgotten.

Up at the travelers' camp, I found Angie and some of the others had taken the offer of a day's work shifting some rotten straw from a barn and had left early that morning. Charley had stayed behind, and he explained to me how his damaged leg restricted the physical work he could do. It turns out that he'd jumped from a multistory car park, thinking he could fly when he was high as a kite.

"Lucien's gone too," he said.

Furious, I told him I thought it was totally irresponsible taking a small boy to bale loading where he could get squashed.

"You mustn't worry so much. Angie's a great mum, you know. People change," He added.

He made tea and I sat with him on one of the logs they had dragged from the woods. He continued sewing, large hands on the ends of scarred arms holding the needle gently, mending the tear in the tent with surprising deftness.

"People do change," he repeated. The repair was neat—tiny, almost invisible stitches in a carefully matched cotton reattached the zip to the tent lining, evenly spaced, evenly taut. He checked his work by running the zip carefully up and down. "Mended."

"Will it hold?" I asked.

"As long as someone keeps an eye on it, yes."

Charley limped with me as far as the track. "Tell me about these nuns of Angie's," he said.

"You can't see them from here," I told him. "They're down in the dip."

"I know that, but what do they believe?"

Good question.

"Do you think they'll stay long?" he asked.

"No idea," I replied. "And you, and Angie and Lucien? How long will you stay?"

"No idea either." He laughed. "But we'll need to move on at the end of the summer, find somewhere warmer to live, like the birds."

I could not risk another encounter with Sister Amelia, not without losing all the glue, safety pins, and drawing pins which had kept everything together this far, but nor could I face the day in front which seemed to show me in all its emptiness what it would be like when Lucien and all the swallows were gone.

Back at the cottage, I picked up a bucket of cleaning things and found a new packet of bicarbonate and thought how old-fashioned we'd become as a society, the smiling faces of the 1940s housewife being the new chic, gracing adverts on everything from vinegar to powdered milk and exhorting us to summon up that wartime spirit as the nation faced its new enemy. Suitably armed, I went to the barn, determined that Angie would never have an excuse to leave. No one had slept in it for a long time—friends who might have come and stayed had stayed away instead, and tourists were the last thing on our minds, although I am sure we could have let it out for a fortune if we had chosen. "One week in Paradise—only £150 self-catering." The only problem would be getting people to leave; The Well had been a story of entrances and exits, but there was no logic as to who left and who stayed.

———

The guards have changed the barn, of course, enlarging the living quarters and putting up partition walls, adding another toilet and putting in a whole load of electronic gadgets. Not so much a barn now as a barracks.

———

That day, I cleaned the barn, scrubbed the sink, threw out the sliver of soap left on the basin and poured cleaner into the toilet which had been unflushed for so long that it had left a brown rim around the bowl. I chipped away at the blue mold between the shower tray and the wall which was blotching the white tiles until they looked like old slices of bread at the bottom of the packet.

With clean sheets from the airing cupboard, I made the bed, running my hands over and smoothing the fresh pillowcases, wondering about Angie and Charley and imagining them setting up home here. Then I lay on the bed, aching with the awareness of my solitude, half hearing a line from a poem on the edge of my memory. *The glacier knocks in the cupboard, the desert sighs in the bed.* That was it. Auden. I had taught that in London and wondered then how the throbbing adolescents before me were meant to understand the bleakness of the sexually impoverished marriage. I spoke the rest of the verse out loud into the silence: "*And the crack in the tea-cup opens a lane to the land of the dead.*"

I undid the top button of my jeans and slid my hand between my legs, letting the sharp urge catch my breath. As my finger worked its method, my eyes fixed on the whitewashed ceiling until I saw a spider spinning a web down from the cracked oak beam above my head, its bulbous body turning and turning in the shaft of light, closer and closer. Suddenly the fear of the touch of its legs on my face made me scream and I tore my hand from jeans and scratched frantically at my face, not knowing where the spider had gone. The moment was over. I stood up, buttoned my jeans, straightened the duvet, and left, unsatisfied.

Outside, the smirking day made me feel filthy and restless. There were things that needed doing, there always were. Things that I had begun to think of as tedious, like clearing the nettles from the young trees or weeding the herb bed, but the only respite I could think of was visiting the Sisters. As time went on, I fought the desire like an addict closes the door and leans against it to shut out the dealer, but on this occasion I went back inside the barn and counted the knives, forks, spoons, mugs, cups, saucers, dinner plates, side plates, and bowls which were kept in the bottom of the dresser ready for the fictitious holiday guests. That way, I got as far as lunch.

By suppertime, another domino had fallen. I told Mark I'd cleaned the barn in case Angie and Lucien should want to stay. He said he'd been up to the nuns' camp and had a quick word. He thought they looked harmless enough. There might even be benefits, he joked, there would be extra pairs of eyes to keep a lookout and, anyway, it would be a brave man who wanted to break into The Well now that it was occupied by two of the nation's most reviled groups: travelers and religious nutcases. I laughed along, and when he said he'd even promised them a hose attachment for the water trough tap by the hedge, I offered to take it up to them. Peace was breaking out all around us, but founded on Pyrrhic victories and hasty attempts at reconciliation. I found the hose adapter in the barn and stuck my head around the back door before I went to the Sisters.

"So you're really not going to make them leave?" I called.

Mark was working at his desk. "Not for now!" he shouted back.

I turned the small plastic nozzle over and over again in my hand, hesitating, half in, half out of the cottage. "It's just that . . ."

"What do you want?" he called from the study.

"Nothing! I'm fine!" I said, and headed up the track, where I could make out the travelers' tents and vans and hear children calling. One of the voices was Lucien's, I'd recognize it anywhere. A year later, I would spend twelve hours listening for it and never hear it again. I could also make out a faint glow from the dip where the campers were. Lucien's raucous screams versus the singing of the Sisters: I chose the Sisters. They were standing in a group, and it was as if they knew I had arrived even without seeing me, because each of them took a silent step backwards, enlarging the circle just enough to make a space for me.

"Come and join us, Ruth," said Amelia.

The older woman smiled reassuringly. "We're probably not as odd as we seem. It's just like evensong, really."

I hesitated, and then joined their vespers. Sister Amelia was leading the chanting again.

Behold the Rose of Jericho.
Behold the Rose of Jericho.
Behold the Rose!

A handful of dust—that is what the Rose of Jericho looked like to me the first time I saw it. Sister Amelia lifted it, kissed it, and passed it on to the older woman on her left; she in turn repeated the gesture and passed it to a girl who looked about Angie's age, with crimson cropped hair and black eyes. It was coming round towards me just like the reading out loud goes around the class at school, and I had no idea what I was going to do when it reached me. The girl kissed it, turned, and looked at me. I copied, held out my hands, and received the Rose. I couldn't have done anything else. I raised the bundle of dry sticks to my mouth and pretended to kiss it. When I opened my eyes, Sister Amelia was smiling at me. I may have left after the last Amen, but I never really went away. I had taken part.

———————

The next time Hugh comes, he asks if I still have a Rose of Jericho. He is intrigued. I have, as it happens. When it was all over, I kept one, as a reminder of what not to believe. Now I fetch it, going down on one knee in front of Hugh before proffering a handful of dead twigs in the palm of my hand, bark flaking like dandruff onto the carpet.

"Behold, the Rose of Jericho."

Hugh leans forward, reaching out his hands tentatively as if unsure whether to take it or not.

"Hold it. It's pretty indestructible. That's the whole point."

"This is the Rose of Jericho? Would you believe it? It doesn't look enough to launch a religion, but I suppose five loaves and two fishes weren't much to write home about either." Gently, he breaks a twig off from the clump and snaps it in two.

"Not an ounce of sap in it, no roots, but you say it's alive?"

"It is a miracle plant. It does what it says on the tin. You can find it dead as a dodo on the dried bed of the Red Sea, half buried by sand in the deserts in Egypt—no roots, nothing, until one day"—I pause for effect and look up at the sky—"it rains." He follows my gaze and I continue. "The rain brings it back to life. Each of these dry little sticks unfurls until the whole mess of dead twigs is transformed by green shoots and hundreds of tiny white flowers."

"For how long?"

"Until the rain stops."

"And then?"

"It dies again. Or at least reverts to looking dead."

"That's what I'd heard, but I've never seen one." He weighs it, as if he too finds it hard to believe that something so featherlight can hold such heaviness. "It is a beautiful thing, Ruth. I am glad you have kept it."

"You can have it if you want it. Or if the Sisters are still going, you can order one online. They sourced a good little supply route from Syria. £14.99, if I remember correctly. Cheap at the price, for a miracle."

Hugh holds the Rose back out towards me, but I am sitting on my hands.

"Come on, humor a man in his dotage. Let's put it outside again. I'd love to see it flower in the rain."

Anon calls through the door that it is time. I help Hugh to his feet, holding out my arm and feeling his weight as he pulls himself up. He takes a few seconds to steady himself, fumbling for his stick. We make our way slowly outside, him with stick in one hand and Rose in the other. Anon looks bemused, to say the least.

"This is a wonderful plant, Adrian. Some people call it the resurrection plant. We can all learn from this plant."

Anon peers doubtfully at the clump of dead twigs. "If you say so, sir."

"I do. Now, how about here?" He indicates a large flowerpot which stands at the corner of the house. We planted it up the first spring, but now it contains only the earth, brown and redundant, sunk some inches below the rim. "Ruth, even you can't count this as gardening."

Hugh stoops with difficulty and lays the Rose of Jericho on the bare earth and there it sits, as though a small boy has found a deserted birds' nest and wishes for eggs.

"When I trashed the house," I explain to Anon, "this was what I was looking for."

CHAPTER FOURTEEN

I f there was speculation that Mark had always been a pervert, there was equal speculation that I had always been a religious fanatic, at least that's what was implied in the press and online. The candles I kept on the mantelpiece at home in London became the paraphernalia of a religious obsessive (according to a close neighbor); my visits to small country churches when on holiday in Devon were evidence of a compulsive need to worship (according to a vicar who didn't want to be named); even the Christmas cards I sent with an image of the Virgin Mary were incontrovertible proof of my desire to follow in her footsteps (according to an old school friend). But the truth is I'd never been a regular churchgoer and I was very much the novice when I first joined the Sisters' evening devotions. Prayer moved in me then like the nursery rhymes I used to know by heart, or which I later sang to Angie, or so recently read to Lucien, the rhythmic recitation reducing meaning to feeling until I was wrapped up in a blanket of bland reassurance. *Ladybird, ladybird, fly away home, your house is on fire and your children are gone.* That will haunt me now, *go round and round the garden, like a teddy bear . . . one step, two step, knife you under there.*

Of course, it wasn't just about the worship. The nearest I can come to describing those early weeks was that it was like a sort of book club. In the space of little more than one day, I went from being acutely lonely to having the ready-made company of un-conventional, but intelligent women 24/7 on my doorstep. It was London all over again, without the exhaust fumes and the dog shit. If Mark was doing his man thing, slouched on the sofa, watching TV, laughing at comedians as if the great maternal BBC could pacify the thirsty with a diet of childish, outdated repeats, then I could pass hours among the civilizing company of women. Amelia was always an enigma from the first time I saw her, and Eve, well, she was like a lot of women I'd known and not particularly liked as casual acquain-tances in London—all spin, style, and shoulder pads, and curiously out of place in this Wellington boot of a convent. The money was hers, of course—I did not know that then—but that can't have been all that mattered to her.

Jack and Dorothy, despite being poles apart, were both my kind of women. Three women meet at a well: a sixty-something Cana-dian widow, a forty-something back-to-the-land grandmother, and a twenty-something victim of domestic violence with a personality disorder—the start of yet another joke. And yes, we did make each other laugh, and we could talk for hours about anything: men, the meaning of life, The Well. And, of course, we talked about their faith, what Dorothy called "their curious feeling that something special was happening" when they all first met in Wales and how they knew now they had been called by God to bear witness to the Rose and bring the hope of salvation to a people parched of faith in a time of drought. I listened, challenged, questioned, and did not always agree, not then. Did they call themselves Christians? This was a new Christianity. Why just women? The Old Testament was male, the New Testament was transitional, and this is the Testament of the Rose, which is the witness of women. I did attend their so-called evensongs but, if anything, it was almost an intellectual game on my part, although I underestimated many things: the stakes, for a start; the gradual erosion and replacement of the rules; the fact that no game is ever won or lost on logic alone; and above all, the power one player can hold over the outcome.

Angie joined our debates sometimes, dismissing my occasional cynical moments, saying I just needed to learn to submit to a higher power. My habit would have been to retort that she'd spent a lifetime in unhealthy submission to stronger forces, but my habits were undermined already and I loved her for her readiness to listen. She really felt like my daughter on those occasions, just as I used to see other mothers and daughters in London, stopping for semiskimmed lattes in shopping malls, leaning towards each other over small round tables in coffee shops, bags at their feet, physical features mirrored in each other in the subdued lighting. Every now and again, some of her friends from the community would come with her, but I would be watching her, cross-legged and skinny on the grass and daring to feel proud of her — of her passionate contributions to our arguments about climate and capitalism, of her compassionate listening when Jack shared her traumatic story, proud of the confident way she rolled up the sleeves of her fleece to peel potatoes. Lucien and Henni came with her, somersaulting down the slope behind us, begging permission to poke around the campers which were a source of perpetual fascination, and Jack in particular was kind, allowing the boys to play house in her van. Sister Amelia came out one evening, watched them cartwheeling and asked me what my granddaughter's name was.

"Grandson," I corrected, laughing.

"Oh. I thought her name was Lucy."

"Lucien. But don't worry, it's the hair, I think. He could easily be mistaken for a girl."

"So when you said that all this will pass to Luce one day, you were referring to him. To a boy."

"Of course. Why?"

"Only that I believe this is a woman's land, Ruth. It should pass from woman to woman."

Nothing in life had prepared me for Sister Amelia.

It was not just me. She held the attention of everyone who stood in her shadow. I was not surprised to learn that it was Sister Amelia who had been the leader in Wales, gathering together this disparate group of women who were all retreating from something, offering them a way forward, the seductive scent of a calling.

"I gave up everything for the Rose," Sister Amelia told me in her low voice, which meant people always had to get close to her to hear. "I had things to go back for, people, possessions, but I knew there was a higher purpose for me. Even if no one had joined me, I wouldn't have done anything different."

"Extraordinary, when you think about it," I said to Mark one evening, trying to explain what the Sisters were all about. "She sacrificed everything for this calling. You know, she's a really intelligent woman, incredibly well-read, and yet she has such conviction. She did what most of us just talk about. She gave it all up and came here to The Well because she believes it's the right thing to do."

"So did we."

"Oh, come on, Mark, you know what I mean."

"I can see she's a very powerful woman," he acknowledged, flicking through his seed catalogs, "but that doesn't make her right."

The other sisters had their own stories. Eve gave up a penthouse apartment in a converted warehouse and her thriving PR business; Jack left her violent partner; Dorothy said goodbye to her lovely grandchildren in Canada. They gave up money and friendships and ways of ordering the knives and forks in long familiar table drawers because of Sister Amelia. They became the Sisters of the Rose of Jericho because of Sister Amelia. And I became one of them also, initially wading in slowly, until one evening I found that I could no longer touch the bottom, and to go back was more difficult than to go over.

Certain episodes of worship stand out in my memory. Early on, there was one evening when I got down there to find Sister Amelia distant and already absorbed in prayer, on her knees before the plain wood altar which they had made from logs and on which sat the little wooden box which contained the dry Rose of Jericho. Her head was thrown back, almost as if her hair were pinning her to the ground behind her, almost as if she were in pain; her long neck stretched on the rack and her eyes closed, her thin, brown arms hung from her sides as if disconnected. The others were waiting, dressed like her, not in their usual jeans and sweatshirts but in simple, gray cotton shifts which I had not seen before. It unified them in simplicity and humility. They did not offer me a gown and I felt put out, excluded from their enlightenment and envious of their peace, one hand in the pocket of my trousers, the other fiddling with the beads around my neck which struck me as gaudy. I still have those beads. They are not gaudy at all, they are pale glass and fragile, but context is everything.

The next night I stayed away, a toddler waiting to see if someone will chase after her. Amelia did not come looking for me, so I gave in and went to her, joining their prayer circle. Again Amelia was praying apart, again we waited for her; the nuns were still in a way I could not be, shifting from foot to foot as if movement reminded me of myself, flicking my hair back off my face, scratching the insect bite on the inside of my elbow. Finally, Sister Amelia rocked back onto her heels, paused, and then rose in one fluid movement. The Spirit of the Rose was welcomed and I willed myself to feel her move me also and there she was: a tightness of breath, a sense of my own heart beating like the wings of a hummingbird, the fingertip touch of a whisper on my spine. It was, as Amelia said, a beginning.

Amelia schooled me in the discipline of worship. She reminded me how to notice my breath, how to abandon thinking, chanting in her low voice, guiding my senses through my own body, noting how the earth received my feet, the strength in my calves, the tension in my thighs reaching into my womb, the emptiness in my stomach, the rise and fall of my breathing, and the thread in my neck that reached to the sky and directed my eyes to the sun. Through this and through the singing, I felt a growing sense of release, a little stronger every time, and I returned to the house each night lighter, light-headed, maybe. But release was not enough, she said, and one evening as the prayers drew to an end, Sister Amelia moved to a new, unfamiliar phase of worship, her voice shaking.

"Behold, look on this woman for the Lord hath blessed her."

Sister Amelia looked straight at me, through me. All of the Sisters dropped to their knees, their heads falling on the ground, arms in front of them.

"Behold, look on this woman for the Lord hath blessed her. Behold, look on this woman, who is the fifth woman."

Amelia fetched the box from the altar and lifted the lid. "Behold the Rose of Jericho."

I felt a great wind rush me, it took my breath. I swayed like a sapling in the eye of the storm of their belief. I fell to the ground. When I was ready to stand again, I felt faint and Sister Amelia held me, and I knew such peace, such certainty that for the first time in over a year, I knew I could stay at The Well and live.

She was always raising the stakes, Sister Amelia. When we read together as a group, we talked with her, responded to her challenges, and pondered her pronouncements. When she was not with us, we talked about her endlessly, agreed that she was a life-affirming woman. And when she was just with me, the two of us walking and talking as we often did, leaving the others preparing the dinner or sweeping out the campers, then she was irresistible.

"How do you see your future with Mark?" she asked once. We were following the tractor paths through the winter wheat, the plants brushing our bare legs. "It's like this, Ruth," she continued, "like this." She bent down and picked up one of the young shoots. "We are so fragile," she said, "so vulnerable to disease."

I didn't understand.

"Are you frightened of him?" she asked.

"No, of course not! He's stressed at the moment, that's true, he's more volatile, but frightened of him, never."

She let the silence undermine my protestations before continuing. "Mark will leave one day, he must. I worry about what will be left when he is gone. He will have taken what he wants and left nothing but stubble." She snapped the stem and let the broken stalk fall from her hands.

"You've got that wrong," I replied. "It's me that wants to leave, he's the one who wants to stay." But even as I said it, I realized that equation no longer balanced.

The path between the fields narrowed and we walked on, single file, me behind Amelia until we reached the brook at the boundary of The Well.

Even our stream was shallow and in places quite dry, because it had not rained for a week or so at The Well. I had even secretly begun to wonder if the drought had finally come to us. Did I hope that might be true, even then? Maybe. It is difficult to tell what is now and what was then. Nevertheless, rain or no rain, the hedgerow which followed the stream was still thriving, with ragged robins and sweet violets deep in the moss bank and the briar rose tangling from the boughs of the may blossom. Amelia behaved as if all this was hers, as if she knew everything.

"Look at the hawk!" she said, pointing to the sky.

"That's not a hawk," I said, reclaiming my world. "Much rarer than that! It's a nightjar. Mark pointed him out to me the other night and we've been tracking him. He looks like a hawk, but notice how he flaps and then glides, flaps and then glides—there, he's gone!"

"The nightjar is a troublemaker," said Amelia. "Mythology says he sneaks into people's places at night and steals the things that are precious to them. Sucks the goats' milk dry—that's his name, goatsucker! And then," she said, pointing at the fence below the willow, "there's the wren!"

"I do know a wren when I see one!" I replied.

"Ah! But what do you see when you see a wren?" she asked, but did not wait for my reply. "Some people see the traitor bird whose song betrayed St Stephen—that's why they stone the wrens to death on December 26."

"How horrible, I didn't know that," I admitted, then added a little maliciously, "You've scared him off with your stories."

Amelia wasn't listening to me. "But do you know what I see when I see a wren? I see the divine, the king of birds, a messenger between this world and that of our Mother!"

"I do know that sailors carried a wren's feather as a charm against drowning," I said.

"The Well is full of messages and warnings," she said, "you must learn to read them. The wren warns me about Mark."

It was my turn to challenge her. "So tell me what they say. What is it about him that makes you worried?"

"He eclipses your spirit."

But I didn't feel eclipsed by Mark; if anything, he was the one retreating behind the clouds. As Mark made fewer and fewer demands on me, Sister Amelia wanted more and more, and it occurred to me, for the first time, that she was jealous. I told her that I was changing my mind about some things.

"Talk to me about it," she said. "God speaks to me through you, Ruth. I shall call you my little wren. I want to listen."

"We have our problems, Mark and I, that's obvious. But you must understand how difficult this is for us. I know he probably seems bad-tempered and narrow-minded, but he's not. He's very thoughtful. He says science will never be enough on its own, he admits that, but he has never dismissed outright what you believe, he says . . ."

Amelia raised her hand to my mouth and silenced me. "Listen to yourself, Ruth. He says this, he says that. This is not the voice of the Rose; this is not your voice."

I felt her hair on my bare shoulders as she leaned in towards me. I think about that now, the two of us, sitting on stones at the edge of the stream, her fingers on my lips, my hand on her wrist. I am cross-legged, with her leaning towards me, eyes meeting, averting, retouching. Gently, I lowered her hand from my mouth and released it.

"Can't I speak for myself?" I asked.

Sister Amelia sat silent for a long time. I could not tell if she was thinking or praying or regretting the move she made. I think she was praying; whatever else I may feel about what happened between us, whatever else I may know now about things she did later, whatever else she may have done that I do not know about yet, I believe that then she believed and that was her only motivation.

Finally she spoke. "I have never told anyone else this. The first time the Rose appeared to me, I believed I was the only one she was looking for, the chosen one, because I was arrogant then and couldn't see beyond myself. Then came the others, but we were still not complete. Then, when we heard about The Well, everything fitted. You, Ruth; Brigitta, like the order where we were staying; Rose, your maiden name. I was just being asked to prepare the way, and if I'm honest, I wanted to be more than the prophet. This is a very hard to thing to say, Ruth"—she took my hand again and held it tighter this time—"but you are also chosen, your self must be subsumed by the Rose. You can't have attachments to other people. Your attachment must be to the Rose. You will not have a voice of your own. But I don't pretend for one moment that it is an easy thing—to be a chosen one."

———

That was the first time she used those words. Chosen one. I wonder about Amelia. Not Dorothy. Eve? I never really felt comfortable with her, but nothing more. Jack? She loved playing with Lucien and used to talk about how she wanted kids of her own one day. No, it always comes back to Amelia, if any of them. Some facts I know; I researched them before they took me away and learned them by rote so they could not be confiscated. Ten years ago, there were over a thousand men suspected of murder, barely more than a hundred women. So the odds are against it being her—or me, for that matter. But then, most children are murdered by their parents, and if not their biological parents, then someone acting in that capacity, which swings the odds back again, the finger pointing to Mark or me. At this stage, I am the lowest common denominator. But I can recite another paragraph: "Killings of children by a natural parent are committed in roughly equal proportions by mothers and fathers, but where the child is killed by someone other than a parent, males strongly predominate." Mark, then. Spin the arrow. Amelia. Again, spin it again. Ah, me.

At the very idea, I vomit.

CHAPTER FIFTEEN

Hugh answers none of my questions. I don't understand this. What would it cost him? I dare not ask Boy: he seems to be avoiding me, as much as it's possible for a guard to avoid his prisoner. I am also embarrassed and yet I would not undo that moment for anything. To have been desired by a man, to have felt desire for a man, that was so special, it was as if someone lost had been found. But the adolescent flutter is over. I am old enough to be his mother, I tell myself, and that should be my role, protecting him from himself, from me, from The Well, making no demands on him that I would not make on my own child. For a moment I am so idealistic that I envisage I might be, once again, altruistic.

In practice I cannot ask Boy anyway. The chances are the Internet here is monitored and he could never safely use it on my behalf. The more I look back, the more I don't know. Aspects of my ludicrous sentence have become ordinary, like the monotonous diet based on some government-approved shopping list cut and pasted week after week or the hours spent listening to the CD Boy's mother sent me, the ten great truncated classics anesthetizing the room, all the difficult bits cut out. But I am parched; my thirst for answers is obsessing me, swelling my throat and making the veins in my head throb even as the rain continues to fall. I can dream up solutions, mirages with the name I need written on water, but when I arrive, there is only shifting sand and a dry wind. Wind can drive you mad, I know, and I am so close again to insanity it would not take much. The guards are outside and I resolve to talk to them, but as soon as I am through the back door, I go back to check it is closed. Not locked—it's not for me to own the keys any longer—but closed. Sometimes, when I am not sure of anything, I have to go back five times. Today it is only twice.

"I would like to discuss communications." I approach Three and Boy, who have their heads stuck under the hood of their Land Rover. I know it's not broken. They have been turning the engine on and off and listening to it in much the same way that I listen to that CD—it is something to do. On hearing my voice, Boy turns quickly and bangs the back of his head on metal. When he lifts his hand to his hair, it comes away bloody.

"Shit!"

I want to say, sit down, let me see how deep it is, part his cropped, spiky hair and tell him it's nothing to worry about.

Three wipes his hands on an old piece of cloth which I recognize as part of one of the curtains Mark and I had in the house in London. "Yes?"

"I said I would like to discuss communications."

Boy is leaning against the passenger seat, testing his head, leaving it all to Three.

"Communications with whom exactly?"

"Post, primarily. Among other things."

"What other things?"

"Post, to start with."

"We could discuss post, if you want to. We could make an appointment. I'll make a record of a formal interview, if you like. Give you a copy of my notes. It would be a short meeting, though, wouldn't it?"

"Why?"

"Because you haven't had any post, have you? It would be hard to spin out a full agenda around the fact that no one appears to want to write to you."

I look at Boy for support, but he is staring at the ground.

Three notices. "Soldier? Don't tell me you forgot to deliver the post when you popped round for one of your chats with Ruth?" Three folds the oily cloth neatly, smoothes the crease. "Funnily enough, we were chatting just the other afternoon about that film, *The Postman Always Rings Twice*, weren't we, *Boy*?" He smirks as he emphasizes the name. "Doesn't matter if you haven't seen it. The title is fairly self-explanatory. But we're not here for Film Club. You wanted to talk about the post. Shall we make a time? Do you have your diary with you?"

The words are cackling like jackdaws, disorienting me. "I do not have the addresses of everyone I would like to write to. I would like to request permission to email my contact list—or some of them and you could view it, edit it if needs be—simply to inform them that I am allowed to receive post and to remind them of my address."

Slapping the Land Rover hood, Three doubles up laughing. "Sorry." He makes a show of wiping his eyes. "Sorry, I shouldn't laugh. Not professional, but do you really think they could have forgotten your address?"

In the same way that a child writes to Father Christmas at the North Pole, anyone, anywhere could probably scribble my name on the front of an envelope and send it to The Well, England, and it would get here. As I retreat to the house, Three calls after me, "I also have some issues around communication which need to be addressed."

I look back. Boy has gone.

"I may need to make some changes to your permissions. Let's talk later." Three slams the door of the Land Rover and, wiping his hands, smirks at me.

There used to be a woman somewhere out in the Far East who

was under house arrest. From time to time her case would appear on the news, prompted by protest marches or elections. It didn't occur to me then that the photo of this resolute and passionate woman must have been from the archives. No one could have eyes like that after twelve years staring at walls. If you took a picture of me now, after just twelve weeks, even if it was taken somewhere open, like in the garden, then once developed you would see the white roses, the gate half open behind me, the handle of the wheelbarrow jutting into the bottom left-hand corner by mistake, the fallen branch on which I am sitting, but there would be little trace of me, just the hint of a blur, as if the photographer was trying to convince you that ghosts have faces.

What is it doing to me, this peculiar imprisonment? Sometimes, I pause halfway up the stairs, close my eyes and stretch out my arms so my flat hands push against the damp walls on either side of me. Then I weaken and softly, so softly, feel the flaking skin of paint peel from under my fingertips, an explorer in the primeval cave of my own history, searching for signs of earlier civilizations. At other times, if it is a clear night, I wait here at this kitchen table in the dark until the moonlight is shining straight through the window behind me, creating for five minutes only a silver screen all of my own on the wall in front of me. Once, the shadow of a glove which I'd hung from the nail on the windowsill grew grotesque and threatening and reached for the hairs on the back of my neck, and I thought to myself, this is a strangling hand. Another time, the silhouette of one of the guards patrolling outside the cottage came to life in a black-and-white story, and I told myself, there is a puppet who knows me well. But tonight was the worst: an owl swept low over the house and a sudden great spread of wings flew in and feathered the room. With animal instinct I covered my face to protect myself from its beating and I covered my ears so I could not hear it haunting me. I am a cavewoman, entertained by shadows. One day, I have to believe, one day, I will turn round and that will be the day I have the answer. But for now, all I can do is look at the wall and call it home.

There is no doubt that Three knows about the moment with Boy, that Boy knows that Three knows; he has been busying himself with data and rain gauges and seems to have little time for talking, averting his eyes if our paths cross. Whatever the truth, Three is planning to punish me and all I can do is wait for it to happen and feel the sand running through my egg timer days in the fields, so I walk while I still can, and think. Checking doors, walking, and tapping three times have become my therapy. If he takes the walking away, I will be back to pacing, which is different. I wander all the way around the perimeter of First Field, marking my territory, noting the poppies which have flowered among last year's crop and picking the red campion from the hedgerow. So much red, I think, but I never noticed the warning flags, nor did I listen to the people shouting from the shore. Looking back, Dorothy was one of those, waving her arms and cupping her hands to her mouth, in the hope that I'd hear her.

———————

I was painting the downstairs windows. Looking at them now, I can't believe how quickly the woodwork has deteriorated, testament to the fact that I never put the hard work in, didn't bother with the sanding down, the wire brush, the undercoats. At that time the Sisters almost never came up to the cottage, so it was unusual to see Dorothy passing the house, waving and holding up a bag of something, so I called her over. Of all the Sisters, I admired her the most, it seemed to me that she had lived long enough not to have to bother with what other people thought of her and therefore she was someone to be trusted.

"Feverfew," she explained, and held out the leaves to me. "For Jack. It helps her migraine. There's a lot of it beyond the old pheasantry."

"I'd heard it was a womb stimulant," I joked.

She laughed. "It's powerful stuff, but it's more likely to cure my arthritis than make me fall pregnant at my time of life. Why, do you want some?"

"At my age? You're joking." It wasn't what I thought, just what I said.

Dorothy didn't reply. She just sat on the front doorstep as I continued painting, allowing the time to pass. "Steady work," she said eventually, indicating the pots and brushes.

"That's the thing about rain," I said, "it rots the windows so quickly."

"I don't know, the things we have to put up with living in paradise."

That was another thing about Dorothy; she had a sense of humor about our peculiar situation, although she was careful not to let it loose when Amelia was around. Typical of her, she offered to start on the other side for me. We talked our way through the morning, dipping and painting, running our brushes slowly down the narrow edges and fluted sills, the paint bubbling up and popping, drips running slowly down the bars, leaving a raised mark against the fresh new coat. Dorothy worked carefully and I remembered that she painted watercolors of The Well down in her camper. She wrapped an old rag over the top of her finger, dipped it in the turps, and cleaned up the drips as she went as if it was the Sistine Chapel.

"So, now Mark wants to sell," she said.

"That's the first I've heard of it."

"Sorry. It's just that Sister Amelia told me that the two of you had been talking about him leaving."

"People are offering a lot of money. Lottery numbers. It is tempting. The Well hasn't quite worked out as we thought it would."

"How do you mean?"

"How long have you got?" I asked her. "The isolation, the publicity, the security, the pressure, the bureaucracy, the legal threats . . .

this was meant to be our second honeymoon, Dorothy, but it's turning into one grand divorce court."

"Mark loves you very much; at least that's how it seems to me when you talk about him."

"Do you think so?"

"I do."

"I think you're right. But I'm not so sure how I feel about him. He's changing. It's like living with a beautiful mountain that's just woken up to the fact that really it's a volcano."

"He doesn't really have anyone to talk to apart from you. That must be really hard for him."

"Do you know . . . ?" I hesitated. Dorothy rested her paintbrush on the tin, wiped her hands on her trousers. "Sometimes I used to wish it wouldn't rain," I continued. "That we had drought like everyone else. Then we could be desperate like the rest of the country, but at least we'd be desperate together."

"Used to?" she asked.

"Until all of you came along and I experienced the Rose. I do believe, Dorothy, like you . . ." I looked from the windowsill at the handful of fresh herbs, heard the rainwater dripping from the gutter into the water tank, and repeated the words to myself. I do believe. It was the first time I had said it out loud and it was true. I was a believer.

"But . . . ?" Dorothy prompted me, intuitive as always.

"But it can't be right that I have to choose between The Well and Mark."

"Who says you have to?"

"Sister Amelia. Because it's a place sacred for women. Because Mark doesn't believe. Because the Rose demands complete dedication, because, thousands of reasons . . ."

I am not someone who cries easily. My lack of tears have been interpreted in many ways, particularly the fact that I have not cried since they found Lucien, but I cried then, with Dorothy to hold me, her paint-stained fingers making handprints on the back of my shirt as she hugged me and leaving traces of white as she pushed my hair out of my eyes.

"We'll pray about it," she said. "I am sure there is an answer. Trust the Rose."

I did. Trust the Rose, that is. If you say that word enough, you end up with just the rust. The flaking paint and the rust.

———

Memories like this punctuate my walks, but my search gives them purpose, the search not only for Lucien's rose necklace but also for the green sweater that was never found. Police dogs may have crisscrossed these fields, noses down, tails up, but no one knows this place like I do, its hidden alleys and camouflaged passageways. Today I make my way through the old pheasant pens—each rotten sack beneath a sheet of corrugated iron is a sleeve, each piece of baler twine caught on barbed wire, a thread. When I walk, I no longer look up to the grand sky but peer in on the minutiae which mock me: the green of the reeds, the shape of the hanging jacket in the shadow, the empty feed sack flapping in the wind. But perspective depends on purpose and mine is a close-up lens with just the one focus: a man's green sweater.

It is in this mind-set that I reach the bottom of the field, where the guards have been clearing low boughs brought down on the electric fence by George's Wood. They have sawn them off and dragged them a little way into the field, ready to be cleared, but there is no one working here now. Sitting on one of them, facing south, catching the full warmth of the sun, scuffing the earth with my foot and sending the ants scurrying, I imagine how Mark would have been eyeing up next year's logs. There is a lot of life in dead trees, Mark used to say. He became so knowledgeable about how it all works, from the sparrow hawk winging into its nest in the Douglas fir, down to the earwig feeding on mold from the fallen branch. I miss that understanding; I became so reliant on experience. A hundred yards away, a hare has emerged from the scrub at the edge of the field. It is motionless as a statue among the shifting grass, alert to the slightest change in the vibrations under its paws, to the variations in the sound waves carried across the hillside by the southerly breeze. The hare cannot see well when it is looking straight ahead, and so it runs in circles. Dorothy told me that. Sister Amelia told me something else: that it used to be believed you could kill a hare only with a silver cross or by drowning it, because hares were witches in disguise.

The hare spies something and then, suddenly, Boy is behind me. The hare is gone. He stands there with his chain saw, helmet on his head, visor pushed up above his eyes, and heavy gloves on his hands. "Seventy miles an hour, that's how fast they can go. Did you know that?"

"No." I look at the place where the hare once was.

"Fast enough," he says.

"Not always," I reply. "There are always things like foxes, predators who make the most of their weaknesses."

"Do you think he'll come back?"

"Not while you're here. You didn't post the letter, did you?"

He puts the chain saw and the helmet down, pulling off the gloves. "I am sorry," he says.

"You do what you are paid to do. I expect you all had a good time laughing at it. You're a bastard, Boy. I trusted you. You'd think I would have learned that lesson by now."

"Sarge watched the whole thing played back. He made me hand it over. I've said I'm sorry."

Sick in my stomach at the idea of Three watching that moment and not understanding it, I take my anger out on Boy. "You have no idea what it cost me, that letter. To write it. To ask you to post it. And afterwards—what happened between us, I wanted to explain, but I haven't had a chance."

There is a flicker of movement in the far hedge, but it is a rabbit, not a hare.

Boy sits down on the other end of the log. "I'm really sorry about that. I hope you don't think I'd ever take advantage of the fact that you're . . ."

"A prisoner? And you're my guard?"

Boy shrugs and kicks his boots against the wood to get the mud off, his face flushed. I turn away to collect myself and then look him in the eye. "I didn't mean that. I don't think you're like that at all, Boy. It was an amazing moment for me, in all sorts of ways you won't understand until you're old and gray and nodding by the fire. But it's over. Don't worry." I try a laugh for size. "I'm not a predatory woman."

"If you write again," Boy says, "this time, I will make sure it is posted. I promise."

"Don't, you don't need to."

"I do. The way you've been treated, by the government, I mean, legally it's not right. I've always been an activist so I'm not going to just stand by. I want to help you, but you'll be confined to the house and I'll be posted if Sarge has any more evidence. So I have to be distant. We have to be careful."

I look back into the wood. "What are you doing in there?"

"Just keeping the branches off the electric fence. I'm working down here alone until Adrian comes on duty. Should be about ten minutes. He doesn't care anyway. And Sarge has gone to Middleton."

My back is stiff from sitting on the log and the sun has moved behind the tall pine at the edge of the forest, placing me in the shade.

"There are things lost in these woods, Boy. A carved rose, a green sweater. If you want to help, keep your eyes open when you're working down here. Answers, that's all that matters to me now."

A woodpecker, somewhere out of sight, taps out its indecipherable code. The valley is loud with other voices; the earth is unstable when I stand.

"And I will write to Mark again, then. Post it if you can, if it's safe for you." I walk away, look back to thank him and see him arming himself again with his helmet, visor, and gauntlets. I make my way unsteadily up the field. The Land Rover is coming towards me, bumping over the grass towards the felling. Three is driving. My heart races. Did Boy lie to me about that? It's always been a problem at The Well, knowing whom to trust.

––––––––––

Dear Mark,

I have written once before, but I know now that it was never sent. You might not have got it anyway because I sent it to Will's house in London. Something tells me that you are not in London at all but have returned to your uncle's farm. You were always happiest in the country.

I always thought you were a better person than me. I think that is probably still true, but I just don't know.

I have been going over what happened here. That is the task I have set myself, to make sense of it all. Somehow, we have to find out the truth and we hold different pieces of the jigsaw. The final picture cannot be as hideous as this heap of fractured images. You have to tell me what you know. You owe it to me.

One more thing. If you have heard from Angie, please tell me. Not knowing how she is, that is my second sentence.

All my love,
R

P.S. I could tell you lots about The Well—how much the new hedge you planted has grown, how much blossom there is in the

*orchard this year. Whoever is innocent could start again here, that
is still a possibility for someone . . .*

Take that, Boy, and post it, if you want to save the world.

I go to bed and Mark is in the bedroom, sleeping with me, the
shape of him haunting me with an ache of equal grief and fear.

CHAPTER SIXTEEN

I took to making supper earlier so I could go and join the Sisters sooner. Initially, we would carry our plates and drinks to the old card table under the trees at the top of the garden (drinks—by which I mean a glass of water for me and most of a bottle of our homemade cider for Mark). The earlier routine suited Mark because he said farmers needed the lengthening summer evenings; he spoke as if I wasn't a farmer any longer. He would come in off the field, wash up for supper, and go back out again. His mind would be on balers and making the lean-to rainproof for when he got the hay in, or, if he had got to his emails, composing a response to the next legal challenge for keeping the government off our land. We were now agreed, although for different reasons, that moving was not an option. My mind was somewhere, but never on the food. I was eating less and less, dividing the omelet unequally, slipping the chips into the bin. I preferred to pray on an empty stomach and then later, light-headed from long meditation, I was all spirit and had no appetite.

"You haven't finished."

"You're getting too thin."

"You'll make yourself ill, you know."

My evening journey from one world to another developed its own rituals. I would stand with my back to the house, my eyes focused on the path ahead. When I started walking, I would start counting in fives. Five times five paces, and at the end of each five times five, I would pray one line from the Dedication of the Rose.

It was very hot one week, impossibly hot. In the outside world, the relentless rise in the temperature at last made the drought look like a drought, with no more of these gray, quietly stubborn skies and temperatures average for the time of year, but the stuff of the buildup in apocalyptic films. There were disasters in tunnels on the London Underground; the elderly died of heatstroke and neighbors traced them only through the smell seeping under the tower block doorways. There was sporadic rioting in simmering cities, and photos of reservoirs like drained baths, the line of scum and residual hair all that was left of the comfortable past.

At The Well, ours was a more traditional heat wave. Mark and Lucien spent the mornings stripped to the waist, repairing the old shed; Lucien, brown backed and thrilled to be useful, passing up the tools, sorting out the nails by size. Sometimes he wandered up to the Sisters with me, but was shy with them, often peeping out from behind the oak halfway up the field rather than coming down into the camp. He got heatstroke and we were plagued by wasps at lunchtime; my shoulders were sunburned and the strap of my cotton top rubbed against the flesh. I hadn't slept well for several nights, pulling the thin sheet up to cover my nakedness, tossing it off to find relief from the sweat. Next door, I would hear Mark getting up for a glass of water, then listen to the footsteps going back to the little bedroom. The Sisters' campers were torture chambers for them; Sister Amelia told me she was taking her mat outside and lying under the stars, often joined by Eve and Jack, who never slept easily. Awake in the cottage, I ached to join them.

One night, the prayers started like any other evening—sitting in a circle, joined hands, eyes closed. Jack was on my left. Her hand was clammy and slid against my wedding ring as we felt our fingers into place. On my right, I was aware of Dorothy adjusting her position, straightening her back. I remember the flints in the ground sticking

into my ankles but not feeling able to move as the group found its
lung, exhaled its tension, inhaled its inspiration, until the body was
at ease with itself and the silence.

Sister Eve led our meditation: "My beloved is unto me as a cluster
of camphire in the vineyards of En-gedi. Behold, thou art fair, my
love; behold, thou art fair; thou hast doves' eyes. Behold, thou art
fair, my beloved, yea, pleasant: also our bed is green. The beams of
our house are cedar, and our rafters of fir."

When the verses had settled with the sun, the Sisters spoke or sang
as the spirit moved them and I joined in the responses, feeling my
way tentatively around the dark waters of their worship, holding onto
the edge. I don't think I made any contribution that evening (I rarely
did), nor do I remember Jack leading, but when Sister Amelia held
the Rose high, I was with them as the circle closed in, all self-con-
sciousness melted away as I felt hands around my waist, bodies pressing my body, my fingers entangled in Amelia's beautiful hair. Each
of the Sisters' unique invocations mingled like a million languages,
cadences rising and falling in counterpoint, vowels and consonants
meeting and parting and making space for expressions so guttural
they were barely words, yet contained in them was meaning—I was
sure there was meaning. And when this happened, as it did happen
sometimes, the chaos of the individual orisons would somehow, like
sand in the wind, be blown into form, and before we knew how or
why, we were in unison.

Suddenly, the unity of the limbs of the great body was shattered
by an arm flinging itself violently into the air. Jack's clenched fist
caught me hard under the chin. I staggered backwards. A high-
pitched screech of agony scarred the evening, and there was Jack,
tearing at her gray shift, ripping at the cotton until it fell from her
jerking shoulders onto the stamped ground. I watched as if this was
a film. A near-naked woman throwing her head back at such a crazy
angle, her eyes must surely fly from their sockets, arms as wide as if

they were no longer connected to her collarbones, which in turn must surely dislocate from her neck, all limbs unleashed from the core. The others froze too, motionless figures on a painted backdrop against the urgency of the fit. Jack slumped. For a second it seemed as if the hard ground must crack apart her exposed ribs and spine and splinter her skeleton. She writhed, the screaming transposed into an ululation, a sound thrusted from deep within the throat which was at the same time language and not-language.

Looking at the slathering beast at my feet, fear and a sense of impotence paralyzed me, until I heard a voice telling me to quiet her. My nausea deserted me and I saw myself stepping forwards as if in a trance, falling to my knees alongside her body and taking her spluttering head in my hands until the rasping gasps become music which passed through my palms into my soul, and all I felt was lightness and all I heard was the song and the voice. That voice which was not recognizable to me then and yet was more familiar than anyone else I have ever listened to, and that voice was telling me that this was the beginning.

We sat for a long time, Jack with her head in my lap, me stroking her hair, the Sisters emptied and uplifted by the visitation, lying like exhausted children in the long grass, already damp with dew. Jack remembered almost nothing of her experience, except a great sense of peace, deeper than she had ever known, coming in like the sea over the rocks in summer.

"That peace came through you," Sister Amelia said to me later. "You were the channel for the Spirit of the Rose."

"Not just me," I protested, "it was all of us."

Eve agreed. "No one person is special. It's the strength of our sisterhood," she said. "The power of our communion."

But in my head, the voice was with Amelia on this. She disagreed with Eve. "No, this was you, Ruth, you alone. This is just the beginning."

I want to think about Voice, but I do not know if I dare, because it may be to think about Voice will be to invite her back and I do not have a spare room. Three marches into the kitchen, a handful of letters in his hand. I am wringing out my knickers in the sink. He stands in the doorway and I push them under the soapy water, but even so he grins pointedly. "Your priest is not coming today."

Clasping my hands under the water, I resolve not to cry in front of him, nor will I risk speaking, nor will I ask him about the letters he has put facedown on the table.

"Did you hear? I said the priest is not coming. Not today. Maybe not next week either. Maybe never again, who knows? Still, if you insist, I expect we can always find another. One priest must be much like another, I imagine, and the whole country's overrun with religious maniacs nowadays."

He makes some comment about coming back later to talk about the permissions and steps out into the daylight. The letters are still on the table. I dry my hands.

He returns. "So sorry, I forgot these."

Pulling the plug on the water in the sink, I realize that I had forgotten to tap five times. If only I had tapped, Hugh would be here. I had planned to talk to Hugh about Voice.

In the orchard I spend the rest of the morning making a chain, threading daisies, buttercups, dandelions; campion, cow parsley, and Queen Anne's lace. I slit their stalks with my thumbnail, noticing the beads of sap seep onto my skin. It makes for an uneven chain: the weaker stalks of the buttercups cannot bear the penetration of the dandelions; the whites, yellows, and pinks make no sensible pattern, it does not know how to end. I lift my chain, letting the links drop onto each other, mute manacles.

I was sure Hugh was going to bring me information from the

Internet today. The Rose of Jericho has flowered after last night's rain; I wanted to show him the Rose. Three didn't say why he wasn't coming. He wasn't well last time. Or maybe we said something about the Internet which was caught on camera. Do they have some way of monitoring what we talk about, even out here in the orchard? I rip at the unruly grass which was growing wild up the bench, convinced that they have hidden their tracking devices among weeds and the willow herb. I snatch at the nettles with my bare hands and they blister white at the sting and I think to myself that these are the hands of a madwoman who has done mad things and even the priest realizes she is beyond his help. Voice would have agreed with that.

––––––––

After that first evening with Sister Jack, I heard Voice more and more frequently, but I told no one about it.

"When you pray," I asked Dorothy and Jack, "does anyone reply?"

They were sitting on the grass, stitching white cotton into robes.

"The Rose replies," said Dorothy, "but you wouldn't say it's a voice I can literally hear. But you've heard her, haven't you, Jack?"

Jack's hand was guiding the needle in and out of the cotton, tightening the thread which kept it all together. "There are different sorts of voices," she said, "and it's all about knowing the difference. When I'm ill, the voices are loud, kind of vulgar, I can sort of half see their owners out of the corner of my eye. Meds used to sort of dull them, distance them a bit, but I don't take the pills any longer. I never felt like me when I was on them and, anyway, Amelia, the Rose, they're a lot more powerful than any chemical crap." She paused for a moment as the cotton slid out of the eye, licked the end, rethreaded it, and continued in an unfamiliar tone. "Do this or else. You'll be sorry if you don't. No one will believe you. That sort of thing. If you've ever been a victim, you'd recognize my voices."

"When did they start?"

"When I was about seventeen, and then on and off ever since. The psychiatrist put it down to me having seen my parents beat the shit out of each other when I was little. And then, of course, so predictable, I get with a man who beats the crap out of me. That's me. I always end up letting other people control me."

"Used to," said Dorothy.

"Yeah, used to. I'm working on it, now I actually believe in something myself." She broke off the thread with her teeth and tucked the needle in the cotton reel.

I hadn't been a victim. Not then.

"And the other voice?" I ask.

"The still, small voice of calm, I suppose."

"That sounds a little clichéd."

"It does." Jack finished tying off the end of the thread. "But it's kind of hard to find any other way of describing it. When that voice talks, I'll do anything she tells me, because she's the true voice. Simple as that."

"Anything?"

"I think so."

"So how is that not control?"

Jack thought for a moment, looked at Dorothy, then laughed. "No. Don't say anything. I can answer this myself. It's faith, Ruth. That's the difference. Faith, from deep inside." She got to her feet. "God, this is like being back at school in a religious education lesson. Come on, stand up."

Jack held the hemmed gown up against me. I spread my arms wide like an angel in a nativity play.

"You'll do." She laughed. "All you need now is a halo."

Jack's description of her voices didn't help me much. At times I was frightened of Voice, as I came to call her, this someone who was me but was not me, inside me but outside also; but at other times, she was my guide and I missed her when she was away. Although for a while, Voice kept herself to the times of day allocated to religious experience, she soon became bored with that limited arena.

Looking out the window, wondering why Mark has taken so long in town:

He has been talking to the bank about selling The Well. Ask him if you don't believe me.

Starting work on the accounts which I promised I'd have finished by the evening:

It's not about the money, Ruth. Take yourself out to the field and pray. The money will get you nowhere.

It's not about the food, Ruth. Only the Rose will feed you.

It's not about loving Mark, Ruth. Only the Rose can save you now.

It's not about your daughter, Ruth. Angie has never forgiven you. She never will. Only the Rose can forgive you now.

If Voice had been my sister, she would have been my older sister. When we were getting on badly, she would always win the argument. But when we were friends, we would have borrowed each other's clothes and straightened each other's hair, finished each other's sentences. Mark worried, that much I do know because I followed her advice and checked up on his phone and discovered the last missed call was from the surgery. We had been lucky since we had moved to The Well. We had been healthy and I was consumed with guilt that I was spying on his mobile and he might be ill.

"You had a missed call on your mobile. I forgot to mention it."

"Who from?"

"The surgery."

"Don't know what they want."

"Are you OK?" I persisted. "Aren't you well?"

"Me? No, I'm fine," he replied.

Later that evening, he sat on my side of the bed and reached out to touch me, but Voice asked me what was I doing, letting him lay his fingers on me like that and I froze. He took his hand away and held it in the air for a second or two, before letting it drop to his lap, where it lay like a prosthetic limb.

"I'm tired, that's all," I said.

The cliché slid around between us like a lump of ice. "Who is it you're talking to?" he asked.

I rolled away from him to face the window, where the faintest of new moons was ghosting the horizon. "I don't know what you're going on about."

Don't tell him about me; he'll say I don't exist.

"It's as if there isn't just you and me in this cottage, it's like you are living with someone else. We can be chatting, and then suddenly you're gone, away with the fairies, as if you're listening to someone else. For goodness sake, Ruth, sometimes you talk out loud and there's nobody there."

He is a nonbeliever, pray for him.

"I pray, Mark. I pray because I believe. That's all. I pray for you, for our land, for the country. You've got to admit, there's a lot of things to pray for right now." I still couldn't look at him.

His Internet history recorded on the laptop read like this (I know because I looked):

mh.co.uk/pseudohallucinations/stress

hardtolivewith.co.uk/psychosis/hallucinations/auditory

myfinemind.co.uk/support/paranoia

I overheard him talking to Angie one morning. I was upstairs, eavesdropping. They were below in the kitchen. Angie had come begging for eggs; Lucien was bouncing a ball against the sitting room door.

"Does Mum ever talk to you about the Sisters and the Rose and all that?"

"Yeah. Sometimes."

"Do you or Charley go down there to this worship or whatever it is? Or do any of the others go?"

"Not really. Not to their worship anyway." The cupboard door slams. "Aren't there any egg boxes?" Then Angie continued. "We go and talk about stuff, but for most of us, we're just not in the right place yet to make like, major life-changing commitments. One day maybe."

"What do you think about your mother going? Lucien, stop that."

"It makes her happy. What's wrong with that?"

"She doesn't look happy. Sometimes I think she's becoming quite paranoid."

"Which is another way of saying she feels you're getting at her, just because she's got a belief."

"Lucien, stop that now! You're going to break something. So you believe all this Rose stuff?"

"Some of it."

"Out! Now!"

"Don't shout at him."

"Typical of you, to pick and choose."

"Back off, Dad. You're too cynical."

"What's cynical?"

"Nothing, love, don't worry about it."

"Lucien, for Christ's sake, take that ball outside."

"Someone who refuses to believe something even though it's staring him in the face," finished Angie.

The fridge door closed and I heard Angie leaving, but then she must have thought twice because I heard her calling back.

"Oh, and by the way, Dad, ever heard of the expression: people who live in glass houses shouldn't throw stones?"

Mark was shouting after her. "You can't just walk away, what exactly do you mean by that?"

Their row continued beneath the bedroom window.

"You think she's paranoid, Mark. Look at yourself in the mirror! You fly off the handle at the slightest thing. If you want her to see a shrink about being paranoid, you should check in with an anger management course."

"You should know," he yelled after her. "We've spent more money on therapists for you over the years than . . ." His voice dropped. "Fuck you!" I heard the door slam and the clink of bottle on glass. It was only 11 a.m.

I did not even know he had gone into Lenford. Increasingly, I found myself keeping out of his way when he was like that, and besides, I was with Sister Amelia and time meant little to me when we were together, so when my mobile went at about half past five, it was unexpected.

It was Mark. He needed me to collect him, from the police station.

Leave him there, said Voice. *Why rescue him? You're better off without him, he is the one who should be locked up.*

"You will miss meditations," said Amelia. "Do you have to go? One of these days, he will have to take responsibility for his own errors."

Fiddling with the key in my hand, I hesitated.

"If someone needs to, let me go." Amelia wrapped her arms around me. "You'll never cope with the antagonism out there. When did you last face the world beyond The Well?" Stepping back, she pushed my hair away from my face. "And why should you cope with it? Your place is here."

She's right. You'll never manage. You're right to be scared. You're weak.

"I don't know why you should have to go . . ."

Amelia held her hand out. "Well, perhaps you're right. I'll put the key back in the Land Rover. Come and pray for him, that's the way

to help him, Ruth. Action is the easy choice. Thought, contemplation—that is where the real power for change lies."

My phone indicated a further message: *Please come. M.*

He has never turned his back on me when I needed him. Closing
my eyes to block out the doubting Thomas of a voice, I took a deep
breath and then texted back: *On my way.*

Once in the driver's seat, I was shaking, not just because I didn't
really know what had happened, not just because I could see Amelia
and Eve in the rear mirror, holding hands, but also because I could
hardly remember the last time I had left The Well. The Land Rover
lurched up the drive, stuttering in the wrong gear, Voice telling me
turn back. At the gate, the police were arguing with someone in a van.

"I need to get out," I said. "I need to get Mark!"

It seems they knew something had happened. That's why they
were there, why the local press were there as well. They padlocked
the gate behind me and I grappled in the pocket in the driver's door,
wondering if the sunglasses were still there from when we used to go
fishing, thinking they might provide some disguise, hoping that they
would lessen the glare from this bare, blinding outside world. But
they weren't.

Voice was relentless and almost impossible to challenge. *Go back.
You can't do this. How are you going to cope in Lenford? Everyone will
look at you. They're looking at you now. Look at them looking at you.*

It was true. As I rounded the hairpin bend, Perry Clardle and a
teenager were standing in their yard, pointing as I drove past; with
no pub to run, I realized he must be unemployed like 28 percent
of the population. Farther down the hill I had to slow to pass an
elderly couple whose name I had forgotten, walking their dog, their
faces shocked as they saw who was driving. *It's her,* I imagined them
saying to each other, *how dare she.* And did I dare drive down that
dusty lane, the hedges brittle on either side, and the gardens of the
bungalows along the main road oblongs of gray wasteland? And how

did I have the gall to turn right by the Kings Head, boarded up and covered with graffiti, or cross the bridge into Lenford with the river-bed beneath it sprouting thistles and litter? Where was the love of the Rose in the High Street—the florists gone, the shoe shop gone, the tourist information office closed down? This is a film, I thought, a stage set—it is The Well, only The Well that is real. I pulled up in the police station car park and had to sit for a minute to slow my racing thoughts before I could get out.

At the entrance, the door was locked; you had to talk through an intercom to get in. I pressed the buzzer, but there was no response. A small group of people were gathering on the other side of the traffic lights, looking at me, and although the green man was flashing, they did not cross the road but stood, arms folded, chins thrust forward. I pressed it again, hard, twice.

"It's Ruth Ardingly," I said. "I had a call from my husband."

There was a buzz, the door opened, and I stepped inside and felt my heart calm a little at the reassuring click of it locking behind me. The woman in civilian clothes behind the glass said I should wait on one of the blue chairs opposite. I sat, a rack of leaflets to my left, a further locked door in front of me.

"Know your limits!" An explanation of the new domestic and commercial unit rates for water consumption.

"Drought Crime is serious Crime. If you know someone using water illegally, you can contact DROUGHTLINE anonymously on 0800 700 900."

God knows how many calls they had received about us.

She knows who you are, said Voice.

"Can you tell me what happened?" I tapped on the glass. "Is my husband all right?"

"I can't say, I'm afraid," she replied. "Someone will be with you shortly."

It seemed I had been waiting forever and was about to summon the courage to knock on the partition again when the second door opened and a police officer came out, followed by Mark. His T-shirt was bloodstained, and his nose, always slightly hooked, looked swollen. In fact his whole face was a mess.

"Let's go," he said.

"Are you . . . ?"

"I want to go home," he said, pushing past my outstretched hand.

The policeman pressed the door release switch and we stepped back out into the light where a police car already had its engine running and blue lights flashing. The driver stuck his head out through the window and said it wasn't his idea of good use of public money, but he'd been told to give us an escort in case there was trouble. Mark climbed tentatively into the passenger side of the Land Rover, without speaking.

"What about the car?" I asked him.

"Leave it," he said. "I can't drive like this."

We followed the police out of the car park. Inside the Land Rover it was silent, except that my head was loud with Voice, but outside, the group of people by the traffic lights had grown and they shouted as we left: "Fucking Headcase," "Pervert." A few seconds later, as we passed cars queuing at the petrol station, a man with a shaved head yelled, "Water-legger," and sounded his horn, and a couple of the other cars joined him in a blast of hate-fueled condemnation.

"What have you done?" I asked him. No reply.

The gate was opened for us and we careered back into our bewildering homeland, leaving the baked gray fields behind us and returning to our Technicolor, digitally enhanced comic strip of a farm. The police didn't stop at the bottom, they did a three-point turn and left.

Lock him out, suggested Voice.

I didn't need to. Mark was in the house only a matter of minutes before he left again and climbed over the gate into First Field. I saw the flare of a match, and the smell of cigarette smoke drifted back towards me, and then he was gone before I had a chance to talk to him. Not one word of thanks for going to collect him, even though he must have known how hard it was for me. Angie had seen the police and came down to see what was going on, although there wasn't much I could tell her, except that I was worried and angry, that I didn't know where he'd gone, that he looked in a state.

"He'll be back," she said. "Come and see me in the morning, tell me what went on," and she also left.

I would have liked her to have sat with me, mother and daughter, during those long hours when I waited for him to return. She is a selfish cow, I thought to myself, if you think of all the hours we've sat waiting for her in police stations and hospitals. He is a selfish bastard too, I continued to myself, he can go, for all I care, I'd be better off now without him, smoking, drinking, going to pieces. And that wasn't Voice, that was pure me. As the dull purple of late evening blurred the outline of the forests and stirred the bats in the eaves of the barn, I began to think he wasn't coming back at all and, as he had nowhere to go, or so I thought, it occurred to me that he might never be coming back, that he had, as they say, done something stupid. I tried to check the gun cupboard but couldn't find the key.

It will be a gun, said Voice. *There will be a lot of blood.*

It was now properly dark and the moon was already showing above the oak. I will go to the Sisters, I thought, they'll help me. I got to my knees, thanked the Rose for her guidance, pulled on a cardigan, and slipped out of the house, shaking. Be careful what you wish for, Ruth, that is what I was thinking.

The thump of him climbing the gate behind me made me jump and all I could make out of him was his moon shadow and the sound of his coughing.

"Mark!"

"Where were you going?" he asked.

"To . . . the Sisters," I began, realizing too late how that sounded.

"I came back because I thought you might be worried." He laughed. "Stupid me."

Go.

"You OK?" I asked.

"Never been better," he replied and went inside.

Welcome back—that was what Amelia said when I got down to the campers. After night worship, when I returned, he was asleep in the little bedroom and it wasn't until the morning that I understood what had happened.

He had been in Lenford when some bloke had started on him. Nothing unusual, happened all the time when he went into shops, he said.

"I never realized," I said.

"No, I don't expect you did," he said. "The bloke was bad-mouthing you."

"Me?"

"Yes, you. Or do you think I have sole rights on being abused in the street?"

"I didn't know, I just assumed . . ."

"I'm sure you did. Well, let me tell you what they said and you can see how it feels."

Whore. Witch. Dyke. Parasite. That sort of thing. So Mark had lost it. Usually, he said, he was able to walk on by, but this time it got to him, he had swung at him, the man retaliated, they fought, the police were called, the other guy went to the hospital to get stitches while Mark ended up in the police station. Just another Wednesday afternoon in Little Britain, he tried to joke.

"Did they charge you?" I asked.

"Disorder in a public place, that's all. I'll add it to our growing list of upcoming court appearances."

Tentatively, I broached the subject of how to get the car back, but that triggered another outburst.

"Why don't you do something useful for a change?" he stormed. "Why does it always have to be me?"

A couple of days later Amelia said she was going in for supplies and offered to see if she could collect the car. She thought it was unfair of Mark to make me pay for the consequences of his behavior. Again. She said she would protect me from the stress of leaving The Well or the pain of enduring the rejection of the very people I was helping every time I worshipped. I was speechless with relief; I had been dreading having to go back to Lenford, given up even pretending that I could cope out there on my own. Eve was the one who managed to drive it back. She left it for us by the barn, without saying a word, and there it was, like a monstrous exhibit in a museum of modern art: the windows were smashed; the aerial snapped; it was viciously daubed with filth and slander against us, The Well, the Rose—I don't know how they knew about the Rose. When I pulled the back door, the twisted metal grated against the frame and there was a sickening smell of stale smoke, the springs protruding through the blackened seat like charred ribs.

"We can't afford another," said Mark. "This is the last straw."

"Surely you can press charges?"

"I do more law now I'm a farmer than I ever did before," said Mark, kicking the car before walking away.

Look at the car, said Voice. *You will look the same when they finally find you.*

Amelia said, you can burn down all the structures in the world, but the Rose never dies.

———————

I tried smoking them out once, the Sisters, like hornets. If they have built a new nest, Hugh will tell me, when he returns, if he returns.

CHAPTER SEVENTEEN

It rained this morning. I wander into the orchard where the blossoms on all the trees—apple, damson, plum—have opened just a little, the buds white but pink-fringed now they are so close to blooming. Just a little rain and such a grand response. They hold their boughs above my head like a guard of honor at a wedding, and when a blackbird flies off, startled by my arrival, a slight shower of raindrops anoints me. My boots are brushed by the long wet grasses until the knees of my jeans are a darker blue from the damp and I sit on my bench, appreciating the resistance of the cold stone pushing up against my weight, insisting on gravity. I don't know how long I am there or what I am doing except that I am grateful for the silence, the absence of Voice. I resume my chain of flowers.

"So, you can pick flowers but you can't grow vegetables? Where's the logic in that?"

The question catches me unawares. Boy and I have hardly spoken since we sat on the felled branches, but the letter had gone from the table when I woke in the morning. I haven't asked, he hasn't said. Now he is in the little plot behind the orchard, looking over the gate. He has his sleeves rolled up and the back of his white shirt is saturated with sweat. It looks as though he has been digging, and the spade is resting against the fence that used to keep the rabbits out of the vegetables. He seems to be expecting an answer, but he doesn't wait long and resumes weeding, methodically working his way up a row of seedlings. When he reaches the end, he rakes the small pile of discarded nettles and couch grass to one side, brushes the mud off his hands, then steps carefully around the edge of the planted rows to pick up an old black plastic seed tray. On it are five or six small terra-cotta flowerpots, planted up; they have the familiar two tender leaves of young courgettes. He must have planted the seeds his mother gave me and stuck them on a windowsill. I imagine him in the barn, Three fixated by the split screen showing a dozen camera angles, Anon playing cards with himself, and Boy watering the courgettes like the plant monitor at school: your turn to look after the garden.

"It's a bit early for planting those out," I call over the hedge, but he doesn't look up. He hasn't heard me. I repeat myself, just a little bit louder. "We used to start them off in the greenhouse and then not even harden them off until the end of May."

"Not really an option now, is it?" Boy indicates the broken-down shell of the greenhouse behind him. "What happened here?"

Holding tight to the security of my horticultural explanations, I continue. "It was because of the wind up here," I shout a bit louder. "And the risk of a late frost. Oh, go on; ignore the advice of a stupid old woman. What does she know about farming anyway."

He has turned back to his work, forgetting me and himself in The Well that is a black widow of a property, enticing you before swallowing you whole and spitting out the bits that stick in the throat. I have lost a lot of men to The Well and now here she is flirting again.

Listening to the scratching of the trowel and the squeak of his boots as he crouches, I deafen myself to everything except the territorial robin. I scream silently at Boy because the glass is shattered and he has the arrogance to assume he has the right to work this land. I cry inwardly for him because what he is doing is futile, save for providing a few beans for a casserole at the end of a summer, when the days are shortening and the leaves falling. I yearn to join him, but that would be breaking my word.

Back in the house, I sleep because that is all I have to fill my days. When I wake, it is dusk. I have been asleep a long time, my head is dull, my mouth sackcloth; I drink a long glass of water. Out the window, the languid evening is spreading herself in pink and gold satin over the curve of the earth. She blows the scent of a sweet old-time summer across the room and I breathe in evenings long gone: hosepipes on the lawn in London and Lucien running in rainbows; strawberries; a pub, somewhere by the Thames and Mark and I and a group of friends, celebrating something special, long forgotten. I splash water on my face and feel my way out into the silk-soft air. In my head, I play an old recording of a long-forgotten orchestra, with the persistent ewes nagging their lambs to come back before dark, the scratch-picking of the hens, the touch of one petal from the pear tree settling on the dew-damp grass, and the pulse of fruit forming like the half-heard, half-felt vibrations of a cello. With a blanket, I climb to the brow of First Field and sit, suspended in the sky above the flickering valleys beneath me. Amelia coached me like her prodigy, but strangely it is Angie I think of now. Angie a few years ago on holiday with us in Wales, telling me about her most recent treatment and the yoga they practiced on the ward, saying sit like this, Mum, it really works, legs crossed, placing my hands upon my knees, turning my palms outwards, both of us breathing in a conscious recognition of being alive. It works for a while. I blow out the candles on my forty years one by one until the past drifts away with the smoke and I am in the present and all that I have been and everyone I have known and loved and lost, yes, even Lucien, they are part of the flaming sky and the kind clouds. This could be prayer. Maybe all is well with Angie; she seems close to me. Maybe I should work the land. Maybe it is possible to live with uncertainty.

So in love with the night, I cannot bear to go inside but instead drag the old sun lounger from the shed out into the garden so that I can lie on my back and watch the stars; it is one of those nights when the meteors shower like storms over mountains, all sound lost, but light remains. I can feel the smallness of my breath, the ridges of the wooden chair hard against my back, the cool air on my bare feet. We used to watch the August meteors from the cliffs in Cornwall, on another holiday, very long ago, Angie asleep in my arms, Mark with his head on my lap. It was such moments we thought we might recapture at The Well, and here I am now, netting moths with candles.

It is the late shift and Boy is standing watch by the barn. He hesitates and then comes over. "I didn't want to intrude," he says, "but I have been waiting all evening for an opportunity."

"I'm sorry," I interrupt. "I wasn't very helpful this morning. Go ahead and do the garden, if you think it's worth it."

"It's definitely worth it, but . . ."

It feels good to apologize, even for something small, so I keep going while I can. "And I was horrible the other day, about the letter, it's just that it's so frustrating, I've been searching so hard for those things I told you about."

"That's what I want to see you about." Boy checks over his shoulder and squats down beside the sun lounger. "I found something this afternoon when I was on duty. It's probably nothing."

He pulls the something from the pocket of his army jacket and hands it to me. It feels like a ball of string, but he shines his torch on it and I see why he has brought it. It is a small amount of green wool, tidied as if it has been wound round and round a hand and then finished with a bow to keep it in place.

"Did you find it like this, all wound up?"

"I spotted it because I saw the end of it. I thought it might have been from the green sweater you talked about. You know, someone might have snagged it on something. But then when I pulled it, I realized it was attached to the rest. It's weird, the way it's crinkled; it does look as though it's already been knitted once and undone."

Slowly, I undo the knot and pull on the end, so it unravels slowly, almost as if I expect it to knit itself back into Mark's green sweater. "Where was it?"

"At that place where the stream backs up, just beyond where the Sisters used to be. The scientist contingent ordered us to clear the leaves because it's all blocked, and it was there, as if it had been washed down. But there wasn't anything else, I looked."

It is the right sort of green, at least I think it would have been, but it's now soiled and ingrained with dirt. But that is all I can say about it. I will not discard it, because Boy offers this gift with all sincerity, but in truth, even tonight when hope is possible, I cannot believe it is anything other than a false dawn. If it can't be evidence, it can be an olive branch.

"Thank you," I say. "I'm not sure it's the same as the sweater, but thank you for looking."

It is as though him finding a piece of green wool which means nothing has used up the odds of me finding a piece of green wool which might mean something, which is absurd, I know, but nevertheless that is the way my mind works at the moment. Fighting to regain something of the optimism I felt earlier, I direct Boy's gaze to one of the shooting stars and I point them out to him as if he were a child, all rancor over the post and the garden gone, the disappointment that is the wool dropped in the darkness. He cannot be much younger than Angie; maybe this is how we might have talked, Angie and her friends and me, if she had been a different sort of daughter.

"These are the Eta Aquarids," he says, "part of my now famous scientific knowledge. It's when Halley's comet appears—once in a lifetime."

"You've come, you source of tears to many mothers," I quote. "It's from *The Anglo- Saxon Chronicle*. I studied them at university."

"The comet always was an omen, good or bad," Boy comments. "Like the Battle of Hastings, just depends if you were Harold or William. It's the same with all so-called celestial portents." Standing up and stepping away, he triggers the security light which exposes us as nothing more or less than a soldier and a prisoner. It prompts him to pick up the torch and clip his radio back on his belt.

"Good night," I say, "and thank you again." But he is already disappearing on his rounds, the beam sweeping the hedges and his heavy-booted footsteps startling creatures rustling along the edge of the wood. The light goes off.

Like a baby who throws its hands into the air, suddenly reminded by absence that it no longer has the womb to contain it, I grasp at the dark and then I pick up the wool and go indoors. Inside, the rotten core of me lurches and reminds me that all that hope was nothing more than a yarn or a star glimpsed fleetingly before the clouds black in from the west.

CHAPTER EIGHTEEN

In daylight, the wool mocks me and I hate it for its lack of significance. I imagine some old woman finishing off her knit one, pearl one gloves for her grandson, never knowing that the remnant dropped by chance would, for a brief moment, give another grandmother hope of the truth. The wool goes round and round my neck seven or eight times, but being weakened by its life among detritus, lacks resolve and snaps at the first sign of pressure, leaving only red rings of failure. Worse, Hugh is still unwell, apparently. I was a better visitor than him: Granny in her last days at the nursing home, a skeleton propped up in a high-backed blue plastic chair, dislocated head nodding on a spring; Mum, her nightie hanging limp over her flattened chest; Angie in rehab, Angie with a black eye and a domestic violence worker, Angie in labor. Maybe it is a woman's thing—all over the world women come in and out of each other's huts, tower blocks, shantytown houses made of corrugated iron and newspaper, neat suburban terraces. Looking out at the empty drive, I realize how very much I want to be visited.

Yesterday, I thought I heard my mobile ring and went to rummage in my bag, in the way that the slam of a back door prompts the widow to put the kettle on. I am sure there was talk of being allowed one phone call a day to one of my approved numbers, but the truth is I have no numbers. Internet I would value, even though I am now more than ever aware of what a web it weaves around the lonely. Still, there are lots of things I could do on the Internet which would not contravene the isolation of my imprisonment: how could it hurt if I were to spend time Googling myself, just to see who I am now, or I could log on to watchpaintdry.com and see if it is more interesting than this, or I might allow myself to create a virtual garden and industriously weed my rows of digital vegetables, accelerate the pace of the growth, then click and drag them into my basket—where would be the harm in that? "No connection available." That is a phrase which seems to make sense to me at the moment.

When other people talk of my conversion, they have in their minds that picture, with the rainbow, the one that someone once described, without a trace of irony, as iconic. For me, the process started twenty-four hours before that moment. I had become somewhat addicted to the Sisters' company, finding my own unreliable and the unpredictable presence of Voice disconcerting, so I went down to the campers so as not to be alone. Things that day seemed different. There was no clatter of plates or smell of fresh bread, no T-shirts and jeans, no chatter. The Sisters were hushed and drifting in gray robes, shadows in the shade of the oaks. Sister Amelia came out of her camper, barefoot, light and smiling at me, and I was a teenage girl with a crush all over again. She explained that the next day's worship would be special and would be held at the Wellspring. The Sisters knelt, bowed their heads, and Sister Amelia wound long strips of white cotton sheet around their eyes. Finally, she beckoned me over and held the one remaining piece of material out to me.

"You must leave us now," she said. "Prepare as best you can. Fast. Come wearing white. Come barefoot. Come alone."

The silence at the cottage seemed the loudest silence I had ever heard, except now I know there is a silence louder than the lack of speech. Mark was out all that day, hoping to pick up a horse box at a farm auction; he hated pecking around in the remains of bankrupt farmers' tenancies, like a chicken in a scrapyard, but money was tight and he said we needed it to take the lambs to the abattoir. That made it easy to observe the vow of silence; we weren't exactly overrun with people dropping round for tea. In the bedroom, I tied the sheeting around my own head, a child playing blindman's buff with herself, and sat on the wooden floor, facing the open window, feeling the heat of the sun on my face.

Initially my thoughts were sparrows, flighty and easily scared. I was so hot, my back ached, my aloneness felt a punishment rather than a privilege, but after some time—and who knows how long—I felt a dampness in the room which was followed by a coolness, then I could see, and what I could see was an old-fashioned brown leather briefcase on the floor in front of me. I had never seen it before or since, but it was so real I could trace my initials engraved on the lid, weigh the tiny key in my outstretched hand, feel the stiffness of the catches against my thumb. Inside was a jumble of old pictures of varying sizes, in different frames. The first was a miniature, depicting in exquisite detail a woman in the desert carrying an earthenware vessel for water. In the second painting, in a cheap, metallic frame, another woman, this one in poor, dull clothes and with unkempt hair, slumped on the end of an unmade bed, cowering in front of a golden pillar of light. The third was a rolled canvas, so big I had to stand up to be able to hold it, and as I did so, the oil paint cracked and the room was full of the flaking gold and blue of disintegrating angels taking flight from a woman in white kneeling in a peeling garden, the thrust of their thunder-ing wings threatening to crush me. I ripped at the blindfold, flail-ing my limbs heavily on the floor, screaming at my voice trapped in a constricted throat.

It is as clear to me now as it was then, and as inexplicable.

Someone was calling me. There was no briefcase. I was aware I needed words, struggled to find some, held tight to them.

"Up here!"

Mark had come home. I heaved myself up onto the bed just in time as his head loomed around the bedroom door. Looking away, I said I felt ill, and when he came closer to the bed to kiss me, I retched. I said I didn't feel like supper and was sorry I hadn't made anything for him, but that I just needed to lie quietly in the bedroom with the shutters closed. It was the sun, he said, it had lost its capacity to be gentle with us. Anyone who stayed out too long would get heatstroke. He lay beside me for a while, on his back with his hands behind his head. I wanted to turn over and for him to earth me, but as I turned towards him, the other inside spoke to me and I withdrew. The moment was past.

The day drifted into night, although the heat clung on. I was not hungry any longer; I sucked on the darkness like a baby on the end of his muslin. The next morning I did not wake until late. Mark had left me water and an apple by the bed and a note saying he was repairing the barn and would be back to check on me at lunchtime — that he loved me. I sipped the water, feeling it settle in the cracks on my lips, and left the fruit untouched.

The strip of cotton lay on the floor and I picked it up, tempted to blind myself again, and was weaving it in and out of my fingers, staring out the window, when I saw them: four tiny figures in white, processing through the corn. *They are going without you,* Voice warned me, *and you are the fifth.* In theory, I had a choice, but in practice the soles of my feet pushed me upwards, the joints in my knees locked me steady as I descended the stairs, the strength of my spine held me upright as I walked through the fields and the magnetic poles held my eyes on the horizon. I do not know where my mind was.

The heat was unbearable that day, its weight a blanket thrown over a cage to silence a shrieking parrot. The buzzards were saving their energy for dusk, and the sheep hugged the thin line of black shade that ruled down the side of the hedges. Angie and all the travelers had gone to a festival and Mark was treating the barn doors with preservative, so the place felt deserted.

Some things I recall. Sitting on the doorstep. It must have been a halfway house, a point where turning back was still possible. Ants, trailing steadily across the gravel, a wren inching its way up the cooler side of the oak, pecking for parasites, the drone of a hornet going in and out of its nest in the wall—small things, making their presence felt in that vast, constipated wilderness. And in the dip between George's Wood and the Hedditch, a slow, silent procession of women in white.

I wore a white cotton sundress. White, Sister Amelia had said. And barefoot, I remembered, the stones on the drive scorching my feet like hot coals.

Did Mark hear the slam of the back door up at the house when I left? Perhaps he put his brush down and thought to himself that I must be feeling better, up and about. Maybe he hoped I might be coming down with a drink, like I used to, when we were in it together, or maybe he picked up the brush and wondered why he was bothering at all to preserve a rotting stable when he did not envisage another winter at The Well, with cows steaming in the straw and the hay in the manger.

Leaving the glare of the field behind, I entered the forest, the sudden darkness like the interior of a foreign church on a hot day. As light and sight found their natural equilibrium, I thought I saw a flicker of white and then there was a young roe deer in the shadows, quivering, staring straight at me, its entire being wired for flight. But it did not run; rather it gently picked a path through the undergrowth down to the water. I followed. When I arrived at the water, the doe had vanished. There, a softer gleam poured liquid gold through the black pines and the Sisters were spread evenly around the edge of the pond, motionless, mesmerized by their own perfect reflections. I joined them. We waited, the heat on our heads feeding off our hunger until we all swayed slightly in our lightness.

Look at me, standing in a stained sundress in the middle of a wood, about to join four women whom I hardly knew for a baptism into a belief I hardly understood. Even then I did not fool myself that this was some spectator sport, a tourist visiting a temple, inhaling the jasmine and tasting the smoke from pyres, before walking out into the traffic and taking a cab back to the hotel. No. Although it was never named, this was all about me, as I knew in my heart of hearts it was going to be. The Sisters encircled me as the limbs of one body, one unbuttoning the eight tiny pearls down the front of my sundress, another taking the hem and drawing it over my head, a third releasing my hair where it caught on a hook. I looked to Sister Amelia for reassurance, but her eyes were one-way mirrors. They led me into the water and I did not resist. On the surface the caddis flies and alder bugs took flight and hid themselves in the reeds, the newts eased between the weeds; beneath our feet the sediment stirred, disturbing the gastrotrichs and protozoa, the hydra, crustaceans, and caddis fly larvae. Sister Amelia raised her hand and they waited for the water to settle around the translucent dresses clinging to their legs. Sister Amelia lowered her hand and the Sisters lowered me into the water, my body arched and gasping, one at my head, two at my waist, one at my feet; then they raised me up again with a rush of water draining from me, running down my face, trickling over my chest, swirling between my legs. Again they lowered me and raised me. I arched. Then a third time they raised me and lowered me, and the fourth found me elsewhere in the way that only the dying or the transported are absent.

On the fifth and final occasion, they withdrew, slipping out from me, and I felt that leaving like an exhalation. I lay, arms and legs wide, like a child in the sea, head back, eyes closed, hair like silk. The Sisters leant forward and cupped the water in their hands and sprinkled it over me, showering down through the sunlight until I saw a rainbow had formed over me and knew that the Rose had come.

The weeping women led me, drained and exhausted, from the water, all of us lurching and slipping on the sucking mud. Sister Amelia watched me shivering and moaning among the fungus at the foot of the ancient oak, hugging my knees, with the twigs and the dead leaves clinging to my wet body, and then she started to sing and the others joined in, their gasping finding form in their song of praise of the Rose of Jericho, louder and louder, deeper and deeper their ecstasy.

"Behold, she blossoms with a thousand white flowers.

Behold, the Rose of Jericho."

Finally, I was laid down like a slack-stringed puppet with disconnected joints, my sagging breasts and loose stomach strewn with wood anemones and white violets.

"You are a chosen one," said Sister Amelia.

The Sisters picked the woodland relics from my skin, dressed me, fastened my buttons, tied back my hair, and then stepped away from me. I lifted my head with a new strength.

"I am ready," I said.

Back through the forest to the wooden gate, on out into the sunlight, across the field of corn I walked with them.

"Behold the Rose of Jericho," the Sisters sang, their hands outstretched to the rain-swollen sky.

Mark would not have heard us, working with the radio on. The travelers didn't get back until late. I imagine the policeman at the gate, clocking off, satisfied that the sightseers were gone for the day and only the usual two or three were gathered in their pop-up tents on the verge, still waiting for the day of revelation, no idea that inside one of those tents the screen on a phone was lighting up. One Mes-

sage Received. *Click.* Sisters, behold the promise of the Rose of Jericho. One Image Received. *Click.* A rainbow over a woman floating
in a pond. Forwarded around the country in minutes. She is come.
That woman was me.

———

The first of the writings came to me unsolicited when I got back
to the cottage—strange episodes of unknowing, leaving behind
pages which varied between lyrical and hysterical, often scrawled
in colored crayons. I hid the notebook in the box of fishing things,
knowing that Mark would never look there again, and that is where I
find it now, on top of the broken tumble dryer in the back passage. I
take out the top tray of flies and hold them between my thumb and
finger, naming them as if at a memorial service for the river: gold
ribbed hare's ear, the coachman, woolly bugger, and blue wing olive.
Beneath that, there are the reels, gut, line, knife and priest and, beneath them, the notebook.

What was I when I left my house this morning?
An empty vessel discarded in a desert of alien corn.
clay chipped, glaze dulled, unfilled, unheld.

How does it hold me up this water?
The Rose holds me up.
How do I not drown in this water?
The Spirit of the Rose is my lightness.
How do I love this water?
I float on the love of the Rose.
How do I see in this water?
With the water comes light.

What am I when I rise from the water?
Myself streams away from me
And I am gone.

What was this foreign language, this unauthored poetry, written in an uneven hand that I cannot believe was my own?

I can speak, but in an unheard music
like rivers in the evening rolling over pebbles,
like the sigh of the black peat serenading the spring,
like the quiet rain dripping from ash bough to pool
or waterfalls in summer, rainbowing the rocks,
like the low lure beneath the silence of the Wellspring.

Months, that's all it took—a few months to transform that birthing pool into a grave and write a different story.

CHAPTER NINETEEN

It is eight o'clock precisely. I have been awake for a while, watching a brash red fox strut the hedge. No hunt now, no shotguns; even the slamming of the barn door does not make him run. He looks over his shoulder and saunters off into the labyrinth in the wood. Three comes into view, followed by Boy. Pulling on a sweater, I run downstairs, hope and fear as always fighting it out in conflicting hypotheses. Boy and Three are already in the kitchen; the creases in Boy's trousers are sharper, the buckle on his belt shines just that little bit brighter. Three does not even remove his cap. He hands over to Boy, as he puts it, and Boy in a voice which I do not recognize, delivers the news that I have been dreading: that I am once again to be confined to the house. There was no point in asking why, but Three commands Boy to explain anyway.

"The original terms of the House Arrest Order specified under section 3(f) that if anyone thought . . ."

"Language, soldier, language. Read from it if you can't resist the temptation to render everything civilian." Three hands Boy a printout, with a section highlighted, then props himself up on the table as Boy begins to read through the pages of the fine print.

"'In circumstances where the senior officer in charge, or in his absence, such officer as may have been temporarily delegated the role of the senior officer or any other officer taking on those responsibilities as part of duties as described in the Armed Services (Drought Emergency Amendment) Act, whether that Officer or soldier be a member of the Armed Forces, or the Territorial Services or Her Majesty's Emergency Drought Relief Community Conscripts . . .'"

"Oh, for God's sake!" I make to leave the kitchen and go back upstairs, but Three blocks my way.

"You're not leaving."

"Get off! I'll do what I want." I try to push past, banking on the belief that Three will not physically intervene, but I am wrong. He seizes my right arm, bends it round behind my back, and pushes me onto a chair and holds onto my flesh just a little too long. "Nice. I see what you mean, Boy."

"You can't do this!"

Boy does not meet my eyes. Three lets go of me as if I was infectious. "This is just the problem, isn't it, Ruth? That you have come to forget that you are a prisoner of Her Majesty's Government, that you were tried and convicted of serious crimes. That in a time of national crisis you sought to manipulate the water supply for your own benefit and that you are still under suspicion for the murder of your own grandson . . ."

"That is not true."

"That you are under house arrest and that you cannot, I repeat, cannot do what you like. That is the whole point of locking people up. That and letting the rest of us sleep easy in our beds. Soldier, continue reading the prisoner the amended terms and conditions of her house arrest."

There is no sign in Boy's voice that he is anything other than a conscript—it is a pilotless drone. When they have left, I stand in the shower and try to wash Three's fingerprints from my wrist, and then I return to bed. There is nowhere else to go.

What price a night on a bench, stargazing with a teenage guard? Six pieces of silver. An orchard, a field, a forest, a sky.

Twenty-four hours in bed and now I expect Three will send for the shrink again, that will be his next kick. Twenty-four hours makes it Sunday. I dress, but get back into bed to wait. At last I hear him. Hugh is back. He finds me mentally frail, I find him physically weak; combined we are human. With characteristic understatement, he describes his stroke as a minor blip, says his daughter is fussy and grumbles that nobody nowadays knows how to milk a cow. Now I am downstairs with him, me curled up like the old woman I am on the sofa, him in his armchair, I realize how deeply pleased I am to see him, how unconditional his visits are.

"The vegetable garden is looking good," he offers. It seems he has not been told.

"I found out it was Boy's work," I explain. "Apparently he wants to be a landscape gardener when he grows up, so he's landed on his feet. Come to the only place in the country where you can still choose that as an apprenticeship."

"I've seen some beautiful gardens in the desert," says Hugh, reaching for the mug, then, after something of a pause, "What made you change your mind?"

"About the gardening?"

"About the gardening."

"I hadn't changed my mind. I didn't garden. Now, even if I wanted to, I can't. I've left it too late. They've changed the perimeters and I'm not allowed out of the house."

He nods. "I thought they might," he says, in a voice lacking in indignation. I suppose his parishioners have told him much worse in the past; he must have seen much worse in his time in Africa— mine is a tedious, inconsequential suffering in the greater scheme of things. Hugh's chest is rising and falling slowly, each breath a deliberate commitment, the pauses between some words are long and I wonder if his speech has suffered a little as a result of his stroke.

"I haven't asked about you," I say, and reach over, putting my hand on his arm. "I am sorry. I am something of a Robinson Crusoe here. I have forgotten how to think about other people. How are you?"

"You're telling me you haven't found a Man Friday yet?"

"No, I've found nothing. No footprints in the sand, no empty canoes. This is pretty much what the guidebook says, a real-life desert island."

Hugh smiles and answers my original question. "I am fine, very few after-effects really. My left arm isn't quite what it was, and my speech—have you noticed? I find it a little trying at times, but I don't need to preach any longer, at least not to anyone except you."

I am desperate to ask him about the Internet, but the electronic eye is blinking in the corner and I am weighing up the serious risk of them banning Hugh's visits against my addiction to information.

I opt for ambivalence. "How's the research going?"

"My search produced no matches, as they say. Lots of references, discussion, that sort of thing, but not exactly what I'm looking for."

The disappointment I would have expected to feel at his evasiveness, at the fact that he has turned up empty-handed, is not here because I am so relieved he is back with me and that he is well. Looking at this fat, old priest and knowing the comfort he brings me, I understand that this is what ministry looks like: no virtual prayers, but rather the offer of one man to take on the suffering of another; no thousands worshipping online, but a few, waiting in line for a quiet communion, their feet shuffling on flagstones worn by a thousand years of faith; no icons to download, but a cross. No visions, for all I know, probably no voices either, no obvious replies or advice from on high, a room full of quite ordinary sorrow, shared.

———

Not so the Sisters. I had been on the Rose site often enough with them when I was at the campers, following their links to texts and readings, watching Sister Amelia write the "Thought for the Day," listening to Eve record the Sisters singing and then enhance the meditative chants until it sounded like a choir and then put it as a link to worship together. At home, I avoided using it. Mark had been on the site once and lost his temper when he saw photos of The Well uploaded with pictures of his hayfields and captions about the Blessed Land.

"What gives them the right to act as if they own this place?"

Me responding that nobody owns this place, Mark, we are just guardians. Him tearing a framed photo of us standing in front of the cottage off the wall and smashing it on the tiles on the kitchen floor and shouting, there, we never bought it, we don't own it, I don't spend fourteen hours a day farming it, it's nothing to do with us, it belongs to your sodding nuns. Me, later, rescuing the picture and hammering the nail back into the crumbling plaster.

The day after the service at the Wellspring, Sister Amelia invited me into the hub, said she had something she wanted to show me. The hub was the camper which acted as the engine room of the spiritual spaceship, wires trailing to the solar charger, printouts of spreadsheets weighted down with the Song of Solomon and with Eve as the chief engineer in communication with earth in front of the laptop. Next to her, sitting on the stool, her hair piled up in a bun, her legs crossed, the first three buttons on her white blouse left undone, Sister Amelia could almost have been in any office, anywhere, tapping out the hours in a heat wave until a five o'clock drink in a little local wine bar with a terrace in the center of some airless city. She asked Eve to move over so that I could see, put in her password, and brought up SistersoftheRoseofJericho.com. The image of me, held by the water of The Well and showered by the fragments of a rainbow, dominated the page. I felt my cheeks, my jawbone, my neck and then grasped my hands together. Yes. That was me.

"Over three thousand hits this morning alone. Watch the counter."

In the corner of the screen the figure which recorded the number of hits was clicking relentlessly upwards even as we watched. It had a life of its own. Impossible to think it had any connection to me, impossible to think that each of those numbers represented a person in another place watching me on a film on a computer.

"The word has spread, Ruth. She is moving through the world on the unseen byways of the Internet, the spirit is breathing through us. They are waiting to hear from you, Ruth. You must talk to them."

"Me? How?"

I think now that if I had been driven to stadiums, called up to address crowds of thousands crying and chanting in their desperation for an answer, interviewed by the press, and featured on breakfast TV, then it might have become clearer to me what I was getting into. But, and it is no excuse, it was all so distant. These thousands were not gathered before me as real people, placing their hope in me—they were site subscribers, paid-up online members sitting on their own in their soporific offices and sterile bedrooms, checking their BlackBerrys while traveling to hospital appointments on late buses, scratching at their gravel gardens with redundant trowels. We could copy and paste them, delete them, store their details, accept or reject their bids for salvation with a click of the mouse. I may have been the chosen one, but I was a novice in this free-market, religious economy.

Eve wasn't. She put her PR experience to good use. "I'm suggesting we live-stream at dusk. People will have left work and it's more atmospheric." She examined a chipped nail and corrected herself. "What I mean is that sometimes it's easier to focus on what matters."

Emboldened, I showed them the writing which had poured from me the night before.

"Super. We'll upload it immediately," said Eve. Sister Amelia said she should read it first, to see if anything needed . . . Needed what? Amending? Correcting? No. What strength, what conviction I had.

This was the word of the Rose. It had been dictated to me and could not be improved. I put the poetry on the table and left them in the tense silence to read it.

The second blog was no less visionary:

Next I am shown the earth under a footprint of gold.
Come closer.
This is not something you can see from standing.
Lie like a child on your flat stomach.
Rest your chin on your hands and attend the soil.
Write the name of Rose in the earth with your finger.
If the land is bare, it is because you have not attended.

Attend to what is written in the dirt.
Attend to your fires, to the burning effigy,
a guy with no revolution in his mind.

The thumb of the believer strikes the flint.
The breath of the believer blows the flame.
And in the conflagration I see the hand that saves me,
seed, pale and pooled on the leaves of a dandelion,
and a Rose which unfurls and spreads its dryness to the sky
ready for the soft water to touch, for the flowering.

———

Hugh is a natural listener. Not for him classes in mirroring body language or nonjudgmental affirmative silence. He makes no comment but simply asks "May I?" and I get up and pass him the notebook, reflecting that there are words that still seem to belong here, the gentle words like leaves and seed. It is hard to think that those other violent insurgent words ever found their home at The Well, this quiet land, keeper of a history of sorts, home to woodpeckers and buttercups.

"So that was the famous First Incantation?" asks Hugh, turning the pages, one by one, slowly.

It was. It had a life of its own, that poem. It defined what was to become the Dusk Worships, the familiar prayer position of the faithful, the writing of the Rose in the soil, the practice of meditating on a handful of dust. But more dangerous than any of those, the hatred of men, the burning of male effigies and the fire-fueled protests against the men in the government that it provoked. I should undergo a second baptism and take the name of Herod.

Hugh flicks back through the notebook and seems to reread one page. "This hatred of men, Ruth, it's so intense. Was it men as a species? What about Mark?"

"Mark was more like a toddler than a man by then," I replied.

"What about young Lucien, then? He would have grown up."

"But he didn't, did he?"

Hugh does not respond but quotes instead from my notebook. "*'We are dry women, but when we kiss the Rose, our lips are touched with dew and we flower also.'* If men were so bad, Ruth, did you find compensation, shall we say, in the love of women? Even an old High Church Irishman like me can see how that could happen."

"You know the history of mysticism better than me, I suspect."

"You give me too much credit." Hugh waited patiently.

Having taken back the writings from him, I look around the room for a suitable place to put them and, not seeing anywhere, throw them in the basket by the stove where we have always put everything that needed burning. "I've told you before, there are more questions than answers here. Besides, I'm not sure the line between spiritual and physical ecstasy has been agreed by the Royal College of Psychiatrists—or by the pope, for that matter." Hugh doesn't reply but nods instead, shifting a little uncomfortably in his chair. I take him a cushion. "It wasn't just another country, Hugh, it was another planet. These were just words, hieroglyphics on A4 lined paper."

We sit for a few minutes, the thick stone walls of the cottage now a barrier, forbidding entry to the rustle of the breeze or the hum of thunder flies. "I did write them. There must have been a part of me that created them. What happened to them all, do you think?"

Hugh looks over to me. "Who? The words?"

"The faithful. The ones who bought the T-shirts and downloaded the hymns."

"The same as has happened to you. Conviction, dereliction, maybe the restoration of hope. Because, despite this whole clampdown, Ruth, I detect a little more hope in you nowadays, compared to my first visit, at least."

"That's because you're back," I said.

"T-shirts? Did they really buy T-shirts?" Hugh asks suddenly.

"Oh, yes, and more. Mugs, biros, calendars with pictures of The Well for every month of the year—even pants, for all I know. Some of it was shipped out from the site; other items, like the T-shirts, Eve said were contracted out, so somewhere I presume there's a warehouse full of fakery. You could take a look on eBay, Hugh! See if you can't bring me a fridge magnet with my face on it next time you come. It could act as a reminder for me in case I should ever think of believing in anything again."

"What happened to the money, do you think?" asked Hugh.

"That I don't know. People subscribed and donated. Eve talked about all that with Amelia. I think she liked to think there were things not shared with me. Amelia did try to persuade me to buy out Mark's share, for the Sisters to form a charity and buy the whole thing. But that was later. There must have been a lot of money for her to be talking like that, but I never really got involved."

"So many unknowns." He is turning the pages of his Bible carefully, scanning the verses, until it seems he reaches what he has been searching for. "Time is running out for us, wingèd chariots and so forth. Do you mind if I read from this?"

"Carry on."

"Ecclesiastes. Nothing about a handful of dust. Something much more useful to remember in life. I think of it almost every time I walk over the hill there.

"'To everything there is a season, and a time to every purpose under the heaven: a time to be born, and a time to die; a time to plant, and a time to pluck up that which is planted; a time to kill, and a time to heal; a time to break down, and a time to build up; a time to weep, and a time to laugh; a time to mourn, and a time to dance . . .'"

"That's one bit of the Bible I do know," I say.

"You know it and you don't know it," he replies.

CHAPTER TWENTY

An unnaturally cold wind for June has blasted across the country and, according to Anon, has led to a flurry of speculation that something has shifted in the heavens and it is going to rain. Maybe it is not the heavens moving, but more probably the high pressure that has squatted over Europe for so long, fending off the Atlantic fronts that used to batter at the door of our western coasts. Our own rain-swollen westerlies must come in disguise, or how else would they break the embargo? Nobody seems to know. Certainly not the meteorologists who are studying each minute variation in the pressure charts like fortune tellers reading the lines on a punter's hand, or the scientists at the top of the drive, waving their wands in the sky like wizards. The banging doors and the relentless rattling of the window frames is making everyone restless, even Boy is pacing out by the barn. I stick my head out of the back door.

"You OK?" I call against the wind.

"Fine." He comes over to talk. "Bored, that's all. Seriously bored and devoid of a social life. I've finished my last book and can't face one more game of two-handed poker with Adrian."

I feel sorry for him, stuck here just the wrong side of his future. He takes up my offer to borrow something, comes in with the door slamming behind him and the dust blowing in with him, and I show him the shelves with the books covered in cobwebs and leave him to it.

"Found anything?" I call from the kitchen where I am avoiding the titles and the memories of who read them last and when and where.

Boy sticks his head around the door. "I've always wanted to read this," he says. He holds up a copy of *Long Walk to Freedom*, catches the expression on my face, and then grimaces. "God, sorry, I'm so tactless."

"Get out of here. Take it, read it. He was an amazing man. Come to think of it, I should probably read it again myself when you've finished."

But I won't. I am fascinated by my own inability to either manage my imprisonment or envisage a future. I'm no Mandela, with his reading and thinking and writing notes in the margins of his Shakespeare, and I can't imagine I'll be any more effective if and when I ever get released. If it starts raining again, it's possible I might be freed—although not innocent. I wonder what I would do then. The thinking moves me from my *Groundhog Day* grammar to the "what-if?" A future. Try as I might to be, to breathe, to live in the present, this present continuous, this "ing," is not enough. Eating. Waiting. Tapping. I am not enough. I will be, may be.

The unanswered, unaskable question, then, is whether I would stay here at all, if I were free to leave. I see myself flogging the country, tracking down Mark and Sister Amelia to sniff out the scent of guilt, only to find the trail led to my own fingers, with their nails bitten and black. And if I were ever to leave here, it begs the question of what was the point of not having left before. So, after all that self-discipline, I have returned to the what-might-have-been. It is a magnet and I have little resistance left in me.

The ill wind started this thinking, collaborating with the guards to keep me inside. Although it is summer, it feels like autumn and blows in with it memories of the day when Angie left and Lucien stayed behind with us, for safekeeping. That again was a strange storm, whipping rainless across the country like a November gale at the beginning of September, sending dry trees crashing over pavements, with mothers walking their children for their first day at school, into bedrooms where the unsuspecting unemployed were sleeping away their empty days, onto a couple sitting on a park bench with rings on their fingers and bells on their toes unaware of the crack in the branch above them.

It was against this wind that I struggled up to the track to see Lucien. The sheep that usually came out to follow me held close to the hedge and I followed their example, so it was not until I was quite near that I could tell the camp was preparing to leave. Most of the small sleeping tents were already packed up, reduced to inconsequential packages of nylon, the nights spent in them, the dreams dreamt there, the arms enfolded, all compressed into a convenient size. Four of the travelers were fighting to take down the big store tent, shouting instructions which got blown away and clinging on to the canvas which rampaged in the gale. Elsewhere, people were squeezing the last six months into small spaces: bicycles onto the backs of the camper vans, mattresses onto the roofs of cars, sleeping bags into recycled supermarket carriers, saucepans stacked one into another like Russian dolls, inflatable water carriers deflated. Set to music it would have been a grand chorus scene in an opera, with all the crowd and the minor parts working in unison and it seemed as though any minute they would turn to face the front and burst into song for their curtain call.

As far as I was concerned, Angie was center stage, taking down a makeshift washing line, standing on tiptoes to undo the knot which held the rope to the branch of the plum tree in the hedge, her midriff exposed, wearing nothing but a silly little top and a pair of jeans regardless of the weather. She always was a teenager, I thought, always will be. I scanned the scene for Lucien and heard him before I saw him. Even if he and the other children had been given some responsible role in this communal effort to move on, they had long given up on it. There they were, two at a time on his blue bike, at the top of the slope.

"Ready, steady, go!"

They were off, hurtling down the hill with screams, the loose tires skidding off the hillocks, the one on the back clutching on for dear life, the one in the front with his feet on the pedals, knuckles white and tight on bent handlebars. Oh, the winning, the winning, emboldened by the maddening wind. And, of course, as soon as they got to the bottom, they were marching back up to the top of the hill and then back down again.

And when they were up, they were up; and when they were down, they were down—Angie found me once singing that to Lucien when he was a baby. That's called the rhyme of the ancient addict, Angie said to me, it's what we sing when we're thieving.

"Look at me, Granny R. Watch me!" shouted Lucien from the top of the hill.

"Watch me, Granny R," called Henni.

Turning away at the point at which they decided to try three on a bike, I put the bag of potatoes I'd brought with me down next to where Angie and Lucien's tent had been, now just a rectangle of yellow grass, and went over to help her with the washing line, pulling on the branch so she could reach the wire.

"Are we the only people in England who have trouble getting the washing dry?" She laughed above the wind.

"Why are you taking it down?" I asked, unnecessarily.

"Leave only footprints; take only photographs," shouted Angie. It takes a certain mentality to move on, to enjoy the space left empty as much as the one occupied.

"You didn't say you were leaving." I hadn't had Angie back long, and even then the connection between us had been tenuous. I couldn't help thinking that it had held this long because she had her tent and I had mine and because The Well had given us a common cause. Love alone had not been enough for a very long time.

She protested that she wasn't going to just up sticks and let me come up here with my soup and find a set of tire tracks and a thank-you letter.

I have it still, that second thank-you letter, signed by all of them, signed by Lucien. It's not so much a card as a collage. They had taken a large piece of card and covered it with a geometric design made entirely out of things from The Well: half acorn shells and the petals of wild roses, plaited reeds from the Hedditch brook, and five crimson balsam poplar leaves spread out symmetrically like jewels. Some of the pieces have fallen off now. I put my finger in a gap where a beech nut once was and feel nothing but the dried glue which kept it all together once. If nothing else, it reminds me that I am imprisoned in a world not only of infinite loss but also of infinite beauty.

Angie's mind was made up. They had been offered work at a late festival, setting up and taking it down afterwards somewhere in Norfolk. Then they reckoned a friend of Charley's could get some seasonal work for quite a few of them at a Christmas factory in Scotland, cutting trees, making holly wreaths, that sort of thing.

"You don't need to leave here to find work," I protested, but she could hardly hear. "Let's get out of this dreadful wind."

We climbed into Charley's van and slammed the door, letting the slightly damp warmth calm things down. "I was saying you don't need to go to some hideous Christmas rip-off factory, for God's sake, making wreaths with plastic berries. We've got the real thing here. Every tree in the orchard is weighed down with mistletoe. Harvest it. I can pay you, if you need money. Mistletoe from The Well could spread great thoughtfulness." There was me, justifying turning my paradise into a commercial enterprise, for my own profit.

But the Norfolk job would be fun, the lineup was unbelievable and it paid well. The Scottish job had accommodation, two large mobile homes and a barn. She had to admit it was just too cold to spend the winter under canvas at The Well. I told her I'd thought about that and got the barn all ready for her and Lucien, and Charley if he wanted to stay, but she said, "We are a group, Mum, we need to stay together, because by staying together then we stay clean."

Can't your mother do that for you? That was what I wanted to ask, but the years had already answered that question. "We'll be back," she said, jangling the keys in the ignition.

I took a deep breath, preparing to bring out from deep inside me what I had been fantasizing about ever since they arrived. "Lucien could stay here," I offered.

I don't know if I even expected her to consider it, but suddenly she was saying something about Henni going to his dad's because he wanted him to go to school properly and learn something and not keep moving around and then there was education welfare, on to them about attendance, maybe Lucien would be lonely, maybe it was a good idea.

I turned sideways in the cramped seat to face her. "Would you mind?"

"I don't know, Mum. Things have been better between us, haven't they?"

"So much better."

She turned to look straight at me. "And what about between you and Mark? Lucien's had enough rows in his lifetime. I want him to know what it's like to be peaceful."

"We're OK, Angie. Yes, it's stressful at times, but we've come through worse than this . . ."

And she looked away again. I could so quickly lose her. I rephrased. "You know what I mean. We've managed twenty years of ups and downs. We're not going to let this defeat us."

Angie got out her tobacco and started rolling a cigarette. "But it's like Mark says, your head's sort of somewhere else at the moment, isn't it?"

I resisted the desire to comment on her smoking. "How do you mean?"

"Well, who would come first? Lucien—or the Sisters?" She flicked her lighter a couple of times and the flame flickered in the dull light of the van. "It's not that I'd blame you for that choice or anything. But there's some heavy stuff going on around here, you're important to all that. You might have to make choices."

"Do you think the Rose would make me choose between her and my grandson? Angie, love's not like that. I'm probably more able to love Lucien now than I ever have been."

Angie inhaled deeply, opened the window an inch to flick out the ash and the wind rushed in, blowing her hair over her face. "And Mark seems better now, don't you think?"

"The bruises have gone."

"I meant less angry, since the thing in Lenford."

I didn't think that, but I wasn't going to say so because I didn't want Angie to have any excuse not to leave Lucien with me.

"And then the Sisters," she continued. "Dorothy's great, isn't she, like a sort of great-granny? So I suppose there'd be loads of you keeping an eye on him."

She is going to agree, I thought. Please, God, let her say yes.

"What about Sister Amelia?" she continued.

"What about her?"

"Nothing." She wiped a space on the steamed-up window to look over to the boys and their crazy game. "I don't know. I just get the impression she'd rather he didn't exist. It would be different if he was a girl."

"You don't need to worry about her," I said. "She's a purist, but she'll cope."

"And in a weird way," said Angie, moving on, "I think The Well will look after him."

"It will," I agreed, smiling at her. "The Well will keep us safe."

She stubbed out her cigarette in the little silver ashtray. "Let's ask him what he thinks."

How clearly that scene plays out before me now. The wind snatches the van door from our hands as soon as we open it and I fight to close it again. Angie calls Lucien, shouting louder and louder to get herself heard. He looks up, runs over to us, runs fast as if he wants me to see how fast he can run, his thin legs pounding the ground, helter-skeltering down the hill, arrives out of breath and laughing and falls on the grass, spreadeagled. Angie says, "Oh, what shall we do, Granny R, it looks as though Lucien's dead!" And he jumps up and says just kidding. Then he sits cross-legged and listens. Not only are his legs thin, but his face is too. It makes his eyes look bigger. I tell him he looks all skin and bone for someone who's just turned five. He decides that he'd like to stay with me and Granddad, hugs Angie, says he'll miss her and will she be back for Christmas and if she does she ought to know that he's going to ask Santa for a pennywhistle. And then he's gone, back to the bike and Henni and I am so happy I too run madly down the hill to the Sisters to share the good news.

They come out of the campers, holding their hair out of their faces. Eve chases after a prayer sheet blowing across the grass.

"Good news!" I shouted. "Good news!"

They hugged me in turn, while Sister Amelia stood slightly apart and then returned to her camper without commenting. I followed her in, closed the book in her hands, and told her to talk to me, not to retreat into silence. She asked me how long Lucien would be staying and I told her as long as he needed to, maybe the winter, maybe forever, maybe one day his children would cartwheel down First Field on a blustery day in early autumn and all this would be his.

"This is a land for women, Ruth. The women shall inherit the earth."

Angie and the campers wanted to leave midafternoon. I ran home and went straight upstairs to the little bedroom; it was cold, but even so I opened the window to breathe new life into the space and the hessian curtains flapped, almost knocking over the lamp on the table under the window. Mark's pajamas were on the bed along with a couple of his books, so I swept all that away and dumped it back in our room. Then I stripped the bed and remade it with Lucien's favorite bee duvet, took the junk out of the drawers in the bottom of the wardrobe so he'd have somewhere for this things, and got to my knees and thanked the Rose for giving me Lucien.

Rose, Bless the hands which will hold him.
Rose, bless the voice which will call him.
Rose, bless the eyes which will watch over him
Rose, bless the ears which will hear his cry in the nighttime
and the lips which will kiss him to sleep again.

After lunch, Mark and I walked up the track together to fetch Lucien, just a little apart from each other but joined for once by a common pleasure. He seemed as thrilled as I was that Lucien was going to stay. Two of the vans had already left by the time we reached them, and it seemed a rather pathetic group that stood huddled for shelter, waiting for us. Lucien ran towards us and hugged Mark.

"I'm coming to live with you," he cried. "Mum says I can be your helper."

He was a boy who was used to swapping adults, and the whole-hearted way he attached himself to whoever was entrusted with him next was both endearing and disturbing.

"Give Mummy a hug," said Angie.

A sculptor could capture it, maybe, these two bodies hewn from the same rock, his arms around her neck, fiddling with her stone necklace, her arms around his waist so slight that they went all the way round and touched the other side; his hair against her hair, his feet just off the ground for a moment. Words move, but a sculpture could make that moment into stone, the first of the autumn leaves caught forever in midair, the red kite captured on the same circling current and the half-shrouded shafts of light from the sun falling always on the poplars, shot through with silver.

That is the point at which it should have rained. Not just at The Well, but down in the valley, rainwater running in the gutters in Middleton, the owner of the secondhand furniture shop rescuing his four matching painted chairs and a stripped pine bookcase; not just in the valley, but over the hills to Wales where the walkers would pull their waterproofs out of the day bags and stride just a little bit faster, bent just a little bit lower against the storm, back down to the harbor for chips in newspaper and mugs of tea; not just in Wales, but in London where the photos of tourists would show rain bouncing off the high-tide Thames, or in northern Spain where the steep gullies of the Picos would send torrents down to Ribadesella; and on into North Africa, where the girls would walk back to the villages, water carriers full on their heads, leaving damp footprints in the dust as they go.

However, there was not even enough water in the world for tears: we should have all been crying, but we were dry-eyed and ignorant. Angie waved goodbye with promises of letters and Mark said she should renege on her principles and get a mobile, but she said not to worry, she'd keep in touch. Lucien blew kisses on the wind, interspersed with reminders about pennywhistles and chocolate. I wanted so much to hug her, but somehow Charley was starting the engine and she was in the front seat and we managed a stupid sort of touching of fingers as she struggled to wind down the old-fashioned window. I remembered I had something for her and ran alongside the van, saying wait a moment, I've got something for you.

But the van bumped off over the rough ground, up onto the track, and she called out of the window, "I'll follow the Rose when I can, Mum."

Ahead, the policeman had seen them coming and had already unlocked the padlock on the main gate, so there was the briefest pause as they looked left and right onto the lane, a toot of the horn, a hand waving through the window, and they were gone. I kept my distance from the lane in those days. Sister Amelia told me it was probably better for me not to encounter the followers camped out on the roadside, waiting for a glimpse of the chosen one, and I agreed with her, though probably for different reasons. So I gave up the chase and retreated.

"What was it, Granny R, that you wanted to give Mummy?" Thank God for Lucien, I thought, and turned all my attention to him.

"It was just this, a little thing to wish her well on her travels, that's all." I showed Lucien the tiny rose I had whittled with a knife from a piece of yew and polished with oil and resin, threaded with a long strand of leather.

"It's beautiful."

"I made it myself," I said.

"I could have it for her."

"Of course you could." So I gave it to him, bending down to tie it around his neck, tucking it under his T-shirt. "That'll keep you safe," I promised. I stood up quickly as Mark came back from chatting to the policeman, put my finger to my lips and winked at Lucien, who tried, unsuccessfully, to wink back.

Mark pushed the bike with one hand, I swung the little bag over my shoulder, and we walked back down the track, swinging Lucien between us. Sister Dorothy waved from the water trough, and behind her stood Sister Amelia like a statue, hands clasped closed in front of her.

"I've got lots of friends here, haven't I, Granny?" asked Lucien.

The gale blew itself out without bringing any rain and I chose not to join the Sisters for vespers, but to meditate on my own in the orchard. Voice was silenced as my thoughts flowered from the deep content that Lucien was safe and asleep inside with me. I invoked the Spirit of the Rose and I heard the Rose reply that all would be well. I thanked the Rose for lending me Lucien. I did not know she would want him back so soon.

The guards are talking about me, but I don't know what they are saying—the words are distorted as though I am listening through water. It seems Anon found me crawling up the track on all fours, soaked from the driving rain, insisting that Angie and Lucien were leaving today and I had to say goodbye. Somehow, Anon and Boy got me upstairs and put me to bed. My head clears. Boy is telling Anon that there is no need to inform Three, or call the doctor.

"He'll see from the alarm record that she was out of area," Anon says.

"He won't. He's playing with the others up at the experiment plots. He thinks they're real soldiers."

Anon is looking out the window. "He notices everything."

Boy closes the shutters. "I'll record it as a breach but not a serious incident. Leave it to me. I'll stay here and make sure she doesn't get ill."

"You're sailing close to the wind, brother." But Anon leaves all the same. He doesn't want a hand on the tiller when the boat goes down.

Boy sits in a chair in the corner of the room, at a distance from me, conscious of the camera's red eye recording everything, but his being there anchors me and even if I can't lay my head on his shoulder, even if I can't ask him to hug me or hold me, I know that his physical presence is enough to prevent me from slipping under the surface.

"Thank you," I whisper.

Boy stays awake for me. My chaotic thoughts still, like a quietening pool, and I go back to those memories, to the first nights with Lucien.

———

Mark and I put him to bed. We tucked him up tight and sat together as we read him *The Sleepy Water Vole*, and then we went downstairs and the two of us had a drink together. Slightly drunk on more than alcohol, Mark came back to our bed and we made love. For the last time.

If you were to draw a graph, the night of Lucien's coming to stay would be an unpredicted spike in the otherwise relentless downward trajectory which mapped our marriage. The high would seem all the more unlikely because of the trough which followed, with only a few days in between spent with an even line at a normal point on the scale. Our routine changed—it had to—you don't have a small boy come to live with you and expect everything to remain the same. Mark said the early lunch and high tea were incompatible with work needing to be done on the farm with the days shortening. He put the "new timetable" down to my desire to spend more time with Sister Amelia, with Lucien, with anyone but him. I pointed out that Lucien was starving by noon and half asleep by seven. It didn't matter much who was right or wrong, the result was the same: we spent our days as if we lived in two different time zones, neither prepared to put the clocks back. The nights were no easier. Lucien was unsettled and had been with us a few days when he woke again, crying.

"I'm going to bring him in here," I said.

"If you do that once, he'll be in here every night."

Looking at Mark across the unruffled sheet between us, I pointed out the obvious. "It wouldn't be as though he was interrupting anything," I said.

Lucien snuggled into our bed, his warm body close to mine, his hand resting on my chest so lightly, so full of faith that I dared not move all night for fear of breaking the spell. I lay like that, pretending to be asleep, even as I felt the bed move and saw Mark's shadow leaving.

"Did you sleep in my bed, Mark?"

"I did."

Breakfast. Lucien and Mark at the kitchen table. I was putting ham in some rolls for Mark to take down to the Hedditch field where he was clearing brambles. "That was kind of Mark, wasn't it?" I commented.

"Will you sleep there again tonight?" Lucien turned the empty shell from his boiled egg upside down and started battering it with his spoon. The bread fell apart as I spread the butter, holding my breath for Mark's answer.

"No," I heard Mark reply. I breathed out slowly, warily.

"Where will you sleep, then?" Lucien persisted. "We could both cuddle up, we're good at hugging, aren't we? There's room for two of us in my bed."

"No!" But that shout was from me, not Mark, and I don't know where it came from.

He stood up, very slowly, very silently, just the scrape of plate on the table as he pushed it away, the scratch of the chair on the stone floor, and Lucien staring up at him, sensing something, not sure what.

"That troubles you, does it, Granny R? The idea of me and Lucien sharing a bed? Do you want to say why? Perhaps you ought to warn him?"

"Shut up, Mark." I leant over Lucien and cut up his toast. "Grand-pa's being a silly-billy," I said, the hand holding the knife shaking visibly.

"How about I move out to the barn, to a safe distance, how about that?"

Now with my back to him, standing at the kitchen counter, I returned to fiddling in the cupboard over my head and muttered something about whatever you think is best.

"Then you and Granny can be together, Lucien. That's what you want, isn't it, Granny? Just you and Lucien. And we mustn't forget Amelia, of course."

Here he comes, screamed Voice, *run*. But I didn't run and I didn't reply.

"Is Amelia coming to live with us too?" asked Lucien quietly.

Without turning round, I took a jar from the shelf and put it on the counter, tried to think about the chutney, about apple chutney, if only I could open that, that would be something, but Voice was relentless, shouting at me about fire and knives. "Has anyone seen the thing that opens jars?" I asked, controlling my words, praying wildly in my head for the Rose to still the storm.

"I didn't quite catch that." Mark was close to me, close enough to disturb the air around me.

Behind me, Lucien was kicking the table leg over and over again, the kettle spat its boiling displeasure, and the tap dripped the seconds away. I heard all that, but I didn't hear him come at me. Mark grabbed my shoulder, swung me round so I was looking at him, our faces inches apart, his possessed and stretched across the canvas of his skull. Instinctively, I raised my hand to protect myself, but he grabbed that wrist, then the other, forced my hands high in his makeshift handcuffs, reading me my rights in a whisper, close to my ear and hissing. Then, when he had finished, he threw me across the room, my head catching the edge of the cupboard door and bleeding, my rib cage cracking against the counter. When I pulled myself up, he was gone and Lucien was crying at the table.

"We can't put this back together again now, can we, Granny R?" he sobbed, picking at the splintered remains of the eggshell. "Was it me who upset Mark? Was it my fault?"

To think that I ever promised to look after him.

CHAPTER TWENTY-ONE

It wasn't until it happened that I realized Mark's moving out was a relief. The barn was my equivalent of an arm's length safety plan. A couple of days later, leaning towards the mirror in the bathroom to examine the bruise on the side of my face more closely, I acknowledged to myself that I didn't miss him. The makeup didn't conceal anything from Sister Amelia. She pushed the hair from my face, kissed the swelling, and whispered in my ear, "I told you so, Ruth, he has to go." Dorothy was the only one who questioned my reaction to his moving out. Talk to him, she urged, twenty years is a long time to love someone and see it gone in a moment. It must be part of the Rose's plan, I told her, and Dorothy replied that sometimes it was hard to know the difference between the Rose's plan, our own agenda, or someone else's agenda. But I wrote my own sermons in those days. Then, as far as the party was concerned, Lucien was the cause for celebration, Amelia my partner, the Sisters my fellow revelers, and Voice the sound track to which I danced. What else did I need?

There never is such a thing as total separation in a family and there wasn't then. Angie kept to her word and did phone, often enough, although by no means regularly despite what I said to her about children liking to know what's going to happen when.

"Mummy's on the phone!"

Listening in, I could hear Lucien telling her he missed her, asking her how long until Christmas, and I would hold my breath, but then he would say that he was very happy, that Granny and Mark were very well, that we were all very busy. Some of that was true, I hope, I pray. Lucien did seem content to be our go-between, trotting between the barn and the cottage with messages or food, or to spend time with Mark if I was in prayer. After the fight, Lucien really did seem to accept our arrangements without question, being used to a veritable thesaurus of ways of living and loving, and he relished the time he spent hanging out with Mark, helping him with the animals, digging and planting and pruning.

"You can be my dad," he said to Mark once.

"How do you mean?" asked Mark.

"I don't know my dad and Mummy said you couldn't have children, so you're not her real dad. But you can be my dad, can't you?"

Mark told me about that conversation, said it was typical of Angie to load Lucien up with things he didn't need to know at his age.

———

I sift through conversations with Mark as if they are a sort of audible photograph album, chucking the ones that are little more than repeats of ordinary views, holding some up to the light the better to make sense of the detail, the doubt.

———

Lucien and me, wrapped up together on the sofa, watching *Bambi*.

"Mark says I'm very, very special. What do you think he means?"

———

Soundscape. Tractor engine. Turned off. Wind. Sheep in the distance.

"Look at my plowing, Granny R!"

Mark was planting up First Field with winter wheat, Lucien sitting on his knee on the front of the tractor, his woolly hat pulled down over his sticking-out ears.

"Bounce me up and down again, Mark!"

Mark got down, taking the ignition key, leaving Lucien playing with the gear stick.

"He's so happy here now, isn't he?" I said.

"Hmm."

"What do you mean by that?"

"I think he misses his mum, that's all."

I take a step or two away from the tractor, calling out to Lucien to be careful. "What do you mean? Has he said something?"

"I don't think he'd want to upset you, Ruth. Yes, he loves it here. But it's not straightforward, is it? He is safer with Angie."

————

Dusk. Coming downstairs and jumping out of my skin, bumping into Mark unexpectedly standing in the half-light in the kitchen. He looked unshaven, smelt unwashed—for all I know he was sleeping in his clothes and drinking too much, like a tramp in a tunnel. I wanted to sit him down, pull his shirt up over his head, hands aloft like a five-year-old, and run him a bath. I wanted him to leave.

"I've come to kiss Lucien good night," he said.

And I let him.

————

And another time I remember, but it's all in the wrong order. Dark this time. Mark came over and we talked in the porch under the sensor light, as if he were a door-to-door salesman with a variety of life insurance policies on offer. It can't have been long after he moved out, because I remember him pushing the hood of my fleece down to look at the bruise on my head, and I flinched. He took my hand.

"I'm so sorry," he said. "It will never happen again, whatever goes on between us. I can't believe I did it."

Our hands lay loosely with each other, the slightest pressure would have meant something, but they fell apart, retreated to their owners' pockets, although I at least was willing them on, aching with the memory of holding hands in other places in other times: in the hospital when Angie was born, walking by the sea in Italy on holiday, the day we moved in here.

Mark spoke first, returning to his pitch. "What would you do here," he asked, "if I went, if Lucien was gone as well?"

"You might be going," I told him, "but Lucien isn't going anywhere."

"You can't have it all, Ruth. Lucien, Amelia, me . . ."

"Why not?"

"As far as I can see, the Sisters believe Lucien should be gone. I think he should be gone too, you think I should be gone. That pretty much leaves you on your own."

"Don't you dare threaten to send Lucien away," I said. "You're just jealous."

"You're right," he said, "I am."

Jealousy. That was one of the possible motives they ascribed to him, when he was in the frame.

With Mark in the barn, Amelia became a more frequent visitor to the cottage. She didn't come in, not at first. Initially, our long one-to-ones would take us meandering in a circle through the fields and back to the campers, then we started to come back via the house and stand and chat outside, with Amelia saying no, she wouldn't come in, it wasn't right, then we sat in the garden and then, one day when a keen northeast wind was ripping the leaves from the oak, she came inside.

"It's just how I imagined it," she said, standing in the way that a prospective purchaser does when looking around the house—as we did I suppose, when we first arrived. I took what she said as a compliment and thanked her, but she corrected me. "No. I mean, it is beautiful, just like you're beautiful, but there's not enough of you in here." She peered into the study.

"That's Mark's study," I explained. She looked at me pointedly, and I added that he hadn't moved his stuff from there into the barn, yet. She stumbled over Lucien's Lego castle, and I found myself explaining that his bedroom was very small.

She examined each of the photos on the wall. "Not many of you," she commented, and I said that I was usually the one taking the pictures. She got out her phone and before I had time to even protest, she said she'd soon put that right, clicked the camera, and then leant in to take a selfie of the two of us, laughing like teenagers in a photo booth.

She picked up the glass heron. "A present from Mark?" she assumed.

I took a pile of Mark's books and fishing magazines from the study over to the barn when he was out and left them by the woodpile, under the shelter, not wanting to go in. And I printed out the photo Amelia messaged me and Blu-Tacked it to the mirror in my bedroom, so whenever I looked at myself, I saw myself twice: once in an ordinary way and once as a curiously young-looking, startled woman with electrified blue eyes and a small mouth, half open, as if about to ask a question. A woman seen through the eyes of somebody else. She never sent me the other picture of the two of us; she kept it for herself. The heron stayed where it was, fixing me with its beak.

Amelia hung a spare coat in the back passage and kept some of her tea which she made herself from nettles and elderberries in a screw-top jar in the cupboard, and before too long she had a place where she usually sat. And there, at the table, we spent hours so deeply immersed in our conversation it was if we were together at the bottom of a dark lake, wrapped in water and cut off from the intrusive sky and irrelevant sounds of the outside world.

"Lucien, will Granny let you play outside? It's a lovely day."

"Why don't you send Lucien over to Mark? He might like the company."

We talked a lot about Mark. That is what women do, isn't it?

When relationships go wrong, they talk to each other: analyze, predict, hypothesize. We used to do it in the pub in London, supporting each other in the way that women do through affairs and divorce, through falling in love and walking away—so that's what we did, Amelia and I. She had the role of what I suppose a counselor might call "the critical friend," or that's how it seemed. She challenged me on my response to his violence.

"He has only ever hit me that one time, Amelia, that doesn't make a personality, it doesn't make a pattern."

"I disagree." Amelia never ate or drank anything at the table. She sat straight but earthed like a yoga practitioner, her hands still and joined on her lap, her eyes always focused even when mine slid away. "He's done it once, he'll do it again. And there's the incident in Lenford. He hasn't got his own way, and men, like toddlers, resort to tantrums and beating their women with their fists when that happens."

Amelia's antagonism towards Mark reached a peak one afternoon when Lucien and I had taken a rug down to the bottom field to read together. Our quiet time was broken by a commotion of some sort in the distance, barking and screeching like fighting foxes. Lucien clutched the book tight. I told him to carry the rug and wait when he got to the gate, then I struggled to run all the way, my heart thudding, rapidly trying to make sense of the scene I could half hear and now half see up at the house.

Mark and Amelia were standing by the front door, a door we never used. Both there, both together, although I had no idea why. Amelia could have been a Spanish *imagen*, the sort they carry through the streets on Semana Santa, motionless and foreboding, carved in white against the wood; Mark was all mud-brown and movement, heavy boots for kicking, pacing, arms flung up and out, and fists raised.

Fragments of sentences, but only from him. Amelia's responses, if there were any, were lost to the air.

Not yours . . .

What, want, what . . .

I can't see through . . .

Leaving the gate open, I pushed myself to go faster across the last field, knowing I had to get there in time. I called out once—stop it!—but had no power to push the words out. Close enough to see them and their expressions, hear the rest of the sentences, all I wanted was for them both to leave, for them to separate.

"Go away!" I screamed. "Just go!"

Amelia responded first. "You see, Mark, she just wants you gone."

Near enough now to smell his rage, I could see Mark's body was wired, the muscles on the back of his shoulders pumping as if they had a life of their own, and his beautiful face snarling, burning. "I'm not going anywhere, Amelia. This is my fucking house. I know what you're up to but you're not getting it."

"It, Mark? Or her?"

"I can call the police, get you evicted, you and all your she-devils . . ." Mark was reaching for his phone.

"Don't, Mark." I spoke deliberately, slowing my pace, my hand out for the phone.

He stepped away from me, shaking his head, a cornered animal, those with the nets closing in around him, turning between Amelia at the front door and me, this way and that.

"You see, Ruth has invited me in." Amelia smiled, her hands held open in the sign of the peace.

Mark lunged at her, grabbed her loose cotton top which ripped in his hands. I pulled at him—stop it, stop it, you'll regret it, anything I could think of saying, anything—but it was as if he couldn't let go of her, his fists clenched around the cloth. I pried them off, one by one, little finger first to ease the release of the rest, and then he fell back and Amelia was left standing, upright and unshaken, her pale breast just visible through the rip in her clothing. Lucien was trembling at the gate, his face half hidden in the tartan rug.

Mark kept himself to the barn and to the farm after that. Amelia came often and we settled into a pattern of living—work, worship, friendship. The only role I had which she resented was the one she could not control: I had not only become a mother again but also a teacher and I loved every single, separate, precious moment of both of my jobs.

I had promised Angie I would try to get Lucien into school, but I didn't even bother to try. He was a long way behind, not just because his attendance had been so poor. As a teacher, I knew that if he went to school they would find labels for him—ADHD, dyslexic—and they would put him on lists and on stages on those lists and fill in the boxes with comments about alcohol and drug use during pregnancy and developmental delay. Lucien needed only one label: grandson. The Well was for him an idyllic school and the Wellspring the best classroom of all. He was fascinated: we built an ant farm; we captured the rain which fell in the nighttime and studied evaporation in the daytime; we wrote poetry describing the sunsets; we did the maths for the number of eggs we should have collected by Christmas. One morning we were down at the well pond studying mushrooms, poring over my field guide to identify the prince and field mushrooms, honey fungus and penny buns, when Amelia appeared.

"What's happening here?" Her horror was audible. "This is a sacred place."

"Granny R is teaching me all about mushrooms," said Lucien. "Some of them are really, really evil!" he added with the glint in his eye of a boy who had recently discovered the cartoon world of superheroes and villains.

"I've been telling him about the death cap," I explained. "They were growing under this oak tree last year. They're the really tricky ones, because you eat them, get really ill for twenty-four hours or so, but then you feel better without realizing they're destroying your liver."

Lucien broke in with ghoulish delight. "And this," he said, running over to some bushes, "this is really, really poisonous. It's called deadly nightshade and if you even touch the berries, you die! Like this!" Lucien put his hands around his neck and fell to the ground with a suitably impressive death rattle. He jumped up, laughing, but then turned more seriously to Amelia. "I thought you said this was a holy place. Why's it got so many bad things in it?"

"Who is to say what is good or bad, Lucien? Every living thing has its purpose, according to the Rose," said Amelia. "It's just that we don't always understand it."

"You mean like the magic?" Lucien was full of questions about The Well and its magic, as he called it.

"I wouldn't call it magic myself, Lucien, nor would your grand-mother. We would say it is the work of the Rose. Praise her!"

"How do you know?"

"Sometimes I have been here and seen her."

"With your own eyes?"

"With my spiritual eyes."

"Do I have spiritual eyes?"

"A boy's eyes are different from a girl's eyes. One day, one night, I will bring you here and we will wait and we'll see if you can feel the magic for yourself."

"Please! Tonight? How about tonight?"

"Oh, no. It will be one night when you're least expecting it. I'll call up to your window and we'll creep downstairs and come to The Well by the light of the moon and—well, let's see what happens then."

"With Granny R?"

"If she wants to. But it could be our adventure—just the two of us."

Lucien took my hand.

"Why not?" I said. "Wouldn't that be something?"

It is surely impossible, unthinkable.

CHAPTER TWENTY-TWO

That is the question I put to Hugh.

"Impossible? Who is to tell what is impossible. This is impossible, Ruth. Look out your window at the impossible taking place before our very eyes. Unthinkable, now that's a different thing altogether."

We are sitting at the kitchen table and through the open window we can smell a soft rain falling and hear its fingertip percussion on the roof of the Land Rover.

"I don't think about the rain much anymore," I tell him.

"I do," he replies. He takes my hands across the table with unexpected strength. "I pray a lot about this rain, about what it means, about the Lord bringing me to you and what I am meant to be offering."

"Answers?" I suggest.

"And there are plenty of those in the good book." He releases my hands and takes his Bible from the ubiquitous plastic bag, passes it to me, and I can see its wafer-thin pages are bulked out by a folded piece of writing paper. Hugh catches my eye, glances towards the camera, and with difficulty inches his way around the table so he is standing between me and the lens. "Read on," he says loudly.

The letter is addressed to Hugh, from a Catholic priest in a town about twenty miles from here. It thanks him for his inquiry and confirms that yes, Dorothy Donnelly, one of the Sisters of the Rose of Jericho, did indeed approach him for confession shortly after the terrible events at The Well. My hands are shaking so badly that I have to follow the words on the page with my finger.

> *I have no need to remind you that I cannot divulge what passed between me and the confessor and that whatever was said lies between us and God. I do not believe, however, that I break that sacred trust if I were to say that, distressed as she was, this good woman had committed no heinous crime herself, but feared rather that she had not witnessed as the Lord would wish. The sister came to me just the once, but she left me an address in Canada, intimating that she intended to shortly return there to rejoin her family in her home country. What I am prepared to do is to write to her there to gain her permission to forward her address to yourself, explaining the circumstances and your reasons for asking and knowing that you ask in faith. Should I receive a reply, I will contact you again.*
>
> *We live in strange times and I pray for you and your work with Ruth that she may know the love the one true God extends to all who truly repent.*

The signature is illegible. Hugh folds the letter, slips it into his pocket, and limps slowly to the window, holding onto the counter to steady himself. I want it for myself, to reread it, to keep it in a tight fist and arm myself with the hope it offers: that Dorothy is innocent is no news, that she knows something about that night may be something or nothing, but my rapid heartbeat tells me that this is the beginning of the end of my search, and that from the confines of my prison, I am reaching out and closing in.

"Here." I hold out the Bible.

"That's for you. You can keep that," he says. He knows full well that I would swap this bestseller for the note in his pocket, but he does not rise to the bait. "You're always saying you want answers, Ruth. Well, you could do a lot worse than start with the good book." I assume he is playing to the gallery, but he continues in a serious tone. "I have marked the occasional passage to get you going—no, not now, later, when I am gone."

Too late. I have already started to flick through the pages to where a red thread bookmark lies. Isaiah: Chapter One. "Come now, and let us reason together, saith the Lord: though your sins be as scarlet, they shall be as white as snow; though they be red like crimson, they shall be as wool." I look up at Hugh. His hand may tremble, his leg may be unsteady, but he meets my gaze without flinching.

"Repent." I struggle to recall the last line of the priest's letter to Hugh, something about those who truly repent. "Repent," I repeat. "You are like him. You think it was me?"

"We all have need of forgiveness, Ruth, all of us."

"So you come here week after week for my confession? That's it. A government-appointed priest—I might have guessed. And perhaps you'll get a convert thrown in for good measure." I slam the Bible onto the table, get up, and throw open the back door, holding it wide for his exit, watch as slowly, painfully, he gathers up his bag, his hat, his coat and silently moves towards me. At first, I think it is because his breathing is labored, but then I realize he is weeping, an old man weeping and the room itself seems to heave with sadness and even the rain outside is crying quietly. I close the door against the lamenting world.

"I am so sorry, Hugh," I begin. "I didn't . . ."

"And so am I," he replies. "I am also sorry. I've got this all wrong."

"What do you mean?"

"What am I doing, on a wild-goose chase for hints and red herrings . . ." He stops, blows his nose, and laughs. "That's a dreadful mixed metaphor if ever there was one. Seriously, though, there is a terrible irony in a priest Googling for the truth, don't you think?" I look away as he continues. "All I've been doing is avoiding the truth, not wanting to go there, as the young say, for fear of you telling me to stay away. I've been a little bit bewitched by you myself, Ruth."

"Next time . . . ?" I begin.

"Next time, no more sins of omission for me. We'll start all over again." He puts his handkerchief away, takes my hand, and says, "The peace of the Lord be always with you." And also with you—that is the required, familiar response, but those words have no place on my tongue and remain unspoken. The priest, who is a wise man, believes I have sinned. Enough. I have no right to offer anyone peace. Does he know what I have done, or is he just guessing? I think he knows, but I don't know how, just as deep down I know what I have done, but I don't know how.

When Hugh has gone, all that is left of him is the black book. Present blessings unspoken; truths offered unread.

I was a truth broker once, dealing in shares on the manic futures market which swept the country parched of certainties; I put in long hours at the office, using my ex as a child minder—not so different from women the world over then. Our worship was still streamed live at dusk, lit by flares and candles, and I thought of them all at their screens, the office staff, working late, ready to minimize the page when the boss came round, the mothers slipping up to their bedrooms while their partners watched the news, old ladies in their armchairs, teenagers with their friends, all over the country. Because that's what the figures told us. I spent time with Amelia and Eve in the hub, the gas heater on, the air thick and fuggy in the camper, typing up the blog with my words from the morning, adjusting the website, checking the accounts. Eve was someone who somehow managed the impossible, living immersed in the Rose at The Well and operating as a member of the real world, even if at arm's length. Her work in the States had given her an unshakable conviction that there was nothing incompatible between faith and profit and that every venture needed to invest to secure its future and its lateral diversification. Dorothy said the Rose had a purpose for everyone, and everyone had a language to describe that purpose: hers was painting, mine was words, Jack's was the language of tongues, Eve's was the language of finance. And Amelia's? Charisma, said Dorothy. Amelia speaks through her charisma.

My role as wordsmith for the enterprise was onerous and draining. With Lucien safely asleep next door, I would spend most of the night awake in my room, relying on the stove downstairs and the thickest fleece to keep warm, wearing fingerless gloves as I worked on my laptop, responding to the prayers of the thousands who now worshipped the Rose. Sister Amelia would quite often have selected those which needed a response from me, others she would answer herself on my behalf. The cries of loneliness and sadness flashed up on the screen like a roll call at the gates of purgatory, from all over the UK, increasingly from all over the world.

Pray for us, Mother Ruth, because my partner has lost his job.

My son has done a bad thing. May the Rose forgive him.

The Rose is bringing rain. I felt it on my hands this morning. Bless the Rose.

I am a widow. All I have left now is the Rose. Pray for me in my loneliness.

The hours passed in a mesmerizing blur. Sometimes I would wake in the morning, on the floor not in my bed, and have no recollection of the night passed, the only evidence being the trail of messages on the Internet history. As one prayer was answered, another appeared, the virtual candles lit and flickering on the screen, begging attention.

Click on The Rose as you pray for rain.

In the past hour alone—1,115 prayers for rain. Yet still it did not rain in the rest of the country. When it rained at The Well during stream worship, the worshippers flooded the site: sitting in their dry kitchens, overlooking their sterile riverbeds and festering canals where the shopping trolleys stuck up from the mud like the skeletons of parched amphibians; gathered in their prayer circles in churches where the graveyards sprouted plastic flowers and the headstones leaned to one side, the ground subsiding beneath them; clicking again in the middle of the night, listening to the wind banging on the front doors which had been locked to keep out burglars, rattling the empty rabbit hutch at the end of the garden. In their thousands, they selected the link which allowed them to listen to the rain hammering on the tin roof of the barn, the rain gurgling from the gutters down the drains, the rain marking time, drop by drop into the bucket left out for the scraps, as the shower eased. If we could have let them smell the rain, if we could have sent its wetness down the wires, we would have done.

Create a shortcut to the Rose,

we urged.

Just click on the icon.

As we received more government notices, Sister Amelia scanned them in and posted them on the campaign link on our website. The Sisters and I tweeted our followers about every new official communication. We urged them to write to the MPs, and they wrote. We urged them to march, and they marched. We organized a day of peaceful prayer for the protection of The Well, and they gathered outside town halls and offices, on Whitehall and at war memorials, with live footage of worship at The Well on large screens, to pray for The Well, for rain, for the Sisters. In the barn, Mark phoned the solicitor whom we could no longer afford and who no longer believed we could win.

Increasingly, Lucien joined me in everything I did and filled my day. Voice was very quiet at that time and easily challenged, and it was Lucien I listened to. I wrote about him in my blog, contemplating the innocence he represented in my online meditation for the day. I tweeted what he wrote underneath his picture of a rainbow for one of our lessons: "The Well is like a miracle because things happen here that only God can do." When Angie called, she said someone who was a follower of the Rose up in Scotland had told her about the tweet. In answer to my worry, she said she didn't mind at all, she thought it was rather special, but what about Sister Amelia?

"What about her?"

"I just remember her saying how it was better if Lucien was kept away from things."

"I didn't know the two of you had talked."

"Yes, she used to come up to the camp every now and again."

I didn't know that and couldn't quite understand why it mattered to me that I didn't know, but Angie was right about one thing: Sister Amelia did not agree with the tweet.

"Eve's been showing me some of the comments on the forum," she said. "Our worshippers worry about Lucien. Look, she's printed out some of their prayers and comments for us to discuss."

How will the chosen one resolve her dilemma: her heart is with her grandson, her knowledge of the way precludes his inheritance. Pray for her.

I see how the chosen one worships the boy. Boys become men. Beware!

I do not think the boy should be allowed at worship. I am sorry if this is a wrong thought.

For the first time in the history of religion, women have a chance to lead. The existence of a possible inheritor of the blessed land in the form of a male is a pollution at the very heart of The Well.

I closed the lid of the laptop. "There are some sick and misguided people out there, Amelia. You know that."

"If they worship the Rose, they are on the road to true knowl-edge—anything else is a blind alley."

She asked me, at the very least, to leave him behind when I wor-shipped, not to mention him in my public prayers or blog because it wasn't helping our cause, but more important, I needed to be plan-ning for his leaving The Well if I was to be true to the Rose.

"And not be true to myself?" I asked.

"It is autumn, Ruth," she said. "Let the leaves that don't belong on the tree fly in the wind and be gone. Be true to the Rose. To the Sisters," she said, then took me in her arms, her breath like a cloth on my bare neck. "Be true to me, that is enough."

November was indeed a bitter month across the country. Most trees had been skeletal for months and the ground hard, but still it rained at The Well and leaves blustered in the gales in our autumn. I was both attached to and detached from the way things were beyond our sanctuary: connected through the incoming stream of helpless-ness that flooded the Rose site, but disconnected from what that was like, day in, day out, for nearly all of the people, nearly all of the time. Mark, I think, was going out more at night, I guessed to illegal drinking dens where homemade booze was cheap, but maybe there were other attractions out there. Or if he was not out, he was alone in the barn, perhaps listening to music, perhaps flicking through the twenty-four-hour news on the Internet, or other sites, who knows. What I do know is that he continued to work obsessively during the short daylight hours.

One such day he was chopping logs. I was loading some in the wheelbarrow for my fire and he was throwing some towards the barn for his.

"Can you imagine what it would be like if we had to pay for heating?" he said, clapping his hands together against the cold. "It was minus six last night in London."

"We couldn't do it," I said, pausing from loading for a moment, thinking how easily we could talk like this, in the no-man's-land between the house and the barn, in the middle territory of wood and winter wheat and how to store parsnips. "We don't know how lucky we are."

He raised his eyebrows.

"Oh, you know what I mean," I said.

"It doesn't just happen, Ruth. We might live apart, but I can't do all the farming on my own. If we're going to live here and stay warm and feed ourselves and Lucien, you've got to do your part."

The logs rumbled out of the wheelbarrow onto the porch and I thought—they can stay there, in a heap, I can stack them later. I made some coffee and took a mug out to Mark as well. He took off his gloves, propped himself up on the saw bench, and hugged the cup, steam rising and merging into the low winter cloud which had hung over us for days.

I sat on an upturned round of ash. "I'm sorry I've been so wrapped up in things. Lucien and the Rose. There's a lot to do."

"I know. That's what I'm trying to say."

The words between us were tightening again and I tried to ease the pressure. "OK. Perhaps if you told me something specific which I could do, then I could make sure I did it. Otherwise I feel I'm always treading on your toes or doing it all wrong."

"I've started the plowing," Mark said, "so that's fine, and I've repaired the fence so we can run a new batch of piglets in the woods. Some of the root crops need pulling and storing. Have I told you—I thought we, I thought I might dig a willow trench, since we could grow that here, no one else can. It would be quite lucrative if it worked . . ."

"And the ewes?" I asked, encouraged by his things-to-do list.

"What about them?" He chucked the rest of the coffee onto the ground and picked up the axe.

"The mating?" I struggled for the right word. "The, what do you call it, the tupping?"

He brought the axe down hard and the log split, splintering into two pieces. "No, I haven't done that."

"You haven't done that? What, you mean there won't be any lambs next spring? Why not?"

He stressed the personal pronoun bitterly in his reply. "*I* haven't done it because *I* couldn't see the point of looking that far ahead."

No lambs, then. I would have to tell Lucien there were going to be no lambs. What sort of a spring is that? It was so unlike Mark to have given up on part of the farm. It was as if he was a model, coming apart in my hands. I had to put him back together, the man I thought he was, so I bit my lip and swallowed my instinctive reply and asked again what I could do to help.

"I'll dig the vegetable garden over," he said, "but it would be great if you could clean out the greenhouse. If we don't do that, we'll get diseases in the seedlings next year."

It might not be lambs, but it was something. "OK. I promise I'll do that in the next couple of days. Promise."

"Thank you," he said, resting his axe on the wood, loading the next barrow load for me.

How do I account for hours spent at The Well? Here, of all places, the seasons continued to matter. Dusk and dawn were our touchstones. But days themselves merged without names until they became weeks, and nights, whole nights could not be accounted for in the ledger book of how I spent my time other than in dreams and delirium. So it was probably about four or five days later that I thought I heard a sound like breaking glass, but the weather outside was extreme, lurid sunlight competing against clouds purple in the face and threatening and the wind had been battering for hours, so it was hard to distinguish what was going on. At the same time, Lucien ran down the stairs crying. Mark was smashing things in the garden, and he could see him from his bedroom window.

"Stay inside, Lucien!"

Hail stung my face and hammered on the roof of the derelict car, but that was just the snare drum to the base thump of the mallet swinging again and again and the discordant chords of the shattering glass. Mark, in only a T-shirt and jeans, was destroying the greenhouse, blow after blow, his feet crunching on the broken panes, shards sticking out from the splintered skeleton of the frame and ripping his clothes, piercing his skin, blood trickling down his brown arms, dripping onto the false snow of the lying hail. Cowering behind the hedge, I could only watch until he was spent and all that was left was a low concrete wall and a shell of a structure of squares and rectangles of metal, sticking crazily into the air like a bombed-out building. The storm moved on, the wind dropped, and the hail eased; the garish light illuminated the man, looking at the blood on his hands.

"I kept my word," he sobbed. "Look!" He swung round, pointing at the recently dug raised beds. "You said you'd clean out the green-house and I believed you. You promised."

There was nothing I could say.

"I used to say you'd have to choose one day between me and

Angie. But I was wrong. You had to choose between me and her—Amelia. And now I know, you've chosen."

He stumbled past me; he had tried to wipe the tears but in doing so had smeared his face with blood.

"Stop, Mark! Where are you going?"

"I don't know where I'm going, but I'm going, Ruth. I'm leaving."

Later, when I went to the barn to stare at the mess inside it, the emptiness of it, the dark stains on the handles and on the washbasin, the absence of a coat on the peg, I realized—he had left The Well.

CHAPTER TWENTY-THREE

Loss and the human condition. I think I read a book about that once, or heard a lecture on the radio, maybe driving to work in the rain, in another country, at another time. The relief guards have arrived. I notice that it's never a woman now, although I don't know if that is just chance. Boy will be gone for a week, returning to the dry lands, to what I imagine is the bitter struggle going on out there, the battle for jobs, water privileges, petrol, space, sky, hope. In theory, I should be pleased to see the back of Three, but he has his place in this ecosystem I call home: he gives me something to hate. I can't oppose the buzzards, the kitchen sink, the dandelion clocks disappearing on the wind, or the graying of the dusk. Accommodate, reconcile, compromise, navigate, capitalize. I can and must do all those things to hold territory, but there are no punch bags here except myself or the logs waiting to be split—and Three. I will even miss Anon, head down below the parapet, all camouflage and blending in. In some ways, of all of them I would like him to go and not come back because I cannot stand the idea that anyone can walk this land and not be in some way changed by it.

Boy's leaving is a wrench. How much better to be chained in a cellar, the tiny gap carved in the old stone high above my head, letting in the smallest light sufficient only to mark the days, but nothing of the world outside, nothing to torture you with what you cannot have, the honest touch of another person, for instance, the possibility of relating. It must be another truth of the human condition that the other man's prison is always greener. This is half my thinking. There is another half that I hardly dare recognize. I take it as a sign of my increasing resilience that I can watch Boy and Anon standing under the thick-leaved oak in their shirtsleeves, holdalls slung over their shoulders, chatting to the new arrivals, knowing they are leaving, believing in their coming back. I will be allowed outside again. I have even been thinking of suggesting that the guards keep hens. *An Anatomy of Hope*—that was another title, but if not, perhaps I could write it myself one day.

Interestingly, there seems to be some argument between Three and Boy—Anon has moved away, of course; it appears that Boy loses because with bad grace he dumps his case, takes a piece of paper from Three, and comes towards the house. I run downstairs to meet him, singing a stupid song from my childhood, all too aware of Three just yards from the back door.

They're changing guard at Buckingham Palace!
Christopher Robin went down with Alice!
Alice is marrying one of guards,
A soldier's life is terribly hard, said Alice!

"Ruth, for God's sake, stop it."

He wants to be off. Well, let him go. "So sorry to hold you up. Did you pop in for a reason?"

"Sarge told me to give you this." He hands over yet another piece of paper which I can't even be bothered to read. He reminds me of a sulky pupil handing in inadequate homework.

I toss it into the bin. "Can't you précis it for me? I am tired of the small print."

"It's to do with alterations to the permissions for a visiting priest."

This I cannot believe. This I will fight. They have no right to stop Hugh coming and I do have the right to a priest. It was established at the beginning, and now my last tenuous fingertip connection is being removed.

"No, Boy. Surely not." I reach out to grasp his arm. "Hugh won't agree, you know, he'll come anyway."

"He won't, Ruth."

"He'll take it up with the authorities; he won't take this lying down."

"He won't because he's dead."

The horn blares outside and Anon shouts something about missing a train. Three's shadow falls across the doorway. "Soldier! Get in the transport now!"

Boy pries my fingers from his sleeve. "I'll be back," he whispers.

"Now!"

In front of the house there is some sort of handover salute between Three and the senior soldier of the new guard, then Three gets in the driver's side, revs the engine, and swerves out of the gateway. I can only assume Boy climbed in the back. The relief soldier comes to the door and says something about revisiting and clarifying permissions with me later this afternoon, since things seem to have changed since he was last here. I close the door.

He won't. He won't because he's dead.

The news fits me so badly, it occurs to me it is not my news at all and belongs to somebody else. I pick the printout from the bin and lay it on the table. As I thought, most of it is indecipherable jargon, but the second paragraph down confirms what Boy has told me:

> . . . *that visiting rights granted to* _____ *(complete name of visitor as requested on permission form HMP (PR) iii).*
>
> *Under category* _____ *(complete category under which permission was granted, i.e., medical/religious/humanitarian/ asylum).*
>
> *Have been rescinded for the following reason(s):_____ (complete giving full details for reasons for rescinding of permission and state whether temporary or permanent).*

And that the detainee has been informed of their rights under the Drought Emergency Regulations Act (Detainees) Amendment Act (section 4) to appeal against said decision, the time scales if applicable and any assistance, legal or otherwise, which may be available under the Representation of Detainees (DEPA) Amendment Act (section 4).

Casually, in a cheap biro running out of ink, someone has scrawled Hugh's name across the top space, misspelled his surname, left out the Reverend: they have reduced all his visits here to a single circle around the word "religious." Then it appears they have started to write "dead" and thought better of it, for a form such as this, and turned the "a" into "c" and the "d" into an "e" and declared Hugh deceased. They could not have seen the irony in bowing to bureaucracy by underlining the word "permanent," nor the irony of giving me the right to appeal against the death of a good man.

Visits
Kindness
Link to the outside world
Yellow roses
Anticipation
Future tense
Milk
A link to Dorothy
Jokes
Prayers

These things are gone now.

Hugh and I had talked about my insomnia a lot, and he had given me advice which I had been following, especially since being confined to the house. Together we had devised a routine—Hugh's routine, I called it—and slowly, night after night, it had worked its magic and darkness had fallen like a blanket around my shoulders rather than the hood over my head. Hugh's routine went like this. When I finished supper—usually eggs or soup, cooked and eaten without enjoyment or ceremony or company—I would close the curtains in the sitting room and turn on the reading lamp behind the pink sofa and play the *Greatest Classical Hits* CD all the way through, once. When the final notes of the Nunc Dimittis sung by the choir of King's College relinquished their hold on the room, I turned out the lights downstairs and, like a child, went upstairs, cleaned my teeth, folded my clothes, read one psalm, and turned out the light. Sleep and I were becoming reacquainted. Don't worry, said sleep, the next ten hours will pass without you counting, you will not know you even lived them. In those hours you can neither commit any new crimes nor remember any old. You will be merely carrying out your obligation to live, but having to endure none of the pain of doing so. Your life span will be passing, and when you wake, another fraction of it will have been accounted for and the debt paid. You need never live those hours again.

But Hugh is dead, he has taken with him his routine; he offered me his blessing and now it is too late to accept it or return it. The only visit which ended in recrimination was the last. After such progress, regression; sleep is impossible once more. Again, I am in a poisonous relationship and condemned to share my bed with a flickering partner who hovers in the corner of my eye, who lifts the covers and invites others to come creeping between the sheets with icy hands and colder memories in the early hours of the morning. The sound track to the visions is played on the wind-up gramophone I inherited from my great-aunt, the tunes and voices slowing and distorting as the handle winds down, the heavy claw scratching the vinyl with its single fingernail as it grinds its way across the recording of my failures.

There is no one left. Angie gone. Mark gone. Boy gone. Hugh gone. Listen to the tolling of the bell. Gone. Gone. Gone. I have only myself and I forge a new routine all of my own. This is a routine devised for a world in which there is neither day nor night, no hours, no minutes, no life or death. All is sameness. The knack is to lie like a rug on the floor and let time wipe its feet on your face. Lucien gone.

Outside, around me The Well exhausts itself with growing, cells multiplying in the ivy grappling up the trees, the grass growing taller and taller until it can barely sustain the weight of each ambitious blade, flowers opening wider and wider until the petals can no longer hold on to the core and float to the ground. The fledglings have left without saying goodbye, the deer move out from the shadows of the woods and crop the fields systematically, moving on in watchful ranks and beneath the feet of the booted guards, ants, horn beetles, woodlice, daddy longlegs, maggots, false widow spiders, caterpillars, slugs, and the brown-lipped snails who take their house arrest with them when they travel. And I do nothing.

I have watched many sunrises. More sunsets, probably, but also many sunrises and one thing does not change: the unexpected ordinariness of the arrival of the day. The sun is like a guest. You are sure it is him, you can see him coming from far away, dressed for an occasion of great splendor, you recognize the shimmering gown, and he is bearing a gift wrapped up in gold foil, your name on the card. As he comes over the hill, there is a red ripple of excitement, he extends his hands and the light flashes off the rings on his fingers as he hands you the present, but then he takes off his cloak and as it is thrown over the back of the chair, you see the underside of the embroidery, all loose threads and no pattern; and you unwrap the parcel and the paper is gold on one side only and flat and white underneath, the next layer is brown paper and string, the next is yesterday's newspaper scrunched up in a ball around the twelve hours of bleach-white living which we call day.

I get up from my floor and stand against the window, remembering how I used to kneel to pray at sunrise not so long ago. I can hear Sister Amelia's voice leading me out of myself and into the curling mist:

The flowering of the day,
Like the flowering of the Rose,
is welcome.
Sun like faith over the horizon, welcome.
Mist like hope along the river, welcome.

Hope will never come my way again. Hugh is dead. Here we are, me and the day sitting together in the kitchen with not much left to say to each other, both tired already, even though we have only just got started. At some point I have doodled names on the piece of paper and surrounded them with flowers with long tendrils and twisting stems. I am not alone. I can feel it behind me, breathing. Then it touches me. This touching is too complicated for daylight. He slips away. I know the leaving of his hands, the weightlessness of where his head has been, the chill on my cheek where he is gone. I am not lonely while I have my phantoms beside me. Sometimes it is Mark: he leaves his paperwork on the desk and comes over to pull me to my feet, but just as I rise, he is gone and I fall back down again. And Voice, Voice keeps me company again, reminding me that Lucien is playing in the lambing shed—can't I hear the bales falling?—or that Lucien is drowning in the bath—and can't I hear the taps running?—or that Mark has taken Lucien—and can't I hear the Land Rover, leaving without me? Angie doesn't come often and Hugh not at all. He is dead, Ruth. He won't because he is dead.

Pray for us now and at the hour of death.

Now is the time to go to that place in the past. There will be no better time, or worse time. There is a time for everything, and now is the time to think about the dead and the dying.

CHAPTER TWENTY-FOUR

H eal thyself. That's what they say, isn't it? I don't know if I could have healed myself, but I do know I could barely have recognized myself by the end of that week, the final week. Sister Eve told us we needed to "refocus to retain the energy and forward momentum of our online campaign" and we decided that there would be eight days of retreat and meditation, starting on December 8 with the Feast of the Immaculate Conception and culminating with the saint's day for Santa Maria di Rosa on the 15th. It was agreed she was the perfect new emblem for a new look.

With the planned week of worship drawing near, I no longer had the option of asking Mark to keep an eye on Lucien and I became a nun with a child-care problem. Mark had been gone almost a month, and after being initially disconcerted by his absence, Lucien seemed to believe my lies and we settled into our routine like an old married couple. Voice was quieter then, and Amelia was often around and even seemed to be winning Lucien over, bringing him owl feathers to add to his collection in his room and holly with bright red berries to help him decorate the house for Christmas.

"Is Amelia your best friend, Granny R?" Lucien asked, standing on a chair to poke the glossy sprigs behind the pictures.

"Do you know, I think she probably is. Be careful on that."

"She's not mine," he said, jumping down. "I haven't got a best friend at the moment."

I thought I was enough; I didn't really listen to him. He stayed in the cottage when I went to dusk worship and he never seemed worried to be on his own and I never worried about him, but the week of commitment was going to demand all of me, all of the time. When Mark had been around, he had frequently said that if I couldn't prioritize Lucien, then next time Angie called I should tell her to come and get him. I worried that he was at that moment seeking her out and I would return to the house to see Lucien with his backpack, getting into the back of Charley's van, waving goodbye, but the fear was not enough to conquer the mad, mounting hysteria of those days, because I was ringmaster, trapeze artist, and clown in my very own circus, while Lucien sat in the audience swinging his legs and sucking his thumb.

The opening act was on the Thursday night and Friday morning, with the Feast of the Immaculate Conception. Online activity had been feverish, the number of hits higher than ever, the Rose chat rooms loud with the conversations of the faithful. It had taken a drought to drain the materialism from Christmas, but most of the country had no idea which religion to turn to in its place, and I don't think the Rose was the only one experiencing a surge of interest—news reports showed even the leaking Victorian churches in city centers filling up to the brim.

Dawn was late, dusk early in the dying days of the year, but the mornings were medieval blue and gold, and our first worship of the day was streamed live to the accompaniment of mallards in flight. Above our vespers, swirls of starlings converged and separated against the sunset before settling on the Douglas fir and Scots pine, drawn in black ink against the evening. I passed the Friday night at home, checking on Lucien's soft breathing in the room next to mine, before kneeling on the rough wood, naked and freezing cold, trembling

with exhaustion. Saturday, day three of our extravaganza, saw us worshipping the mistletoe, taking our webcam to the gnarled trunks and
leafless branches of our beautiful apple trees. Followers were able
to buy sprigs of mistletoe online which were supposedly from The
Well and I waxed lyrical about the plant's druid history while Sister
Amelia drew attention to the berries: "the female which fruits when
everything around her is bare and barren for winter."

On the fourth day, we created the page for the Christmas Rose,
Eve leading the singing of medieval lyrics exalting Mary long into
the darkness, our praying hands and shrouds lit by the flares which
represented in flame the pattern of our sacred flower and we saw that
it was good. When I got back to the cottage that night, I branded
myself with the Rose. I do not remember the burning.

Did the days know where their relentless march would take them?
Day five, exalted spiritually, exhausted physically, we held high the
life of our Lady of Guadalupe and sat huddled in the warmth of the
hub camper, watching the links spread to Mexico and prayers in
Spanish scroll through the site.

Geography is no barrier to belief—andreabeliever

Bendiga la rosa—oliva@nuevavida.

And so it was the sixth day came. The 13th of December. Lucien
woke me. There would never be a seventh day, never be a day of rest.
It was late. I had been up all night praying and writing, and had been
to worship in the morning. It was colder, the wind had swung round
to the north and the blue skies had been replaced by steel gray; beneath our feet there was ice for puddles. I think it was the cold, as
much as the tiredness, which had finally driven me to my bed when
I got back, and for the first time in days I had fallen asleep. The faint
tugging I felt on my arm was a reminder of a physical world which I

had abandoned, but I rolled over and there was Lucien. He climbed into bed with me, snuggled up tight to me.

"What cold hands you have." I laughed.

He grinned madly at me. "And what big teeth you have, Grandmother." Then he said, "I miss you."

I hugged him even tighter, his woolly sweater tickling my nose, his bare tummy warm and soft against my body. "I'm so sorry, Lucien. Have you been lonely?"

"Mummy hasn't phoned for a long time," he said, "but I'm not really lonely, don't worry."

Pulling on my thick fleece, I took Lucien downstairs and made slices of toast dripping with honey for him and great mugs of hot, sweet tea. One day, I told him, we'll be able to have hot chocolate with proper milk again, but he said he couldn't remember what that was like. Then I told him that there were only two more days, then the week of worship would be over and then I would be all his. Promise? Promise. "And when will Mummy be back?" Lucien asked. "I'm sure she'll call very soon," I said, "and then we'll see when she's coming for Christmas."

"And when will Mark be back?"

———

Our worship that evening was at the Wellspring. The procession from the camp started at 4 p.m. and we followed our familiar pilgrimage, chanting and carrying candles and flares to be placed around the edge of the water. In those iron-gray days, the heron watched us motionless from the far bank and the overwintering coots hid among the tall, dry bulrushes. I reached down and touched the icy water and thought there will be no immersion at this service.

Suddenly, Sister Dorothy's voice broke our quiet preparations. "Who's that? There's someone there!"

We strained to make sense of the footfall crunching through the dead wood and brambles.

Jack grabbed me, trembling; she was not well again and often seemed distracted by distressing things or people we could not see or hear. "It's something evil," she whispered. "Don't leave me."

"Get out! In the name of the Rose, get out!" commanded Sister Amelia.

Lucien, with hat and gloves and a stick for beating back the brambles, stumbled into the clearing. "Surprise!" he shouted. "Mark's come back, Granny R. It's only us!"

Mark. Behind him, Mark, crashing out of the thick darkness of the wood, out of all proportion to the silence, coarse and heavy in boots and an ex-army jacket, storming our lightness, stamping back onto my thin ice.

"We came to see the magic," cried Lucien. "Sister Amelia, can you see the magic now?"

I looked from Amelia to Mark and back again. "Mark! What are you doing back? What are you doing here?"

Dorothy came to my rescue. It was she who took Lucien by the hand, led him away from us around to the other side of the Wellspring, let him light a candle, pointed out the long-billed snipe running out from among the tufts of frozen grass as I summoned Mark back from the edge of the pond into the forest. We squared up between the tall oaks and hissed at each other.

"Shall I tell you why I came back?"

"Please do."

"Because Lucien asked me to."

"You're lying. How?"

"I rang your mobile, Ruth. Stupid me, I wanted to talk, but guess what? Lucien answered and said you weren't there and you wouldn't be back 'til late."

"He was fine."

"He was crying."

Glancing back over my shoulder, through the branches, Dorothy was crouched down with her arms around Lucien, his head on her shoulder. Eve was comforting Jack, whispering in her ear, and Amelia was staring directly at me.

"It's not good enough," Mark said. Then he moved closer, speaking straight into my ear. "I can't get hold of Angie, but if she calls, Ruth, you need to get her here, before it's too late."

"Don't threaten me."

"I'm not." He turned away, punched the trunk of the nearest tree but then sagged to the forest floor, squatting on the dead leaves and brittle twigs, head in his hands. "Just listen to what I am saying. I wanted so much to come back, but I can't stay. I can't cope with Lucien, it's too much to expect, but I can't leave him like this. Something's going to give. I have to go. He has to go."

Sister Amelia crept up on us and now echoed his words, but for different reasons. "He is right. The boy has to go. This is the final intrusion," she said, and then spoke directly to Mark. "You must both go. Leave the Wellspring and The Well and take the boy with you. You do not belong here. It is a living blasphemy."

"Not now, Amelia . . ." I started to say.

But we were interrupted by Lucien's crying.

"You promised." He was sobbing, breaking away from Dorothy's hug. "You and you and you, you've all promised to bring me here and see the magic and you've all lied."

One of the people around that pond kept that promise and brought him back, but only the water knows who.

"Come here, Lucien," said Jack, holding out her hand. She pulled him close, whispered in his ear, and tickled him. "No more tears? Promise?"

Lucien squirmed, halfway between giggling and crying. "All right, I'll go away now if that's what you want." He threw a stone into the pond and ran off into the wood, tripping over the rotten branches and kicking one of the unlit flares as he went. Mark shouted after him to wait.

My indecision lasted barely a second as Amelia slipped her hand in mine. "I won't be long, Lucien," I called after him, "I promise!" And I allowed Amelia to lead me back to the water.

To worship after such conflict was not easy. Tears streamed from Sister Amelia's gray eyes and her pain hurt me, piercing me all the more because of the love I thought she had shown me, the care I thought she had taken of me. Voice was loud and incoherent in my head, peace difficult to come by, and it was a conscious effort to erase the image of Mark from The Well and pray, but eventually I came to that place of ecstasy again, all the more beautiful for the time it had taken to reach it, ravished by the Rose, every nerve ending quivering with knowledge, all else was as nothing. Before we parted, in unspoken agreement Sister Amelia and I hung back and let the others go ahead, and I whispered that I was sorry and she pulled me close and we kissed as sisters kiss and then we kissed again.

Crossing the plowed field, clods of mud clung to my boots and I was weighed down and exhausted as I struggled up the hill and faint by the time I got back to the house. The kitchen seemed a strange place, cluttered with small, physical objects I hardly recognized and I struggled to do something as simple as boiling the kettle. In the sitting room, the fire was almost out, the log basket full, but I could not connect the act of putting the log in the stove with warming up. Once I realized how cold I was, I started shivering uncontrollably, jerking and spilling the tea on my robe, feeling it soaking through to my jeans. My jaw seized up and my teeth chattered and it occurred to me that I was having some sort of fit, but there was nobody there to keep my burnt tongue from slipping down my throat and suffocating me. I swallowed consciously, determined to make each instinctive act of remaining alive purposeful. I stood up. I put the mug on the mantelpiece and pushed it one or two inches back towards the wall. I walked towards the staircase, hands out in front of me, feeling my way to the banisters. Working my way, hand over hand, I climbed the stairs one at a time until I reached the top and I made it into the bathroom. It was dark. Slumped on the floor, I leant against the wall to collect myself, then managed to crawl towards the bath, using one hand to grip the cold, white rim and the other to feel for the links of the chain for the plug. Link by link I inched my fingers up the metal, until I felt the rubber plug catch the other side of the tap. I released it and heard it swing against the bottom of the bath. Reaching down, I pushed it into place and turned on the taps, listening to the splattering water and the familiar lurching of the pipework in the airing cupboard. Downstairs, the well pump shuddered and sucked at the still pools in the bedrock hundreds of feet beneath the house.

With a returning awareness of the physical world, I started to undress. Great clumps of ridged mud fell onto the carpet as I struggled to untie the laces which had tightened into impossible knots. My robe slipped easily over my head, but my jeans were damp and tight and I could not trust myself to stand up, so I wriggled like a child on the floor, pulling them down my legs until it all came off at once— pants, socks, jeans—and lay like a half-finished Guy Fawkes dummy. My numb fingers unfastened my bra and I lifted my leg over the bath and felt the sharp heat on one foot, then the other, felt the veins in my calves and then my thighs grow red and swollen as they returned to life. I lowered myself in until I was sitting, then lying, until my head sank under the water and my hair floated behind me and I was warm again, so warm.

The water drained from me in a rush as I sat up, terrified and gasping for breath; it streamed from my hair down my back, it blinded my eyes, and I tasted it in my mouth. The bath surged to and fro with a crazy perpetual motion as if it wanted to persuade me to go back down, but in time it retained its equilibrium and so did I. The sliver of a moon coming through the window was enough for me to start to make sense again of the edges of the room, my breath slowed and deepened, my jaw relaxed, and I stretched my legs and flexed my toes. I was very hungry, of that I was sure, and my own consciousness edged back into my mind telling me I should eat. Were there eggs in the rack and had I made safe the chickens for the night or had the fox laid waste the pen? And then there is Mark, said Voice, Mark is back and where is Lucien?

"Lucien?" I shouted. "Lucien?"

Lucien had been at the Wellspring, Sister Amelia had wanted him gone, Mark had taken him away. He must be with Mark, he was safe. I had no idea how long ago it was that they left. Out of the bath, I dried, dressed quickly in clean clothes and toweled my hair roughly, just enough to stop the drips dampening the back of my neck, but kept the water in the bath for Lucien. I left the boots on the floor, thinking I'd have to deal with the mess in the morning, and went to find him. All grandmother now, I ran to the barn where the clock said it was quarter past eight, the stove was roaring, steam was rising from something boiling on the two-ring cooker, and Lucien was standing on a chair, naked except for sneakers on his feet and the little wooden rose around his neck. He was stirring something in a bowl on the table.

"Granny R! We're making you a surprise!" he shouted. "Go away! You'll see, go away!"

"What on earth . . . ?"

Mark pointed at the jeans, pants, and shirt hanging over a chair by the radiator. "The first attempt went all over him," he said, then he lunged towards Lucien. "Careful. It'll happen all over again."

"Mark helped me take off my clothes and wash all over," said Lucien. "He said we could wash away all the evidence and nobody would ever know. That's what you said, wasn't it, Mark?"

"I did indeed," said Mark, who then turned his back on Lucien. "What the hell is that?" he whispered, pointing at the rose necklace around Lucien's neck.

Not now, I mouthed back, then continued out loud, "I'm so sorry, Mark," I said. "I had no idea of the time. I came back and had a bath and . . ."

Mark wiped his hands. "Well, we've had a great time together, haven't we, Lucien?"

The barn was probably a mess before Lucien got there, but now there were hundreds of bits of paper from Mark's printer all over the floor, each with a token scribble of a picture on it before Lucien had moved onto the next like a form of speed-painting. I picked up one, then another, then another. They all had the same motif. Lots and lots of M's, Lucien said. For Mummy, Mark explained.

"I better get Lucien off to bed," I said.

Lucien's face collapsed into an overtired scowl. "I'm not going to bed. I'm staying up tonight. You can go to bed. Get out." He got off the chair and started pushing me at the knees. "Go on, Granny R, get out."

Mark raised his eyebrows at me.

"And I'm going to the Wellspring again when you're not there," Lucien shouted. "Because it's not just yours and anyone can go there whenever they like, Mark says so."

Mark felt the damp jeans and then got his own old green sweater from the bed and pulled it over Lucien's head and rolled the sleeves up.

"It's like a huge dress," moaned Lucien.

"It's cold outside," said Mark, and then he picked him up, so easily, so strong, and Lucien laid his head on his shoulder. "I'll carry you over."

The little boy and the man, making their way across the icy yard to the cottage, with me losing my footing behind. Mark opened the door, stepped back into the cottage, carried him upstairs, and was sitting with him on the edge of his bed as if nothing had changed since he was a baby and lived with us in London.

"Shall I tell Granny our secret?" Lucien was rubbing his eyes and reaching for his special duck.

I am standing at the door. Voice likes secrets. "What secret is this?" asks Voice and I say it out loud for her.

"Oh, no," said Mark.

Lucien shook his head slowly in agreement.

"But we can tell her that we've made her supper," Mark said. "We thought you'd be very tired because you'd walked so far and you haven't had much time to eat recently."

Lucien is holding his duck tight. "I've got lots of secrets, Granny R."

Lucien was in that impossible state, overexcited and overexhausted, wide awake and half asleep at the same time, so I decided to abandon the normal bedtime routines and I left him in Mark's green sweater, pulled off his sneakers, untied the knot on the leather band which held his little wooden rose around his neck and placed it carefully on his bedside table, then pulled the duvet snug around him and kissed his forehead. One kiss. One last kiss. A Judas kiss. He was restless, so I read the Noah story, with just the night-light on, letting the rhythm of the two-by-two fold its pattern over the night and put in order the day that had gone and present the rainbow as hope for the day to come. Then when his breathing had slowed and his beautiful eyes had closed, I asked for the Rose's blessing on Lucien and crept from the room. I pulled the door so it was almost shut, as usual, and that was how I left him. I know that was how I left him. I left him.

I went to the barn to have supper with Mark because Lucien had made it. And maybe because I was exhausted and needed something physical to hold me to the ground, after the slip-sliding week I had just experienced. And I felt worried for Mark, because there was something desperate in his face that night; a part of me loved him because he had come back—and remember, I had loved him for a long, long time. And it looked like an olive branch, even if now I see it in my mind's eye as a crown of thorns.

We sat like a couple in a rented holiday cottage who suddenly find they have too much time and too much silence on their hands. Mark and Lucien had made parsnip soup, which I sipped, feeling it sit uncomfortably on my shrunken stomach. I tried to resist the wine he had brought back with him; he took a great gulp as if he was summoning courage.

"Awhile ago," he said, "you tried to persuade me that we should sell up and get out while we could and I said no. But I was wrong, Ruth. Yes, I came back because of Lucien on the phone, but I wanted to come back and talk anyway. And what I want to say tonight is yes, let's do it, let's take what we can and go and start again somewhere else. Maybe it's not too late." He looked up from his glass, vulnerability in his eyes and pain in the way he closed them to hear my answer.

"It is too late, Mark" I said. "I can't leave now."

We gave way to the silence again, aware of not only our differences but also of the history of our closeness, living up here as attendants in our own theme park.

Mark started clearing the table, creating noise with the plates and knives, returning to the same question that seemed to plague him. "Is this it, then?" he asked. "You will stay here at The Well forever? With her? Nothing will take you away?"

"Only if that is what the Rose wants."

"The Rose? Or Amelia? That's it? You'll let her erase twenty years of love just like that. Gone."

"The Rose!" I repeat.

"And Lucien?" He spoke with his back to me.

"The Well will always be here for Lucien and Lucien for The Well. He is the future. The Rose is close to him, I feel it."

"You think Angie will agree with you?"

"Leave her out of it," I screamed at him.

Crashing the frying pan into the sink, Mark turned to face me. "You are kidding yourself. Whether or not your Rose is real, I don't know. But what I do know is that you are fooling yourself. The Sisters don't believe that about Lucien. Sister Amelia hates him, really hates him—you saw it yourself this evening down at the spring. Sometimes I wonder what she might do to him, she's such a religious freak. Face it. A male inheritance is not part of their vision. Your grandson is nothing but an obstacle on the road to their fucking paradise."

My lips were dry. I looked over my shoulder at the door. *He has done it before*, said Voice.

"Don't walk out now," he ranted, but then he backed away, holding his hands out as if I were a vampire. "Don't push me too far, Ruth," he said. "You push people too far . . ."

"What do you mean?"

"You put us together, me and Lucien, and pull us apart as if you're a puppet master. I love you too much, Ruth. I love him too much. It's all gone wrong and there'll be no going back now. Just like before."

"I don't understand, please . . ."

"You can't understand anything any longer. I've said it before: you can't have it all." Suddenly the threat was gone and he was crying, great gasps shaking his body, and I went to him, held him, put my head on his juddering chest. All I could do was pray, and the Rose filled the room with petal-scented peace in much the same way that some people say ghosts do.

He held me tighter and I felt him hard against my thigh. "One last night?" he sobbed. "After so many years of loving you, just one last night. Please."

Twisting my body, I left his embrace and shook my head.

"Enough!" he said, and moved away from me also. "Go. Things will be clearer in the morning."

As I was almost at the door, he suddenly shouted, "No, stop.

You've got to stay." He opened the oven and presented an apple cake to me. "Lucien would never forgive us for forgetting his surprise. We've got to eat it, for his sake."

That was my last supper, the cake that Lucien made. Had I known, I would have taken an eternity to break off the corner with my spoon, to scoop the warm yellow custard onto the sponge and rest it on my tongue; I would have sold my soul for the lightness and the sweetness; I would have invited the eggs and the flour, the sugar and the apple to become part of me, dissolved into my body, mingled with my saliva, digested by my enzymes, transported by my blood until this cake that he had made was indistinguishable from each individual cell of my body.

I didn't know. Voice asked me what I was doing eating so much. I smeared it around my plate and left some lumps under my spoon, offering to wash up before Mark could notice. I scoured the pan in which it was made, letting the water run over it and wash away all trace of his small hands, the wooden spoon he had held, the tongue which had licked it. Mark wiped the table clean and I let the washing-up water carry all traces of him away.

When I got back into the cottage, I pulled the back door behind me. I did not lock it; I never did. Having put a large log on the wood-burning stove to keep it going until the morning and turned out the lights, leaving just the sudden flare of the flames in the black room, I crept upstairs, went into the bathroom, and noticed the bath where the water was now gray with a slight film of soap and a few strands of my hair. I didn't drain it, knowing the noise might wake Lucien next door, and I left the pile of wet clothes on the floor. I was so tired that I decided to sleep first and wake early to answer the prayers of the faithful and finish the blog for the penultimate day of our week of worship, so I clicked in the top right-hand corner of theSistersoftheRose.com and watched it shrink to nothing in far less than a second and confirmed that I wanted to shut down.

The last thing I did, in a way the last thing I ever did, even after I had taken one final look at the full moon, even after I had closed the shutters in my bedroom, even after I had knelt and thanked the Rose for the day and blessing for the night to come, the last thing I did was tiptoe onto the landing and peer through the half-open door to Lucien's bedroom. His night-light was on and the curtains, although thick, were allowing a slit of moonlight to cross the floor and catch the glint of the mirror on the opposite wall. I didn't go in. I never did. I stood stock-still as always, riveted by the magic of a sleeping child, listening for the rhythmic rise and fall of his breath, watching for the slight shuffling of the duvet, the sucking of tongue on thumb. Then I went to bed and slept as I had not slept for a long time. It is because I know now what can happen while you sleep that I will never sleep again.

CHAPTER TWENTY-FIVE

There is no such thing as waking these days, just a blurring of different ways of being alive; after that morning, there would never be another awakening.

That day, my resolution had been to get up at 4 a.m. to answer the prayers and prepare the readings which I had failed to do the evening before. Why did I sleep through that deadline that night? Maybe because my body had been busy, working with the devil in the bleakest hours of the night and I had not long been in bed. Sometimes I want to rip my skin apart just to see inside the real me and know what I am made of, but I lack the talons and have to make do with surface scratches on my arms, which barely bleed.

I woke late. Too late. I had already missed dawn worship, but if I hurried I could get to the Sisters for the readings. There was no sign of Lucien, but the day before had been long and these dark mornings smudged the edges between night and day. I was grateful to be able to get dressed in peace, Lucien had become so attention seeking recently. I knelt briefly to pray. That day became a catalog of firsts and lasts—this was the last time I prayed in faith rather than desperation. Downstairs, despite my clattering in the kitchen, Lucien had still not come down. I called upstairs; the last thing I wanted was to have to get Mark to look after him again and give him the excuse to summon Angie or the excuse to stay longer. The radio was on with its tedious catalog of drought-fueled misery, so I turned it down and called again and, getting no reply, went halfway up the stairs and called again, then up to his room. I pushed open the door. The night-light was still on, the curtains still closed. His bed was empty.

"Lucien?" I shouted, although where I thought he could be in a tiny two-bed cottage with only one staircase, I don't know. I looked in the bathroom where last night's water looked stagnant but undisturbed and my gown lay to one side like a sodden shroud. At least he had not fallen in. I looked in our bedroom, pulling back the duvet, waiting for him to boo out on me. My chest tightened, but at the same time I told myself to breathe deeply and calm down: this was something all mothers felt at some point, the flutter of the unthinkable, that they had lost their child. But they never had—hardly ever.

Back into the kitchen, as if somehow against the law of nature he could have come downstairs and got himself to the table and started his cereal without me having noticed him on the stairs. He was not there. It was obvious that he'd woken up early, when I was still asleep, and slipped outside. His brown coat and Wellington boots were still in the back passage, as were his shoes, but I didn't put it past him going out in bare feet even on such a day as this. The back door was unlocked and outside seemed to me a strange place, as if the frosted oak was an illustration and the pheasants a sound track. Of course, he would have gone to Mark! I could not deny he had been so pleased that Mark was back. I knocked and pushed the barn door simultaneously. Inside the main room, Mark had tidied a bit, the washing up put away, the coloring paper with all the M's was gone, presumably into the wood-burning stove. Lucien's jeans were still on the clothes horse, but Mark's coat was not on the peg and it was only when I went outside again that I realized the Land Rover was gone. Logic. Rewind. Lucien had got up early, found me still asleep, and gone over to the barn. Mark must have needed something in Middleton and taken Lucien with him for the ride. That was how it must be.

I scanned the field in front, feeling its bleakness, the sheep huddled around the hay, two crows fighting off the buzzard over the Hedditch cover. I was cold, very cold, and the ground was hard beneath my feet. I went back inside, dithering and ineffectual, his mobile went to answerphone, but it would if he had just gone into Middleton, the reception was dreadful there. Overhead, a huge heron lazily flew up from the direction of the pond and headed towards the lane and away from The Well. Then I understood. The naked boy, the last laugh, the "pushed too far." Something terrible had happened; he had taken Lucien from me and gone.

You are all alone now, said Voice. I started to run up the empty track.

"Come back!" I screamed and then, there it was, the Land Rover coming towards me. I felt so foolish for thinking what I had thought. I stopped, watching as the car swung up onto the gravel and Mark got out of the driver's seat, carrying a newspaper: I remember thinking how he'd never gone to buy a paper in the morning before, how he had hated the media ever since the problems at work, even more since we moved here. Later I thought, why would he have gone into Middleton, faced all that all over again, just for a paper? But at the time it seemed irrelevant why; all that mattered was that he was going to go round and open the door for Lucien.

"Why didn't you tell me you had Lucien?" I went towards the car to get him myself, because he had to be in the car, there was nowhere else he could be. "I've been worried sick."

"What are you talking about?" he asked.

"Where is he, Mark?" I shouted, opening the rear door and seeing a backseat that had nothing more than a heap of wood and nails and mallets. "What have you done with him?"

The logical solutions were all gone. I started to run, just to run. Down the slope towards the lambing barn—he must be there, perhaps he'd made a house out of hay—but the lambing barn was all settled dust in the half-light and undisturbed. So I ran on to the tractor shed, he must be there, sitting on the tractor in his pajamas, hands on the wheel, but I'd forgotten the tractor was down by the hay. So I shouted to Mark, I'm going down to the tractor, and started stumbling over the rutted mud.

Mark held my arm like a vise. "What's going on, Ruth?"

"I woke up and he wasn't in his bed. He's gone, Mark. Gone!"

Mark looked shocked—I am sure he was shocked. "Well, was he OK last night? Did you check on him when you got back to the cottage?"

"Of course I checked on him. What do you think . . ."

"I don't understand. Where can he be? He must be somewhere."

Mark's composure was gone, and when I spoke next it was to reassure him as much as myself. "It's OK. We'll find him. He's just wandered off, that's all. He's used to doing that, isn't he? He did that all the time when he was with Angie."

"You're right." Mark threw the paper back onto the driver's seat. "We need to be systematic. You need to get a coat, for a start."

He put his arms around me and held me very tight. His heart was beating fast, loudly, and I could tell from long experience that he was trying hard to control his breathing. Such enforced togetherness. So short-lived.

"I'm going upstairs to get another sweater," I said, but when I got to my bedroom, I fell to my knees.

"I have done so much for you," I said slowly, spitting the words out one by one. "I have given up everything for you: my husband, my dream, everything. I have never asked for anything in return, but now I am asking. Find Lucien. Give me back Lucien."

The echo of my words sounded blackmailing and threatening,

and Voice said I'd better repent, making demands like that, who did I think I was. Then I was so scared that I might offend this god of the drought who possessed me and about whom I knew so little.

"Sorry," I said. "I am so worried. I know that you love each and every one of us and that whatever happens is part of your plan. Help me to trust the Rose this morning. Amen."

The sound of that amen was very loud in the empty room. Where do you go after amen?

I went to Mark. He was on the phone.

"He wasn't in his bed when she woke up this morning. We are sure he's just wandered off somewhere on the farm . . ."

To the police.

"Why?" I ranted. "He's just somewhere out in the fields. It's not like we're in the middle of London and he's going to get grabbed by some pervert or get lost. Why did you call the police without asking me? I have prayed." I screamed at him, "I hate the police snooping around The Well."

"This isn't about you and The Well, Ruth; nothing to do with your sodding Sisters or the Rose or any other bullshit. It's about finding Lucien, nothing else, no one else and I think the police might just be a little bit more helpful than your prayers."

For a second, we could hear the clock ticking and the squawk of one of the hens outside. Then he continued in a quieter voice, saying that in these cases it was always better to let the police know sooner rather than later. I agreed, although the whole thing seemed to be escalating into a film which was fast-forwarding without me in it. I told him I was going up to the Sisters, to see if he was with them. Mark was astonished that I hadn't asked them already.

We set off, calling as we went. Lucien. Lucien. Our voices were loud in the workless, waterless valleys that stretched beyond The Well. Dorothy was already making her way down the track before we reached them.

"Is something wrong, Ruth? We missed you at prayers."

We ran to the campers. It was obvious Lucien was not there. Eve said they had all been up since dawn—Jack hadn't been well, difficult to manage, so Sister Amelia had moved her from Dorothy's into her own camper and it had taken some time to settle her. They would certainly have seen something if Lucien had been around. I'll check the campers, Mark said, just in case. Sister Ruth can check the campers, interrupted Amelia, and Mark kicked the laundry basket and started back up the hill. Lucien adored Dorothy and Jack, was wary of Amelia and Eve, but loved all their campers equally: the way the beds folded up into the walls, the way the tops of the bench seats opened up into secret chests, the way the toilet looked like a fridge. So the Sisters and I checked the campers, with their steamed-up windows and smells of bodies and damp, their mystical writings laid out on the hinged tables and the smoke from the mugs of herbal tea rising up into the winter air. Jack was curled up in a fetal position on the bed in Sister Amelia's camper, oblivious of the creak of the opening door and the blast of cold air. Dorothy covered her with a blanket and she didn't stir.

"She's been vomiting," whispered Amelia. "I've given her something to help her get some sleep. We mustn't wake her. The stress of all this will be too much for her." Sister Amelia took a glass from the table and put it in the sink, felt Jack's forehead with the back of her hand, picked a robe up off the floor and took it outside to dry in the winter sun. "She'll be all right," she said, and blessed her with the sign of the Rose.

Lucien was not there, but there was nothing else to do but look. Dorothy rang the prayer bell three times and it tolled its unusual call to arms like a death knell over the quiet morning. She said the Sisters should organize themselves to walk the woods and she asked for the blessing of the Rose on their search, but Sister Amelia insisted that Eve stay in the hub and reconfigure the site so that a prerecorded reading could be shared with the followers expecting the seventh day of preparation.

"We need everyone to help," I said.

"So does the Rose," she replied. "I'll search the Wellwood. The Rose is with us. She won't let anything happen to Lucien."

"What you said," I sobbed, "about the Rose not letting anything happen. How do you know? You of all people—you said that the Rose doesn't want men any longer. You want him gone anyway, so why would she save my grandson?"

Sister Amelia laid her arm on mine and spoke quietly. "Remember whatever has happened, it is her plan and it is a good plan. God himself, the first time, lost his only son."

I remember asking, "Do you know something, Amelia? Because if you do, you must tell me." And she said, "Why are you asking me, Ruth, why aren't you asking Mark?" Then she was embracing me and confirming how she loved me, that everything she did and had ever done was because I was her chosen one.

"He wouldn't have gone onto the lane, would he?" asked Dorothy, meeting back at the house, having gone through Smithy's Holt and found nothing. He wouldn't have willingly gone anywhere else now. We had looked in all the places he would have gone and he wasn't there.

"I drove that way this morning to get a paper," said Mark, going on to explain rather elaborately that he'd heard the early morning news and mention of a rainstorm in Yorkshire and he'd wanted the details. "It doesn't seem quite so important now," he concluded, adding that he hadn't seen anything. By which I suppose he meant he hadn't seen my grandson in his great big green sweater walking down the main road. I was beginning to think that someone might have taken him, someone with a grudge against The Well, or the press, or one of those mad people who wrote to us and offered us millions to sell.

"He'd still be alive, though, there'd be no point in someone like that harming him," I was saying, but Voice was reminding me what the car looked like when they found it—burnt out and mutilated— and what Bru looked like when I found him, saliva and poison dripping from his soft muzzle. "They wouldn't harm him, would they?" I was asking when we heard the sirens.

Blue lights and sirens across this quiet land. The 360-degree view which had sold us this place started to rotate as evenly as the flashing light, mocking me with its expanse and our irrelevance; we had always been nothing more than fleas crawling on its skin, ever since we first dreamed of owning it.

The arrival of the police made everything real, but unreal. The kitchen became a sort of headquarters, invaded by strangers in boots coming in and going out and making tea, more tea, talking about rustling undergrowth and footprints and broken-down hedges and dropped gloves and the sound of crying that turned out to be the mewing of the buzzards—the words falling all over the floor and being swept into the bin with every other used-up possibility. The policemen seemed huge and black, overwhelming the space with their synthetic voices on the radios and talk of scrambling a helicopter. The rest of the Sisters came back, empty-handed. I went through the morning and the night before with the police over and over again, and the more I repeated it, the less I knew that I had ever lived before this moment, that anything was real.

Had I locked the back door?

Why did my husband sleep in the barn?

Did I actually hear him breathing?

Did he usually sleep in a man's sweater?

What kind of grandmother was I?

Was there anything missing from his room?

I thought not, but I would need to look to be sure. I asked to be left alone in his room, but they said no—for my own protection, for the preservation of the scene—so I tried to work through it methodically. There was the mirror where the moon had been reflected, his toy chest, closed but with everything in it as usual, the jigsaw pieces, unmade, on the floor, stuffed under the table, along with the incomplete set of felt-tips he'd used to write M's over and over again in the barn. There on the floor by his bed was his special duck. And then . . . I stared at the space, tracing it with my finger. Don't touch too much, said the policewoman. Is there something missing? Behind her, Sister Amelia had come upstairs and was watching from the doorway. I looked at them both, then back at the table, then I felt on the floor, looked under the bed, and my hand went to my own neck.

"There is something missing," I said. "But he'd never have put it on. He couldn't tie the knot. It was too fiddly."

"What's that?" the policewoman asked kindly, but her voice was urgent.

"The Rose," said Sister Amelia, but the policewoman ignored her and looked at me.

"Yes, a rose. A little wooden rose I made, hung on a piece of leather. He wore it sometimes—well, always—but he couldn't put it on himself, he used to ask me to help him. I took it off for him last night when I put him to bed."

Was it really last night?

Two other officers were already pounding up the stairs, one of them plain-clothed, pushing Sister Amelia out of the way and saying excuse me.

"Why did you give him a rose?"

"It is a sign of the Rose's love for him."

"Was he special, then, to your religion?"

"He is special. We are all special."

The officer's resistance was like a wall. "But women are more special than men, am I right—in your religion, I mean?"

"Different," I said hopelessly, my mind too drenched in worry to be able to explain.

"So this ritual you had yesterday," he continued, "did that involve the lad? Would he have put the rose on for that?"

You don't understand, I kept saying, it isn't like that.

On and on they went, these people with their questions. The police seemed to have multiplied. They were all talking, I was repeating myself. I seemed to have to say everything again and again; I didn't know if I was imagining it and was just locked in a world where there was no sound but Voice and perpetual echoes. Lucien, Lucien. A little wooden rose. A little wooden rose. Half past eight. Half past eight. My grandson, my grandson. I don't know. I don't know. I don't know. Ask Mark, why don't you ask Mark?

The police found it hard to accept that we had no way of contacting Angie directly, impossible to believe that someone nowadays didn't have a mobile and that we used to wait for her to ring us; they were right, of course, it was madness that we ever agreed that was all right, but it was how Angie had wanted it. Everything I had ever done seemed in doubt. People moved around me like humans must look to goldfish, distorted and silent.

"What are you all doing in here, swimming in circles?" I screamed. "Get out, get out and look for him!"

I barged my way out of the kitchen, out of the back door, out, over the stile.

"No!" I shouted at Mark, who made to come with me. "I want to be on my own."

Stumbling over First Field, I could hear the policewoman panting behind me. She must have been asked to stay close to me because who knows what I was capable of.

As soon as I reached the brow of the field, I knew I was going to find him. I gathered speed as I dropped off the side of the hill; I could still hear the calling, the occasional whistle, and I wanted to hear someone shouting, we've got him, he's here, he's safe, and to feel my feet running back up to the house, but I knew I wouldn't hear that. That was no longer possible. The search could have lasted days, been on the national news with me tear-stained and with a cracked voice appealing for information, and the police finding Angie on her farm in Scotland and driving her down in a police car on empty motorways. Maybe even the village would have joined in, putting aside their accusations of witchcraft for the sake of a child. But I knew that wouldn't happen now. I was close to him. My feet were taking me to Lucien. I could feel him calling me. How was it that I knew where he was?

When I reached the edge of Wellwood, I forgot where the little stile was, scrabbling along the barbed wire and brambles, leaving blood from my fingers as I went. In desperation I climbed the fence and my coat caught on the barbs, my legs were unsteady on landing, and then I pushed my way through the undergrowth. Roots and strangling brambles tripped me up, and above, low-hanging branches from dead trees caught in my hair and yanked me back. But it was just a wood, an oblivious wood. I found myself back on our pilgrimage path, still narrow but well trodden now; it took me closer to the pond, the dampness suffusing the air. It was almost tropical the way things grew here, even in winter; there was an emerald gleam to the ferns and underfoot the stony soil of the forest, the crunch of nuts and scuttle of dry leaves gave way to a softness, a slight give in the surface of the earth. I slowed down.

Bodies float, I thought, they floated on the surface with their arms outstretched and flowers from weeds in their hair, but when I stared into the black pool, the blank gaze of the undisturbed surface met me and I experienced an agony of relief. I was wrong. A mallard flew up suddenly from the other side and was gone and even the distant shouting seemed to stop, leaving this cathedral midnight silent, the arches of the great trees above it holding up the sky, their thin black branches leading the windows between them, letting in the winter light which shone on this my baptismal font. For a moment, Lucien stood beside me, holding my hand, pointing at tadpoles, then he smiled and slipped away under the water. And then I could see him, beneath the surface where he lay, head down and hanging, barely visible, a pale shadow of a naked boy imprinted on a shroud of water.

CHAPTER TWENTY-SIX

Heaviness, that is what I remember about the first day after that day: the dark itself weighty and anonymous, having neither time nor person to lift it; words, like my head, lying leaden on a pillow; even the silence was thick.

A half memory of walking in front of my mother's car on a cliff road in dense fog, shining a torch from side to side. "Be careful," I am shouting. "You are too close to the edge."

Thirst sticking my tongue to my lips.

Two people, a man and a woman (who was not the other who sat with me sometimes), talking. That other had gone, leaving no trace. Someone else had left, but I was not so clear who, just a sense that they too would never be back. Angie was always coming and going, but it was not her who was missing, although I did need to get in touch with her about something. Perhaps Mark could do that for me. They talked without listening to each other, the man and the woman in the corner of the room. It's the smell that's different, he said. I didn't believe it, sir, when they said about this place on the news. It feels as though I haven't smelled rain on grass since I was a kid. Let me know when she wakes up. I thought I was awake. My eyes told me this was my bedroom at The Well. Something had happened to bring these people here—a lot of people—they ran all over the fields and shouted because they had lost something, or someone. Then I remembered. Lucien was dead.

Unfamiliar words and procedures. Days full of circles, questions, headlines, moments of absurd ordinariness and debilitating tremors of loss which came from deep within the earth, leaving jagged cracks down the flaking walls of my mind.

I put him to bed. I woke up. He was gone. I found him dead.

What made you think he'd be at the Wellspring?

I don't know. Maybe because he was always fascinated by it.

What was your status with the cult?

I am one of the chosen ones.

Chosen by whom?

I don't know.

How did you know you were chosen?

I was told.

By who?

By the Rose. By Voice. By Sister Amelia. I don't know.

Who is Voice?

No one's Voice. It's just a voice.

Tell us about Sister Amelia. Who is she?

I don't know.

Tell us about Mark.

I don't know what to say.

Why did your husband leave?

I don't know.

Why did your husband come back?

I don't know.

Are you aware of the previous allegations made against your husband?

Of course.

Where is your daughter?

I don't know.

Did you kill your grandson?

I don't know.

You don't seem to know very much at all.

Where is Mark? I asked them, but they didn't give me a straight answer.

One thing I did know was how to log on to todaysheadlines.co.uk.

- *"Women shall inherit the earth from women": is this why Lucien died?*
- *A member of the Rose of Jericho sect yesterday revealed evidence showing that the woman known as Sister Amelia had been talking of the need to expel Lucien Ardingly . . .*
- *Police suspect ritual drowning in child murder case.*
- *Police would today neither confirm nor deny reports that the boy was blindfold when his body was found. They are following leads suggesting . . .*
- *Pictures seen here, taken from the religious sect's web page, show . . .*
- *Drought and Death go hand in hand: Johan Matzinsky exposes the hidden costs of the ongoing climate crisis.*
- *Drowned boy had mental health difficulties.*

I clicked on the link.

Drowned boy had mental health difficulties

Medical experts today are speculating that five-year-old Lucien Ardingly, who drowned on The Well on Friday was born with fetal alcohol syndrome and may have had significant emotional and mental problems. These could have led to him harming himself either deliberately or accidentally. These factors, combined with poor parenting and a traveler lifestyle, may well have led to feelings of low self-worth. "It is likely his state of mind deteriorated when he was deserted by his mother and left in the hands of a grandmother already suffering from delusions of grandeur," said Melanie

Unwine, Consultant Child Psychologist. (See p. 7: Why are so many of our children committing suicide?)

I didn't see page 7. I returned to the main site.

• *Did this Grandmother sleepwalk her way to murder?*
• *Grandpa or Pedo Pa?*

I hesitated, then expanded the headline.

Fact: Ardingly is not the boy's real grandfather.

Fact: Ardingly had moved out of the family cottage and lived a solitary existence in a barn on the isolated property.

Fact: Ardingly is suspected of having removed all the boy's clothes while looking after him the night before he was murdered.

The most frightening fact of all: Mark Ardingly was investigated for child pornography when he worked for a local authority and was NEVER CONVICTED.

The police need to be asking questions — NOW!

The taste of doubt. The police confirmed that the only footprints found by the Wellspring were those of the Sisters, Sister Amelia, Mark, Lucien, and me, no drought-deranged outsiders, no vengeful locals. Him or me, then. Or the Sisters.

"What about the Sisters? Sister Amelia?" I asked the policewoman.

"They have been released without charge as well."

"As well as who?"

"As well as your husband."

"Where was he then?"

"You'll have to ask him. I am not at liberty to say."

I did ask him. He told me. The medium of the Internet, which had painted him as a potential pedophile and thrown our lives into chaos in London, had this time put on a suit and tie and provided him with an alibi. Analysis of his laptop had shown he had been online at, as the pathologist chose to call it, the "likely time of death." There were Google searches recorded for flats to rent, Christmas tree farms in Scotland, our solicitor's address, Alcoholics Anonymous, how to drown yourself . . . and there was a half-finished letter evidently addressed to me, last edited at 2:07 a.m. I didn't ask about the letter; I knew what it was. Apparently, Mark told me, computer evidence like this is not "conclusive," as the police say, but it was enough to let him off the hook for the time being.

Nothing has been conclusive since that night, but conclusions are all that I am interested in now.

There were things I wanted to ask the Sisters as well, and at some point I was given permission to visit them. I found them the same, but different, and my questions stuck in my throat. Sister Amelia was in the hub with Eve, updating the site because the followers were worried, their faith wavering, but their hope for rain uncompromised. They told me how they had been questioned, but in the end, of course, as Amelia said, no Sister is ever alone. They were all each other's alibis—that's how the police framed it; they were all each sister's keeper, according to the word of the Rose. Later, I sat for a while alone with Dorothy, who was tearstained and shrunken, wrapped tightly in a blanket. She told me that they had questioned her repeatedly, not just about what she had been doing but about the others too, and she had become confused. Some things seemed significant only in hindsight; she said she had never felt old until then.

"It was straightforward about Eve and Amelia, they just went to bed as usual, but Jack?" She dried her eyes and started making some herbal tea. "I didn't know what to do. She begged me."

"What was wrong?" Sitting at the little fold-down table, I stared at the watercolor half painted on the pad in front of me, mesmerized by the way it captured the winter rain falling at an angle across the bare poplars, struck by the desolate feeling which came from this painting of heaven.

I was barely listening, but Dorothy continued talking regardless. "Sleep is very hard for her. I often wake and find her gone, so it wasn't unusual. But she's been so ill, Ruth. She was a complete mess while the police were around, totally paranoid and deluded. I wondered if it triggered bad memories for her, you know, when she was a child. She kept saying the police would have her sectioned."

"So what are you worried about, Dorothy?"

"I prayed, Ruth. I prayed so hard, but I couldn't hear the answer. Do you remember asking me once if anyone ever spoke back when I prayed? Well, this time, nothing. But I had to say something. So I said she was here, asleep with me, in this camper, all night, until dawn when she got up and went out to pray."

"Where does she go when she can't sleep?"

"Usually to the hub, now it's cold. In the summer, she just sat outside and looked at the stars until she felt calm again. She couldn't harm anyone, Ruth, you and I know that."

I took the mug from her, inhaled the sweet lavender of forgetfulness and rosemary of remembrance. "Dorothy, you are the most truthful person I know. You mustn't worry."

"I think I have told them everything," she sobbed.

The door opened and the cold air rushed in, making us wrap the rugs around us just a little bit tighter, holding on to the writings on the table to stop the answers blowing away. "I am sure you did," said Sister Amelia.

―――――

My boy gone? Never to sit with me again here? On the sofa, reading together? Never?

―――――

A postmortem report—Contents:

Autopsy Fact Sheet
Historical Summary
Examination Type, Date, Time, Place, Assistants, Attendees
Presentation, Clothing, Personal Effects, Associated Items
Evidence of Medical Intervention
Postmortem Changes
Postmortem Imaging Studies
Identification
Evidence of Injury
External Examination
Internal Examination
Histology Cassette Listing
Microscopic Descriptions
Toxicology Results, Laboratory Results, Ancillary Procedure
　　　Results
Pathologic Diagnoses
Summary and Comments

Cause of Death Statement:

　　Freshwater aspiration leading to systemic hypoxemia, causing myocardial depression; reflex pulmonary vasoconstriction and altered pulmonary capillary permeability contributing to pulmonary edema; a fall onto the back of the head resulting in an abraded scalp surface, the undermined areas of scalp infiltrated with liquefied fat.

An interim certificate of fact of death has been issued by the coroner.

Inquest adjourned.

Body released for burial.

CHAPTER TWENTY-SEVEN

Dates—December 25, December 31, January 1—all passed, unmarked. Lucien's funeral was the first and last time we were all together: Mark, Angie, and me. I think now of the missing fathers—of Angie's father, Lucien's father, Mark's father. Even my own father comes before me as an absence, fathering away in test tubes behind blue curtains in an attempt to further the line. There were mothers missing as well.

The police had finally traced Angie, but she wanted nothing to do with me, that's what they said.

"She is going to find it hard to come here," I remember him saying. "You must see that. The fact that nobody's been charged. It will just be too hard for her."

When he had stopped crying, Mark shaved, had his hair cut, and moved back in from the barn. He was close to me at those times, physically close to me. He held me when I could hardly stand, he sat with his hand on mine, he slept on the sofa just so I could hear him breathing in the night. He listened to my silence and to my noise, the harsh sobbing from a hoarse throat and a sandpaper soul. And when the Sisters came to visit, I heard him, from my bedroom window, lying for me: "She is sleeping. She will come to find you when she is ready."

Mark lied for me and about me too. "I'm sorry," he said, "but that's the message. I am only the messenger."

Did he want me for himself? How could he possibly have wanted me physically those weeks following Lucien's drowning—I was red-eyed and hysterical, the only bodily contact I craved being that of my own nails scratching my own skin to see my own blood bubble. How could he possibly have wanted a wife who he thought might have murdered her grandson?

"It's a long time since you needed me," he said, helping me to bed.

"She bleeds," the Sisters said on the blog. "She bleeds for the loss of innocent life."

———

It took me a long time, but I finally put into words the unmentionable question.

Mark had braved the world outside our gates, driven to a supermarket some way away and replenished our supplies. He was trying to get me to eat a little, but my stomach knotted at the smell of food. Nevertheless I was sitting with him, the warmth of the Rayburn pretending that the kitchen could once again be the heart of a house. Mark had returned to a conversation we had been having earlier, admitting that on the night of Lucien's death, after I had left, he had written to his solicitor, putting his half of The Well in trust and had put the deposit down on a bed-sit.

"It's not good for us—for you—to stay here. You must see that. You're like a prisoner here. You should leave."

"Here is as good and as bad as anywhere else."

"I agree anywhere will be difficult, but away from here there is at least the chance of recovery." The word alone was enough to drive me from the room, but he caught me and sat me down again. "OK, not recovery. I'm sorry. But at least a space to think."

The rubber omelet lay on my plate like a piece of plastic food from a toddler's kitchen play set. I could not make any connection between it, the eggs that had been broken for it, and our hens which had laid the eggs. Someone would need to look after the hens if I went. I don't know who that would be. Where would I go? But they were all paltry questions compared to the one which ground my cells to dust.

"Do you think I could have done it?"

"Not now, Ruth."

I repeated the question, my mouth contorting in an exaggerated fashion as though he was a lip-reader. "I am asking you if you think I killed Lucien."

Mark had finished eating. He got up and stood with his back against the Rayburn, his hands wrapped stiffly around the silver rail that ran the length of the cooker. His prolonged pause was enough.

I felt the prongs of the fork against the thin skin of my wrist. "I take it you do."

"I don't know what you want me to say."

"The truth."

So he answered truthfully, or so I thought, using the grammar of comparatives and mathematics of probability. More likely, less likely, unlikely. That the Ruth he knew and had been married to for over twenty years loved Lucien more than anything—he knew that to his cost. Almost more than anything.

"What do you mean by almost?" I was now the inquisitor, fierce in my devotion to unpalatable answers.

"Could you honestly say which was more important to you—Lucien or your Rose?"

"I know now," I said.

"But then you were a different woman. So if you are asking me if Ruth could have done this to Lucien, I'd have to ask you, which Ruth?"

He held my hair back as I vomited.

He never asked me if I thought he had done it.

Where should you bury the boy you probably killed, or what is left of the body of the boy after they have taken him and carved him up like a frog on a school bench, as if that could ever explain what had happened? You could take him down from the cross, roll the boulder in front of the tomb, and sit there and weep. You could give him to The Well because The Well would water his grave and let buttercups grow on the unnatural mound. Sister Amelia thought the service should be here. It seems she wrote to me every day—songs, prayers, blessings, advice, psalms, poems, parables, letters—but only a few of them slipped past my censor.

> *My Ruth,*
> *We have been praying about Lucien, about how She would want us to mark his passing. Let him be laid to rest with the Blessing of the Rose to remind us that just as the Rose lies in the desert earth, seemingly dead to all who pass a straggle of sticks on a dusty highway, so Lucien seems dead to us, his little body no longer breathing the breath we recognize. But like the Rose, he lives.*
> *I told you once that everything that blooms on the earth is already written in the bud: believe this and you will find peace. We await your return.*
>
> *Amelia*

Texts of all sorts, she wrote, none of them true. Mark found the letter and told me that what Sister Amelia wanted was nothing more and nothing less than a sacrificial burial mound over which she could gloat. I don't know which was more horrifying—the possible truth in what he said or the fact that he was disturbed enough to even think it.

In the end it wasn't my decision—I was not capable of making decisions. I wanted to keep Lucien's body in my bed until the decay of the rotting bones seeped its poison into my living frame and took me with him. I wanted to burn his body on a fire on the top of First Field and let the ashes drift on the wind across the drought-dried land of this country until we were all nothing but particles of hopelessness, and then I would shout at the green well, you are a deceiver of men. I wanted to stand in the bland atheism of a suburban crematorium, as I did for my mother and for my father, and know that there is traffic and deodorant and queues of mourners muddling up their dead and weeds in the gravel of the graves and that is all. I wanted all of these things and nothing. I did not want to bury him at all. I wanted him back. Though you speak with the tongues of men and angels, but have not love, you are nothing. Though you bury children with bells and rituals, but have not Lucien, you have nothing.

"I am going to contact Angie," Mark told me. "We need to talk about the funeral."

Mark went to collect her from the station. I waited, looking out the window at the hateful rain, feeling physically sick. Finally, they arrived. I stood out in the raw north wind, watching the car slewing its way down the track now riddled with puddles and greasy with mud. There was a driver and a passenger. My husband. My daughter. They had been a long time, far longer than it took to drive from Middleton Parkway. They had been talking, about me, presumably.

Mark got out of the car first and went back to open the door for Angie. She climbed out like an old woman does on coming home from the hospital, uncertain that her legs will carry her to the familiar front door or that she will ever be able to resume the life she had before it all went black.

I fell to my knees. "Forgive me; say you'll forgive me."

"Please get up, Ruth," Mark said. "I don't think we need any more kneeling."

Even my kneeling was misconstrued. I got to my feet. Angie froze, inches from me, a blank measureless distance away from me, as if her stare had brought down a glass pane between us. Mark moved to the fence and looked out over the fields, where he stood like a visitor—all closeness had vanished in the space of the journey. Angie had homework once, when she was in primary school, all about proverbs. A bird in the hand, watched pots, stitches in time—we were a fount of wisdom, but even then I'm not sure anyone cited the unspeakable: two's company, three's none. It came back to me there, standing in the drive, knowing the "auld" alliances had shifted again. Angie started shivering uncontrollably, so Mark led her inside and sat her on the sofa, and I could see in her face the bloated dullness of overmedicated grief. And something else, the thing I feared: her eyes were pinprick black, she licked her lips continuously—they say if you know an addict well enough, you'll recognize her ticks. When I sat down next to her, I raised the sleeve of her thick, llama wool sweater. She jerked her arm away and ran from me across the room, pushing the armchair between me and her, shaking in the corner, screaming at me, clawing at the cushions.

"What the fuck did you think I was going to do, Mum? Pray?"

And . . .

"You killed him. Whatever happened, I will always, always hold you responsible for the fact that the only thing I ever loved is gone."

And . . .

"I loved him so much. You've no idea how much I loved him."

And . . .

"You should have drowned in that fucking pond, it should have been you."

And and and . . . before sinking out of sight into the dust and dropped coins in the corner of the room.

Mark prowled around the silence. He straightened the photo of us on day one at The Well, he adjusted the airflow to the stove so that it roared, he ran his finger along the top of his desk and pulled open and pushed shut the drawers, with their receipts and dried-out biros and old issues of *Trout and Salmon*. He escorted Angie from her hiding place to the stool in front of the stove, where she sat consumed by the flames.

After a long time, a very long time, she spoke again. "I'm sorry, Dad, but I've got to."

Mark looked at me and then turned his back on us. "I know you have to," he said.

She swallowed, then spoke robotically. "On the way back from the station, Dad and I promised each other that all we would talk about would be arrangements for the funeral. Everything else would be too difficult, that's what I thought." Angie sat picking at her cuticles until they bled, and wiped her hands on her long skirt. "But I can't stop myself. You need to tell me what happened."

Forcing my hands away from my eyes, I shook my head and was about to speak, but she interrupted.

"I know what the police have told me, and Mark and the press and the world and his wife—but you? Nothing." The mechanical voice was spluttering. "You cut me out. Once you knew I had a phone again, you made one call, screaming like a banshee, like it was your son who was floating facedown in a bog, then nothing. Not a word." Pause. She hit herself, hard on the head with her fist, again and again. "Now, right now. I want to hear it from you. In words of one syllable. You owe me that much. What went on here?"

I curled up even tighter. "I don't know."

"I just don't believe that. Deep down, you must know something."

"I don't. I promise you I don't. And you never got in touch with me. How was I meant to explain? How do you think I feel? People say I did it, that I did it in a trance . . ."

"She was not asking how you feel. She asked a simple question. This is not all about you." As Mark swung round, pointing his finger at me, his elbow caught the glass heron on the half-moon table and it smashed, the light from the window picking out some of the shards on the wooden floor like dew on the flints in the plowed fields.

My mouth watered—I wanted this violence. Voice was telling me that Mark was coming to beat me and I was answering back, yes, beat me so hard that blood pours from gashes across my face and scars me, so that other people will see the stigmata and say, there goes the woman who said she was a saint but has turned out to be a murderer. He had done it once. Don't let him hold back now. I craved punishment, but my longed-for torturer collapsed in the armchair, all fight gone.

Silent in a sea of broken glass, I bent down and started picking up the shards one by one. "I don't know what happened," I said finally, as I knelt. "If I knew, I would tell you. Please believe me. I spend every second reliving that day, that night, trying to find the one moment when I could have done something differently and Lucien, Lucien . . ."

"Would be here now," Angie finished my sentence sarcastically. "Do you know what, Mum, you never thought I should have had him. You didn't either, Mark. You thought I should have quietly gone down the clinic like every other teenage pregnant schoolgirl. Well, you've got the end you wanted now, haven't you?"

It wasn't true. I loved Lucien from the moment I heard he was going to be.

"And then you thought you could do a better job than me. Don't worry, Mark's told me everything, how you drove him out of the house, how he had to look after Lucien, feed him, bathe him, while you prayed for the rest of the fucking world. Everyone else's favorite holy mother . . ."

Mark's eyes met mine. Oh, yes, they had been talking in the car.

"And he told me all about how he rang up and Lucien, my son, answered your phone and was crying because he was on his own." She started crying herself and that was unbearable and it was almost impossible to make sense of the words. "You said you'd choose him. You promised. You said The Well would keep him safe, I remember you saying that, exactly that. You should have told me when I phoned if you couldn't cope."

"We should never have let you go without leaving us a contact number—" started Mark.

But Angie interrupted, anger now providing coherence. "Why did I ever think you would do a better job with him than you did with me?"

"Angie!" Mark moved over and took my place next to her, his hand around her shoulders. "Not now, let's not go there again. Let's talk about the funeral and then leave. That's what you came here for."

Standing there with a fistful of broken glass in front of the two of them all wrapped together, I couldn't let it go unsaid, the one truth in all of this. "You know I loved Lucien, Angie. When you weren't well . . ."

"When I was off my face, when I was stoned, when I was fucked . . . say it, Mum, like it is."

"When you were using, I tried to be like . . ."

"Like a mother to him."

The bitterness eventually exhausted itself and curled up in front of the fire. We sat, the three of us, Mark and Angie on the sofa, me on the floor, back against the wall, and we whispered our thoughts about the funeral so as not to reawaken it. Mark suggested the church at Little Lennisford.

"The C of E church. It's the only safe place because it's the one thing none of us believe in," he said.

CHAPTER TWENTY-EIGHT

Word of the world outside reached me mainly via Mark and the policeman at the door. Apparently, the whole camp of followers of the Rose which had set up all along the verges of the lane—their pop-up tents tied to the hedges, snapping branches off the hesitantly budding hawthorns, the wheels of their camper vans obliterating the early snowdrops—had been cleared by the police. I had seen them, briefly, as I was driven to the police station, and they had started the chant when they realized who was in the car:

"Behold the Rose of Jericho!"

By the time I was driven back a day later, the entrance to The Well looked even more like something from a drug-induced hallucination, crowded with day-trippers, some of whom came to the shrine with motorway service station roses, others who fought with the police to bang on the hood of the car in order to berate a child killer. Some, I guess, came simply to dip their toe in the rippling pond of drama in the otherwise flat surface of their lives. To me, in the back of the police car, this was a virtual reality scenario in which I had no avatar.

They told me about fifty or so online followers had materialized and traveled from across the country to "be together at this time of crisis." They had been given permission to camp in the fields on the other side of the lane, and who can blame the farmer, who must have hoped that either their magic or their money would rub off on him. On one of the rare occasions I ventured out of the cottage, I saw the flicker of their bonfire and flares in the distance. According to the Internet, they weren't alone. Tiny tented camps had sprung up wherever there was a patch of vacant ground close to a community standpipe. The images showed women standing around braziers handing out roses to commuters, lampposts strung with banners proclaiming THE ROSE BECAUSE IT RAINS! Some with a picture of the chosen one and the slogan INNOCENCE PERSONIFIED written underneath.

YesterdayinParliament.com reported that MPs struggled to express condolences, but it was clear that they neither wanted to condone the sect nor offend those caught up in the rising tide of religious fervor in the country. Instead, the MPs, while not wishing in any way to prejudice the ongoing inquiry into the tragic death of Lucien Ardingly, asked earnestly whether everything possible was being done to ascertain the reason for the continued fertility of the land at The Well; they put down questions for the under secretary of state for education about the effectiveness of home-school liaison in rural primary schools and provision for the monitoring of the education of traveler children; they demanded data on social services assessments of children in informal kinship care; they asked the minister for gender equality to place on record her opinion of single-sex religious cults; and they quizzed the home secretary about the arrangements that were to be put in place to ensure that Lucien Ardingly could be buried with dignity at a private ceremony, as the family had requested. Most of all, they wanted assurances from the prime minister that nothing like this would ever be allowed to happen again.

Dignity. Private. Family. How to achieve such things in those circumstances?

On the morning of Lucien's funeral, while it was still dark, diversions were put in place around Middleton. The entire four-acre field between the old Bridge pub and the river had been set aside for the press, who were now parked up in their vans with masts and satellite equipment. Apparently, they broadcast throughout the night. Who for? I asked the policeman stamping his feet on duty at the front door. He told me audiences were very hungry first thing in the morning. Those attending the funeral needed to be on a list of approved mourners. Even the organist needed clearance.

"And are you going to stay the night before the funeral, here at The Well?" asked the Detective Inspector with the thankless task of making a cortège run smoothly.

"Does it matter?" asked Angie.

"It's just that it's easier for us to protect you if you're here—there's a clean run with an escort down the lane to the main road and straight through to the church. If you're still staying at the motor lodge at Middleton, it makes it a bit more complicated, that's all. We can't close the dual carriageway."

She couldn't stay here. No one could sleep here.

Mark made the decision. "I will stay with Angie in the Travel Lodge," he said. "We will drive up here early in the morning and then we can all go together to the church."

"Together?" asked Angie.

Mark nodded at her, then asked the DI, "Will that work?"

The DI stood up also. "We'll make it work, sir," he said.

I will sleep alone, then, I thought, tonight and for the rest of my life.

The medication they'd given me wiped out both my memory and my ability to anticipate, so it was the sweep of car headlights and two slamming doors which woke me to a day which I greeted with a combination of relief and vomiting. Downstairs I could hear someone filling the kettle. I opened the shutters as my first step towards acknowledging the birth of the most deformed of mornings. Mark was sitting on the stile to First Field. Had it all gone to plan, he would have been preparing to lamb, but the barren sheep loitered around the hedges as if conscious of their purposeless existence. It was not raining, but snowing. Births, marriages, and deaths—and all of them shrouded in snow. I could almost count the flakes as they landed on the black sleeve of Mark's coat, his turned-up collar and his dark hair holding their form for the briefest of seconds, but before I could make sense of it, the flurry was over and Mark had come back into the house.

Sitting on the top stairs, I eavesdropped on my own husband and daughter.

"You've got snowflakes on your hair."

"Is Mum up?"

The clinking of a spoon on a mug.

"I can't go up there again."

Two hours, more than two hours without ceasing she had wailed in his bedroom the evening before, with Mark shut in his study and me out on the porch in the dry-eyed darkness, both in our terrible, separate silences, hearing it, before Mark had persuaded her to leave. Keening, they call it in Ireland, and that is the right word, the endless knife-sharp pain of it.

"Don't worry. I'll go in a minute. There's no need for her to wake up yet, the day will be long enough anyway."

The spitting of the kettle, newly filled, being put back on the Rayburn.

"Fucking mess this place."

Tap running. Crash of pans being put in the cupboard. I imagined her scrubbing the surfaces, like me, desperate for cleanliness. I got up slowly, but the floorboards creaked under my feet.

"That's her."

The tap was left running, so the pump thundered into action, summoning water from The Well. I pulled Mark's old dressing gown around me, reluctant to get dressed, and got as far as the doorway to the kitchen. Angie ignored me. "Do you think if I leave it long enough, it will run out?" she said. "Then that'll be the end of it all."

"Your mother asked me that once." Mark gently pried her hands off the taps, turned them off, and then hugged her as she sobbed. Only when they moved apart did I feel able to step forward.

Someone had organized a formal undertaker's car.

"I think Lucien would have liked it," said Mark, sensing Angie's hatred of the thing. "He liked the idea that there was the right sort of car for the right sort of job."

"Remember how cross he got because the window cleaner arrived in a van that looked like the postman," I said.

"When was that?" said Angie.

"I don't know, love. London some time. Must have been when we were looking after him." Words chosen by a devil with a long-handled fork.

"I can't do it, Mark," sobbed Angie, and I didn't really know what she was talking about and what they were talking to the police about until I saw Mark helping her into the back of the unmarked escort car and calling back to me that he was sorry and it was only as far as the church, before he joined her and slammed the door. I got into the funeral car and sat on my own in the middle of the long backseat, big enough for three, four at a push. Ahead, the police motorcyclist skidded slightly on the mud at the junction of the track with the lane and the cars slowed. Then I saw them, the Sisters and not just Sister Amelia and the others, but all the Sisters from the camp over the road as well, dressed in white and lining either side of the lane. In front, Mark was leaning out of the car window and shouting, but the sound was turned down inside my coffin.

We crawled past them, each face tearstained, each hand holding high a Rose of Jericho, each mouth moving silently in prayer. Dorothy looked as an old woman should at a time of grieving; Jack, dust and leaves falling from her Rose as her hands shook; both of them hand in hand with Eve, trying hard to stare the future in the face. Suddenly, Sister Amelia stepped out in front of us, arms outstretched, forcing the car to stop.

"Behold a Chosen One of the Rose of Jericho!" she cried.

The driver was blaring his horn, several police ran towards Amelia and dragged her out of the way, her long hair knotted in their hands, her white robe scuffed up to her hips, and her bare feet scraping the gravel. Some of the Sisters ran to help her, scratching at the policeman and screaming, tugging Sister Amelia's hands; others took up the chant, louder and louder.

"Behold a Chosen One, the Rose of Jericho! Behold the innocent!"

Hiding my eyes in my hands, I rocked back and forward in my solitary black cavern. "No! No! No!" I repeated over and over again until the rhythm of the journey told me that we had gathered speed and had left the Sisters behind. In my head I fought with Voice, who wanted to come to the funeral.

The endless aisle was mine alone; Mark and Angie had walked on ahead, arm in arm, and were already seated. The half-turned faces of the strangers in the congregation bloated and contorted in my sight as I passed, and I heard the whispering cease and resume like the silence between waves as I was pulled towards the altar, eyeball to eyeball with the crucified Christ. I slipped apologetically into the pew to sit beside the two who were my husband and my daughter. Whatever they all thought, these people who had come to mourn, we had one thing in common, we were all ill at ease with death and religion, uncomfortable with the offer made by a thousand years of stone and stained glass. Someone had filled the plain country church with lilies, and their scent blended with the smell of damp hymn books and polish and the low moan of the organ. Some of the travelers had come, including Charley; if anyone was going to help Angie get clean again, I thought it would be him. They had brought their kids, girls in woolly tights and long skirts with bunches of snowdrops in their hands, and boys in jeans, unable to sit still. Henni came up to Angie and said he had brought along a photo of Lucien's bike. He thought he might stick it to the coffin with Blu-Tack because Lucien would like that, to take a picture of his bike with him when he went. Angie nodded, kissing him on the head, and said it was very kind and he should do that. So the vicar and all the mourners and the policemen at the back of the church and the lady vetted and brought in to play the organ and me and Mark and Angie all watched as Henni walked the length of the aisle in his squeaking sneakers and stuck the photo of the bike to the lid of the wicker coffin.

The coffin was small, so impossibly small.

There were hymns—I am not sure who chose them. "Lord of all hopefulness, Lord of all joy, whose trust, ever childlike, no cares could destroy . . ." "A thousand ages in your sight are like an evening gone." Standing up. *Gone*, said Voice. Sitting down. Kneeling down. Gone, gone, gone. Sitting up. My body a robot, my mind a black screen virus. Mark holding Angie, Angie weeping and weeping, and me, not a tear to be dragged from my dry sockets. Not even in the graveyard, where the diggers had brought in a mechanical digger the day before to help them get through the packed, dry earth; not even as they lowered the coffin; not even when Angie kissed his special duck and dropped it into the dull grave; not even when the children threw their flowers into the chasm.

Not even now.

Wordless, Angie left me at the graveside. I turned around and she was gone, leaving no promises or forgiveness behind her. A doctor and a policeman took me back to The Well. Mark apparently managed the wake in the village hall and then left without ever coming back here again. The doctor was a kind man. He stayed with me, told me later that the statement had been a good idea; he hoped it might put an end to the queues of people waiting to pay their respects.

Statement?

The family would like to thank everyone for their kindness and sympathy expressed over recent weeks. They cannot find the words to say what a gap the death of Lucien has left behind in their lives. He was the most wonderful son and grandson anyone could hope for and loved by everyone who ever met him. They know that there has been a lot of speculation throughout the country about The Well and about the family's future plans for the farm. What is important to the family is that this special land is now used in such a way as will best benefit the rest of the country suffering so terribly as a result of the drought, and then Lucien's death may not have been in vain. They will therefore be leaving the land shortly and making legal arrangements for the change of ownership to a charitable trust.

The family now ask to be left to grieve their terrible loss in private.

"It was sensible of Mark to write it," said the doctor. "He said he thought you had enough on your plate without having to write statements for the press."

That was his public valedictory speech; for me he had a different message.

Dear Ruth,

This is the hardest letter I shall ever have to write, but I cannot put it off any longer. I am leaving. By the time you read this, I will have left and this time I will not be coming back. I am sorry.

I wanted to stay. The Well was a dream for both of us to start with. It didn't belong to you or me, but it has driven us apart. We've tried every permutation now. Together in the house, then separate bedrooms, then separate houses, the next logical step was always going to be for one of us to go, but then all this. The last few weeks I kidded myself that you needed me again, but I was

wrong. You have not needed me for a long time. You have had
your daughter, your grandson, your sisters, your god—I have been
way down your list for a very long time. Since Lucien's death you
have allowed me to feed you and count your pills, but that is not
enough and I am going.

If I could share your beliefs, I would, but I can't. I don't have
any other answers, as you so often remind me, but I think that
to rely on some godcentric explanation of how and why we have
ended up at The Well is weakness, not strength. It is delusional.
As I have tried to tell you so many times, out of love not malice,
you are being exploited by Sister Amelia. I hope you stay away
from her. You need medical help. Unlike Angie, I do not think the
Sisters are harmless.

I think we agree on one thing—that The Well is bigger than
us. I've invested everything in it as our smallholding, but it's not
a small thing, is it? It is not and never really has been ours to
own—if it offers answers to the drought, they belong to everyone.
So I have signed my half of the Government Temporary Lease
Order and lodged it with our solicitors. I have not received any
money for this yet. It never was to do with the money. Surely you
know me well enough to believe that. This March would have
been our wedding anniversary. You have meant everything to me,
and perhaps that is why it has been impossible to accept anything
less than all of you.

Do you remember those lists you used to write for me and
Angie, if you were away for a conference? Jazz dance on Thursday, don't forget the lasagne in the freezer, Angie's reading book
due back Friday—all that. I want to write one for you—check the
sheep every day for foot rot, the supplement for the Tamworths is
running out, the brake lights on the trailer need fixing . . . I want
to remind you to look after yourself, to eat properly, to lock the
back door, not to use jump leads on the Land Rover, to steer clear

of the Internet . . . but you haven't done any of these things for months, so what's the point in me saying it now. So what if they all die? For my own sanity I need to be able to walk away, so I will stop now. I need to look after my own grief. You can look after yourself.

I have left all the paperwork, financial information, etc., in my desk. I've downloaded all The Well paperwork onto your laptop in a file called Leaving. There is some money in the bank, but it won't last forever—at some point we will need to talk about that. Maybe I will ask the solicitor to get in touch. Do not try to contact me. I will not reply. It is over.

I don't know what I'm going to do. Will says he knows someone who may need some law work done, but my heart will not be in it.

You have left me as surely as I have left you. I am sorry I hit you. I am not a violent man, but you have punched me so hard that there are times when I can no longer breathe. Maybe this will all be over soon. Maybe it will start to rain. But until we know who murdered our grandson, it is impossible to think of forgiveness. I hope against hope it was not you.

You can have all my love, I will never need it for anyone else.

Mark

CHAPTER TWENTY-NINE

Remembrance comes at a cost and does not travel alone. I wake up with its companion beside me, its cold body spooned against mine despite the heat of the day, its rancid breath against the back of my neck causing me to pull my knees up to my chest and howl like a dog. Before Hugh's death, I was beginning to think it might have packed up its leaden suitcases, laden with grief and deceit, and dragged them down the stairs and out. But it was hiding all along, biding its time, and here it is again.

Staring at the ceiling, I mock my small steps forwards with my strides backwards. At some point during the morning I turn onto my side, look out the window, and see the wheat sprouting among the thistles in First Field and the regimented experimental crops on the government plots. Here are the functions of all living things. Be born. Feed. Defecate. Grow. Reproduce. Die. The rats which scuttle near the compost heap are more accomplished at all of these functions than I will ever be. They do not, as far as I know, kill themselves.

My hand reaches for my thigh and feels the raised welt of the branded pattern there; it does this often, my hand, as if it is worried I might forget something. At this moment it strikes me as likely that I could have killed Lucien. His face appears from the knot and twist of the grain of the floorboards and confirms my guilt, not some abstract moral responsibility but the physical act: waking him up in the early hours of the morning, putting my finger over his mouth to shush him, whispering in his ear about a dawn adventure. I lace his sneakers for him, double bows and ends tucked in. He is sleepy. I hang the rose around his neck and in the dim light my fingers know how to tie the knot by heart. I search for his hand hidden under the long sleeve of the green sweater and then lead him down the stairs. He is awake now and excited.

"Where are we going, Granny R, and why?"

"Look how dark it is, Granny R."

It is very dark and very cold. There are no stars. There is no moon. We hold hands, Lucien so he cannot get lost in the night, me all the better to lose him. At the top of the field, we look out over Cadogan Hill; there are no lights on in the distant farmhouses, no one wants to wake to see this.

Voice tells us to hurry. Dawn will break soon.

"Are we going to the Well, Granny R, is that where we're going?"

We are going to the Well.

He is frightened now, climbing the stile into the wood. I can feel the tightness of his grip on my hand as he clutches on to the one thing that will harm him. We arrive at the black water and Lucien bends down and touches the surface with his hand. It is slow to wake up and recoils drowsily to the edges of the pond where it cowers in the reeds; the water itself does not want to shake hands with evil.

"You're not going to leave me here, are you, Granny R?"

Yes and no.

"How deep it is, Granny R. Can you touch the bottom?"

Yes, and rise again.

We sit on the cold earth and he leans against me, saying he feels a little sick and can we go home now, come again another time, but I tell him the water makes everything all right.

"Will we see the magic?"

Yes, I say, but we have to do things properly for the magic to work. Follow me.

Hand in hand, we stand in the cold waters of the Wellspring, the mud sludge sucking us in, Lucien giggling and shivering. One more step. One more step along the road we go, one more step along the world I know. From the old things to the new, keep me traveling along with you. I start to sing to him, quietly, and he joins in because he knows this song. He sings like a girl. He has hair like a girl, I feel it in my fingers. But he has the genitals of a boy. Deeper, says Voice, go deeper.

"How cold it is, Granny R."

I tell him that when you are cold, the best thing is to go deeper. The cold, the pain you have in your tummy, the fear you feel in your fists, when you are in deep enough, they all disappear with the magic. You just have to believe.

"I do believe, Granny R, honestly. I do believe, but I'm very cold."

Trust me.

He lies back against my arms, but when the water splashes on his face, he screams. Suddenly he has a thousand arms and fingers and they are scratching at my clothes and pulling my hair. Stumbling in the dark, I lurch into him, he beats me, kicks me in the breast, we fight like drunks, he half stands, half slips, and his head flies backwards, crack, against the old moss steps and then he slumps, slides into the water. I hold his perfect, bleeding head under the surface. Just once, feebly, his hands reach out for something to cling to, but finding nothing they open to float like flowers. He stills, becomes beautiful again, and I allow his pale face to surface to meet the moonlight, his lips puckered like a rosebud.

Voice says I have done well, and then I am home in my bed and the house itself is weightless and outside the dawn is colored like a rainbow.

———

"Ruth, are you OK?"

"I didn't know you were back."

Boy feels my forehead. "You're very hot."

Rolling away from him, I huddle under the duvet, shaking. He thinks I am ill. He is right, I am sick to the core.

"What's been going on this last week? I read the log; you've hardly got up . . ."

"You need to leave me."

"I'll go and get you some paracetamol. You need a doctor."

"No. And I don't want your paracetamol. And, you know what, Boy, I don't want you either. Go back to your barracks."

Boy puts his head in his hands. Grabbing his arm, I lean forward and press my advantage. "For God's sake, go. It's pathetic—me a menopausal head case and you nothing but an adolescent looking for a cause. You've picked the wrong one. And do you know what? Sooner or later you'll conform, get a house and a job and wife and kids, and all this will be a story you tell at supper parties."

My fists pummel him as hard as my words, beating against his oh-so-traditional successful youth, his ordinariness, his future, hating him because he has so little to lose, so much life left to live, and I have lost it all already—and Lucien never even got to try. But he does not flinch under my blows and he does not leave and I cannot carry on, so I collapse, exhausted, and turn away from him. Sit there, I think, if you must, and catch my disease. In the silence which follows, the thing that really needs to be said stirs in my stomach and organizes itself into words.

"I have spent the week remembering the worst times. But it's been worth it. I think I killed Lucien," I tell him. "I think I have remembered it all."

Still, he won't leave. His shoulders are a little lower, his chest rises a little higher when he breathes. He doesn't look at me when he speaks.

"What do you remember?"

"Details. How I tied his laces, how he hit his head, how I held him under, my footprints in the mud." I sit up, cross-legged. "It's a relief. I can tell everyone now, be charged, go to prison. It will all be so straightforward. And no"—I stop him interrupting—"don't say I didn't do it, because you have never quite got it, how mad I am, how miserable, how delusional. Actually"—it seems I have been searching a lifetime for the right word and suddenly I find it—"how selfish."

Boy moves away and sits on the broad windowsill where the light behind silhouettes him and his shadow falls across the bed. It means I cannot see his face very well, but his voice gives away the fact that he is struggling.

Boy speaks slowly, in a measured tone. "I think you are a very beautiful woman—not like that, I don't mean physically, I mean all of you. I don't know if you murdered Lucien, I've never been sure. You never tied his laces in a double bow, did you? He hated that, it said so in the press—that you would never have tied his laces in a double bow. Then there's the sweater and the wooden rose, you've never remembered where they are. And footprints mean nothing. Everyone—Amelia, all the Sisters, Mark, Lucien, you, the world and his wife—was at the Wellspring that evening."

"You just don't want to believe it, Boy. But you must. Piles of wet clothes in the garden, me exhausted in the morning. And who else would Lucien have gone with, in the middle of the night? I didn't know what I was doing half the time when I was awake, let alone when I was asleep. Face it, Boy, I could have done it."

Boy throws open the window to let some air in, then paces to the other end of the bedroom and stands defiantly. "And it wasn't just you in the frame, there's Mark—from what I gathered in the news, he had pretty much lost the plot by then. And what about the Sisters?" He presses on through my silence. "A cult like that can do anything; think of all the unbelievable things that have been done in the name of religion throughout history. I've told you I don't get religion. I never met these Sisters. I don't doubt they were good people, you seemed to trust them, but that's the thing, isn't it? Those mass suicides in Texas, suicide bombs, 9/11 for God's sake . . ."

"No lectures, please. I've thought about all those things too. Yes, there are other people, other ways of telling the story," I acknowledge. "It doesn't make this version any the less true."

Boy ignores me, sits back down on the bed and takes my hands in his. "I don't know if you killed him or not. Even if you did, it wouldn't change things, because it wouldn't be the real you who had done that. I don't know how to put it."

"Well, don't bother to try, it won't change anything." I pull back, he holds on tight.

"It's like thinking it was my mother, or someone like that, who people are saying has done something awful. Even if she'd done it, it wouldn't change the fact that she's my mother and I know she's an amazing person. Do you see? It would have been another Ruth, one who was stressed, ill. You were put under massive pressure by the government wanting the land and the rain and your marriage falling apart, quite apart from the Sisters and all their crap. You read about it all the time, people who can't be held responsible for their own actions."

There is a short silence. Here we are, handcuffed to each other to fulfill our own needs. I break away. "In the end there are some things you can't change with speeches, Boy, and one of them is guilt."

The next morning when I wake he is not on duty. No Boy. I am filled with dread, thinking that we were too close yesterday and Three has read into that what he wanted to see and has got Boy redeployed—but I am panicking unnecessarily. Anon reminds me that Boy has gone to Hugh's funeral. I wanted to go myself to ask for his forgiveness, but I didn't even bother to apply for permission: I would have just been a freak show at someone else's private grief. There is one piece of good news. Apparently the notice which restricted me to the house has now been lifted. The ways of God have remained a mystery to me, but no more so than the ways of this government's judiciary. Nevertheless, it makes a difference. It means I can mourn in the orchard, where Hugh and I sat for so many hours; I am sad that he never tasted the wild raspberries in the hedge behind the bench, nor did I get the chance to give him a bag of gooseberries to take home to have with some cream from his beloved Jersey cow. How he would have loved that. He gave me so much and I never thanked him.

In this mood, I am ill prepared for Boy who comes back from the funeral proper a little drunk, all yesterday's seriousness forgotten. Apparently Hugh had left express orders that the mourners be allowed to polish off his substantial collection of rare Irish malt whiskeys and Boy gives a graphic and verbose description of the wake, saying it was a pretty happy occasion — a thanksgiving for a life well lived. Boy says he hopes he gets a send-off like that and collapses in a heap on the bench by the back door. I point out that it might be sooner than he thinks given the state he's in.

"Did you bring me back a wee dram in a party bag?" I add.

"No. Just some fruitcake. And a cow."

"A cow?"

"A cow."

It is not the drink talking. Hugh left instructions that on his death his beloved cow should come to live at The Well, and Hugh's daughter will be delivering her, just so long as she gets permission, which she has, apparently.

"His beautiful cow, for me?"

"All yours."

"I don't deserve her.'

"Well, you've got her whether you want her or not."

"When? Boy, be sensible! I mean it."

"Tomorrow." Boy turns a little green and lurches off to the barn.

It is an act of great kindness, typical of Hugh, and for a time I think I cannot accept it, but then I realize that the greatest insult to Hugh would be to reject it. Mark would have known more than me, but I do what I can. I am sweaty and have red weals on my palms from dragging straw up from the bottom stable to the barn, broken nails from repairing the fence in the paddock, and I stink like a public loo, having devoted the best part of an hour and a liter bottle of disinfectant scrubbing out two metal pails, but since I have spent most of an afternoon busy, two sensations overwhelm me: tiredness and hunger. Hugh's gifts always had hidden messages.

I fidget my way through the morning. It is drizzling softly, so I sit under the porch, flicking through an issue of Mark's old *Smallholders' Weekly* with advice on your first dairy cow. Then the trailer arrives and Hugh's daughter introduces herself as Sam—two women of a certain age, we stand in the sun swapping names and small talk.

"I'm so sorry about your father," I say. "I wanted to write, but I couldn't think of anything that would be good enough to say. I am sort of out of the habit of writing."

"It doesn't matter. We had hundreds of letters. I suppose I'm going to have to reply to them all. Dad was very fond of his visits here. I used to drop him at the end of the track and he'd joke he was going into time travel mode. I can see why now. It's as though the past two years simply haven't happened here. Did it rain here this morning?"

"Just drizzled."

"Drizzled." Sam let the word linger in her mouth like fine wine. "But it wasn't just the place—it was seeing you. He was fond of you."

"He was a very good man."

"A good man who did good things. That's what's going on his gravestone." She turned away for a moment, and in a rush I realize how much I miss the company of women. I put my hand on her elbow. It feels awkward and I wonder if I'm so out of practice that I've got everything wrong, like a traveler in a foreign land who is not sure of the significance of gestures—but she smiles.

"Guess we'd better get her out," she says.

Anon helps Sam lower the back of the trailer. Once it hits the ground, all Boy's Christmases have come at once. He puts his hand on the cow's golden flank and keeps her steady as Sam pushes and coaxes her backwards down the ramp. Anon beats a hasty retreat, as animals make him wheezy. At the bottom, Boy holds her halter and she looks around placidly, her huge dark eyes taking in her new home.

"Cow heaven," says Sam.

Annalisa is, as Hugh always said, quite beautiful: her breath is soft on my hand and she smells of *The Child's Guide to Farms.* Sam holds out the halter rope to me and I lead my first cow slowly towards her five-star barn. If only Mark could be here; a cow was for year three on the dream plan. Boy and Anon are busy latching up the ramp, and Sam follows me to the barn, carrying a dustbin liner.

She says loudly, "Here are various bits and bobs you may need." She looks over her shoulder and then speaks more quietly. "I'm not sure what you're allowed and what's forbidden—he was always talking about the bureaucratic restrictions—so I've left a couple of things in the food sacks which may interest you. He did a lot of research, you know, before his death. I don't know if he meant for you to have it or not. I had to make that choice. It may be nothing."

Sam says goodbye and hugs me; I'd like her to come again, but that's too much of an imposition, so I say nothing.

There is not much milk this evening; I think the traveling has affected her yield and I am an unskilled dairymaid. Even so, the sweet milk froths round the shining metal bucket and I carry it to the house with pride, remembering Hugh's first visit. Boy joins me to help with the bedding down. We stand looking at her, warmed by her body and stilled by the steady crunch of her chewing our own sweet hay. We wonder if she will get lonely.

Boy is shaking out the dustbin liner, trying to be helpful. "There's something in here," he says as a plastic wallet falls to the ground.

"It's nothing important," I lie, picking it up quickly. This wallet could hold answers, information at the very least, an address for Angie, something from Mark, an update on the Sisters. I know Boy means well, but I will not risk losing this. "I'll read it later on my own."

It strikes me he is a little resentful, being shut out of his boy's own adventure. He leaves reluctantly and I am alone.

It turns out there are only two pages. "Notes for Ruth," it says at the top of the first one I look at; then "the Sisters?" underlined. This is all about the Sisters, then, nothing about my Angie or Mark. I cannot believe it was so impossible for Hugh to have traced Mark, and if he had found Mark, then Mark would have known something about Angie. That leaves just the one explanation: that Mark refused to talk to Hugh. The conclusion is unbearable; I return to the paperwork about the Sisters.

Beneath the heading is a list of Internet sites, as if Hugh was Googling them; there is one that he has underlined twice, emphatically: Sistersoftheinlandsea.com. Beneath that is about half a page of jottings, as though he was making notes at the same time as looking at the site: "Blog—very similar. Picture of the Sisters' ritual by sea, tall one—Amelia. They have reinvented themselves." Then an arrow pointing to the word "Norfolk" and some illegible scribbles running vertically up the margin about Christian feminist tradition and a couple of Bible references to the Song of Solomon and Ecclesiastes. He has also written "Saints Days (???)," but nothing more specific. Between the pages is a photo of Amelia, taken from a newspaper. Although it is black and white, her hair still looks auburn to me, and she is as tall as ever, standing windswept on a beach, a long white gown full like a sail in the wind, her arms out as if in worship. I hold it close to my eyes, run my finger up her arm to her finger, touch it; I note the lie of the cloth against her breast, trace the faint line of a necklace she is wearing to the cleavage which conceals its pendant. If a blind man can read meaning in Braille, why can't I read the truth here? Despite the shafts of light over the sea behind her, there is nothing in this picture to illuminate me, but one thing is clear: Sister Amelia has set up shop again. Although it is depressing and disorienting to see my miracle reproduced with such factory efficiency, it is little more than a personal humiliation. I look at the next page.

This is a printout from a twenty-four-hour news site. As opposed to just printing an article, Hugh has printed the whole page. There are links down one side, pictures of well-known presenters down the other, a link to what's on live in the corner, the result of which is that the news article itself is in a tiny font and difficult to decipher in the low light of the barn. We always kept a flashlight down here. Mark said matches and hay were a poor combination. My arm remembers the movement, reaches up, fumbles on the little wooden shelf to the left of the door, and there it is, and it still works. Cautiously, I move outside and check that there is no one around before turning it on. The beam illuminates the midges, makes it easier to spot the bats, but nothing else becomes clearer. The main news article is about a house fire in Portsmouth in which three people died and protests about the fire brigade's lack of access to water. I guess he meant to print out something else, maybe one of the links, and got in a muddle. I run my eyes down the links: State of the Markets—record low—click here; Drought Update—technical difficulties cause ten-month delay for water purification system—click here; At Home/Regional/Eastern—woman sectioned after attempted murder at seaside camp—click here; International News—Paris calm after nights of riots—click here. None of it makes any sense to me, so I turn over and squint at the immaculate handwriting on the back, which simply reads Exodus 20 and a D and three more words: the Ten Commandments. They enter my mind like those PowerPoint slides, where someone has text randomly appearing on the screen, from left, right, below, above, letter by letter, magnifying and shrinking; they flash before me in the order of the level of my guilt.

Thou shalt not kill.

Thou shalt not commit adultery.

Thou shalt not worship graven images.

Those are just the things I have done; there are many other things that I have left undone.

I was hoping for so much more, but my disappointment is tempered by a realization that I am relieved Hugh hadn't brought these empty pages to me on one of his visits. I would have been angry with him.

The sum of it is this: I spent a year surrounded by fakery. I try to imagine the Sisters, camped up on the seashore, a new altar for the Rose, Eve updating the site, Sister Amelia identifying another woman to be the fifth. I don't know about Jack. Not Dorothy, of course. D—that is what the D is for—D for Dorothy. I check the bits of paper again. There should be a reply from that priest she saw: he was going to write to her; Dorothy would certainly write back. But there is nothing. I wonder why Dorothy left when the rest of them stayed. Perhaps she just lost her faith, saw it all for the sham it was. She told me she had lied; did she tell me all of the truth? Thou shalt not bear false witness. Or perhaps she left because of what happened here, because of the way it all ended for them, for us.

Hugh's papers are hidden back in the dustbin liner in the stable, the torch is out, the darkness is complete. The way it all ended—that is what I recollect now. Mark was both right and wrong about the hay and the matches.

CHAPTER THIRTY

The medieval mystics had a word for it—derelict. It's a good word, conjuring up as it does empty stables with their rotting planks leaning outwards like gaping teeth, their innards just rusting machinery and corroded pipework. Dereliction. The state of not feeling cared for. After the funeral, a deep, debilitating depression rendered me passive and incompetent. With Mark gone, I was like a domestic animal left tethered in the stall when the villagers have fled the plague. The police patrolled the property, ensuring the search for the sweater, the rose, and anything else that could be used in evidence would not be disturbed. Their dogs scoured the hillside and the coverts, noses down, tails up: "a southwest wind and a cloudy sky, makes the scent lie breast high"—that's what they used to say round here when the quarry was a fox and the huntsmen blew for home at the end of day. The Sisters left food and herbs on the doorstep, Amelia wrote messages, but I told the police I wanted nothing to do with them. I kept the door locked, never allowed them in, nor did I eat their offerings or read Amelia's texts. Sometimes I slept fitfully during the day, but I only ever ventured out at dusk, as if, like Canute, I could hold back the waves of night, and then when darkness came, I paced the hours away. The Rayburn went out from lack of oil, I did not bother with the stove but recreated instead the torpor of the hibernating dormice and hedgehogs, which I both envied and imitated. I existed, that was probably the most that could be said about me.

All tethers were cut. I lost myself in hours and hours of obsessive searching online, believing if I followed enough links that somewhere out there in the billions of bytes of information must be the truth about that night. Compassless in a maze of irrelevant information, I would wake up and find myself on a blog from Japan, written by a grieving mother whose son had been decapitated by a monster with a samurai sword; on a message board for victims of crime in Adelaide, South Australia; on a site which boasted more than ten thousand images of dead children. How I got to these places, I don't know; leaving them was even harder. I returned again and again to the social-networking page which had sprung up in Lucien's name, featuring a photo of him from when he was traveling with Angie, standing in a dry riverbed building a tower of pebbles. Over three thousand messages had been left on his page. Once I started to read them, I could not stop and I would wake some hours later, the laptop out of battery, me out of my mind.

Finally, I decided to face my own demons. I brought up the site of the Sisters of the Rose and scrolled down to Sister Amelia's blog.

Pray for the Chosen One, for the Judas preyed on her!

He pretended to minister to her!

He offered her food but starved her!

He gave her his hand in marriage but isolated her from those who truly loved her!

Like all men, he pretended to nurture but sought to conquer!

He spoke the language of science and was deaf to the word of God!

I clicked on a date from earlier in the week.

Sisters of the Rose, do not believe the propaganda you are reading
in the world's press. The prophet is never recognized in her own
country! The authorities would have you believe that a Chosen
One is guilty, but I know, we know she loves like a woman. And
the authorities would have you believe that the Rose commands
the Sisters to rid The Well of boys, but I know, we know only a
man would have the poison in his mind to kiss a child, then kill
him. Pray, Sisters of the Rose, that the Judas of The Well will be
unmasked!

It dawned on me it was Mark they were talking about, and I seemed
to hear his voice, before the funeral, protesting, "I can't live with
people saying I am a child killer." His voice is cracking. "I loved
Lucien. He was very special to me." I was worried he might kill himself, but he didn't, did he?

I sat captivated by an image of me at the Wellspring on the screen,
my hands cupped and water falling through them like diamonds, my
eyes closed in ecstasy. Me and yet not me. A virtual me. A version of
me. I clicked on the link to my Word of the Day, expecting the last
entry to be the day before Lucien's death, but my writings had apparently continued.

Friday: These things I know, Sisters—that the boy I loved is with
the Rose and that the drought in my heart will be touched by rain!

Saturday: Why do the mothers allow such suffering? The child
orphaned in the tsunami asks the waves. The boy who has lost his
sister to malaria asks the mosquito. The wife widowed by a bomb
in a bus asks the politicians. Mothers, why such suffering? I have
no answer, but only to say that just as each of you suffers and has
known suffering, so do I! I suffer with you!

Sunday: Be ready, Sisters, for soon I will issue an invitation. The rain falls more strongly than ever! Be ready, Sisters, and stay awake for the calling!

I did not write this drivel. I was not certain of much, but I was certain of that. The only person who could have written it—tried to impersonate me—was Sister Amelia. I had read enough of her missives over time to recognize her prose anywhere, all first person and exclamation marks. Pulling on an old coat from the back passage, I struck out across the field until I reached the single oak where I had first seen the Sisters all those months ago. Beneath me, the campers were like the pale humps of grotesque sheep perverting my pastures. There was a light on in Sister Jack and Sister Eve's van and I imagined them reading the Song. I could go down there, I thought, and join them, stepping into the warmth and sickly smell of the Calor gas heater. Jack would make me a mug of camomile tea; Eve would shift up on the little bench seat so I could squeeze in, and nothing much would have changed. We would talk. Was their faith still strong? Surely their paradise must have withered and rotted as mine had. Perhaps that's what they were doing down there, in their cells—planning their escape. My eyes were drawn to the hub, where, although there was no candle, there was the recognizable white stare of the computer screen, and I thought of Sister Amelia now as a guard, not a guardian, directing the blinding searchlight of her campaign into every corner of each woman's doubt. It occurred to me that what she was doing in there was quite possibly typing up my so-called Word of the Day.

The only thing that mattered to me was to stop her. Stumbling down the hill in the dark, faster and faster, I slipped on the wet grass. I got up again, though my ankle was painful and my head swam for a second. I hurtled on, the ground pounding up through my legs, until I burst through the door and into the suffocating hub. Amelia was there, her hair loose, lying back against the pillows on her bed, with the laptop propped up on her bare knees and her man-sized shirt hanging loose and low over her bare breasts, her photo of the two of us Blu-Tacked to the wall beside her.

"Ruth, you've come. I knew you would come back to me."

Amelia was laughing, rising towards me, when I flung myself on the bed, snatched the picture and tore it in two, grabbed the laptop and threw it across the tiny space so it hit the table and landed on the floor. I got off the bed, picked it up, and hit the delete button over and over again. "Gone! Gone!" I screamed.

Then Eve was in the doorway, her hands at her face. "What's wrong?" she cried.

"This is," I screamed, tearing paper from the printer and screwing up the pages. "You are."

Amelia stood, rigid, her face now inscrutable.

"You are," I repeated, pointing at Amelia directly. "You are a liar, a spin doctor!"

Amelia spoke slowly. "I think I know. It must be the Word of the Day.

"Which I didn't write, did I, Amelia?"

Amelia closed the door firmly behind Eve, to keep the warmth in, she said, so that the others would not be disturbed. "They're very exhausted," she explained, "spiritually this has been a tiring time for all of us."

"Go on, admit it. Tell Eve. You wrote it and made it all up."

"No!" Amelia's voice was harder, but no louder. "We prayed, Ruth. All of us. Not just me. Eve will say the same. It was all of us. We act as one."

Eve sat down on the bench seat, trying to get the table to collapse to make more room, but I had bent the hinges and it hung like a broken wing. She nodded. "We prayed, Ruth, so that the Rose would give us your words, because you had been silenced. Amelia and I together, we prayed."

"I have no idea what you are talking about," I said.

Eve looked at Amelia, who nodded, so she continued. She said the Sisters knew that Mark was acting as a barrier; he refused to let any of them visit me after Lucien's death. And not just visit, she said, they baked for me every day, they poured healing herbs into bottles and left them for me, to help me sleep, Jack had written me a poem—but they thought Mark threw them away.

"Where is Jack?" I asked. "Has she left?"

"She is not well," Eve explained. "She became so stressed after everything, her problems returned—banging her head, cutting her arms, crying all night. Usually Sister Amelia nurses her in her camper, giving her rhubarb root to calm her. The rest of us pray for her, but we don't visit."

"And where's Dorothy?"

"Resting."

"But to go back to what you were asking," Amelia said, closer now, sitting straight-backed on the end of the bed, "we also knew that nothing of what you wanted to say to us, to all the Sisters of the Rose waiting across the country, that none of that was being communicated either."

"And it was important we didn't lose momentum," said Eve. "So we prayed; the rain fell, the Rose flowered, and I wrote the words: it was as if someone else was holding the pen, giving me the text, and we were up and running again. It was a miracle."

I sat down next to her. Misguided they may have been, but what evidence did I have that she—either of them, any of them—had ever done anything other than try to love me and look after me when I needed help. Amelia softened, ran her hand down my back and under my jacket, resting it warm on my lower back.

"We're glad you've come back to us, aren't we, Eve?" She rested her head on my shoulder and her hair lay on my shoulders like a prayer shawl. "I know how hard it has been for you. But we will help you through it, that's what sisters do." She brushed my hair from my face. "And now there's just us at The Well, Ruth, women free to worship, we will find peace, I promise you. We mustn't squander what the Rose has given us."

Amelia poured over me like water, but I was a cold stone. My hands stayed in my pockets and in there I could feel the remnants of our dream: baler twine for tying up gates, tacks for nailing wire to posts in the sheep run, pellets of chicken feed, a tissue for wiping the tears from my eyes when walking against the east wind.

I stood up, feeling the space where her head had been, the print of her palm tattooed on my flesh. "I'm going to write my own piece for today, Amelia, and this is what I am going to say. There is no Rose. There is no chosen one. There is no second chance. There are nails and wood and tears. You have whipped up a storm on this strange plot of earth and yes, you are the siren at the center of it all."

Dorothy was waiting outside, at the bottom of the steps. I ignored her and went past Amelia's camper, where I caught sight of a hand moving the curtains, nothing more, and pitied Jack her captivity. Dorothy made as if to follow me; she started calling as if she had something to say to me, and when, breathless, I reached the oak, I saw that she had come partway up the hill behind me but had now halted, looking after me as if caught in the indecision of purgatory. Behind her, the other two were stoking the fire, embracing each other in the smoke. I did not look back again. I looked up at the stars instead, my mind made up.

CHAPTER THIRTY-ONE

For once I was methodical in my madness. I took the key from the ring by the Rayburn, the matches from the mantelpiece in the sitting room, and the flashlight from the back passage. Once outside, I undid the padlock on the shed and shone the light over the toolbox, the coils of rabbit wire, and tins of half-used paint. In the corner, the beam picked out the pair of stilts we had given Lucien for his fifth birthday, standing like dismembered legs in the shadows. I reached my hands through the cobwebs and picked up a plastic airplane with a broken wing, pushed the propeller and watched it spin and then held it to my nose as if it might smell of his faith that it would fly. The plane launched, glided, and came to rest lightly on fishing nets. In its place, I took a full five-liter can of petrol and a dust sheet covered in splashes of blue paint left over from the time we decorated his bedroom, shortly after we first moved in.

Those things I carried, with difficulty, to the single oak: the matches, the dust sheet, and the petrol can. The lights in the campers were out now, although the fire flamed a little more strongly than before. They must have built it up to light their prayers, to reassure themselves that they could see the world clearly, even in this very dark darkness—Amelia probably told them that the dereliction of the saints was the forerunner to glory. They were going to know glory now.

It was a work of art I created in the camp and, like most art, it was meticulous, hard work. I dragged three bales all the way from the stack and broke them into segments. Then I spread the hay from their fire in the center of the camp out in spokes to the circle of campers, dousing it as I went, the sour smell of the petrol canceling the sweetness of the hay. The last of the trails led to Amelia's camper. It was not enough. Slinking beneath her camper like a fox in a hen-house, I ripped up the sheet—dust and flakes of paint danced in the torchlight. Then I soaked the strips of white cotton in petrol. If the tearing of the cloth did not wake her, then surely the smell of the diesel would; if not that, then the ringing when I knocked a bucket against the Calor gas bottle; if not that, then the glare of my intent as I struck the matches. The cloth would not catch. I took the screwed-up paper from my pocket and lit that, holding it so the flame licked upwards, fanned by the night breeze, burning my wrist, then I placed that under the floor of the camper. One end of the sheet flirted with the flame and caught fire, illuminating piles of cardboard boxes stored on bricks on the bare earth beneath the van, boxes which I assumed contained roses and leaflets, T-shirts and posters, probably pictures of me. I wriggled out from underneath the van, then ran to the center of the camp and pulled the hay into the embers at the edge of the campfire.

There was no more to do. I climbed as far as the oak, leant against the hard trunk, and imagined a field of grass, emptied of all of them, and just me here at The Well, living out my sentence, alone. As, indeed, it has come to pass.

If it would just burn. At first there was only smoke, curling up from under Amelia's camper. I was worried the fire would go out and was on the point of going back down to relight it when I saw the flame licking up and down the side of the metal like a pole dancer. Without warning, my homemade medieval hell was suddenly un-leashed in an orgy of wild dance and destruction, fanned by the oxygen of hatred and the whip of the wind. At the same time, in the center of the camp, the spokes of my wheel of hay caught fire and the orange sparks ran along the trails like scorched rats.

It was beautiful—caught on the film of my memory as a still shot—at the top of the dark night, the stars, the silhouette of the bare oak and down in the dip, a flaming rose.

Dorothy. That was surely Dorothy, running past Eve's camper, banging on the door and screaming. She lurched towards Amelia's, reached the steps, and didn't hesitate. The fire rising up through the gaps in the iron must have melted the soles of her rubber boots with its hot tongues. Not Dorothy. I never wanted to hurt her. And where was Jack, was she still sleeping in Amelia's camper? I watched Dorothy reaching out for the handle, pulling her hand away but then wrapping the sleeve of her sweater over her fingers and shaking the door violently.

"Get out! Amelia! Amelia, there's a fire!" Her voice screeched like a little owl across the night.

Behind her, the others had fled their campers and were stamping on the fire trails like Victorian pictures of savages, etched in black and white, with color added later, seminaked humans leaping in the flames of their heresy, beating the ground with coats and blankets in a frantic choreography.

Eve was shouting "Water! Get water!" and running with a plastic container in each hand towards the tap. There was not enough water in the world, not even at the rain-blessed Well, to quench a fire such as this.

Ah, at last—Amelia. Dorothy was grabbing her, shouting at her to jump, not to step on the metal, then they were down on the smoldering grass and the two women with their heads bowed and their hands over their mouths hunched away from the flaming camper which had opened its home to the red stranger at the door and invited him in to rape and plunder at will. The explosion of the first gas canister blew them off their feet. I forgot about the gas. There will be another explosion, I thought. There were two canisters. Run, Dorothy, run. The second caught them just as they scrabbled as far as the other Sisters. How they huddled in fear, so close to their altar.

There was Eve. The water from the tap was pouring over the top of the carrier, running over her feet, trickling its way as a moonlit stream down the hill, in and out of the tufts of grass, inching towards the blazing camp. But Eve was not staring at the fire; she was pointing at me, screaming to someone, anyone.

"It's Ruth, up there, it was Ruth . . ."

There was Jack, safe then, taking Eve by the arm and dragging her down the hill, but no one could tackle this inferno. The metal had become so hot that it was crying out as it contorted into impossible shapes of agony, sometimes screaming like an animal in pain, sometimes folding in on itself in silent submission. Acrid smoke blossomed out of the van, dressed up for a night out in lurid, chemical colors, sparks like bling glittering the nightclub. The Sisters had now surged towards the hub and were heaving at the bricks blocking the wheels, but Amelia stood aside, arms high above her head, holding the Rose aloft. The Rose would burn well.

Blue lights to the side of me. Two fire engines, bumping over the rough ground towards me—toys I would buy for Lucien to put at the bottom of his stocking—the crew, helmets and gloves and ladders, all Lego men. The men locked their plastic arms around Amelia's bare shoulders and pushed her away until she was nothing more than a woman, wrapped in a blanket, standing on the sidelines of an episode of *Casualty*.

Blue lights behind me now. A figure was running up the hill towards the track, picked out in the headlights, waving his arms as two ambulances drew to a halt, a police van behind them. They left their engines running. The police got out of the van wearing bulletproof vests like in an American thriller. On those programs they have a word for what they're doing: spreading out.

The play had unfolded much as I thought it would, from my seat up in the gods: the cast were minimized humans on the giant stage of earth, air, fire, and water. It was all reduced to this.

"Ruth!"

They called again and again, but I did not reply.

"I need you to reply, Ruth, to know you can hear me. Can you hear me, Ruth?"

I could hear them, but I did not need words any longer.

The man's voice was like the rustle of a bag of sweets in the row behind, irritating but irrelevant to the main action. Two, three men were very close to me. The clouds pulled back the curtains on the moon and their shadows lengthened around me.

They took my body up the hill, but I left my eyes behind, watching. The Sisters saw what was happening; they were surging forwards into the searchlights, stretching out their arms as if they could reach me, falling on the ground, weeping. "Ruth!" they cried, "Chosen One of the Rose."

Their arms directed me forwards, my head swiveled round to look back, below, in the sodden, emptied camp. Amelia was alone, still holding the Rose aloft above the embers.

The doors of the ambulance open. The play is finished. We are outside the theater.

I scream. "Stop them!"

I am all fury and physical rage, but they have a great many hands to hold down my limbs. The needle slides into my arm. The waters close over my head.

CHAPTER THIRTY-TWO

S o it was The Well that waved goodbye to me, standing with hands on hips, watching me taken off, drugged and deranged, by men in uniform. Then, not much more than two months later, when the world and its justice had had its day with me, The Well watched me return, peeped through the kitchen window at the prison van bouncing down the drive, observed the guards releasing the handcuffs, then opened the front door for me, made my bed for me, welcomed me home, and kept me here for one hundred and twenty-seven days so far, tucked up tight like a long-stay patient, unwilling to make predictions about a prognosis for my particular disease.

Anon's shadow blocks the evening sunlight which was lighting up the straw as I am forking manure, ready to bring the cow in for the evening milking. There is real pleasure in my new duties and routines and real resentment when it is disturbed. "Do you want something, Anon? I wasn't aware that you were keen on cowpats?"

Anon keeps a safe distance. "Don't shoot me, I'm just the messenger. The gardener wants a word about the vegetable plot, asked me to let you know, that's all."

Propping the fork up against the wheelbarrow, I pause. "The gardener? Do you mean Boy?"

Anon laughs a lot at his own joke; he has put on so much weight doing his indolent job at my bountiful Well that his belly shakes. "That's the one," he says and plods off, wheezing and coughing and calling behind him. "He's out there now."

It seems a strange message, unusual enough to make me leave the stable and go to the fence in the orchard. I call over to Boy, "I gather you've got a problem?"

Boy turns quickly and jumps to his feet, sees me, looks around, beckons me in. "You'll need to take a closer look," he says. "I hope Anon has gone in."

"I don't garden, Boy, you know I won't come in."

"It will be worth it, I promise," he says.

Reluctantly, I push the little wooden gate, remembering how it sticks at halfway open, halfway closed, because we put the hinges on the wrong way round all that time ago and I stand like a foreigner amid the rows of orange-flowering runner beans. "Well?"

Boy slips me a letter. It says it is for a Mr. and Mrs. A. Ranger at an address which is unfamiliar to me. But the handwriting, that I do recognize, the looping *R* is the same as the way it used to be written extra large on birthday cards, with the rest of the words tailing away. If proof were needed of Boy's loyalty, then this would be it; he did post the letter to Mark and he has with him a reply.

"That's my parents' address," Boy is explaining. "I slipped a note in with your letter, telling Mark that was the best way to get a reply to you if he didn't want it opened. Mum's old-fashioned, no emails for her. She still writes to me every couple of weeks and sends stuff. I asked her to forward it on, if a reply ever came."

There will be time enough to thank him, but at this moment, I am drawn to the handwriting, thinking how forensic pathology would be able to tell me how he was feeling when he wrote it, maybe even where he was, the pollen in the air caught in minute samples on paper, sealed in the glue on the envelope, which he must have licked. I sit myself down slowly on an old log. Of all the places to read a reply from Mark, here I am, in his beloved garden, at my feet tiny fragments of glass still glinting in the mud, the shell of the greenhouse behind me.

Now I have only these words.

Dear Ruth,

I got your letter. You are right, I am in Northumberland. Uncle Andrew passed away last month, after a heart attack. It was a terrible shock for Annie and difficult for me. As you know, he was like a father for me and the last thing I could cope with was another bereavement. But life must go on. I am helping Annie look after what's left of the farm. The sheep up here aren't doing too badly, they have taken on some British Alpine goats and of course she's always had her hens. I am doing the occasional piece of work for some local solicitors as well.

To respond to your letter. We all need to find out what happened to Lucien. Nothing can bring him back, but I agree certainty would help so much. It is easier for me, I know, since it is clear where I was and what I was doing that night and that I am innocent. You are in a much harder position, but you ask, so here are my thoughts.

1. Amelia has set up some sort of copycat cult in East Anglia and managed to con some poor drought-stricken victims into following her. It was in the press and there is a little about it—but not much—on the Internet. It looks as though Dorothy has gone back to Canada. I don't know about the mental one. That just leaves that rich bitch businesswoman (Eve?), and they couldn't have done anything without her.

2. It is clear Amelia wanted me out of there, and she succeeded. I think that was because she wanted you and she got you. Who knows what she was capable of doing in order to achieve that. So many things seem to point to her, but the police lost interest in

*her pretty quickly. No evidence, plenty of alibis. They have told
the press that they are not following any leads on anyone living
outside The Well at the time of Lucien's death. I want to believe
it's Amelia, but it looks increasingly unlikely.*

*3. I asked you once before to get help, but you ignored me.
Please, this time, take my advice. I have been finding out about
therapists who can help you retrace things from the past and I can
put you in touch with one if that is helpful. You know I was never
one for that sort of psychobabble, but even I think it has to be
worth a try. Whatever you find out about what you have done, it
cannot be worse for you than not knowing.*

*I am sorry I have not been in touch. I did get a letter some time
ago from some vicar who is visiting you, at your request, if he is to
be believed. I would have thought you had had enough religion
for one lifetime. I have—there was no way I was going to get involved with him. If I am honest, I have to say I cannot face you.*

*Yes, I do miss The Well. I loved that place. I can remember
every tree I planted, every branch I pruned, every single sheep I
lambed, the way the tractor stalled on corners. Everything.*

*You asked about Angie. I can tell you she is with Charley, she
is safe and—if I believe her and that was always the problem—
apparently not using anymore. She says she went down around
the time of the funeral, but Charley has helped her back up. She
has asked me not to tell you where she is. She is not ready yet
to be in touch with you. I know this will break your heart, but I
cannot blame her. At least we are close now and I hope I am some
support for her. Give her time.*

*I'd like to hear from you again, I worry about you and miss you
and am plagued with guilt about leaving you when you needed
me. I may not have liked you very much towards the end, but I
will never stop loving you. I will never love anyone else.*

Mark

So he is alive—and well, as the cliché goes. And my Angie, nothing terrible has happened to Angie. Nothing else, that is. I reread those lines again and again. "She is safe," "she is not ready," and "we are close." Where does that leave me? At The Well, of course. I remember Boy is there.

"Read it." I offer it to Boy.

"You want me to?"

"Yes."

He wipes the mud from his hands on his jeans and takes the letter. I watch his face while he reads, the way he turns over, flicks back, shakes his head.

I want a second opinion. "What do you think?"

"What do you mean, what do I think?"

"What is he trying to say?"

Boy passes me back the letter and runs his hands through his hair. "There's nothing new in what he says, is there? I mean, I Googled some stuff when I was on leave, picked an Internet café where I could use a different account, but to be quite honest, it wasn't worth it. Mark, Hugh, me—none of us have come up with any more outside The Well than you have stuck here."

"So what's he saying?" I repeat, although the answer is clear to me.

"I don't know what you're getting at." Boy picks up the spade and jabs it into the soil.

"Yes, you do, Boy." I fold the letter over again and again. There's something about only ever being able to fold a piece of paper six times, no matter how big it is to start with, everything always ends up in the same impossible conundrum. "Hugh, now Mark, it's clear, everyone thinks it was me. That's what he's saying."

"I think he wants you to think that it was you. What's always puzzled me is why don't you ever think it was him?"

He waits for me to answer, but I am exercising my right to remain silent, so he continues. "You do think it was him, don't you? Sometimes, anyway. It's just you don't dare say it out loud."

Shaking my head, I tell Boy he just doesn't understand: this was Mark, a gardener like him, this was what he loved; I wave crazily at the ordered ranks of courgettes. Mark wasn't mad, he wasn't evil, he wasn't violent . . .

"So what happened to the greenhouse?" Boy looks pointedly at the ruin.

"I drove him to that. Before we came here, he was different, he was . . ." I falter.

"A pedophile?"

I have to get out of this garden. At the gate, I turn round and tell Boy. "I never believed he was a pedophile!"

"Then."

The monosyllable takes its place in this outdoor theater of a courtroom, the implicit question raises its eyebrow at the bench but stays silent.

Boy follows me out of the garden, catches me, takes the letter from my hand, and pushes it out of sight into his pocket. We walk as far as the front of the cottage; there is no one around and we continue our legal wrangling by the back door.

"Ruth, I could argue, objectively, that he was all those things. And—no, let me go on—and who else would Lucien have gone with? He had the chance to dump the green sweater, the wet clothes, the rose necklace on his early-morning trip to buy a newspaper, which you yourself said was totally out of character."

"Stop it." I am going to go inside, shut the door on his logic.

Boy puts his foot in the way. "Why?"

"Because, I don't know why, I just want you to stop." Of course, I have thought about whether it was Mark, but Boy is right, hearing that suspicion voiced out loud is something different and I put my hand out to get my letter back from him, but he keeps it out of my reach.

"I'm not saying it was him. But if it was, then what better way of covering things up than making you mad all over again, convincing you of your own guilt? It's obvious no one is going to pin it on the Sisters." He turns his back to the barns and gives me back my letter. "I've never the met the man, Ruth, but you're always defending his memory, and no man is that good, we're a jealous breed."

I allow myself a day in bed to think about Boy's unthinkable premise, to reread the letter, trying to find the subtext; I was so good at analysis of language when I was paid to teach it, but now, looking for a different sort of remuneration, I am not up to the job. I loved Mark. For a very long time I thought he was a good man, even when others disagreed. He wasn't the sort of man to hurt people, although he did. He hurt me, for a start. He had an alibi, but people can do all sorts of things with computers and rarely get caught, which he knew only too well. I loved him. The reason it is unsayable is this: if it was him, if the laptop accusations were true and that was him, I have lived with and loved a pervert, I've been so embroiled with him that I myself cannot have escaped contamination. Easier, in a way, for it to be anyone but him. Easier, even, in some strange way, for it to be me.

Outside, I can hear banging. Looking out the window, I can see Boy has taken up my idea of keeping chickens and is mending the henhouse, bent double, hammering the wire to the frame, his collar turned up against the dry wind whipping up the dust, surrounding himself with the paraphernalia of the dream of the smallholder. No man is that good.

CHAPTER THIRTY-THREE

Today is August 15. Exactly this time one year ago, I was making a cake. I will make a cake again today as an act of remembrance. I will take the large yellow mixing bowl from the bottom of the dresser. Perhaps when I am finally released I can write a celebrity book called *The House Arrest Cookbook*. The first thing it will say is to make sure you have enough small things: saucepans for one, half-pint mixing bowls, casserole dishes designed for one chicken leg only, although it may be worth keeping one large yellow mixing bowl big enough for mixing a six-year-old's birthday cake, just in case. With some foresight, I have ordered ahead.

Anon queried the shopping list. "Some kind of special occasion?" he asked.

He is not inquisitive enough to be promoted. Anon will go through life knowing enough and no more, which is one way of living—maybe a good one—but whatever he thought of my request, he brought back what he could. Food interests him; he is probably the only person in the UK to have put on weight during the drought. Flour is still easily obtained, if expensive; sugar, providing you are happy to take unrefined, is also not a problem; and hens are quite happy scratching a living from dust and bare earth, so we are now apparently a nation of free-range egg eaters. I have made an attempt at making my own butter from Annalisa's lovely milk.

The ingredients are laid out on the table, reminding me of cookery lessons at school, when we had washed our hands (how casually we must have washed our hands), tied the stiff, plastic aprons behind our backs with uneven bows, and read through the recipe written up on the whiteboard. Diana Reid was my cooking partner. We lost touch long before we moved here. I wonder if she read about me in the press and said to the people in her office, I used to be her cooking partner at school, you know. And everyone would think, I work with someone who went to school with someone who knows that weird woman who thinks she's the chosen one and who killed her grandson in the pond. They would all experience a little frisson of having come so close to madness and got away with it.

I take a spoon and scoop off a block of butter and scrape it into the bowl. There are no scales so the ingredients cannot be weighed and found wanting. I use a tablespoon to measure out the sugar: flat across the top for sugar, heaped for flour—that made twenty-five grams, my mother taught me. Actually, she would have said ounces, I think, but I am making things up. I can't hear her voice any longer. Much as we had our differences, I am glad she never lived to see this: her daughter baking birthday cakes for the dead.

Creaming butter and sugar is hard work. The muscles which I used to pin down the sheep for shearing and balance the wheelbarrow full of stones for repairing the orchard wall withered long ago, and I find myself softening the butter on the Rayburn to make the task easier and swapping the wooden spoon from hand to hand to alleviate my aching arms. The creaming done, I crack the eggs into a bowl and whisk them lightly before adding them slowly to the cake mixture. At first it is beautiful, full of air and a consistency, which reminds me of the Cornish cream the old ladies used to serve at the fete with dollops of jam and crumbling scones and wasps. How full of memories I am today. But then I add the egg too quickly—slapdash Ruthy—and it curdles into slimy islands which slop their way around the bowl and refuse to bind. The flour rescues it, but I don't have baking powder and now I think this cake will be airless and life-less like biscuit. In a second, it has gone from a work of love to an object of hate, and I am close to hurling the yellow mixing bowl and its separating mixture of survival and grief against the wall.

Then Lucien is standing on the chair besides me. He smells of clean laundry. If he could be there, if he could only be there, beautiful on the chair beside me, wanting to put the eggshells back together again and lick the spoon, then I could carry on. I uncurl my hands from their rigid grip on the bowl and breathe deeply, resume folding in the flour, first this way, then that, and slowly it starts to come right again. I resolve not to throw it away. I spoon the mixture into the greased cake tin and put it in the oven, then stand by the sink and watch the wheat unharvested ripple and fly in the hot wind and I think of his hair. The pheasants, fat and unaware of their good fortune, pecking in the straggling grass by the gatepost remind me of him windmilling down the drive, clapping his hands and watching them take off, heavy as jumbo jets. I run my own finger around the bowl and lick it, once for me, once for him, and once for what? For good luck?

Three invades my house.

"What do you want?" I am brave, here in my kitchen, ready to defend my cake against any impostor.

"For once, I thought you would be pleased to see me. But if I'm interrupting something . . ."

Putting the spoons and bowl into the sink, I work hard to manage my expectations. I run the water to wash up. "What is it you wanted to say?"

"It was to inform you that a section 9 visitor's permit has been granted for this afternoon. Fourteen hundred to sixteen hundred hours."

He has played his trump card and he knows it.

"Today?"

"I said this afternoon, fourteen hundred to sixteen hundred."

"You must have known about this and you're telling me now. You are a sadistic bastard!" I smash the bowl onto the draining board.

"You must be aware I have the authority to rescind the permission if you are not in a fit mental state." Three plays with the piece of paper in his hand.

Breathing very deeply, I dry my hands on a cloth, over and over, and manage just the one word more. "Who?"

Three slaps the form on the table and I seize it, read it, there are no names, just small print and dates and timings. "Tell me who." I scream at him as he disappears up the drive, beyond my limit. "You must know who!"

Back inside, the clock moves towards 1:05 p.m. The official slip gives nothing away, no matter how many times I reread it. Boy would have told me if he knew, or if it was anyone interesting. That's the thing about Three, he would break the news like that just to torture me with the hope that it was Angie, or Mark, knowing all the time it was some dreary official or a doctor. The hope that it is someone I love thunders inside me, but I hold tight to more rational explanations—Sam, for instance, come to see how the cow is, maybe she felt sorry for me, and that leads me to think this might be a substitute priest they have dug up from somewhere.

If somebody comes, what will I do with the cake?

The smell of the baking cake fills the kitchen, makes me wonder if I might not one day bake again for somebody else, for children, someone else's children, I don't know whose. I could have cooked more with Angie and worked less and maybe it would have all turned out differently. It might be Angie. In some ways, I think I could manage if it was Angie. I know what I have to do when I see Angie again. But what if it's Mark—the Mark I love or the Mark I hate?

The timer sounds. I jump, but it is the cake, not the visitors.

Bending down and opening the oven door, I take out the cake with shaking hands and, trembling, put it on the table. Perfect. It has risen, golden-topped, cracked but only enough to reveal the moist, steaming sponge inside. Even as it cools, it doesn't collapse. There is plenty of jam left: damson, plum, apple jelly, crab-apple jelly . . . some are labeled *Year 1* or *Year 2* as if we might lose count. Lucien would have wanted strawberry jam, but that was never on offer. Mark made our first batch of damson jelly; Angie, she was a peanut butter kid, so that is no good. I choose damson, I don't know why, and back in the kitchen slice the cake horizontally in two. At last they have allowed me a decent knife. I pointed out to them that the sheds are full of beams to hang myself from or scythes or shears which I could steal in the night and creep up behind them and slit their throats with, so the lack of a decent kitchen knife seemed somewhat futile. I spread the jam over the cake. It crumbles slightly because I haven't been able to wait for it to be ready, but thick with lumps of fruit I sandwich it together again, then run my finger along the blade and lick it, leaving my skin stained purple and crimson. Damson. Mark's favorite.

It is 1:45 p.m. The visitors are due in fifteen minutes. Scrutinizing the paper again, I try to remember whether Three said visitor or visitors. What a difference a plural might make—when two or three are gathered—and then I realize it could be the Sisters. Would they really have given permission to Amelia to come back here, if she asked? There is no sign of anyone arriving down the drive. Anon is out there now, dealing cards for himself in the shade. I cannot imagine what I would say to Amelia. Sweat pours down my face, I lose focus and the room swims in the heat and my mind gasps for knowledge in an anarchy of unknowing.

"Anon!" I call from the doorway. "Do you know who is coming to visit me?"

"I'm afraid I'm not party to that information, but I'll sure let you know as soon as someone turns up. I'm the one on duty. Sarge has gone up to the experimental plots for some top secret security update, or something like that."

The Land Rover is not there and Anon confirms that Boy has headed into town.

Our hedge by the gate has blackberries. I pick some, to commemorate blackberrying and Lucien. I arrange them on the icing with care, angry that I am at risk of losing sight of him in the midst of this impending invasion. I had not really thought what I was going to do with it when it was finished, but now I am faced with the prospect of sharing it. Some lines from Proverbs come to mind uninvited. "If your enemy is hungry, give him food to eat; if he is thirsty, give him water to drink." I shared them with Mark a long time ago, in a different context, in what seems like another country. I am trying to remember how the proverb ends when the buzzer sounds in the barn.

"Looks like they're here," calls Anon.

They?

An unfamiliar blue car bumps down the drive, does a three-point turn under the oak so it ends up parked facing away from the cottage as if ready for a quick getaway.

Who wants to come to such a birthday party as this, with no invitations, no balloons, no birthday boy left to blow out the candles?

The car door opens.

The answer is Mark.

The fact that it is Mark means that it is not Angie. Not Amelia. Not any of those other possibilities. It is Mark. Who it is and who it is not are equally debilitating.

Back inside, I stare from the window, frozen like the doe deer at dusk that sees the marksman raise his rifle but cannot run. Part of me thinks that time has fragmented and re-formed like a kaleidoscope and that Mark standing by the five-barred gate, looking up at the cottage, is quite normal and that he is about to come into the cottage, unpack his shopping, and I will call down, how are things in town, and he will say, I'll be up in a minute. Another part of me thinks that this is Mark, but at some point in the future, and I am the ghost come back to visit old haunts, to inspect the ruins.

Whichever way I try to rationalize it, it cannot be now, unless of course he has changed his mind and he loves me again; unless he has news, unless he has evidence to share which will prove beyond doubt that it was me. Or him. Or her. It cannot be a mistake that he has chosen this day for his return; it used to be in Mark's favor that he never forgot birthdays. He must know I am sad, but I have been sad for a long time and it has not prompted him to comfort me. Mark. Just to hold him, imagine that, for him to say I've come back, I can't live without you. Suspicion corrupts that soft-focus picture. The truth is he has stayed away for far too long, does not love me, has not stopped punishing me, so again the question repeats itself: why come back here now? My mind is rapid cycling, rushing between the conscious thought and the hardwired memories, trying to make sense of this unforeseen appearance. Slowly, an alternative reading of events occurs to me. A piece of received wisdom: that people are drawn back to the scene of their crimes. That special days act like a magnet to the murderer. Perhaps there is sense in this madness after all. It was Boy who said it out loud. Why don't you ever think it was him?

Sitting on the edge of the bed, my foot taps the floor as my knees shake uncontrollably. I am holding my breath; the only thing I can hear is my heart, and then downstairs, the minute adjustments a house makes when someone walks through the door, the almost inaudible foot on the kitchen floor, the air moving to one side to let him pass.

"Ruth, it's Mark."

He calls up again, sounding closer still. He must be standing at the bottom of the stairs. I fix every muscle so I am motionless, as if it is a game of hide-and-seek and I am under the bed and he is prowling. I'm coming to get you.

"Ruth? I know this is a shock. I'll go for a walk for five minutes, then come back. Give you a chance to collect yourself."

Rage is useful to animals, it brings the blood back to the front of the brain: fight becomes the stronger of the two impulses. I follow him with my ears as he leaves via the back door. From the bathroom, I track him strolling out over the field, trying to avoid the crusted cowpats drying in the sun, then I lose sight of him and know that the only way I can spy on him is to look through the window in Lucien's room. I never go in there, but I will now. I throw open the door, three strides is all it takes to get to the window. Mark is on the hill, his hair is shorter; he is tapping an unlit cigarette against the box. He is an unfamiliar man surveying all that he knew once—all that has been destroyed. To my right is the toy box trunk, behind me the empty bed, and in the corner a black bin liner which has never been opened, not since the police returned it.

Enough.

The black plastic rips easily and I reach my hand in as if this were some birthing beast. A red T-shirt. His hoodie. Jeans. They are all clean and smell not of him but of washing powder; these were the clothes they took from the airing cupboard. My hand closes around some sneakers and I put them on the floor beside me, recognizing them as the ones he'd grown out of, with Velcro, not laces. Pants, more T-shirts, an anorak he hated, a pillowcase. All of Lucien ironed out of them. I tear the bin liner farther apart, expose its stillborn contents and pick up the fleece, bury my face in the buttercups and bees. This is Lucien, the Lucien who is gone in a way that is beyond metaphor, because metaphor would imply connection. I breathe in absence, undiluted by any secondary pain or conscious thought, the purity of this moment is all I need to convince myself that it could not have been me.

"Enough," I say out loud.

With clothes strewn all over the floor, this looks again like his room, so I leave the door open. Back in the bathroom, very calmly, I wash my face, brush my hair, and look at myself in the new mirror which Boy has hung over the sink, and see someone capable.

"You can do it," I say out loud to the woman in the mirror and she believes me, I can see it in the way her eyes are resolute now, the way she is biting her lip. Downstairs, I take up my position on the sofa in the sitting room and wait. It is slightly cooler in here than anywhere else, being darker and facing east. Although my palms are warm and damp, I focus on looking ice-cold calm. I have waited to see Mark face-to-face for a long time, only now do I know why.

He calls from the back door. "Ruth?"

"Hello, Mark."

"There you are. You made me jump. I thought I saw you at the upstairs window."

He looks as though he wants to step forward, to hug me, even, but he stops. The funeral stoop is gone; this man walks a little taller, but his face is taut and the tension he carries with him is palpable.

"You were wrong."

"Yes. Yes, I was." We are fiddling awkwardly with the space and time between us. "Did you get my letter?" he continues.

"Yes. Just the one."

He perches next to me on the edge of the sofa and I allow him to take my hand, weighing up the risk. He swallows, audibly. "I'm so sorry, Ruth. I really am."

"I know."

"I wanted to be in touch, to visit you, but I couldn't face it. But . . ." My hand is dropped again and I reclaim it, using it to push my hair out of my face so I can see more clearly.

I am proud that I am still sitting. He is the one pacing now. I am taut like a tiger. "You're here now. Don't get me wrong. There's so much to talk about. So much I want to know. But why today, Mark?"

"Aren't you pleased to see me at all, Ruth?"

"I don't know what I feel, I just don't know. I asked you a question."

He replies with his back to me, a familiar shape framed by the window, the curtain half closed to keep out the light and the heat. "There is a reason," he says, then clears his throat. "It's been hard," he continues, "ever since Lucien's, well, Lucien's death, ever since that . . ."

Now is the time for me to go to him. I put my hand on the back of his neck, massage it slightly, stand close with my breath, causing him to flinch and his shoulders to rise, causing the hairs on my bare arms to prickle. "I have missed you," I whisper. "It must have been so difficult for you too. You probably did what you had to do."

He stiffens against me, we know each other too well and the very muscles in our bodies recognize dishonesty. He continues talking to the glass. "I hope today will be the day when . . ."

My hands drop from his neck and clasp him in an embrace from behind and I rest my head on his jacket; he smells of hay and poorly selected aftershave and what might have been, and this undermines me. I struggle against the siren voice of the way we were, once.

"There's no hurry," I reassure him. "I'm not going anywhere. There's only Anon on duty, I am not sure he can even tell the time. Let's sit at the kitchen table, like we used to."

Turning him to face me compounds my error. In front of me is the Mark I loved and trusted implicitly and it is impossible, almost impossible, to believe he is the wolf in sheep's clothing. I so nearly falter, but with very few words he makes it easy for me.

"You've been baking," he says. "I could smell a cake when I came in. Have I interrupted a special occasion?"

He speaks as if it is a joke, but I know now. It is no coincidence, this timing. The rest of the proverb comes back to me. "You will heap burning coals on his head, and the Lord will reward you." He will know what guilt tastes like.

In the kitchen, I get a couple of plates out and put them on the table. The Rayburn has combined with the searing August temperatures to create a furnace, so he takes off his jacket and puts it over the back of the chair. His checked shirt is sticking slightly to his back, and when he rolls up his sleeves, his arms are still strong and tanned and although he is slumped in the chair, it is clear he is still fit from working the land. He wipes the sweat from his forehead and rubs his red eyes.

"Of course. Lucien's birthday." He keeps his eyes closed for a few moments.

"You couldn't have forgotten," I say, but he shakes his head slowly and I don't know what that means. "Water?" I offer.

"Yes, please."

He drinks sip by sip, sitting in silence before whispering, as if to himself, "It's still so beautiful here, the most beautiful place in the world." He puts the glass down on the table gently, tips it, watches the water circle and settle. "And it still rains. You know, I don't think we ever really got what that meant. I didn't. Not until I left and lived like the rest of the world. I can understand the madness now."

Lifting the cloth which is covering Lucien's birthday cake, protecting it from the flies that buzz continuously nowadays, I am close to collapse. This would have been his birthday cake and he is dead and there is only that one unforgiving, unforgivable truth: I will never ever see him again.

"Ruth."

Except that Mark is sitting at my table, unworthy even to gather up the crumbs.

"Sorry. I was remembering. Here."

The cake sits between us, whole. I pierce the icing with the candles. One. Two. Three. Four. Five. There is one more in my hand. "What do you think? Should I put the sixth candle on, because that is how old he would have been? Or should I leave it at five, because that is how old he was when he was murdered?"

Mark turns the plate around as if to circle the question. Finally he answers, tight throated. "I would leave him at five, as he was, our happy five-year-old grandson. Let's keep that memory."

"I am not allowed matches. You haven't taken up smoking again, have you?"

"No." His eyes slide immediately to his jacket.

"I can't blame you." I reach into the pocket and pull out the cigarettes and a slim book of matches, with the logo of a Manchester hotel on the front. "No need for lies now, Mark."

He mutters something about how he can explain everything, but I know my script. Nothing is stopping me now.

I invite him to light the candles. He is going to cry, but I won't. The first match fails to light. His hand fixates me—the hand that led me up the aisle; the same hand that led the boy to the well. He tries again and one by one the candles hesitate into life. The hand that brought me pleasure; the same hand that purchased pleasure of a wholly different kind with a PIN and a credit card. The flame reaches his fingers before he gets to the last one. The hand that held the head under the water . . .

"Give them to me." I light the last candle myself and, sitting back down on the other side of the table, we watch them burn.

Mark speaks first. "How are you? Really?"

"I'm fine now, Mark. Shall we sing 'Happy Birthday'?"

"For God's sake, Ruth, what is this?" He slams the table and everything flickers, but these are perpetual candles which never go out.

"You came here, Mark. You just happened to arrive in the middle of a birthday party. If you'd called ahead . . ."

"Fine. For Christ's sake, Ruth, I told you to get help."

"I don't need help anymore. I know what I am doing. What's more, Mark, I know what you're doing."

"I'm here for a reason!" he shouts. "Because of Angie."

"Don't bring her into it. Not now it's just the two of us at last."

I pick up the large, sharp knife and make as if to put the point in the very center of the cake—but pause. The table is between us. I walk round and stand behind his chair so that I am leaning over him, put his hands on the knife, my hands over his hands and say, "Let's do this together, Mark, like we did at our wedding."

I am sure he thinks I am mad again and he needs to humor me, but he is wrong. I have never been as sane as this. Just as the knife is going to slice through the cake, I kick the chair. He lurches, caught off guard, grabs at the table, but his fingers slip, he falls to the ground, and the chair crashes on top of him. I push it out of the way and stand over him, with the knife in my hand.

"What the hell? Ruth! Put it down. I was about to tell you that Angie . . ."

He will have the lines and he will have the moves. I am not taking any risks. Kick. Kick him in the head.

"I hate you. I hate you. I know it was you, I know!"

He grabs my leg, but I have kept my left hand on the rail of the Rayburn and he cannot pull me down.

"Murderer! Pervert!"

I stumble. The chair smashes into his face. I am falling towards him, knife raised, stab, stab again, no blood, screaming, yes, but there is no blood. Someone has hold of my arm, forcing it towards the ceiling. I am scratching at him to get off, that he needs to pay, but Mark is up off the floor now, pinning my arms to my sides. My fingers are pried open, I am subdued, I am knifeless, I am held. There is no blood, just damson jam on the lino and the purple stain of blackberries leaking onto white icing. The plate is cracked, the cake split, but the candles still burn.

Boy drags me from the kitchen.

CHAPTER THIRTY-FOUR

H e wants to talk."

"You shouldn't have stopped me."

Boy has brought me into the orchard and sat me on the stone bench. Some time has passed—I am not sure how much. It is incredibly hot and the sweat is inching down my shivering back.

Boy suggests we move into the shade—mad dogs and Englishmen—but I am rooted to the bench by my failure. He takes a deep breath as if he is trying to keep control of himself. "For the past six months you have said that all you want is answers. The truth. Mark must have a reason for coming and you won't talk to him."

This is a pointless argument. Disguised, the answer walked into The Well this afternoon, all wrapped up in self-pity and excuses. It is my failure that the answer will drive away again.

"Ruth, you could have killed him. I'd never forgive myself if it was because of what I said the other day."

"Don't apologize, that was very helpful." If it is possible, I am both frozen still and shaking.

"I'm sorry I wasn't here when he came."

"I didn't need you for this, Boy. This has nothing to do with you and I wish you hadn't shown up. If you hadn't interfered, it would all be over now."

"Listen. I'm not going anywhere now. You'll be OK. I'll stay here with you, if you're frightened of him . . ."

"Frightened?" I burst out laughing. "The only thing we're ever truly frightened of in life, Boy, is the unknown. What have I left to be frightened of? I have finally allowed myself to think the impossible. You're too young to know."

In this heat, nothing moves. No wind rustles the branches, there are no birds; in the field even our lovely cow cannot be bothered to eat but stands sleeping in the shade. Flies. I can hear flies. There must be something dead, somewhere.

A car engine starts somewhere over by the house.

Boy jumps up. "We've got to stop him, Ruth. He'll report what's happened." He pounds across the orchard. "Mark, wait!" he is shouting, crashing through the gate, before he disappears. A moment later the engine is turned off and I move towards the house like an automaton, directed there, with no conscious purpose possible. Boy is standing beside the car, the driver's door open. Anon is hovering by the barn, looking up the drive. He will want Three to come back and rescue him from the out of the ordinary. Inside the car, Mark has his head on the wheel. There are scuffs and smudges all over the back of his shirt and his elbow is grazed like a child who has been in a fight in the playground. When he lifts his head, he notices blood on his cheek and touches it.

"I knew this would be pointless. I said I was never coming back to you and I should have stuck to that." Mark wipes his hands on his trousers, then puts them back ready on the steering wheel, pushes back against it until his arms are straight, relaxes them again, puts his left hand on the gear stick, while his right reaches for the key.

He looks straight at me. "I never knew you hated me that much."

I hold on to the door handle to prevent him from going.

"Turn it off. Let's go inside." Boy is young enough to believe in solutions.

"You guys OK?" Anon. Of course.

Mark puts the car violently into reverse. Boy pulls me out of the way just in time as it swings round towards the drive. Then Mark leans out of the window. "If you want to know the truth, I only came today because Angie said she was coming too and she wanted us all to be together."

"Angie?"

"It didn't occur to me then it was Lucien's birthday. But I don't think that was all. She said she was coming because she had news and something she wanted to show us."

"Angie? Coming here?"

"Yes."

"Why didn't you say?"

"I tried to say, Ruth, but—what a surprise—you weren't listening."

The engine revs and I grapple my way round to the front of the car, my hands spread-eagled on the hood.

"You should have said straightaway."

"I didn't want to say because I didn't want to raise your hopes in case she didn't show up. And I was right. A leopard doesn't change its spots."

"Don't go. What was she going to show us?"

He takes his foot off the accelerator. "I don't know. Perhaps we'll never know. Perhaps it was nothing in the end."

The suspended moment, engine idling, the heat—it is all ripped in half as the alarms suddenly sound behind us, the high-pitched pulse which indicates a break in the perimeter fence.

"What the hell's that?"

"I'll get that sorted!" shouts Anon, heading off towards the control panel in the barn. They go off all the time and he is relieved, not worried, a deer caught on the wire, branches down on the junction box, but the wail sends my pain out over the hills and I am breathless with the panic of confusion and chances sliding away from me.

Mark gets back into gear. "This place really is an asylum."

"Ask her to get in touch with me," I plead, stumbling alongside the car. "Will you come again?"

"Turn that thing off, Adrian," yells Boy.

Mark slows the car. "Not now I know what you really think of me. What you called me. Don't ever try to get in touch with me again. Ever." He pulls away, careering crazily over the drive, looking back at me out of the window. "I mean it this time, Ruth."

"Intrusion in Wellwood, boundary three!" Anon calls from the barn and runs back out, radio in hand, armed. "Not a false."

"Mark," I scream after him, tripping on the stones. "Mark!"

The car bounces up the track, dust clouding out behind it, and stops at the top of the hill. Now that he is going, I will him to come back, flooded with an incoherent sense of compassion, as if all the kindness he ever showed to me was carried out on the tide which has now turned and is coming in again, washing over me. I would call him, I would run after him, but he is too far away. He must just have been taking one last look at his love, The Well, because the car is moving on, almost out of sight now, gone. Mark is gone. I am full of fear for what he might do.

Boy turns to me. "I've got to go with Adrian and check this out. I'll be five minutes, no more. Don't do anything stupid."

The fence takes my weight, then I sit heavily on the stile and stay there, the whine of the siren now reduced to an intermittent beeping, scrambling my thoughts. Staring at the scuffed gravel and tire marks, I see the forensic evidence of a story of leavings and loss, unresolved. In his absence, it was easy to believe it might have been him, but now I am sure it was not Mark. The women, then, that leaves the women who did it.

It looks like a woman being brought up the field between Boy on the right and Anon on the left. They are not holding her; she walks freely with a bag over her shoulder and her hands in her pockets, her boots scuffing the ground beneath a long skirt. You'll wear your shoes out, I used to say, take your hands out of your pockets, hold mine. As Angie gets closer, she raises her right hand as if in greeting. I have heard voices, seen things, so I am not ready to believe it, and even as she reaches me and stands within touching distance of me, but does not touch me, I remember the last time I saw her she was weeping by the side of a grave. I hold tight to my doubt for fear of waking up.

"Our intruder," says Boy.

"Not sure what to do about the paperwork here," Anon prattles on like a voice at the end of a line in a call center. "But I guess we could put it down as a false. After all, you did have permission, ma'am, you just came about it the wrong way."

"Hello, Mum," she says.

There is no reply good enough. She is my daughter, but how can I claim to be her mother, this withered wreck of a woman who turns all flesh to dust?

No words come, but she lets me take her hand in mine. I lift it to my cheek, breathe in the years of her, the birth of her. "Angie."

She takes her hand back, but gently, and I find my voice. "Mark said you were coming, but he's gone, Angie, he's gone and he won't come back. He said you hadn't shown up, so he left."

"Unreliable Angie," she mimics. "I can hear him saying it now. How long has he been gone?" Her eyes trace the path of the drive up the hill.

"Minutes, that's all," I tell her.

"I got Charley to drop me off. I wanted to walk up through the wood, I'd summoned up the courage to visit the Wellspring and, well, take some time there, that sort of thing. I didn't realize it would be wired like this," she explains. She gestures around her at the barn, the antennas, the paraphernalia of imprisonment and that seems to jolt her out of her daze. "You've got to get him back, Mum."

I am shaking my head and crying as I realize the truth. "He won't come back, Angie, not after what I've done."

"Call his mobile," she urges, "someone must have a phone."

Boy hands her his mobile. She checks the signal, calls, cancels, calls again. "For Christ's sake," she says, "answer the phone!"

"I have said some awful things, Angie. He'll never forgive me."

"The person you are calling is unavailable. Please try later," she repeats.

I have felt this lurch of fear before. "What shall we do?"

"Never mind," says Angie. "I wanted us all to be together for this, but if it has to be just us, then that's how it has to be. You look dreadful. Let's go and sit down."

She has news, answers maybe—something about her has changed. I allow myself to look at her eyes, but they are sunk deep and black-ringed with exhaustion, dark pools which swallow any hope I was feeling. Boy suggests we sit in the orchard, saying he'll fetch some water. He has grown up; he recognizes something is happening which he cannot be a part of, or change. He and Anon leave, and I walk with my daughter between the trees, where the hard green apples are forming on the boughs, where the scent of the wild honeysuckle has drugged the birds to silence. We sit on the bench, just the two of us, as mothers and daughters do, but not quite like that. I am terrified of her, that she is the mother of Lucien who died, and I want to hold her, but I am afraid she will disintegrate when I touch her and this moment of sitting alongside each other will be gone. She reaches into her embroidered bag and pulls out a butterfly. For a second, I think it's real, I can't believe how big it is, how still it rests in her palm, then I notice the texture of the silk thread woven in circles of peacock blue for each of the eyes on the symmetrical wings and the sparkle of sequins sewn onto the thorax.

"A sort of birthday present for Lucien," she says. "I was going to leave it at the Wellspring, but then the alarms went off and I didn't get the chance. And this as well." She shows me a simple pennywhistle and blows the first few notes of "Happy Birthday to You" on it.

"This was the Christmas present I promised him. I'd already bought it when . . ." The thrush behind us takes up the song, which is good because neither of us can speak. "I'll take it to his grave instead."

Then Angie pulls a third gift out of her bag, a large brown envelope. "And this," she says, "is for you. Open it, go on."

"Do you know what's in it?"

"This part, yes. It's OK. Open it."

With difficulty, I try to separate the seal without tearing the paper in case it should need to be closed again, but my hands are slippery. Inside there is another white envelope and a small parcel, wrapped up in blue tissue.

"Open the parcel, but be careful what you handle when you unwrap it," says Angie.

The fragile layers open like a flower, petal by petal, in my thick fingers, unfolding from the center outwards until revealed in my hand is a small, carved wooden rose threaded with a cord, the knot intact, the leather severed. I move to pick it up, but Angie stops me, hand on my arm, shaking her head. Instead, I lift the rose in its paper cradle to my face—it is Lucien at bath time, talcum powder and clean towels, hot blackcurrant and bees and buttercups. I have searched without ceasing for this relic. Who was the last person to touch this? Me?

Wrapping the rose up again, I notice how the damp traces of my fingerprints have marked the fragile paper. "Who had this?" I ask at last.

Angie is crying quietly and the name is hard to hear at first. "Sister Jack," she says.

The name drifts out of reach in my mind. "Sister Jack? No, it can't have been Jack. She was my friend, Angie."

"I don't know. I don't know everything."

"Have you spoken to her?"

She wipes her eyes, smudging black mascara onto the hem of

her white top. "I tracked them down. I had to do something. I lost it really, but Charley made me pull myself together and we set about finding them. Anyway, we went to Norfolk and found the Sisters. There weren't many of them. I'd guessed as much from the Internet, the site gets hardly any hits now, like people have given up believing. There were a few new women, who I didn't know, and that cow Amelia didn't want to talk to us, so it seemed like a wasted journey."

"So how did you get this?"

Angie is on her feet now, restless. "Eve, surprisingly. She was still there. I never quite got what was in it for her, but then there she was, coming out of Amelia's camper, and I suppose it made sense. Anyway, she recognized me, caught up with me just as I was leaving the camp, said how sad she was about Lucien and she believed you were innocent and all that crap and then she told me that Jack had been sectioned and how hard that had been for the Sisters because none of them believed it could have been her, not until then."

"So it was Jack." Until now, it has never occurred to me that the truth might be equally, impossibly hard, whoever was guilty.

"Just wait." Angie moves away from me, breaks a twig from the tree and snaps it. "Listen to me for once. I went to visit Jack. She's in a women's psychiatric unit, not a prison, she hasn't been charged—not with . . . not for what happened here anyway—but she was in a bad state, has to have a nurse with her all the time because of self-harming. Her arms . . . you think mine are bad . . . hers are grouted, sliced to pieces."

I have been there, in that place, literally and metaphorically, and my instinctive reaction is that Jack is at best an unreliable source of the truth and that Angie has pinned her hopes on the messages of a madwoman. I try to say so, but Angie is strong in her rebuttal.

"She seemed pretty sane to me. She asked me to come back the next day, said she had things to sort out, and when I went back this envelope was waiting for me with a note telling me to bring this to you. She wouldn't see me again. But she gave me the rose, Mum. And she wrote you this letter."

"What does it say?"

"It is to you. I haven't read it. I opened the rose, of course, she told me what that was, how we mustn't handle it, but I haven't read the letter." She sits down next to me, trembling. "That's what we have to do now." She corrects herself: "That's what you have to do now."

The white envelope lies on the bench in the gap between us, with just the one word, "Ruth," on the front. It is a thing. An object. A noun. But to open it?

"It could say anything, Angie." I pick it up and hold it in two hands, by the corners. "You read it, I can't."

"You have no choice."

CHAPTER THIRTY-FIVE

Dear Ruth,

I do not know where to start. I am so sorry. I didn't know what to do. No one was ever going to believe me, no one ever does, even if I kill myself and leave a note, they'll say I was mad. Nobody believes that I know the truth. I am the only one who knows the truth, but I know you will believe me.

The writing is ill formed, it loops irregularly over the first of the two pieces of A4 lined paper which have been torn raggedly from a pad. At times the red biro has gone through the paper, such is the ferocity of the feeling behind the words. Her voice is recognizable to me from her writing and so, I fear, is her illness. Angie is full of anticipation next to me, but this is all paranoia and delusion. It is my territory; I know it when I meet it.

"What does it say?"

"I don't know about this, Angie," I say. "She's obviously not well."

"Just read it to me, for Christ's sake."

So I read it to Angie, finishing with three words which stand alone, underlined: "I am guilty."

Silence from both of us. Angie speaks in a tone which reminds me of the terrible years, dipped in bitterness; she doesn't look at me, her hair covers her face, she is picking at the flowers on her skirt. "Well, go on, then," she says finally.

> "While you were asleep, I was the one who crept up the stairs.
> "I tiptoed past your door.
> "I woke him up
> "I told him sshh
> "I tied his laces
> "I led him downstairs
> "I took him out into the night
> "That was all me, Ruth. I am so sorry."

Each "I" is circled. It is written like a list or some bizarre rhyme. "Don't believe this, Angie."

"What else is there?"

The letter is shaking in my hand, the lines below full of signs and symbols and hieroglyphics which blur and re-form before my eyes. The curving vowels wrap themselves around my neck and strangle my breathing, the straight lines of the unforgiving consonants pierce me. I dare not even look at my daughter, at the girl who lost her son.

> "Amelia was waiting for us outside the cottage under the oak
> tree just like we had planned. Do you remember when Lucien
> was so upset at the Wellspring because no one had shown him the
> magic and Amelia said to me then, you and me, let's bring him
> here tonight, and I thought that was a good idea, so I did what
> she said and told him and said what she told me to say which was
> that it was our secret and you and Mark weren't to know or the
> magic wouldn't work. He was so excited. He trusted everyone."

Lucien, with his duck, in bed that night. "I've got so many secrets, Granny R . . ."

"I wanted to make him happy, I really did. Then his laces came undone and I tied them up again twice and he said he was cold and I said I'd get him a coat and Amelia said he didn't need a coat because he had a great big man's sweater on and the magic would warm him up, but then she noticed he didn't have the little wooden rose you had carved for him around his neck and she was hissing at me in the darkness about the rose and I had to go back for it, back to his room. My fingers were too cold to tie the knot and she took it from me and she did it. We walked across First Field with me on one side of him and Amelia on the other and it wasn't that dark. He showed me Orion's Belt because he said you'd taught him all the stars and Amelia said the moon had come out to show us the way to the magic and he said he wasn't scared at all and I don't think he was. I think he was excited, and I was happy too, swinging him, me on one side and Amelia on the other, because I thought it would be amazing at the Wellspring and how this might be the end of all the trouble between you and Amelia about Lucien not belonging at The Well. I wanted that for you and for the Rose."

This is possible, what she is writing. It sounds real, but it doesn't make sense. "What do you think happened, Angie?" I whisper. "If there was some awful accident at the Wellspring, why didn't they say at the time?"

Angie still doesn't reply. Struck dumb. We must have used that expression for such trivial things in the past, but now I am worried that she is stricken. But to touch her, to awaken her now? I do not need to. Almost robotically, she takes the letter from me, tucks her legs underneath her and sits cross-legged on the bench, then takes over the reading. I cannot listen with my eyes open.

"And then we got to the stile into the Wellwood and Amelia told me to go. I didn't understand but she said the Rose wanted

just her and Lucien for this special thing and I could see that
Lucien didn't want me to leave and he wouldn't let go of my hand
but I just took her word for it and told him it would be fun and I
helped him get over the stile and then he turned round and waved
me goodbye."

Angie's voice snags like wool in barbed wire: *"Twice he turned*
round to wave me goodbye."

This is a photograph in my mind's eye: a small boy, captured in
black and white at night, halfway into a forest, a pale face half turned
back towards us, a hand half lifted to say goodbye. Lucien. Jack's
story is both compulsive and irrelevant: it may explain everything
but change nothing. I open my eyes. Angie slowly, silently spreads
the letter in front of both of us; she is no longer able to read out loud.

There was a voice in my head saying don't leave him like this.
We talked about voices once, I should have listened to that one.
But I didn't. I listened to Amelia instead.

Angie repeats the name as if it is the first time she has ever heard
it. "Amelia. Amelia."

I am at the bottom of the page now. "Finished?" Angie nods. She
clutches a handful of my shirt and clings on tight. I turn the paper
over. On the back, Jack's writing is more legible and coherent, as if in
the very process of putting events in order she has found some relief.

I don't know how long she was gone. I didn't know what she
expected me to do at the campers. I couldn't sleep. I got in a state,
kept hearing things, seeing things. By the time she got back, I was
so relieved to see her. She was ecstatic. None of us could say no to
her when she was like that, could we? We went into her camper,
lit the candle, but she was wired like a tiger and even her shadow
was overwhelming. I pulled her wet robe over her head, made her

sit by the gas fire, stood behind her and brushed her long, damp
hair. I even knelt in front of her and dried her feet. Then she told
me the green sweater was outside and I should get rid of it. I asked
her why, I asked her where Lucien was. She said he was with the
Rose and I still didn't really know what she was talking about. I
remember asking, did he get wet too and did he put his pajamas
on and had you woken up when they got back and things like
that, even though I think I was beginning to realize something ter-
rible had happened. I just kept talking and she sat there, electri-
fied, then suddenly she grabbed my wrists so tightly she left marks
and she said we had done the right thing.

We. That's what she said. We.

I asked if he was dead and she said yes. I asked again, do you
mean you have killed him and she said, he is at peace with the
Rose, the way is now clear for the Rose, for The Well.

For this place. For these brambles scratching my ankles, for the
squirrel gnawing the bark from the trees, for this watery wasteland —
she killed him. "I asked if he was dead and she said yes." Now there
is nothing left to know. Angie's red eyes are moving left to right, left
to right. I was a teacher once in London, in a cold Portakabin, keeping an eye on my class during silent reading, noticing who had got to
the end. I am not here, anywhere but here, now, reading this, please
God, anything but this.

So I knew he was dead, but it was like it was something hap-
pening somewhere else. Amelia was exhausted then. We sat
together in front of the heater, as if there was nothing wrong, as
if we were sharing a mug of tea after worship. She tugged a loose
thread on the green sweater and it started to unravel, so she pulled
on the wool, hand over hand, and I wound it round my fist, round
and round, until we had unknitted the green sweater and there

was nothing left of it at all. I think she kept a bit in her pocket,
but the rest we burned in the fire.

She hung the little rose around her own neck and I lifted her
long auburn hair and I was the one who tied the knot to secure it.
She never took it off after that. Never.

She had me then. She knew if it was my word against hers,
people would believe her. I believed her. I did not know what to
believe. But I did know. I knew she had murdered Lucien.

We have reached the bottom of the second page.

Angie turns it over and back again. "Do you believe her, Mum?"

I always thought the truth would at least be clear. He did it. She
did it. I did it. But this is a mess, everything has been a mess for so
long and I cannot see a way of it ever becoming clear and honest.
"I've no idea what to think." Her fingers are still clutching at my
shirt. I release her grasp and take her hand in mine. "It might be
true. Or it might have been Jack and she is making all this up about
Amelia because she's scared. It might all be made up." The sun is
behind the chimney now, the other side of the hedge I can hear
the steady crunching of the cow working her way through the long
meadow grass, and I remember Jack on afternoons like this, soaking
the lentils, reading out loud from Sylvia Plath, showing Lucien how
to whistle through grass. "She was ill, you know, but she wasn't violent. Sometimes I thought she was the wisest of all of us."

"There is still one more page," says Angie. The second page is in
black ink and it looks as if it has been written more slowly, maybe
added on later.

Rereading this, I know you will probably find it hard to believe.
I always knew that would be the problem. She was my keeper. I
could have run away when we moved to Norfolk, but that would
not have been any good. I know from what has happened to me in

the past that it's not enough just to say it's happened, just to have the marks. Nobody believes you, all they'll say is that you need evidence. I needed evidence that Amelia killed him and I waited until I could get it. What you are holding in your hand is the evidence. That is why you must not touch it. Look closely.

Angie puts the letter down, reaches down, and takes the little tissue-paper parcel out of her bag, unfurls its leaves, lets it rest on her knee. We study the wooden rose, the leather thong, and then Angie gasps. "Look at the knot, Mum, look at it."

Threaded through the curled and twisted leather are several long strands of auburn hair. The focus is lost on everything else—the words on the paper, Angie's face, the rose itself—all blurred. I have run my fingers through hair such as this.

All at once Angie seems calmer than me, more methodical. She wraps the rose again in the tissue paper, puts it very carefully on the bench, and takes up Jack's letter one more time, her voice a little steadier.

"This is Sister Amelia's hair. I cut the rose from around her neck while she was sleeping. Eve was with her. She woke up, saw me with the scissors, and they called the police. That was how I ended up sectioned. They thought I was trying to kill Amelia, but I did not want her dead. I wanted her convicted, but I did not tell them that. I had to wait until someone who believed me came to find me. I have kept the rose necklace a secret all this time, waiting for you to find me. I told myself I would live that long. Amelia has tried to visit me, I know what she wants, but I have refused."

Angie moves close to me now. "That's true, I saw her there, waiting outside in a car when I collected this letter."

"You saw Amelia?"

"But I didn't speak to her. I don't know if she saw me. Let's finish it." Angie holds the letter so we can both read it, our hands either side of the page, our faces so close our breath becomes one as it leaves us and meets the softness of the orchard air.

I hope this is enough to lock her away forever. It will convict me as well, but I will be glad of that. She knew Lucien wouldn't go with her. He never liked her. So the witch used me to get him. She had planned it all. I did not mean to kill him, but I killed him all the same. But please know that I loved him, he was the sweetest boy I've ever known and if this had not happened, he would have been the kindest of men.

I don't know about Eve, but she could never have spoken out against Amelia. I don't think she is as powerful as she looks. Dorothy suspected something. She lied for me about that night but only out of kindness.

I am not mad as I write this. Our only madness was to believe.

You once held me in your arms when I was frail and this is how I have repaid you.

I hope it sets you free.

Jack

Angie finally starts to sob, shuddering, almost hysterical sorrow sucking the air from her lungs and drowning her in tears. The letter slides onto the grass, rests on the clover, forcing a bee to new flowers. My arms are wide, suspended in fear and hesitation for the shortest of moments, and then they remember what the arms of mothers do, so I wrap her up and hold her together and we sit like this for a very long time, entangled in the horror and grief and relief of knowing. Intermittent questions, rereadings, repetitions flutter in and out of the silence, but none of them makes any difference to the weight of the knowledge.

"Mark!" she chokes finally. "I need to get to him, Mum, he needs to know as well." She gets up as to leave, but I persuade her to take time, not to rush off in the state she's in. I could not count the number of times I have said that in the past, but this time she agrees. She blows her nose with what's left of her last tissue, then rolls a cigarette, her hands shaking and the tobacco sprinkling onto the bench, while I sit beside her, numb.

"Are you all right, Mum?" she asks.

I nod, that's all I can do.

"Are you sure? You look really pale."

"I don't get out much," I manage to joke. I know she needs to go, I know I need to make it possible for her.

It is as if my attempt at a joke has jolted her back into her surroundings. "This place is so weird now. I don't expect you even realize how weird it is." She shakes the buddleia behind the bench and two or three cabbage whites spiral up from the purple flowers. "Fucking paradise, that's what I called it once, didn't I, when we were arguing? I remember that. I said I wasn't going to leave Lucien in your fucking paradise."

Closing my eyes against the words, I can hear her voice collapsing again, but she regains some control. "I'll get things sorted, Mum. I will be back, I promise."

A hug, a kiss, half-choked words about loving her and a leaving. From the rise and fall of her shoulders as she walks away, I can see she has taken a deep breath. Then, just before the gap in the hedge, she turns. She has forgotten the butterfly.

"I could take it down to the Wellspring for you," I offer. "For him. Today."

She nods. "Thank you. I can't do that now," she whispers, almost inaudibly. "And I'm so sorry, Mum, I'm so sorry that I ever thought it was you."

It was me, of course. None of this would ever have happened if it was not for me. And yet it was not me. She is gone, but this parting gift is priceless. It is only because I believe she will come back that I can let her go—because I love her, I do love her. Charley loves her too, I am so glad she has him—it is something to be cherished. The way she was standing when she was under the buddleia, her hand on her belly, her skirt a little tight, I even wondered if she was pregnant. She has taken the envelope and will go to the police—she is so strong now, so purposeful in her grief. I try to picture it, Sister Amelia tall and unrepentant at the door to her camper, the police at the bottom of the steps with questions. Will I ever meet her again to ask her why, to ask her, was it worth it? She kissed me, on more than one occasion, she said she worshipped me as a Chosen One, but it was all, always, the other way around.

My thoughts are interrupted by Anon shouting from the house that Sarge is on his way and they need to repair the breach in the boundary fence. I listen to Boy calling back, the slam of a door, something forgotten, then quiet. They have gone. I am alone with these revelations again; they make for strange company.

It was Sister Amelia. Not me. It being me has been part of me for so long that I am not sure who I am without it. Not Mark, either. But there is the legacy of even having entertained the thought that it could have been him. That cannot ever be unthought; it is one drop of poison in a well.

The Well. Lucien has two graves. Angie will go to the churchyard with her pennywhistle, and later, when the guards have finished down there, I must find it within myself to go again to the Wellspring with the butterfly, knowing now what I know.

It seems to take them a long time, although I don't know why. Maybe it is just that time is going so slowly, waiting. When Boy finally returns from resetting the electric fence, he finds me settling Annalisa for the evening. She has been hard to milk, but now I am feeling a relief of sorts in swatting away the droning thunderflies and shaking out the straw. I ask him how it was in the Wellwood.

"How do you mean?" he says.

"I don't know what I mean. It's silly, I thought it might be different down there, now that we know."

"Can you tell me?" he asks gently.

I can. I take him through Jack's letter, it helps me believe it, saying it out loud, and his questions and comments help me clarify things in my own understanding.

"I always knew it wasn't you," he says when I have finished and I let the lie rest.

"Anyway, that's what I meant," I repeat, "when I asked you what it was like in the Wellwood."

Boy fills the stable bucket and then turns off the tap, but the chime of the dripping water counts us through the quiet, a mantra in this early evening full of flighting thoughts.

After some minutes, Boy lifts the bucket over the stall and places it near the cow. "If you want to know, it was weird," he says.

"Weird?"

"I've always felt OK down there, even though I knew that was where Lucien was found. But this evening"—he struggles for words—"it almost felt like someone was watching me."

There is a new restlessness about tonight, I think. Outside the stable, it is dusk and darkening and the rooks are writing across the silver sky in a sweeping hand, full of the loops and flourishes and strange characters of a foreign alphabet which I cannot understand. I will go to the well and put things right.

CHAPTER THIRTY-SIX

There are differences. For me, the August evening is heavy with heat and even the dew feels warm, but for him it must have been white-cold. And this is a summer sky, just the hint of stars, the promise of the Plow in the northwest, but for him, Orion's Belt would have been sharp as steel, low on the horizon. Each step of the familiar path to the Wellwood is now different. What must he have felt, holding tight to the large hands of these women in the middle of the night, the smell of their thighs, the stubble scratching his legs? And here, at this stile, how frightened must he have been, waving goodbye to Jack, not once, but twice.

I stop at the fence as if it is here that I also saw him for the last time, because everything beyond here, everything that took place on the other side of this fence is conjecture, except how it all ended. I am not sure I can go in, but I cannot turn back now, not when I have made a promise, not when he had no choice but to go on. Behind me, over the field, there is still a sense of the daylight only just taking leave, the glow is slowly fading from the mottled clouds above Montford Forest and a huge moon is cresting the horizon. In front of me, night has pulled the curtains closed and the wood seems black beyond belief. I stand between two times. I climb the stile unsteadily and follow the questions between the trees towards the pond, my eyes growing used to the silhouettes and shadows, and when I get there, light is polishing the silver water—the last of the sunset or the first of the moonbeams. I don't know which, but it is like it has always been—and different.

I had thought that now the story was out, the water itself would thrash and moan, but no, it is still beautiful. Still. Beautiful. The mallards have tucked their heads into their wings and are sleeping on the bank, somewhere in the leaves and branches around me the dragonflies and water boatmen hold tight to their half life, and even the trees themselves seem to breathe more slowly. So I find my way softly to my sitting log, so as not to wake the quiet wood. Just to be here is a start, to remember the other times: Lucien on his tummy with a jam jar full of tadpoles; Lucien trying to catch a damsel fly with his hands; Lucien squatting beneath the fat oak with his book of poisonous plants, look at this one, Granny R, this one must be really deadly! I take the silk butterfly from my pocket. What I would do to have him, if I could, if he could still be, but he is not, will never be again. The hot, honest clamp of grief presses on my head and the tears come again and I want to let the butterfly float on the Wellspring, but I cannot let it go, so I sit in the darkness and hold hands with its loveliness, close to prayer.

Screeching of ducks. Flapping of unseen wings above my head. Rustling. I can't see clearly in this half-light. The dry muffle of weight on dead leaves. Something larger than a squirrel or a fox. I am on my feet and as watchful as a blind man. A glimpse of something pale against the charcoal trunks—and then it is gone and there is no sound and I struggle to think of what there is so white in a wood such as this at night: a badger, the tail of a roe deer, an owl? Whatever it is, it is still there, the other side of the pond, and it is moving again, unevenly, stealthily, but crashing now, snapping branches, brazen, advancing towards me. I am reaching for a stick, brandishing it in front of me, looking behind me, whether or not to run, where to hide. I am right to be afraid. It is Amelia.

A rough beast slouching out of the thicket, breaking free of the thorns clutching her back, standing upright in the clearing opposite me, a wild and bedraggled thing, Amelia, her long white robe mud-stained, her auburn hair tangled, but I can make out her face and it is the face of a woman I know, Amelia. The clearing is in uproar, with every living thing taking flight. With both hands I lift the stick while stepping back, tripping on the log, trying to keep my balance. I have never met a murderer before, and I am afraid, rapidly process-ing information, response, hypothesis, reaction: she is a killer, she probably knows I know she is a killer, she may want to hurt me, she looks unwell, I can run faster than her, I can get help, she will be caught, I will be safe.

"Ruth. My Ruth, you have come at last." She speaks my name as she always has, so that it lasts a long time, so quietly it draws me closer.

And for all that fight or flight, she is still Amelia, my Amelia.

"Ruth. You can't think that I would ever want to hurt you. You, you've meant everything to me."

She would never have wanted to hurt me.

She is coming slowly towards me. I lower the stick and it falls from my hands so they are free to embrace her. We hold each other for a long time. My eyes are closed, I feel her hair, her hand is hot against my back, our breath heaves heavily together, slows, steadies. We step apart, she is smiling, thanking the Rose; I am bewildered by what I have just done. I cannot make sense of myself or of her, the state she is in, the fact that she is here at all.

"How did you get in here?"

"The same way as before. Your daughter let me in."

Angie hadn't mentioned her. I shake my head at her. "That must be a lie, Amelia. Don't lie to me, please."

"I've never lied to you, Ruth. The truth is all that has ever mat-tered to me. The truth and the Rose, they are indistinguishable."

The Rose. After all that has happened, she is still talking about the Rose. I move away from her, sit back on the log, feel myself rocking, staring at the mud and the moss at my feet. I cannot make anything out of it. "Then how?" is all I manage to say and I wait for her reply, but I do not look at her.

"I didn't know if I would be let in if I came on my own, I didn't know if you'd see me, so I followed Angie. She took me by surprise, breaking in through the wood, but she was always was so irrational, wasn't she? As soon as I slipped through the breach in the fence after her, I knew that I wouldn't go up to the house, I would let her tell you her stories, and I would just wait for you here to tell you the truth. I knew you would come eventually." I hear her move and then see her, kneeling down and splashing her face with the water of the Wellspring. "All I had to do was wait and pray," she says.

"That was hours ago." I am aware that my body is shaking even if my voice is not. The thought that she was here at The Well without my knowing turns my earth to quicksand.

"I wasn't going to come at all. I was weak. I was tested and I almost failed. But I was helped by a friend, the Rose spoke to me through her and she persuaded me it was the right thing to do."

"Who?"

Still kneeling, Amelia is pulling something slowly from the front of her robe. "She never really understood the Internet, the blog, the Twitter account—all that went over her head. Hers is an old-fashioned faith, but no less strong for that," she says.

I don't know who is she talking about. Her riddles always caught me and even now she reels me in.

"Sister Dorothy," she says, getting to her feet, holding up a blue airmail envelope.

I stand as well. "Let me read it. I have been waiting so long for a letter from her." After all this time, Dorothy wrote to Amelia and not to me, and I am once again the outsider, on the edge of their worship circle. It seems unlikely, but here she is, Amelia, and here it is, a letter. Not unlikely—unbearable. A thought occurs to me. I hold out my hand over the distance between us. "It's addressed to me, isn't it? Give it to me, Amelia."

"No, she didn't reply to you, Ruth. I think she was worried about the men you had surrounded yourself with. It was right she wrote to me instead."

Amelia's face is impossible to read in this funeral parlor of a wood. "I tried to get in touch with her. I thought she might help me . . ." I begin.

"She told me all about your desperate search for answers. Priests. Ruth, the Rose was always there for you, you shouldn't have forgotten that. But she said, how did she put it . . ." Now Amelia is fumbling behind the tree, her hands find a small sackcloth bag which rattles as she reaches inside, then there is the rasp of a match striking a box and she lights a candle; she was prepared to worship and to wait. The flame flares up and illuminates her eyes, which seem huge, and it catches beads of sweat on her cheeks as she reads. " *'The Sisters of the Rose believe in the power of telling the truth.'* " No, don't interrupt, Ruth, let me get to the end of the letter." The light cowers away from her as she speaks, then steadies itself. *" 'I could reply to Ruth but all I could give her would be the further agony of suspicion and unreliable evidence. You, Amelia, are the only person who can free her from the pain of unknowing because you are the only one who knows the truth.'* " She moves towards me, as if to let me read it for myself. "She still believes, Ruth, until I read that I had almost forgotten who I was. But Dorothy reminded me. I am the one who knows the truth."

Amelia holds the candle to the letter, the flames reach her fingers, and then she drops it so it falls to the ground where it curls up and dies. I am dizzy, I cannot see properly. I have not felt darkness more impenetrable than this and then I feel her touch as she stops me from falling and guides me back to sitting. I can smell her, the familiar lavender on pillows, but something else, something sour like the sheets stripped off the bed from a sick child, and when I raise my head she is standing very close to me.

"You think she still believes?" I am wondering out loud, taking Dorothy's words apart, trying to read the meaning and the purpose in them.

"Of course she still believes. We all do, you too, Ruth. This is just your time in the wilderness."

She towers over me. I have to look up to her to ask. "And did Dorothy know what happened here?"

"Don't torture yourself. Dorothy loved you, respected you. If she could have helped you, she would have done. She didn't need to know everything about Lucien."

His name, spoken by her. Her tongue has seduced me in many different ways and I have my guilt to own in that. But to hear it now, curled around his consonants, lingering over his vowels, the time has come to cut it out. "But I do need to know, Amelia. Even if I hate you for it, I need to know."

A barn owl screeches from deep within the Wellwood; somewhere, maybe in Hedditch or farther away, a rival answers back. She sits down beside me. "Hate, love, the back of the same circle, Ruth. You are shivering. It's getting cold. Let me hold you."

"Don't come any nearer, I can't trust myself."

"You never could. It's not me you're trusting, trust the Rose. Take my hand." Grandmother's footsteps, blindman's buff, her hand lifts slowly towards my face, filthy nails stretch towards my cheek, the palm turns outwards and she strokes my skin with the back of her clammy fingers, once, twice. I flinch, turning my head away, and feel the fondling feather-light and razor-sharp; my eyes close at the pain of it which is hollowing me inside out. She leans in to whisper to me, that hand now following my neck, tracing the line of my collarbone. Those same hands. I do not consent. Suddenly, all thought is gone. I am no more and no less than a somatic nervous system, the hippocampus knows this woman well, and every nerve in my body screams no. Legs push me to standing, hand hits her, slaps her, arms push her, teeth would bite her if they could, eyes see the shape of her rise, fall, stumble, and ears register the slump of her onto the dead ground.

She lies motionless for so long, I wonder if I have really hurt her. The candle and her body transform this meeting into a wake. That would be her parting gift. Her body lies facedown among the dull leaves. I creep forward, my heart loud in my head, I crouch down and there, yes, I can see the rapid, shallow rise and fall in her shoulders, and in the silence of the overheated night, I can just hear the rasp of breath. Finally, like some mythical animal, she wakes. With one arm at a time, she places her wrists bent against the mud and pushes her body back onto her haunches, rocks a little, kneels up.

"Aren't you going to ask how I did it, why I did it?" she whispers.

She is licking her lips, her face is ashen. She retches. She is suffering. I could hold her beautiful hair away from her sickness, rest my hands on her heaving shoulders. She suddenly looks so weak, but now she is scrabbling again for the bag, shaking it. I catch a glimpse of moonlight on metal and and realize she has a mug. She crawls towards the pond, dips it in the water, drinks and drinks and retches and drinks again. When she has slaked her thirst, she gives thanks to the Rose for the water and offers me the cup.

When I shake my head and refuse her communion, she sags, apparently exhausted, and I have a moment to think. Now I understand what Dorothy has done for me. She created this moment, produced and directed this scene from afar, her letter auditioned Amelia for the part and she took it. I know my lines, I just need to get over the stage fright and speak them.

"Why?" I ask.

The sound of the water being poured back from the mug into the

Wellspring is loud, but the silence is even louder. Slowly, very slowly, she stands, the last drops fall from the cup and the candle goes out.

"Why?" I repeat, but the question frightens me and I move away from her answer, around the other side of the pond, which is less familiar to me. I don't know where the roots lie or where the badgers' sets open beneath our feet.

She follows me, calling. "Because of how the Rose meant it to be. Because it was the truth. Because of you." She catches up with me but stops short of my arm's length and drops her voice, pushing her sentences out one by one. "I'm not a murderer, Ruth. Does the world count God a child killer because he sacrificed his only son?" She swallows, wets her mouth, laboring her words. "I didn't kill Lucien, Ruth, I freed him. He didn't suffer. I gave him more than you could ever give him. When the water closed over him, that was the moment The Well was free, and like the Rose of Jericho he was dead but then he lived, he flowered. Happy, Ruth, he is so happy now, I know. The Rose loves me for that." Again, she has to pause, again she struggles to breathe. "And you. The Rose loves us both."

Amelia plunges into the black font that is the Wellspring and it resists her, slapping the mossed stones in anger at the disturbance. "Today is the day of the Assumption." She cups the water, scoops it, throws it into the air over and over again, but this is a sunless chapel, there is no light to catch the falling drops, and this time, there is no rainbow. "And you, you were free, Ruth, to be who you are meant to be, to be with the Rose, with me." Like a decaying statue in a fountain, lit by an uncertain moonlight, she stands with her arms raised in the air, her head pulled back by the river of her hair in that familiar ecstasy.

"*O daughter of Babylon, who art to be destroyed; happy shall she be, that rewardeth thee as thou hast served us.*

"*Happy shall she be, that taketh and dasheth thy little ones against the stones.*"

As if someone has cut the strings, it is suddenly over and she lurches and slugs herself back out of the pond, leaving a wet trail glistening, a pale hump sludged with mud from the pond floor and smeared with weed. She has no weapons left; I am still standing.

"Amelia, he was just a little boy." I look down at her, all drama gone, just the one fact left. "That wasn't right. By the laws of any God, that cannot have been right."

She reaches out to grasp my ankles, but I am too quick.

"And do you know what? I don't know what happened to me when I met you, what I felt for you, but I can tell you this, it was never love." It cannot be hate now either, I think, as I listen to her sobbing, otherwise there will be nothing left of me. I squat down beside her. "Amelia," I start, "we were all mistaken—"

But she is not listening to me. She is staring through me into the gloom. She interrupts me. "Look at them all coming, between the trees."

There is no one there, no one at all. Not even the sound of anyone.

Amelia continues to call and point. "They are all coming because they believe. The Rose of Jericho is flowering for them. Do you still believe in me?"

Ignore her, I tell myself, this is all madness, but she repeats her question again and again, becoming more and more agitated, reaching for me, grasping, clutching.

"Do you still believe?"

The fear I felt when I first saw her returns. I need help, I need the guards down here, but if I go to get them, even if I go just far enough up the hill to scream for them, she will be gone when they arrive. She will have slid back under the surface and no one will believe me that she was ever here at all. It seems impossible that she could escape, but everything she has ever done has been impossible.

In the empty space left by her hallucinations and my indecision comes a strange warbling, a foreign, primeval sound like night frogs or crickets in a hot climate. I can sense that Amelia is also unnerved and that the two of us are transfixed by this high, insistent song. It is not clear where it is coming from. It has moved. First above our heads, then silent, now there it is again. Whatever it is seems to be on the boundary fence which divides The Well from the rest of the world and its persistent call rises and falls without ceasing, like a siren. There it is, it is a bird, taking wing, silhouetted against the moon which has arrived like a visitor at the edge of the wood, and I know from its flight song, the hawkish pitch, and the glide that this is the nightjar, returned, the Puck of a bird, the goatsucker. It is gone. Instantly, I know what I must do. In an instinctive act of faith, I run at that space, at the fence, I thrust my tagged wrists through the barbed wire, the electric shock thumps me and throws me onto my back, my head hits the ground, there is blood and gashes on my arms, but even through this pain and confusion I can hear the one thing that matters: across the fields, through the night, the alarms are screaming for attention.

Dizzy, disoriented, I use a low branch to pull myself to my feet. She is still down. "It's over, they're coming now." The sickness recedes and rises again, and although my blood is dripping onto the rust-brown of last year's leaves, I have found a sort of unfamiliar strength. I shout, "You'll be arrested." I see her future, it is pathetic and its pathos feeds my reeling bitterness. "I'll tell you what will happen then. You'll serve your time in prison, but not like this." I throw my arms out to the forest. "Not like my beautiful prison. You'll have a toilet bolted to the floor and dinner on a plastic tray."

She is laughing; I am right, so I am crying. The forest has never heard such a cacophony: two women, by a pond, in the darkness.

"You'll be nobody in there, Amelia. For years. Forgotten. No visitors. A nobody." I continue my damnation of her, but I am not sure she can hear me. My voice is weakening, my head spinning, but although I seem to be losing control, I am not imagining it, there is shouting. The guards. Two minutes at the most, they'll be here. Has she taken some drug, to be like this, laughing so loudly, so sick? They are approaching, the beams of their flashlights are sweeping between the trees, lighting her up, darkening her again—now you see her, now you don't. They will take her away and I will never see her again.

I realize that what I really want to do is to come face-to-face with her one last time. I trip over branches and stones to reach her before they do, I fall on her, bind my wrists with her long, wet hair, raise her head, pull her sick face close.

I spit at her lips. "Judas."

The clearing was filled with light so hard I had to turn away, and behind the light were the shapes of the guards, guns raised, commanding, demanding that I freeze, that I stand apart, that I let go. It is not that easy. I cannot let go. Out of the shadows, a boy steps forward as if to help, but I call out, "No!" I will let go. One by one, I extract my bloodstained fingers until her hair falls free and I am left staring at the auburn strands in my hand, which are all that is left. I have let go. We both get to our feet.

"This," I say, "is Sister Amelia."

There is confusion. Amelia says nothing, I have nothing left to say. Boy is explaining that Anon has brought only one set of handcuffs, which I suppose were meant for me, but on Three's instructions he moves towards Amelia.

"Wait!" she commands and Anon steps back. Of course. She bends low. I step back. The men are tense. She is breaking off the ends of small branches from the undergrowth behind her, quite methodically, almost like a woman picking flowers for her table. She stands back up, very slowly; she is high again now, like she used to be, she has presence again now, like she used to have at those times of prayer and worship, and I see it in the way we are all still and I feel it in the way we are all waiting for her next move. I am left in the wings, all the lights are on her, setting her hair on fire against the white marble of her face and neck, shining through her wet robe and illuminating her breasts, her ribs, her thighs. She picks berries from the branches, brings them to her lips, kisses them with her eyes closed, and then smiles at me, holds the kiss out to me, unfurls her long fingers and offers me the fruit. I clasp my bleeding fists together, keep my dry mouth tight. I know what grows at The Well and where.

"Goodbye Ruth," she says.

She tosses the berries into the Wellspring and, for a brief moment, a few slight ripples catch the light and sparkle and then the water is still and dim again. She brings her other arm up and holds her wrists out for the handcuffs. I am about to say something, but there is too much shouting, it is confusing, it seems hard to organize the words for what needs to be shared. I am ordered to follow, but I hang back. Boy hesitates, I ask him to go. Three tells him to move and the moment is past. Amelia is manhandled out of the clearing, I hear them crashing their way out of the Wellwood and watch the swing and lurch of the torchlight fade. As she goes, I hear her singing.

What am I when I rise from the water?
Myself streams away from me
And I am gone.

And she is gone.

Wading into the pond, I am surprised by how warm it is and its warmth is seductive. I am in up to my waist. I reach out for the berries and they float beyond my reach. I inch forward, I grasp one, then another and another, until I am sure there are none left and I hurl them from the spring. Then, with one deep breath, I plunge my whole being into the womb of the water and feel the weight and the cloak close over my head and hold me down until I think there will be no end to the pain and the pressure and the blindness, before I burst back out into the miraculous lightness of air, and understand. That was how it was for him—my question is answered.

CHAPTER THIRTY-SEVEN

I t is a very hot afternoon, the thick walls of the cottage have held the sun at bay, but the heat took my breath away when I stepped outside. I slept very deeply last night and right through the morning. I don't know who put me to bed, I remember very little after they took her away, but now I am sitting outside under the shade of the oak. Boy has put up the little card table and has run a bowl of warm water and is bathing the cuts on my arms. I let him; he is gentle and intent in his care, and as he dips the cotton wool and dabs my skin, he tells me that Angie has left a message: Mark is safe. He also fills me in on what happened last night, how they found me collapsed by the spring and carried me home and how it took two of them to hold Amelia, even handcuffed, how they took her away in a police van.

I wince at his first aid. "An ambulance would have been more appropriate—actually no, a hearse. That's what she needed."

"She looked pretty rough," he agrees, "tachycardic, sweating, hallucinating. So did you, for that matter." He takes the bowl and empties the stained water into the hedge. "But you have to be careful after an electric shock."

"No, you don't understand. She'll never stand trial." I have brought Lucien's book of *Poisonous Plants of the British Isles* out with me and I thumb through to find the right page. "That's what she threw in the pond." The picture accurately depicts the deep purple flowers with orange stamens and the rich, dark berries hanging from their vinelike host. "She has eaten deadly nightshade!"

"Deadly nightshade? Are you sure?" Boy turns the pages of the book in disbelief.

"Devil's herb, sorcerer's cherry, call it what you will. It drives you mad with thirst." A woman by the Wellspring, holding out the offer of a tin cup of water and a fistful of fruit—I close my eyes to rid myself of the picture.

"Belladonna, isn't that the same thing?"

"It is. Do you know why it's called belladonna? Women used it to make their cheeks flush or their eyes look enormous."

"That's right, her pupils were really dilated."

"But another myth is that sometimes the deadly nightshade takes the form of an enchantress of great loveliness who it's dangerous to even look upon and fatal to kiss." A second recollection, tactile this time, touching and a tongue around the lips, the licking of lips. I wipe my mouth with the remaining cotton wool. "She will die."

Boy gets out his phone. "I'll call the police. There must be an antidote. She has to live to be charged."

Leaning over the table, I put my hand on his. "There's nothing to be done. She will never stand trial, never be found guilty."

More than that, she has mugged me and run, left me full of hatred and robbed me of the chance to forgive her one day—people say that's how you move on, but I don't know if forgiving the dead has the same effect. She has snatched from me the possibility of pity, the quality of mercy.

Boy hammers the table. "But that can't be allowed to happen, there's no justice in that." He paces up and down. "Things need to be tied up, finished."

"Resolved?" He doesn't hear the smile in my voice. "She'll confess first, she loves me enough to do that."

"But that won't resolve anything."

"I've had my day in court, Boy, and the verdict was—"

Suddenly, Boy is on his feet and so am I, both incredulous, because the Land Rover is being driven down the drive at a crazy speed, thumping into the potholes, crashing against the ruts, horn blasting, radio blaring, and Three is leaning out of the window, shouting, "Come and listen to this! You've got to hear this!"

They skid to a halt, inches from us.

"Jesus! Get a piece of this." Anon is in the passenger seat, sticking his head out the window.

The Amelia story cannot have come out so soon. Anyway, it's not the news, but a ludicrous song from the 1960s: "Raindrops keep falling on my head, because I'm free, nothing's worrying meeeee." Three is now out of the Land Rover, drumming the beat on the hood and crooning. I join him and Boy and listen as the music fades.

"Now we go over to the London Weather Center for an update. George, what have you got for us?"

"Sometimes I thought I'd never hear myself say these words again, Miles, but here it goes. It is raining."

"Say it a bit louder for us, George."

"Yes, Miles, it is raining. Not just raining, in fact, but bucketing down in Northern Ireland and just starting to drizzle in the northwest and the forecast is for these storms to sweep across the British Isles over the next twenty-four hours."

"Fucking hell!" said Boy. "Rain!"

Three tells them to shut up.

"We've been here before, haven't we, George? There were storms last year which petered out. What's different this time?"

"This time, Miles, there is a real shift in the weather pattern. We're ninety percent sure of it. You'll have read in the press that the temperature readings from the Atlantic indicate a long-term change in the currents and that has combined with wind swinging round to the northwest. We really think that this will be more than a one-off soaking. How long it will stay, how long it will take everything to recover, there are a lot of unanswered questions out there, Miles, but we're pretty confident the worst is over."

I look up at the sky. It is not raining here.

"But there's no such thing as a free lunch, George," continues the weatherman. "The country is now gearing itself up for severe flooding . . ."

Three turns the radio down, Anon jumps out, and they are all reaching for their mobiles, texting, checking, and then they run into the barn. The television is turned on, there is a lot of swearing and more whooping. The whooping must be Anon. I guessed a long time ago from the smell on their breath that they had found a way of using our old potatoes for their own illegal brew. They will be drunk soon enough and will have forgotten all about me.

I walk stiffly up the drive, knowing that the alarm will go off as I cross the tagging zone, knowing they will switch it off and keep watching the news. For the first time since I was brought back here, I reach the top of the drive, that place where we stopped the car and gasped all that time ago, and I can look out over The Well and see close up the strips of crops planted by the government research-ers; they fall away either side of me like a striped quilt, their colors luminous in the strange light created by the ferocity of the lowering sun and the blackness of the thunderous clouds. Great shafts of sun-beams burst from cracked seams in the sky, illuminating Montford Forest and the Welsh hills. The wind is picking up and the trees rustle and gossip and pass on the news, the breeze brings with it the sound of car horns blaring over and over again in the village, as though they are heralding a bride, and over the Crag I see the veil descend, which means it's raining there. When she was kneeling, Sister Amelia's hair used to hang over her face like a veil. I did look into her eyes, I did. My eyes into her eyes, blinded.

I could go down to where Angie and Lucien were camped, all

that time ago. Or I could go the other way, see whether the grass has grown over the scorch marks where the Sisters' campers were parked. It was Sister Amelia. I could keep wandering, go as far as the gate, turn right onto the lane, feel the tarmac under my feet, get as far as the main road and let the swish of the traffic push me into the hedge. For God's sake, I could get in the Land Rover, turn the key, and drive. I am free, or will be soon. It was not Mark. The drought is over. It was not me. I am not free from guilt, but I am not guilty and I will be free. I am free from Mark. I am free from Amelia. How will I know when she dies? Maybe I will just know. It is impossible to know what to do with this self that is now me. It is impossible to understand the rain.

It is still not raining here, but it will be soon and I will get ready for that homecoming. There isn't a lot to choose from in my wardrobe, so I put on an old sundress and nothing else and fetch a rug from the wicker basket on the landing. That is all I will take with me when the sun goes down. I will not need a flashlight, I know the way well enough to the place I have chosen; I will not need shoes, I want earth under the soles of my feet; I will not need champagne or music or streamers; if the rain is coming to the rest of the country, that is enough.

When I reach the brow of the hill in First Field, it is as I imagined it would be. I spread the rug carefully and sit in the middle of it, my arms wrapped around my legs and wait. There are doors slamming as Boy goes in and out of the barn; the ring of a mobile phone; a shout across the night, a reply and then quiet, the sort of quietness you get in a theater in that strange moment between the audience settling down and the curtain going up. Anon has a habit of coming out for a cigarette on these unbearably hot evenings, even on ordinary ones. I think Three must be sleeping it off. Despite the heat, I shiver. Somewhere over towards Rose Cottage there is a dog yapping into the night and there is the barn owl again, marking its territory down in

Morgan's Wood. Other than that, the land beyond The Well seems to be getting used to the idea of rain—the thunderous clouds have smothered the hills to the west in their embrace, turning out the lights ready for their consummation.

Tonight there would be meteors and comets were it not for the clouds, but we have no need to make wishes if the forecast is right. Lying back and looking at the few stars still visible in the clouding sky, I feel, for once, my own significance, not the status imposed on me by the Sisters, not the status imposed upon me by the media, not even the status of a prisoner, but my own physical significance. The breeze gets up and goose-bumps my legs, naked under my skirt. The earth supports the weight of my head, and isolated drops of rain are falling as if they are each, individually, committing themselves, and they leave their mark on my thin dress. I wait and watch.

In the distance, the darkness is pierced by the pinprick flicker of lights as if a few stars have broken out of prison and this is the first high land they found as they fell to earth. And there is singing, I think. I am no shepherd and these are no angels, but here is good news. Lights move, they part and come together again, fickle like fireflies before joining in a stronger illumination, and I can see they are flares, carried by people, and the people are circling and swirling, dozens of them, no, hundreds maybe, choreographed for a grand opening ceremony. With them come music, drums, and the banging of spoons on saucepans and pipes and singing. Visions like this have plagued me, been my downfall, so I get to my feet hesitantly, full of fear that here is more trickery, full of hope that it has come to save me. Rain—not heavy—but rain all the same, is starting to fall steadily. It seems different, this rain from another country. I sniff it like a wine taster: a hint of salt, bracken, pavements, perhaps. I am not guilty. These, these crowds now pouring down the drive in the distance, spilling out over the fields and running down the hills in rivers of release, these are people, real people, come to celebrate real rain. Behind the foot revelers come cars, headlights throwing long beams on the luminous grass, horns blaring, radios loud and pumping. The Well is throwing a party. It is clear that my absence is of no consequence to the villagers, or to the Sisters from the site over the road, or to the remaining farmers, or indeed to the hostess herself: The Well. A huge celebration has sprung to life with this cottage as its centerpiece and I am deliriously happy in my anonymity on the hill. Hours pass? I think so. The party ebbs and flows; somehow there is a band down there now, plugged into the kitchen sockets, I guess, the bass guitar throbbing across the field. Every now and again, everyone joins in and swells a familiar chorus—just pop songs, silly songs—an explosion of childlikeness, and I recognize the words from another life and sing along to myself and hug my knees and tap my feet and they all dance in unison, hands in the air, waving their lighters. And there are children, so many children, I can see the outline of them, always running, chasing. I can hear them laughing in this, their second christening. Lucien would have run and laughed and loved like that. A few of the new invaders have come a little closer, but they don't know I'm here, at the top of my hill, wrapped in the clouds; these are the teenagers who kiss, and in the dark places shadowed from the moon by the tall hedges, I know their lovemaking is wet and wonderful.

Somewhere over Montford Forest, thunder stirs up the earth and the lightning is fleeting and hesitant, but the crowd have noticed the messenger and roar their welcome. Soon it is really raining, hard, driving diagonally across the fields and watering their memories of packed-up barbeques and coats over heads as you run for cover and staring out through the doorways of leaking marquees and puddles of water mixing with wine in glasses left beside the storm-blown roses. But here, now, this England is dancing in the rain and I am released.

I do not go down but pull the blanket around me and wait. Although I am stiff in the morning and cold, I wait. The rain has stopped, the cloud has lifted, and a gray daylight is prompting the crowds to leave, draining away in drips and drabs, leaving tire tracks and litter and the glorious detritus of celebration in this our weak, wonderful, washed-out dawn.

CHAPTER THIRTY-EIGHT

Anon gives me updates. The guards up at the experimental plots will be staying on, apparently, although a good part of one crop was washed away in the surface flooding that followed last night's storm. "Seems the government still thinks there are lessons to be learned from your Well," he says, and as always I resist the desire for an ironic reply because he never gets it, never will. He also tells me that Sarge was gone early, redeployed somewhere terribly important no doubt, and Boy, he has also gone, but left a note on the kitchen table. I will read that later. It is right that he has moved away; this is no country for young men. He will look after his mother, love a girl one day soon and make her happy, father children, all just a little bit differently because he spent six months at The Well—and that's my going-away present to him. I feel his leaving like a child on a hilltop releasing a balloon.

Anon is still talking, but he must be used to being ignored by now. He is saying something about the fact that he himself will have checked out by evening; he is also needed elsewhere to cope with the floods and what's being called the National Adjustment Plan. The local police have been asked to "oversee and monitor" my imprisonment and secure the perimeter and he's just hanging on in there for them to show up. The cabinet's emergency committee is meeting to discuss how to deal with the wave of mania which hit the country last night, and Parliament is to be recalled to consider amendments to the Drought Relief Powers. Anon is a veritable mine of information and conversation, for once.

"I guess you'll be a free woman again."

Free. The word feels thin and insubstantial against my teeth; it should have rounder vowels, more breath than this. Nevertheless, I use it again, for practice. "And I hope you'll be a free man as well, before too long."

"I figure on going to the States," he says. "Take a road trip, go to Vegas, it's what I've always wanted to do."

Well, you could have fooled me.

Anon has various bits of paper I am meant to sign. A police car is stuttering down the drive, one of those allocated to the Drought Community Officers. I comment to Anon that I really have been downgraded.

"Don't take it the wrong way," he apologizes, and I suppress my laughter.

Anon takes the file into the barn, saying he needs to make sure the paperwork is in order and then he'll be off. I am not sure of the etiquette of saying goodbye to one's guards. The policeman is sitting in his car. I am hovering awkwardly when Anon comes out with his rucksack.

"One more thing," he says. "There's a message just left on the phone from your ex, saying he has heard from your daughter and he will write soon. Sounds good." He gives me an awkward hug. "That's us done, then, Ruth!" he says. "Signing off for the last time. Private Adrian Lambert—over and out!"

"Good luck, Adrian, good luck!"

Under the porch, I can sit here quietly, listening to the drizzle running down the gutters with nothing more or less than a sense of peace. It is not clear from the message if Mark is coming back, but I can hold hands with his absence for a while and he will write when he is ready. Boy's note is here in front of me and is what I expected, full of commitment and promises of action, contact details for human rights lawyers, mobile phone numbers and email addresses, and a lot of thank-yous, for what he has apparently learned from me and from being here, all of which is well-meant but does not mean as much to me as the fact that he signed himself Luke. He was a physician of sorts and I will miss him.

With no desire to leave The Well—not yet—I spend my days as time should be spent here, doing the small things that matter. I take good care of Annalisa and her milk takes good care of me. I take the trowel and go to Boy's garden and work my way up and down the rows, weeding here, tasting there. The runner beans hang in their hundreds down the bamboo pyramids; the marrows sleep on the wet grass, and even now the land is preparing for winter; carrot tops and potato leaves, the parsnip ferns and red beetroot stalks are lining up for the future. I select two or three courgettes, a handful of tomatoes, and an onion and take them to the kitchen for my lunch, which I prepare slowly, with great care, softening the onion in my butter, slicing the courgette with my knife, stirring the ratatouille with the wooden spoon.

I walk the perimeter in the rain. It is ugly—all wire and charge boxes, cameras, sawn boughs, and trampled hedges—but that will come down soon. There is a different quality to the field where the Sisters were, whether from the burning or the months denied light under campers I don't know, but I crouch down and brush the grass. One day soon I must write to thank Dorothy because she was a good woman and a friend to me, and I am already sorting words in my mind for my letter to Jack. It does not need to be complicated. I do not blame you. You meant no wrong. Please forgive yourself. Moving on, climbing the stile into the Wellwood, I am no longer afraid; I remember Mark's plan for thinning out the conifers and letting the broadleafs grow, and I notice the way the oak and cherry saplings he planted have outgrown their plastic guards, so I release them and let their young branches spread out and find their shape as trees for the first time. The rain which has revitalized the country has also brought a new freshness even to this pond; a single white water lily lies open on the dark water, reflected with rippling symmetry in the rain-dropped mirror, as are the boughs above and the overhanging ferns. The wren is here, silenced for a moment as he watches me, head to one side, before he continues worshipping in this chancel, accompanied only by the choir of swallows and their Nunc Dimittis. There is no one else here, no one watching, no one waiting, no one wandering. All is stillness. I sit beside the water and weep as I have not wept before: I weep for Lucien, but not only for him. Finally, I cup my hands in the Wellspring and use the water to cool my eyes.

"A time to kill and a time to heal," I say out loud, "a time to mourn and a time to dance." These verses are another of Hugh's presents. I know them by heart now, if not in the right order, and another springs to mind. "A time to scatter stones and a time to gather them in." So that is what I do: I gather mossed stones from the wood and shining stones from the water's edge, choosing each one carefully for the way it feels in my hand and for the way it fits with the others, and with these stones I build a small cairn to be a resting place for a silk butterfly.

Later, I sit on the gate by the house where we used to watch the sunsets in the early days, when the sunsets were worth watching. Then, they were part of our routine. Lock away the tools, shut up the hens, put Lucien to bed, check the supper in the oven, and then that space of time, a glass of homemade wine and some silence between the working day and the rest. Each evening would be different. Sometimes in high summer, the sun would slide on its mathematically perfect parabola towards Cadogan, until it met the uneven silhouettes of the forest. Earlier in the year, it set farther round, waving white hankies of wispy cirrus before sinking behind Edward's Castle. Other times, she would not go so gracefully, but bold and aggressive clouds would barge in from the southwest on a wind and a half and shove her aside, and her last stand would be made all the brighter by her dark assailants. The best was when we were surprised, the plain sky promising little, the sun hesitant all day, just retreating after a poor performance, and then suddenly a final surge of flecked beauty before the dusk. Hopkins was our poet then, with his grandeur and "shook foil." There were as many ways for the sun to set as there were evenings on the gate together. There are still sunsets like this one, flickering silver and pink like sea trout, and always have been. It's just that I have neither had eyes to see nor memory left to hold things, until now.

My solitary confinement, if that is the right name for this exquisite freedom, is almost total. The noise is my head is stilled. There is one visitor, the constable, who comes up here every morning to check on me, and he asked if he could get anything for me. Last night, I was wondering about a laptop, but although my finances would probably stretch to it, I'm not sure I am ready. By this morning a much better idea has half formed in my mind. I ask him if he can get an italic pen, some watercolor paints, and a large book, like an album. He makes a second visit, just to bring them to me, saying he hoped I didn't mind but he'd spent a bit, thought I'd like a nice book from what I'd said. We talk a little about what's going on in town, about how the Lenn has subsided and how they are repairing the bridge whose ancient stonework foundations had become unstable in the dried-out earth and then undermined by such flooding.

"The same all over," he comments and goes on to recount an umbrella parade which took place last Saturday, the whole town turning out and spiraling their way through up the main street, like a carnival, he said, what with all the different-colored umbrellas and the Lenford Town Band as well.

"They say they'll make it a regular thing," he says, "every year, the same date, so people won't forget."

"We're all a little bit of history," I agree.

He even says that he has noticed the Taylors have started plowing Tenacre.

"Tom's son, then," I venture.

"That or his brother," replies the policeman. "Sad he didn't live to see the day himself, but nice for his widow that things go on."

So it is we philosophize as day-to-day people do and I feel quite proud of my ordinariness. Finally, I pay him from the weekly allowance I hardly ever use, and he says he looks forward to seeing whatever it is I'm writing. He has done well and bought a beautiful embroidered book of plain paper and I smooth my hands over it, preparing. He is halfway up the track, before he reverses and knocks again on the window. There is something else which he forgot to give me, a newspaper already a couple of days out of date, folded to page eight: "Deadly Nightshade Suicide for Nun Accused of Child Murder." The small article, pushed aside by forecasts and floods and statements from the government, this blurred photo and two square inches of hieroglyphics, might as well be in a foreign language given the sense of bewilderment I feel, laying it on the kitchen table, weighting it down against the autumn wind with a bowl of plums. If—when—I am asked to give evidence at the inquest, I will not know what to say. It does not seem right to keep the cutting; it does not seem right to burn it as if none of this ever happened. One day, I will know what to do with it.

Like a child with a new exercise book at the beginning of the school year, I return to my album and write "The Well" and the date at the top of the first page, in the middle, and underline it. I will spend my waiting weeks cataloging this place. Who knows what it's really like out there, what has been lost in the years of drought, what species, what names, what images? And no one will ever know what it was really like here unless I become a scribe. The readings from the boreholes, the graphs, data, and samples gathered by the government analysts, they say something, but in a different language.

I work systematically, trying to recall the birds that have circled on thermals and held tight to our water, the buzzard and the swallows, the sparrow hawk and the wren, the crested grebe carrying her babies on her back across the pond, the kingfisher, the heron, and the nightjar. Then I let my tongue roll over the names of the flowers that grow here and I work late into the nights illuminating them with my watercolors, curling stems up the consonants, flowers around the vowels like a medieval monk: purple aramanth, bleeding heart, buttercup, red campion, on through the alphabet—deadly nightshade, feverfew, foxglove, harebell, love-lies-bleeding, leopard marsh orchid, sweet violet. In the evenings, with the curtains closed against the dusk and the fire roaring, I record the fox, the stoat that danced on the lawn, my hare and the butterflies, and even the insects and the bees whose hum kept me company and moved the pollen from tree to tree in the orchard. The trees. So many trees, so much blossom. And the mushrooms, I will not leave them out, not any of them, not even the deathcap because all living things have their place here. It seems my work will never be done and my days pass fruitfully. I sleep well at night.

The constable has promised to find me a book of British wildflowers because I think I may not know the right names for some of the things I have seen, so I am looking out the window, hoping he might come soon, when I see a familiar red van, splattered in mud. It is as if nothing had ever changed—the postman gets out, leaving his door open and the engine running, pushes several letters into the rusted blue box hanging by one hinge on the gate, and then revs away again. He must be new. I can't remember the last time we had post delivered all the way down here at the house and I have lost the little key, so I spend a ridiculous half hour with a bent piece of wire coat hanger, fishing for letters, beside myself with anticipation. My first catch is from my solicitor, the second is junk mail offering me interest-free credit on a new sofa, so perhaps the economy will get moving again after all, and the third fish is the greatest prize of all—a letter from Angie. It is so precious, not only because she says again she is sorry she ever thought it was me, not only because she gives me news of Mark, but mostly because she puts PTO at the bottom and "one more thing . . ." With Angie, there was always one more thing.

"Charley and I were wondering if you would mind if we spent the winter at The Well. We could live in the barn? We could help out and who knows, maybe our baby will be born there—due at the beginning of April!"

It has taken me most of the night, but my reply to Angie is written, as is the much harder letter to Mark. At the top of First Field, I stand and listen to the church bell tolling in the valley, distant but not impossibly far away. It must be a Sunday, ten minutes to matins, if I set off now, cut through Smithy's Holt, down the sheep track past the Taylors, cross the lane, through the wrought-iron gates of the church-yard, to the heavy oak door which whispers against the flagstones and into the sun-dusted pews and silence—if I set off now I could be there in time, and afterwards I could walk between the yew trees and the headstones to that smallest of graves with a pennywhistle and pray there. Or I could fall to my knees here, on this hill, which Hugh called the most beautiful altar this side of purgatory. With no words of my own left, I recall the verses he chose once, standing at this place, in the rain, with me and a fistful of corn. In pastures green He lead-eth me the quiet waters by . . . a start, I tell myself, it is at least a start.

Back at the cottage, I tuck my letter to Mark inside the front of my illuminated manuscript and prepare to post the parcel tomorrow. That will be my first act in the new world.

Dear Mark,

I am going to instruct my solicitor to hand over to you my share of The Well. All the world could ever see was my connection to this place, but what they did not see was that you were the only one who knew how it worked, what made it grow. There are awful memories in the bedrooms, in the barn, in the Wellspring, hidden in the soil, washed in its water—we can't deny that, but you have the skill to reap a different harvest here.

We could never re-create the dream; that, in a way, was our first mistake. Things cannot be repeated but only done differently, but we did love each other for a long time and that must count for something. You were steadfast and I was an uneven partner. I am sorry. For every moment that you stuck with me and that I turned my back on you, I am so sorry.

I would like to come back to see you, if you invite me.

Angie and Charley are coming here to stay in the barn for the winter. Maybe this could be home for them and the baby they are expecting. Someone needs to be here in the spring to put buttercups on Lucien's grave.

My house imprisonment was revoked last week. It is funny that on more than one occasion dates I have craved for so long have passed with me hardly noticing. October is a good month to leave, when the forests are gold and the fields ready for plowing; I am not sure where I am going to live, but I have learned something about how I am going to live.

The time is right. With this letter, I am sending you a book. It is a record of the miracles that happened here, even while our backs were turned. With this book, I am returning The Well.

Ruth

ACKNOWLEDGMENTS

There are so many people, who, knowingly or unknowingly, have helped me over the years in so many different ways this page can only acknowledge a tiny proportion of them.

At the start, there were my parents, who chose me, loved me, and read to me and my wonderful brother, Christopher, a true Renaissance man.

Later, at various times, there were some inspirational teachers and fellow students at Clifton, St. Annes College Oxford, Oxford University Department of Continuing Education, and Oxford Brookes University, all of whom helped me learn to read and write.

Next came a plethora of independent publishers who do so much to support new writers, particularly Jan Fortune-Wood at Cinnamon Press. They accepted my short stories and poetry and thereby gave me the confidence to continue writing.

As *The Well* took shape, some people were kind enough to read it and help it on its way, including, amongst others: the trusty members of my book club; the Elephant Rock writing quartet; Anna Davis; and Rachel Phipps from The Woodstock Bookshop. There was also Bella, who, being a dog, was unconditionally positive about the whole thing.

Thank you to Lucy Cavendish College, Cambridge, for their prize for unpublished women's fiction; winning this made all the difference.

As a result—an agent. My heartfelt thanks to Janelle Andrew and the fantastic team at Peter, Fraser, Dunlop, including Rachel, Marilia, and Alexandra. Nelle's unbounded enthusiasm, astute critical eye, and straight talking have been invaluable, and I strongly believe she should be cloned.

And then the inestimable Canongate and the privilege of working with Jamie, Jenny, Natasha, Vicki, and Rafi, who designed the beautiful cover. Particular thanks to my editor, Louisa Joyner, who has brought me gifts of wisdom, experience, knowledge, and kindness in equal measure.

In April 2014, Jamie Byng gathered many of the foreign publishers of *The Well* at The Shed in Notting Hill. I asked them all to sign the menu for me because I was not sure that I would ever again be in the company of so many gifted people who make it their business to bring beautiful books to life. To each and every one of them (and to those who could not make it)—thank you.

Finally, from the world to home. To Christopher, Jeremy, and Jessica who have managed the acrobatic act of being endlessly loving, supportive, and tolerant of neglect whilst keeping their mother's feet firmly on the ground. And to Simon. I hope he knows already that I would have been as nothing in this world if I had not met and married him, but it is worth saying again. And again. Thank you.